PRAISE FOR BEAUTY REBORN

"Lowham adeptly wrangles classic elements of 'Beauty and the Beast' to craft a sensitive and slow-burning retelling. While this lavish version of the original tale is comfortingly familiar, the creator's narrative stands out in its portrayal of themes surrounding trauma and recovery alongside familiar musings on perceived differences between humans and monsters." – Publisher's Weekly

"Beauty herself is an intriguing, well-crafted original, her story building on the tale's perennial theme of consent: She goes willingly to a Beast who does not force her into marriage though his life and humanity depend on it. In that respect, this iteration does not disappoint. Readers who appreciate narrative risk-taking are well served." – Kirkus Reviews

"A darker and bittersweet retelling, laden with an equal dose of humor and tragedy. The author writes with a lyricism that drew me right in." – Compass Book Ratings

“I devoured this book in less than 24-hours I was that engaged. *Beauty Reborn* is an apt title. The main character, Beauty, does undergo a rebirth born out of time, space, and healing, but the fairy tale itself is also reborn through Lowham’s skillful storytelling.” – The Christian Fiction Girl

“This book is so full of emotion! You can just feel the magic and enchantments through Lowham’s words. Even though difficult events happen, you can feel the hope that things will get better.” – The Readathon

“What’s threaded into the pages is a more than just a retelling. It’s a story of resilience and rising above your darkest day. I went into this expecting to not find anything special as a ‘Beauty and the Beast’ retelling has been done 100 different ways, but I found something that made me sit back and think about women who have endured the worst and how they still choose to move forward and hope for better days.” – Rachyl, bookstagrammer @readwithrachyl

“This is such a beautiful story of healing, hope, patience, and true love, not to mention a wonderful retelling of one of my favorites!! The growth that the characters are able to experience is powerful! The romance was slow but captivating, and in the end, I loved the main characters so, so much. The writing was amazing and I can’t wait for the next book!” – Sam Conover, bookstagrammer @see.sam.read

ASTRA REMADE

ELIZABETH LOWHAM

Media inquiries may be sent to contact@elizabethlowham.com.

Learn more at elizabethlowham.com

Hardback edition ISBN 978-1-964042-00-8

Paperback edition ISBN 978-1-964042-01-5

eISBN 978-1-964042-02-2

Book cover: Etheric Designs

Cover images: © Shutterstock

Art direction: Elizabeth Lowham

Interior art: Etheric Designs

Interior formatting: Danyelle Ferguson

Author photo: Aubrey Nicole Photography

ELIZABETH LOWHAM BOOKLIST

BEAUTY REBORN
ASTRA REMADE
CASTERS & CROWNS

To Kathy and Karen,
my own left-handed heroines.

PROLOGUE

THE LITTLE BOY in the tower had no name. He'd had one before, but it hurt when he tried to remember it. His parents couldn't help him remember; they lived somewhere in the castle, and the boy's tower didn't belong to the castle anymore. It was alone now. Just like him.

His tower had three windows and four floors. Outside the three windows, the sky was green. It hadn't always been green.

No, that wasn't right. *This* sky had probably always been green. He'd just lived under a different sky once. That one had been blue.

The little boy preferred blue.

With no blue sky to enjoy—and no castle and no parents—all he had was three windows and four floors. He counted them often, going up and down the circular wooden stairs that followed the curving tower walls. The lowest floor was his favorite. It had two of the three windows, identical, facing each other like soldiers, their battle spilling in rays of pale green light throughout the entire room.

The next floor up didn't have any windows, so it was gloomy and smelled like old socks. He avoided that floor. He avoided the very top one, too, because he had to crouch to walk in it. It had an attic ceiling pressing down at a sharp angle, like a hand pinching in to crush him.

The remaining floor had the third and final window. It was wider than the others, arched on top like a giddy upside-down smile. It made him smile too.

But even with one happy window and two bright-soldier ones, there was something wrong with the tower, something beyond pinching ceilings or old-sock smells. It was too *high*. The lowest floor wasn't on the ground like it should be, like it *used* to be. In fact, it was so far off the ground that if he leaned out a window, the waving grass down below made dizzy patterns that left him feeling sick.

And there was something else wrong with tower. The worst thing of all.

It didn't have a door.

Everything had changed for the boy in one terrible earthquake, an earthquake that had transformed the tower and changed the sky and somehow brought him far, far away from home. No matter how many days he waited, another earthquake didn't come to take him back.

So even with the sick feeling, he finally tried climbing out a window.

The tower held him back with arms he couldn't see, and no matter how he kicked against the unseen power, he couldn't leave. Maybe the tower was lonely. Maybe it was waiting for an earthquake to take it back to join the rest of the castle, and in the meantime, it just couldn't stand to be alone.

The boy knew that feeling.

He wasn't always alone, at least. Ever since he'd arrived under the green sky, a bird had brought him food.

She wasn't really a bird—at least not like the ones Mother fed in her garden—even though she had feathered wings. The garden birds never spoke, but the tower bird had lots to say. She brought him sweet red fruits and crunchy green vegetables, and when he mentioned Mother's garden, she rolled her eyes and muttered something about "human gardens." She didn't like when he asked her questions about birds.

"I'm not a bird," she said, her yellow wing feathers quivering. "Let's get this straight, aye? I'm a Planter."

She did look more human than bird. Except for the wings, she had a body and a face like the boy's, though her skin was darker and patterned with thin, swirling lines, like she'd drawn all over herself. The boy's old nursemaid would have scolded her for that and said, "Ink is bad for skin!" Maybe the Planter didn't have a nursemaid. The lines were beautiful, though, and between the Planter's brown skin and the long, stretching feathers of her yellow wings, she could have been a sunflower in Mother's garden. The boy had always liked sunflowers.

"Not a bird and not a flower," she told him. "I'm a *fairy*. Planters are the only fairy type that matters. Remember that."

Unlike the boy, she had a name. Doll.

"How do Planters get names?" he asked.

"We choose them," Doll said. "Representative of something that defines us."

She said *Doll* came from dollop, because she liked to dollop magic where others sprinkled it. There were other Planters too. Once in a while, they came to peek in the windows, always zipping away as soon as Doll arrived. If the boy was quick, he got to ask them a question before they disappeared. He asked about names.

Renny, with vibrant pink wings, was named for perennials, because he thought it was important to be steadfast. *Gard* claimed no single blossom in a garden was better than the garden as a whole. *Vine* just liked vines.

Welly was the strangest, and no matter how the boy squinted in thought, he couldn't see how *Welly* came from *trowel*, or why trowels were very important to begin with.

The boy looked for his own name. He didn't have trowels or perennials. He asked Doll for a garden—it would have fit on the bright floor of the tower, and Mother always said light was good for plants and people alike—but Doll just cackled at that.

"Humans don't have gardens," she said. At the reminder of his mother's garden, she muttered that it wasn't a real garden, and that was that.

So the boy didn't have a garden, and he didn't have a name. In truth, he didn't have much of anything—not a door or parents or a blue sky. All he had was three windows and four floors.

He should have had a sixth birthday; he'd been waiting for it to come. Every winter after the snow started to fall, his birthday arrived, and Mother decorated the castle with white banners and snow lilies, and he got to eat as many white cream puffs as he wanted. But snow didn't fall from a green sky, so he didn't have a birthday anymore.

That meant he had to find a name. *Had* to.

"If you insist on a name," Doll said, "just be Wart. For the tower."

The boy scrunched his nose. "That doesn't sound like 'tower.'"

"Then be Tower. Or Toper. There—Toper's a nice ring to it, don't you think?"

But the boy didn't want to be Toper, and he certainly didn't want to be *Tower*, because he didn't even *like* the tower. The windows were fine, but every day, he missed the door, and he missed what should have been on the other side of it.

In truth, he hated the tower.

"Can't I leave?" he asked.

"You're payment," Doll said. "Payment has to stay paid."

The boy cried sometimes. When he did it around the Planters, it made them leave, even Doll. Not that she ever stayed long; she flitted in to bring food and then flitted back out. If he asked questions, she would talk, but she never came to just talk.

If he'd just had a friend, he could have talked to them. They would have comforted him when he cried instead of leaving. But he had no friends in the tower. He'd gone up and down the empty stairs enough times to know that.

When Doll brought more vegetables, the boy asked about friends.

"Make one," she said. "Humans like making things."

The boy tried stacking vegetables. He couldn't get arms to stick, but he got a body and head. Until the head rolled away. Fruit worked a little better, at least the flat-circle ones with a tough red peel and juicy sections inside. After he stacked three, he used his thumbnails to dig eye spots into the top fruit's peel.

"Hello, friend," he said. But then he wanted to introduce himself, and without a name, there was nothing to introduce.

After a while of not eating it, the fruit turned fuzzy white and stank worse than socks. He threw it out window number three.

Doll said, "You need better materials, aye. Listen. I never offer humans a harvest from my garden, but you're special. I'll let you harvest as much wood as you want from my pygmy trees. Make something out of that. Just a little thing in return."

She asked for some of his hair. It seemed very strange for anyone to want *hair*, but the boy had plenty, he supposed, hanging over his ears and onto his neck. Sometimes it got in his eyes.

So he said yes.

Doll gave him a knife. Not a big knife like the one Father carried in his belt, just a little knife, with a smooth wooden handle and a stubby blade, sharp only on one side. Cutting off sections of his hair turned out to be fun. He pinched his fingers around a section of reddish-brown locks and felt the tight-tight-give as he pulled the hair taut and slid the blade through. As it cut free, it made a *shiiish* sound.

Plus it made Doll so happy. It was the first time he'd seen her smile widely, showing pointed teeth, and her yellow wings flapped so hard they hummed their own song. She hugged the bottle of hair tight with both arms.

As agreed, Doll brought the boy a stack of wood, and he discovered something even more fun to cut than hair. Wood was tougher, but his knife was sharp. His favorite wood turned a different color when he cut it, revealing a dark purple heart beneath green bark. Over days, he whittled thick branches down to small sticks, then started again. Into the wood of the floor itself, under the light of the two soldier windows, he carved shapes and lines from one wall to the other, crossing and mixing and swirling.

And then he carved a friend.

It was meant to be a bird, but it was too blocky, with a thick body and lumpy head. He cut his finger while trying to make wings, so then he decided he would just imagine wings.

What he couldn't help imagining was Mother's garden. He wished he could show Mother his blocky bird. She would have liked it, even without wings. He hugged it the way he wanted to hug her, and even though it wasn't soft, it felt good to hold a friend while he cried.

After setting Blocky beneath window number one, where she could bask in the warm, pale green light, the boy carved again.

He carved, and he carved.

Doll brought more wood; the boy gave her more hair. The trades expanded, supplying him with tools and other things. Even though he paid, he liked thinking of Doll's things as birthday gifts, since he would have passed a birthday or two if there had been snow to tell him when.

By carving, he filled his tower with enough friends he could never be lonely, all of them standing sentinel around the curving walls and beneath the three windows, most of them shaped like blocky birds—though none were ever as special as Blocky—or like lumpy Planters. The process coated everything in sawdust. It filled the grooves he'd etched in the floor. It made his fruit taste gritty and his clothing itch. It made him sneeze.

Sawdust, he thought.

The boy smiled, giddy like window number three.

When Doll came to bring food, perching on window number one with her yellow wings bright against the green sky, the boy told her he had a name.

"About time, it is," she said. "Let's hear it."

"I'm Dust," he announced proudly.

She pursed her thin lips, squinting at him with yellow eyes. Then she shrugged. "I thought Prune to be the obvious choice, but it's your name. Dust it is."

CHAPTER 1

ASTRA

ON THE DAY I betrayed my family, my father told me a story.

I knew a pearl diver once, he said. *A good man with a family. His rival started selling pearls the size of a man's thumb, claimed he hunted them a hundred feet down, deeper than any other diver dared go. So my friend took hold of a boulder and sank himself to the bottom of the ocean, without enough air to come back. The rival was exposed for false wares, and my friend left behind a widow and two children.*

When I asked him for the point—because Father always had a point in his impromptu sermons—he told me two things.

Consider the voices you're listening to, Astra.

And beware the path you think leads to pearls. It might lead to losing everything.

I gave him my opinion in the slamming of the door.

Within two days, I regretted it, but by that point, I'd already taken hold of the boulder and sank myself to the bottom of the ocean, without enough air to come back.

"Give me a wish, fairy!" I shouted, pointing at my youngest sister. "Make me more beautiful than she."

"Astra, don't!" said Beauty, catching my arm. I shrugged her off. I had never been able to stop my sister in anything; this time, she would not stop me.

The fairy was not as I'd imagined she would look—barely more than a head tall and floating without wings. She was also blue from nose to toes, including her solid blue eyes, void of pupils. Callista had told me every warning against fairies imaginable; she'd said they twisted fate to suit their purposes, they tricked humans into terrible bargains, and they had to be trapped in order to be trusted.

I had not trapped this fairy, but I did not care. The fairy promised Beauty the world and its riches, and before Beauty could claim any of it, I spoke first.

For once in our lives, I claimed my desire *first*, instead of tending to my youngest sister.

"I wish to be so beautiful," I said, "that wealthy men propose at the sight of me."

The man I'd desired most in the world had rejected me in favor of my sister, and I'd stood by to witness it, planning to let him marry Beauty without telling him how I felt at all. But she'd turned her nose up at the very opportunity, and the sour taste she'd left for him poisoned any opportunity I might have had.

No matter my sister's excuses, I knew the true reason for her relationship with and rejection of Stephan. My sister took what I wanted because she could. Why shouldn't she? In our younger years, she'd been spoiled by Mother and Father both —the daughter born after loss, who sometimes made them forget the three children born before it. They told her she could have anything she wanted. So she'd claimed and discarded a lord.

It was my turn to claim something.

And where my family ignored me, where Stephan rejected me, the fairy perked up at my voice. She turned toward me with full attention, gazing down with lovely blue eyes full of promise. The hem of her petite gown trailed shimmering blue magic, the glistening power to achieve *anything*, just waiting to release me from my prison and gift me a new future.

In response to my desire, the fairy spoke the two most joyous words I'd ever heard: "Wish granted."

In an explosion of blue fairy magic, I left my old life behind, and the world around me reformed into something new. It was so jarring, I stumbled, though nothing had pushed me. Hovering beside me, the wingless fairy beamed, gesturing with an arm at the city now surrounding us.

It was as far from my family's poverty-ridden shack as could be imagined.

I stood on rough cobble paving. The smells tickled my nose in familiar ways—a motley market blend of butcher shops and women's perfume and everything in between—but the street itself was not like any in my port city back home. It was narrower and longer than I was used to, with fewer sailors and more housewives.

Without a mirror in public, my only chance to see myself was a barrel of water beside the butcher's shop. I craned to catch my new reflection, leaning out of the way of a string of cured sausages. Then I saw for myself the change I had felt take hold after my wish.

Every bit of me was out of place. Where the other women on the street wore linen and wool, I wore silk. My silver dress carried patterns of glittering black diamonds and swirling white embroidery in pristine stitches so small an insect must have held the needle, yet even so, it had become the *plainest* part of me.

The irises of my eyes churned with depth and vibrancy, the color as alive as a bubbling spring. The plain auburn of my hair now reflected a different shade with every slight turn of my head, mesmerizing in its effect. I touched my hands to my cheeks, finding skin so pristinely smooth it might have been porcelain, free of freckle, scar, or blemish. I tested my expressions and found I could produce neither frown nor scowl, only faint sullenness, still beautiful, like the charming pout of a beloved child.

And my smile . . .

My mother had named me after a pagan deity—Astra, goddess of triumph. Even when my monotheistic father had disparaged the name, she'd insisted. When the goddess Astra was kidnapped by the sea and held beneath the waves, she harnessed the creatures of the depths to fight her battle. When the stars refused to share their beauty, she waged the war that made them bow. The goddess Astra took orders from no one and settled for nothing. She was untouchable. Secure.

When I smiled into the water, I saw the reflection of a goddess, ready to make the stars bow.

"Thank you, fairy." I looked up at the blue sprite hovering

above the bucket, my new smile as radiant in my heart as on my face. "Now, if you would kindly point me to the nearest wealthy man."

For the first time since Mother's death, since Father's bankruptcy, since Beauty's claiming of Stephan, I could feel hope on the horizon. And when the fairy turned her head to the sky, drawing my attention to the turrets of a castle looming above the city, I could *see* it. I could see my future.

Once I returned home with a wealthy husband in tow, my father could no longer accuse me of chasing false pearls.

"Here, wealthy men exist in abundance," said the fairy. "I look forward to viewing the results of your wish." With a grin, she disappeared, only a trail of blue glitter sparkling in the sunlight to show her passing.

My heart beat strongly in my chest. I gathered my skirts and made my way down the street. Everyone turned to stare as I passed; I stopped traffic like a royal procession, inspiring the delighted smiles of children and the open-mouthed stares of parents. Under their gaze, I tossed my hair and gave a venerable wave. My curls caught the sun like mist beneath a waterfall, glittering with the same rainbow hues, fleeting but breathtaking.

One woman fainted.

I laughed. Just as quickly, I restrained myself to silence. Mine was a loud, barking laugh that escaped without permission—the cackle of a creature belonging deep in a forest, dripping mud and crawling through leaves, half-mad with hunger. It was not a delicate mannerism for society, no matter how desperately I worked to tame it. My greatest shame was that, at times, I even snorted like an animal.

I did not snort this time, but fairy magic had not repaired

my laugh. I realized it had changed everything about my outward appearance, yet left my insides the same, and for a moment, I felt like a falsehood, a magnificent tapestry hung to cover the plainest of walls, though the wall remained lurking still.

In that moment of doubt, I froze on the street—just long enough for a cutpurse to take his chances.

The man lunged at me from within an alley. Before I could do more than gasp, he'd cut the small leather pouch from my belt, but as he moved to run, he faltered. He stared at my face with slack jaw and mesmerized eyes.

"Beg *your* pardon," I stammered at last. "But that is not a coin purse. It's my sewing kit. I demand you return it at once!"

My voice snapped him from his reverie, and he dashed back into the shadows, turning a corner into the winding maze of houses. Once beyond the open market, the streets constricted, weaving between houses of timber and brick with such narrow passage I could stand in the center of the path and touch the houses on either side. When I tried to give chase, I found my legs would not carry me faster than a brisk walk. Perhaps my body was still adjusting to the fairy magic.

It was hopeless anyway; the thief was long gone.

I stood frozen on the street once more, and that had not ended well the last time, so I forced myself to walk again, my eyes searching every alley I passed, my shoulders growing tense. Silly though it was, without my sewing kit, I felt naked. Though I possessed not a coin to my name, I'd always been able to carry a needle.

Forcing a slow breath, I lifted my chin. I was panicking over nothing. Once I reached the castle and secured my future, I could buy enough sewing supplies to fill an entire room.

Until then . . . perhaps it would not hurt to have some protection from further incidents.

"Pardon, sirs!" I called out to an approaching guard patrol.

The two men snapped to attention. They wore leather tunics over chainmail, the leather emblazoned with a white-and-yellow crest, the same hawk emblem I'd seen on the castle's banners.

"I desire an escort to the castle," I said. "If you'd be so kind."

The closest of the men paled behind his dark beard, and he looked like he might faint just like the woman in the street. He squeaked air with no sound.

Panic spiked in my chest as I suddenly worried the fairy had taken me across the world. What if it was not only my beauty silencing him but also confusion at my language? What if this city of wealthy men was also—

"Of . . . of course," the second guard choked out, elbowing his companion as the bearded man continued to flounder. The second guard was the taller of the two, and he stood with more composure. "At your service, my lady."

My lady. Me, a lady? Imagine. Even at the height of Father's fortune, I'd not been such; lady was a title reserved for the daughters of barons or higher, not the daughters of merchants, and certainly not the daughters of impoverished peasants.

But once I married a wealthy lord, I would be a lady indeed.

I bit my lip, holding back a girlish squeal. Far up the hill, the castle seemed to beckon to me. Every pair of waving banners became a pair of welcoming arms.

"My lady, if I may . . ." The taller guard glanced up and down the street, brow furrowed. "Where is your retinue?"

"At the castle," I lied, the first words to come to mind. I certainly could not say, *I have no retinue. I am the daughter of bankruptcy, without a coin or even a sewing kit to my name. I am sustained only by a fairy wish.*

The ground felt unsteady beneath my feet. I forced myself to smile.

"We shall escort you at once!" The shorter guard came to his senses at last, his voice erupting in a deep jovial rumble. He bowed and practically tripped over his own feet in his haste to lead me.

But his companion hesitated.

The taller guard was near my age, perhaps a few years older, clean-shaven and serious. He wore a frown even in the presence of my beauty.

"My lady . . ." He hesitated. "You are . . . new to Everspring?"

I'd been caught. My heart began to pound. What could I say to—

"Wait." I shook my head. "Everspring? This . . . this is Everspring?"

Turning, I saw the cramped street with new eyes, the houses packed in so tightly because so many people desired to live at the heart of the kingdom. *Everspring*. Of all the places the fairy could have chosen, she'd brought me to our nation's capital. *Everspring*, said to be the most magnificent city ever built, so stunning that war could not cross its walls because invading armies would drop their weapons at the threshold, forgetting conflict in favor of peace.

I believed it; after all, our kingdom had not seen war in anyone's memory.

Oblivious to my shock, the taller guard persisted in his frown. "If you are new to the city, you mustn't go to the castle."

"Piers!" The bearded guard blushed, stepping closer to his companion. "The lady asks an escort, not counsel."

"But she should know . . ."

I raised an eyebrow as he fell silent. "Know what, sir?"

Piers shook his head. "You must not encounter the king."

"This one." The shorter guard gave a nervous laugh, jostling his companion. Shooting a pointed look in my direction, he lowered his voice, as if I could not hear a whispered conversation when they stood directly beside me on the street. "Piers, *look* at her! She has nothing to fear. Perhaps she'll even overpower His Majesty."

Though Piers continued to frown, he nodded.

"I'll thank you to be plain," I said sharply. "What's this about King Osric?"

"King Osric passed just weeks ago," said Piers. "Kenric now reigns. His coronation festivities are still ongoing for the court."

"Oh, I'd not heard." News was always slow to reach us at the western edge of the kingdom. "What is the measure of Kenric that you should be worried I meet him?"

"A fine man!" the shorter guard rushed to assure me. "He'll surely make the grandest king we've ever seen. Since coronation, he seeks a bride, that's all." Something must have sparked in my eyes at that because he leaned in as if conspiring. "My lady, you would *far* outshine the competition."

Piers frowned as if meaning to contradict, but he only looked away.

A competition to be *queen?*

I could scarcely breathe.

Clearing my throat, I straightened. "I shall take the measure of court and its options for myself, thank you. Please lead on."

CHAPTER 2

DUST

FAIRIES COULD NOT BE TRUSTED. It was a lesson Dust had learned as a child and kept re-learning even as an adult.

Doll leered down at him with malicious yellow eyes. "Take your poison, human."

With reluctance, Dust lifted a black pepper from the wooden bowl in front of him. The pepper itself was only the size of his fingertip, shaped like a raindrop, though its stem extended three times that length. Part of him was tempted to flick the whole thing at Doll to see if it would knock her from her perch on his bedpost. But that would be petty. He'd accepted the game, and he could stomach the consequences.

Dust twirled the stem once before using his teeth to pop the pepper free. It burst in an audible crunch, spreading fire across his tongue and down the back of his throat. He doubled over, coughing as his eyes leaked tears.

"Poor thing," Doll cooed, clearly enjoying herself.

That was good—Dust needed her in a good mood. She would be more likely to grant requests that way, and for weeks, he'd been working up the courage to make a big request. A little pain was more than worth the possible boon. It was the whole reason he'd agreed to a game of friendship peppers in the first place.

The game consisted of two people with a set of eight peppers each, beginning with pink, which each player ate to begin the game, and ending with black, which Dust could say from personal experience burned hot enough to melt the scales off a dragon. The peppers carried no heat at all if players gave completely honest answers, but Doll had asked him a question about something called a stingray, and Dust had never heard of such a creature, so he'd been unable to answer correctly about its migration patterns.

"You"—he pointed an accusing finger at Doll—"claimed ignorance of sea creatures. I trusted that."

The fairy wiggled her shoulders, bobbing her yellow wings with the movement. "Honesty's only required during the game, not before it."

Dust hurriedly drained a cup of flaxseed milk, though it barely doused the heat. He breathed carefully until he could do so without coughing.

Friendship peppers was a game of rapid-fire, back-and-forth questions, and when Dust had agreed to questions concerning the sea, he'd thought he and Doll were on equal footing in knowledge. Instead, Doll had escaped without a scorch while Dust had swallowed fire on five out of seven questions.

At least the game itself had been mild. Planters most commonly used friendship peppers for interrogations, testing the dangers of possible alliances or the intention behind requested harvests. Usually, when he played with Doll, she snuck in a surprise question or two about his efforts to escape the tower. But there hadn't been anything new to report on his escape efforts for a long time, so perhaps she'd given up.

Dust hadn't.

"I'll win the next one," he said.

"Always amusing, that determination of yours."

Dust stood, bringing himself eye-level with Doll on her perch. The Planter was barely a foot tall, but her spindly limbs and thin body gave her the illusion of greater height. It was her presence, too; she'd been an adult while he was a child, and that kind of impression lingered, even years later. To him, Doll would always fill a room, always be the unquestionable authority.

Which was what froze his request on his tongue.

While he dallied, Doll stepped off the bedpost, wings carrying her in a quick *zip* down to the floor where Dust had been sitting. She marched around the wooden bowl with its remaining peppers—two sets of rainbow shades—examining and muttering to herself. When not in use, Planter wings sagged as if boneless, so Doll's longest feathers swept the floor behind her bare feet as she paced.

"This harvest *is* better than last," Doll murmured, "even with the inker infestation during quarter-moon. I've yet to repay Renny for that. Still claiming innocence, but we both know . . ."

She continued prattling on about her garden. Her favorite topic.

She'll leave soon, Dust thought. *It has to be now.*

He took a deep breath, but it did not bolster him. So, like a coward, he settled on the edge of his bed without speaking, tucking his own bare feet up beneath him. He picked at a new hole in the knee of his trousers, dreading the thought of mending. After so many years making his own clothes, he would have expected to be better at it, but not everything was as enjoyable as carving, and besides, there was no point to well-mended clothes with no one to see them. When fairies dressed in leaves, magic, or nothing at all, they had no care for what Dust wore. Fashion was a human tradition, one of many he clung to from his childhood.

Stalling, he chided.

"Doll," he said aloud.

"Hmm?" She looked up at him over her examination of a shiny blue pepper.

"I've been thinkin' I could help in your garden."

More than once, he'd asked to *see* it, but any request to leave the tower met the same refusal: *Payment must stay paid.*

As if an entire lifetime of captivity were a just price for his father's tree.

"Payment—" Doll started, right on cue.

"This *is* payment." Dust put on an easy smile, one that denied the nervous tensing of his stomach. "Else it's free labor. Either way, a benefit to you. I know you've got a garden twice the size of any other Planter; imagine what an extra set of hands could do."

Before he even finished speaking, her attention returned to the pepper. "Humans can't garden, you know this."

"I could if you teach me. I'm a hand with plants, and you know it." He rapped the back of his knuckles on the ornate bedpost for emphasis. The entire bedframe was hand-carved, just like every other piece of furniture in Dust's tower.

"Dead plants." Doll's wings twitched. "You carve my trees, I'll carve you."

"I'm *saying,* point me in a direction, friend—you'll find I'm quite useful."

She lowered the pepper, and Dust's heart raced as she squinted in what seemed to be genuine consideration.

Then she said, "You *are* useful, Dust."

It was not potential gardening skills she referred to. Dust's scalp itched. His hair was sitting on his ears again, slowly creeping down his neck. There was enough for a cut, but he'd resisted offering one, even though holding out was foolish. Without any way to leave the tower, everything he needed had to be purchased, and Doll always found a way to have just what he needed.

"You can keep these." She dropped the pepper into the bowl, where it rolled against a bright red neighbor. "Harvest for the game."

"How generous," Dust drawled. "Suppose I'll challenge Bumble, though I doubt the game'll play the same against someone who doesn't talk."

She gave no response except, "Morningdew, 'fore I forget."

Since Dust paid for morningdew in batches, that need was at least settled until half-moon, but it signaled the conversation's end; she always dropped the feathers on her way out.

Sure enough, Doll flitted out his arched bedroom window without so much as a goodbye or parting glance, her wings humming close enough to Dust's face that he felt a burst of air against his cheek. She'd left behind a single yellow feather, resting across the peppers in the bowl.

Dust sighed. For a moment, he gripped the bedpost, pressing his fingertips into unyielding wood, just *feeling*. He swallowed hard. Then he stood, rolling his shoulders to dispel the remaining emotion. His latest attempt to widen his captivity had failed, but four floors and three windows was much too small a space to share with anything, especially lingering disappointment. It would fill the whole tower if he let it.

There would be other ideas for escape, other opportunities to limit the hold of his curse. For the moment, however, morningdew was not a resource to be wasted.

He scooped up the feather. Viewed closely, flecks of orange speckled the deep yellow-gold coloring, and little droplets of clear liquid beaded along the shaft. Planter wings collected the dew in every flight through their gardens.

Rather than taking the stairs down through his tower, Dust took the window, swinging his legs over the ledge and onto his wooden balcony. The balcony was an old construction, but the eel vine he'd fastened at one edge was still new, meaning it was still a novelty to grasp the slick vine, to jump and feel freedom for a moment before sliding in a quick drop to the second smaller balcony below. The brief adventure flipped his stomach and left him grinning.

For a moment, he stood beneath the wide green sky, looking out at the valley below, the thick, waving grass leading to dense forest and distant landscapes. Wind tousled his hair, bringing with it the scent of moss and moisture. Rain soon. He glanced up at his rooftop to be sure the rain catchers were in place, out of habit more than anything.

Then he ducked through window number two, planting his bare feet on the gritty floor of his woodshop. A multitude of carvings greeted him, half of them painted, half raw wood in all the shades the fairy realm had to offer. With a nod to his personal army, he crossed the room, running his finger fondly over a badger's ear as he passed.

His morningdew mirror waited in its place beside his workbench. The mirror looked like an ordinary thing, just a wide, shallow basin of water held by a carved woman with raised hands. Dust had made the stand a few years earlier, tired of hunching over the basin on the floor.

Taking his place in front of the mirror, Dust dropped the feather. For a single heartbeat, it rested gently atop the water, like a brightly painted canoe on a crystal lake. Then it vanished into a flash of yellow rippling out to the basin's edges.

The mirror came to life. Though the water remained, it was no longer a plain wooden basin he looked down into; instead, he viewed a world far out of reach.

Ocean waves rolled in along a beach with sand as black as night. The shore rose abruptly into towering cliffs colored only by dark, wet moss. A seagull flew past the rocks, starkly white against the oppressive landscape. The view turned, away from the seagull and out to the ocean, where a line of great looming ships sat anchored, sails furled, waiting for voyage. Dust saw an unfamiliar hand with a silver ring as if he were looking down at his own. It reached for another hand, entwining fingers as a man stepped into view.

The man spoke in an unfamiliar language. Dust drank in the sound, a shadow in someone else's conversation, pretending he belonged.

Encountering foreign language was common—morningdew was a wild game of chance, allowing him to look through the eyes of any creature in the human realm, though he could never tell ahead of time who the target would be. He'd seen through the eyes of men, women, and children the world over, from cultures living in homes of ice to people walking the very streets of Everspring. He'd witnessed firsthand the lives of forest animals and deep-sea creatures. If any being possessed eyes, it fell into the lottery of morningdew mirror.

Once the mirror had opened in a place, he could direct it as he pleased. So with a flick of his finger that set the mirror's water rippling, Dust moved his viewpoint, looking from the man's eyes this time. The woman beside him wore her dark hair braided with ivory beads and spoke in a low, murmuring voice. Her side of the conversation disappeared in the crash of ocean waves. Another viewpoint hop led him to a crab with its face in the sand, offering Dust nothing to look at but clumps of black sand flaked with dried seaweed. Above, he found the seagull's eyes, peering down at crews bustling to ready the ships for sailing. Rather than watch any of the crew members, Dust returned to the couple on the beach.

He was never good at filling in the conversations he couldn't understand. *Lovely day. See that wave? That's a large one.* His ears heated just trying. But then the woman drew closer, worry in her face, and the man wrapped his arms around her. Some moments spoke a universal language. Things like, *Don't go.*

It would be a powerful thing, Dust thought, to hear someone say, *Don't go.* It would mean the freedom to leave. And it would mean a reason to stay.

After another moment, he gave the couple their privacy, turning to the upbeat conversations of crew members. He contented himself with listening to the cadence of human voices and the sounds of a roaring blue ocean beneath a reaching blue sky. Though he couldn't feel the ocean foam or smell the scents carried on the breeze, he could see, and he could hear. It was enough. For the moment, his world was wider than four floors and three windows.

CHAPTER 3

ASTRA

AS WE MADE OUR WAY through the city, the bearded guard pointed out noteworthy features of Everspring. He spoke of the city's finest shops—found in the upper market—and its finest vineyards. He prattled for some time about an ornate building called the Chapel of the Tree, which seemed to be of personal interest to him.

Though I tried to focus on his words, I found myself distracted by details in the city, such as the flat rooftops of many houses. There was no gathered snow on any of them, and the citizens took advantage of the space for terraces and canopies. Some grew herbs, little splashes of green against the wood and stone. Back home, the snow was still piled high, the deep of winter having just barely given way to the new year. In Everspring, the air did not sting my face as we walked, and my breath hardly clouded when I spoke.

"Is there no winter here?" I asked Piers. Then I felt silly; it was in the name Everspring, wasn't it?

"We have snowfall," Piers said quietly. "It melts within the hour, my lady."

The bearded guard had stopped to point up at another grand building, saying something about guilds and fellowship within Everspring. We'd climbed a set of stairs to reach the upper city, and I found a wide, circular balcony to my left, which gave a natural vantage point from which to view what we'd left behind.

The maze of the lower city stretched for miles, a gradual slope of cluttered rooftops leading to the city gate, all of it encircled by a massive city wall, at least fifty feet tall, crowned by the jagged teeth of a parapet. A glittering snake of water curved from the north down to the far southeast corner, originating beneath the castle and ending at a lake—an entire *lake* enclosed along with the buildings. I stared at the crystalline water, so still and calm compared to the ocean I knew. Everspring had orchards and gardens, mansions and cottages, an entire sprawling environment packed with chaotic fervor.

It was so different from my home. The ocean reached its fingers far beyond the beach to touch houses, infesting floorboards with sand, weathering walls in salty high winds. Even in its richest areas, my port city had a battered feel to it, like a crustacean hunkered in a shell, waiting out a storm. Everspring, on the other hand, felt like a tulip in bloom, fresh and lively. Its grand walls stood with pride, like a mother hawk standing loving guard over her nest of eggs.

This could be my new home.

Piers stepped up beside me, lowering his voice to a near whisper. "It's not too late to leave, my lady."

I narrowed my eyes on him. "You seem very eager to be rid of me, sir."

He looked away. "It's just that I've seen people be lured in before. Court life may look enticing, but . . ."

For a moment, I was reminded of pearl divers and false treasures. I frowned.

What did a city guard know of what I sought?

The other guard caught up to us both, and I continued forward, my gaze fixed on the castle until, at last, we reached it.

A long bridge above the canal separated the castle from the rest of the city, and a row of guards stood posted at the bridge entrance, with another set at the other end in front of the castle's portcullis. Turrets rose like tiny mountain peaks in the sky, yellow flags fluttering in the path of birds. The castle had a wondrous symmetry, with towers and gardens balanced on each side. It rested like a regal crown atop the city's brow.

There was, however, one blight.

On the western side of the structure, a tower was missing —not in the way of an architect having forgotten to construct it, but rather in the way of a giant having torn it loose. Holes in the castle wall had been hastily bricked with construction materials a different shade from those of the original castle. The broken symmetry was a tragedy in itself, but the lack of any real effort to cover it was worse, like a one-eyed pirate had forgone an eyepatch to leave his empty socket gaping.

The ground that ought to have hosted a tower had been converted to a half-hearted garden composed entirely of a single tree—grotesquely overgrown, drooping beneath the weight of its own wood, branches tangling into the castle structure as if they'd confused themselves for vines. It bore a sickly purple fruit, like figs past ripe.

"What happened to the castle?" I asked Piers.

"That is the Peace Tree," he said, which was hardly an

answer. He only glanced at it from the corner of his eye, as if he, too, were bothered by the visual stain.

"It's long overdue for pruning. Why doesn't the king order it cut down and a new tower built?"

Overhearing, the guards at the castle doors gaped at me in such a way I might have brought news of the plague. Piers hastily made my introductions as a visiting lady. His bearded companion bowed deeply and wished me power—a strange parting. Piers said nothing, only bowed. He seemed as hesitant to look at me as he'd been to view the tree.

Cool air greeted me inside Castle Everspring. A servant stepped forward to assist me, but I had neither bag nor shawl. She waited for orders, staring as much as anyone else I'd passed.

I stared back; I could not think of what orders to give.

At last, I said, "I am in search of wealthy men," and then felt entirely foolish.

The maid never batted an eye. "The king's ball is underway in the throne room. If it pleases you, milady, I shall escort you there at once."

Though I did not mean to, I hesitated. It was so very strange. No one had stopped me to demand a name or a title. The maid standing before me offered to bring me to the *throne room,* to the king himself, without so much as asking my business within the castle. I'd had more hassle attending an event at the lord baron's manor back home.

Of course, I was a different woman now. The most beautiful woman in the kingdom could not belong anywhere *other* than the castle, surely. Everyone must have realized that at a glance.

So I lifted my chin, and I followed the maid into the castle interior. The rugs beneath my feet spoke to enough wealth to excuse the dreary gray of the stone walls, and the portraits and tapestries added to the displays of luxury. We followed halls as winding as the streets of the city. I caught glimpses of polished harps in music rooms and of greenery blooming indoors beneath swirled glass ceilings.

This could be the rest of my life.

I bit my lip, though it did nothing to restrain my giddy smile. At last, we arrived outside a set of arched double doors, propped open and guarded by more men in hawk-crested tunics. The maid curtsied and scurried off. The guards did nothing to bar my entrance, only bowing while trying to conceal their stares.

For a few moments, I hesitated on the hallway rug, my toes poised right at the edge as if it were the darkened line along a beach, dividing dry sand from wet. Inside the doors, a whirl of ballgowns and decorated suit coats swept past, weaving around stone pillars, keeping time to the sound of strings. Laughter burst from one side of the crowd, crashing like a wave against the edge of the room. The dancers moved gracefully out of my sight, like the tide washing out.

Facing down an ocean of uncertainty, I took a step back, and I seemed to step into memory.

Ten Years Earlier

"Astraaa," Beauty's voice distorted my name into a whine. "Come *on*. You're the slowest."

She and her other eight-year-old friends scampered ahead of me, jumping from rock to rock along the shoreline, giggling when one of them slipped and dunked a shoe in the tide, all while I trod carefully on the wet sand, despising the way it caked onto the edges of my boots.

I despised my mother's charge nearly as much. *Astra, go with your sister.*

It was always the same. No matter what *I* wished to be doing, no matter that at this very moment, Mrs. Heartshire was hosting a gathering where I *knew* Denis Cole, the handsome blacksmith's apprentice, would be present. It did not matter, because Beauty needed tending, and whatever Beauty needed, she received.

And, of course, careless for my fear of it, Beauty *needed* to be at the ocean.

Though our city bordered sea, I never ventured out to it by choice. The ocean was a big, unsteady thing that had no care for me and I none for it. Along the beach, even a breeze could not bring true life to the air, so full was it of the pungency of salt and something that had lived too long in a shell.

While Beauty clambered recklessly along rocks, I picked my way carefully. The rocky shoreline set me ill at ease, especially as the boulders grew bigger approaching the towering cliff that gave Widow's Point its name—the overlook where widows could weep for lost ships and the men they'd carried, tears falling to join the dead in the ocean below.

Despite the official name, no one really called our port city and surrounding land Widow's Point. It was just *the city*. The only one that mattered. Home. And I would have much preferred remaining on its orderly streets to clambering along its rockiest shore.

Beauty dropped onto a large, angled boulder with a sigh,

sprawling along its edge, her feet dangling above my head. I approached from a sensible ground level, watching for crabs and other creeping creatures that might pop from hidden burrows beneath my feet. My sister's friends continued to climb and laugh in the distance. Waves sprayed white against the cliff beyond.

Beauty moaned. "They never wait for me! And why do I require a chaperone? And why must my chaperone be *you*?"

At least we were united in mourning.

"Are you finished, then? I should like to return home." I shook my foot. A clump of sand broke free and fell. As the newest wave washed in, I inched to the left before it could touch my partly cleaned shoe.

Beauty laughed. "It's silly you're afraid of the ocean."

"I'm not afraid," I said crossly. "This is a waste of time, that's all."

I was nearly fifteen, and I should have been chasing boys in ballrooms. Instead I was imagining krakens in every wave—Beauty's fault, since I never heard of such monsters until she brought home the stories. Beauty loved to speak of creatures she knew I would find fearful.

My youngest sister climbed atop the slanted rock, balancing precariously. She shielded her eyes to gaze out across the blue. No figure of a ship broke the horizon. Despite myself, my heart fell, though a longer voyage was good news; it meant Father's bartering proceeded well, and he would return with more silk.

"Beauty, get down. It's not safe."

"I told Rob I'd watch for his return. It's his first voyage, you know."

Of course she pined for Rob. Despite the eight-year gap between oldest and youngest sibling in our family, Rob and

Beauty possessed the same level of immaturity and therefore made a perfect pair, bringing chaos to every room they entered. Or perhaps I was only feeling sour because Rob had taken my entire sewing kit with him on the ship. As if sailors had such urgent need to mend their trousers—and to do so using three needles and six thread colors, besides.

Still watching the horizon, Beauty spoke with her affected voice of storytelling. "The strongest sailor forged his odyssey. And battled years 'gainst gods of wind and sea. Past rolling waves which reared as mountains, came he, at last, to white-sand shores. There found he golden youth in fountains, so to conquer evermore."

"Uh-huh." I watched a beady-eyed crab inch through the seaweed, where it thought I couldn't see.

"Suppose Father finds a white-sand shore." Beauty moved her hand from her eyes, stretching her fingertips toward the sea. "Suppose the fountain of youth truly exists, and it's guarded by a dragon, and every story is real. Can you imagine, Astra?"

"You already have me imagining krakens. Now you want to add dragons to the list?"

She grinned down at me. "Imagine this, then—ten years from now, what does your future look like?"

The crab had disappeared. I searched until I spotted it farther down shore.

"I'll be married," I said. "That's my future."

"Astraaa."

"Beautyyy." I snorted. "What did you expect? I'll be married and never set foot on a beach again, white sand or otherwise. There."

She slipped.

It happened in an instant, like the spray of a wave, and I

felt the same cold chill. My sister was there and gone. Her scream was there and gone. The hungry ocean rumbled throughout, continuous.

I dashed forward. In her fall, Beauty had cracked her head against one of the rocks, and the water swirling her hair washed in with white foam and out with bloody red. My stomach lurched.

"Help! Someone, *help*!" I shrieked, drawing the attention of some fishermen up the beach.

I struggled to drag my sister out of the reaching tide. In the back of my mind, a memory lurked. A memory of the day death had taken another sister.

Thankfully, Beauty roused. She coughed and groaned, reaching a hand up to her matted hair. She cried, and I did, too, though the tears on my cheeks were grateful ones.

With the help of a kind fisherman, I got my sister home. After the physician tended Beauty's wounds, Mother sat me firmly in a chair and demanded answers. A lock of auburn hair had come loose from her bun, frazzled beside her angry brown eyes.

"I told her not to climb!" I said. "She never listens!" Though it was truth, it itched like the sand in my shoes. I was the oldest sister. Beauty was my responsibility, yet she always did what she pleased regardless of my voice.

"I'm sure it was an accident, Astra, but one of the reasons I send you along is to keep her from doing things like this! Don't you care if your sister *dies*?" Mother gave a quick gasp, half a sob, pressing her forehead with one hand. Her shoulders fell. "I'm sorry, sweetheart. I'm sorry. I never should have said that. Come here."

She hugged me tightly, kissed my hair, and encouraged me to get ready for sleep.

But even after crawling into bed, sleep did not come. I remembered Isabella.

Isabella had been my second sister, after Callista, before Beauty. She'd never had a chance to walk along a beach or attend a ball; she'd died at birth. Though I'd been a child at the time, I remembered with clarity the coffin my father built, stained with his tears. Isabella's death had become the family secret, the thing always lurking and never spoken of, as if everyone hoped it would simply fade away if not given voice. But there is no growing that can make a five-year-old forget the day they closed her baby sister in a box.

A soft knock came at my door. When I answered, a maid announced with apology that my sister called for me, so in my nightdress, I padded softly down the hall to Beauty's room.

The overeager girl sat propped by her pillows, light brown eyes full of energy, with a stack of parchment in her lap and a candle on her bedside table. She seemed to pay no mind to the bandage wrapped around her forehead.

I regarded her sternly from the doorway, and it did as much good as it had to stop her from climbing on the rocks. She only grinned, brighter than the candle, and gave the excuse, "I couldn't sleep!"

"So you render *me* unable to sleep." I took a seat in Mother's abandoned chair. She must have retired to her own bed since Beauty was clearly not suffering.

"Well, I had to give my answer." She shuffled and rearranged parchment before extending a sheet toward me. "Here."

"Beauty, it's long after dark. I am not *reading*." Though she constantly begged our tutors for additional study passages, I did not even enjoy the required ones. "What is it?"

"It's my answer! What my future looks like ten years from now."

Of course she'd written it down. There could be a thousand books in the world, and Beauty would still be unsatisfied. She spent so much time in reading, I wondered if she'd forgotten that life itself was not a book.

"I could have saved you a page of writing," I said. "Ten years from now, you'll be eighteen. You'll be searching out a husband—and you had better not still be climbing beach rocks."

Thoroughly unchagrined, she glanced down at the parchment. "I did write 'adventure' twice. See, here and here. Forgot about the husband, though. I suppose he'll fit on the back."

"Forgot about . . ." I sighed. "Beauty, you cannot be impractical forever."

"What's impractical? There's more to life than marriage."

"Of course. There's also childbearing."

"Oh, children. I suppose they'll fit on the back as well."

My eyes were too tired to roll. But even as she amused me, my stomach also clenched, remembering the moment, the chill, my sister there and gone.

"Beauty, you have to be *careful*. I thought you'd . . . I mean, you could have died today."

She laughed. "People don't die from falling—unless it's falling beneath the mighty fire blast of a dragon!"

With a huff, I stood. "Goodnight—"

"Wait!" She caught my nightgown in hand. "I meant it about the future. Malthea wrote—she's the best female philosopher—she wrote that without a purpose, people only drift, so we must direct our own futures, like how Father steers his ship. 'Fate is helmed by purpose.' Look, it's right here."

She pushed a new paper into my hands, and despite myself, my eyes skimmed the words. But they did not land on the ones she'd intended.

Instead, I considered in silence: *The world bends to beauty.*

"Goodnight, Beauty," I said softly, letting the parchment glide to rest on the blanket across her knees. She surrendered with a groan, and I returned to my room, divided from my sister by walls and silence.

Ten Years Later

That day after the beach, I'd learned how the world worked. *The world bends to Beauty*.

"My lady?" one of the guards asked.

Lady. I was not the Astra of old, facing down big, unsteady things like an ocean that might swallow me. I had been reinvented. I touched my hair and pressed my hands to my cheeks, feeling the softness, the smoothness.

The beauty.

I was no longer responsible for my sister, my family. I'd left them behind to chase my own dreams with nothing and no one to hold me back.

And it was time to see the world bend.

So I surged into Everspring's throne room.

CHAPTER 4

ASTRA

EVERSPRING'S THRONE ROOM was not lacking in grandeur. Banners depicting the king's white-hawk crest hung from the walls. Sunlight streamed through high windows, the glass so clear, it seemed invisible. Above the center of the floor hung a massive chandelier topped by candles that seemed to burn without smoke, though any stench could not have pierced through the mouth-watering smells of roasted quail and boar set on the food tables.

The tables were arranged to leave a center square of floor uncluttered—an outer ring of socializing and dining and an inner circle of dancing. The orchestra played from up in the rafter balconies, the music seeming to ring down from heaven. King Kenric sat regally at the head of the room, his widowed mother beside him, the pair of royals flanked by a guard on each side.

A gasp went up near me. All it took was one head turning my way, and a wave of attention spread through the room, stilling the crowd. Ladies gaped from behind gloved hands. Lords halted their conversations mid-sentence.

I dipped in my most elegant curtsy, which had grown three times as elegant under fairy magic.

"I am Astra Acton," I declared boldly, disappointed when my projecting voice did not quite carry above the music. Still, those near me heard it. Whispers took root and began to spread through the crowd.

One dark-haired man stood out, his straight nose and jawline as pointed as his attention on me. Even from across the room, his eyes were deep enough to sink in. I lifted one graceful hand to dance my fingers in his direction. He smirked, whispering something to his companion, a round-faced man who also stared in my direction but lacked the same striking appeal.

Just as I decided to approach, a nobleman stepped directly in front of me. He stared without words. I missed my curtsy, but the lord did not seem to notice or care. His bow nearly brought him to the floor.

"Lady Acton." He took my hand with the desperation of a dying man. "I am Lord de la Mar, and I am overtaken by your beauty."

His words brought a flush of pleasure. "My lord—"

"Marry me."

Another gasp from that easily startled woman to my left. Though she was the most vocal, Lord de la Mar's proposal had clearly shocked every nearby courtier, the guards at the door, and even the man himself. I felt only relief. My outward appearance was one thing, but here was the true proof my wish had not failed. Here was the result I'd anticipated.

"My lord—" I began again, only to stop. Though my eager acceptance begged to be spoken, good sense halted it. The man before me was handsome, if only in a dim way, average in build and features. But the gray streaks at his temples betrayed him. Certainly there was a reason he was middle-aged and yet unmarried, and I was no longer a desperate maiden abandoned in a shack. Now I could have my pick of wealthy men. They crowded this very room.

With a growing smile, I said, "I shall certainly consider it."

I stepped into the crowd, leaving Lord de la Mar in his frozen, speechless state. People drew back slightly as I passed, and the staring was the same as it had been on the street, with one addition—I saw other young ladies in glittering gowns measure their own attire against mine. I saw the displeasure grow, dainty hands raised to conceal it. After I passed, their whispers followed like a breeze behind me. I had never inspired such jealousy before, and I knew it was not right to relish it, but relish I did.

My target stepped forward just before I reached him.

"My lady," said the handsome, deep-eyed lord, "what a stunning sight you are. I am Lord Casserly."

"Astra," I said.

"Dance with me."

There was nothing I wanted more.

His round-faced companion stared at me with greedy eyes. "Surely Lady Astra does not need a dance so much as refreshment. Allow me—"

"I would be delighted, Lord Casserly." I placed one hand in his and lifted my skirts with the other. Smugly, Lord Casserly led me to the dance area, pulling me into a rapid three-step pattern which matched the orchestra's upbeat symphony. Despite his striking looks, he was not much of a dancer, holding me uncomfortably tight and falling shy of the beat on each third step. My own grace covered the gap, never allowing me to stumble.

"My lady." Lord Casserly leaned in close, his face flushed in a handsome way. "You must marry me."

I smiled. "I shall certainly—"

"Allow me to list for you my finest qualities."

He did.

Extensively.

A more knowledgeable horseman than any stable master, indeed—oh, but of course, with all the refinement befitting a royal court. Unparalleled in learning. Not from books, of course. Books could be changed under scribing processes. No, Lord Casserly was a man of true learning, the kind of learning gained through heroic life experience, such as the time—

The music ended before he did, and I pulled free of his grasp, curtsying with an emphasis on *curt*. It made no difference; my every move was flawless.

Lord Casserly lifted my hand to kiss the knuckles. "My lady, our engagement shall be the talk of—"

Interrupting him, a nobleman rushed onto the floor, catching my other hand with the desperation of a drowning man. He showered me with praise and confessed how he'd been quite unable to tear his gaze from me since I'd entered. He offered his own proposal. I tried to find in him the reflection of a dream. All I could see was that he was balding, and he used a handkerchief to mop sweat from his forehead.

"If you'll both excuse me," I began, turning my eyes toward the table of food, "I find myself—"

"Unhand her at once, Merteberge," Lord Casserly barked. "The lady and I are having a private conversation."

My smile grew strained. "Gentlemen—"

Another proposal sounded to my right, and I turned to find a press of suitors bearing down on me, overtaking the dance floor. They began to speak over each other, throwing out proposals, begging me to look their way. All of them together painted a rainbow of options dizzying to behold—some thin as a twig, others bursting their own buttons; some so pale they might blur into the sun, others so dark they were a shadow themselves; some as young as Beauty, others senior to my own father. One man was so ancient, I thought he might have risen from the grave just to ask for my hand. What little hair he possessed was barely a wispy cloud, raining age spots across his wrinkled scalp, and a tilted cane struggled to support him, like a single beam holding up the crooked skeleton of a sailing vessel under construction. His proposal accompanied a wide smile void of all teeth.

"Stop it!" I shouted, forgetting manners. The suitors only bore down with more intensity. Hands reached for me from every direction, catching my arms, stretching me like a rack. "*Stop it now*! Release me!"

They either did not hear or did not listen. The music had never resumed, and the argument rose like a hurricane with me at its center, consuming the room. I caught a glimpse of horrified women at the edge of the dance floor, a few of them shouting for their husbands to come to their senses. I nearly swallowed my tongue. *Husbands.* Even married men were vying for me.

A sharp *crack* cut through the voices.

Lord Merteberge collapsed, scattering the other noblemen. His hands cradled his face while blood leaked between his fingers. Lord Casserly stood above him with red-streaked knuckles. Shock momentarily arrested the crowd, but raging expressions promised an upcoming continuation of the violence.

I tried to scream.

But screaming was not beautiful.

"That's enough!" said a booming voice. "Everyone, step away from her."

While I remained frozen, every other person in the room took a single step backward in eerie unison, clearing a space around me and opening my view. Up on the dais, the king himself stood before his wooden throne, revealing rich cushioning and ornate engravings previously hidden. King Kenric wore a neatly trimmed beard and a ruby-encrusted crown atop a head of rich black hair that showed no signs of gray. His coat of red velvet was patterned with stitches of gold fine enough to rival my own gown. That commanding voice was the voice of a king. Unmatched to his voice, however, his bearing was not the majestic demeanor I expected.

It was the dismissive smile that ruined it.

The king spoke brightly, his smile enough to be unnerving, especially considering the dark circumstances. "I fear the warmth of our evening has been dampened by a draft of cold air. Allow me to close the window."

At his gesture, guards stepped up on either side of me. Though I wanted to protest—and heat rose in my face at having been called a *draft*—I was still too stunned by what had transpired. I allowed myself to be the unruly sheep herded from the room.

CHAPTER 5

DUST

Dust leapt out the window.

It was an annual thing. As close to annual as anything could get in the fairy realm, which did not tell time by seasons but rather by a moon which suffered fits of temper and changed its pattern as a result. But whenever half-moon came around, Dust leapt out window number one. He kept it balcony-free for just such a tradition.

For just an instant after leaping, he was flying. The force of his curse vanished, leaving only the force of the ground, the sweet yank of gravity which pulled him toward the grass far below, waiting to catch him with long, waving arms. The wind rushed past his ears in a symphony of freedom.

Then his flight veered sharply, the curse sucking him toward the tower wall.

A *snap* as he struck the rough stone.

Dust hissed through his teeth. Pain throbbed in his wrist. He took a moment of disappointment, a moment of shallow breath, with eyes closed, forehead pressed to the cool stone. His whole body remained motionless, anchored in place by neither rope nor harness, only by the sheer stubbornness of a curse that required him to maintain contact with his tower at all times, even if it meant refusing to let him fall to the ground like any other creature.

Every half-moon, he tried. Every half-moon, he failed.

After his moment of breathing, he shifted to find purchase on the tower wall and used his uninjured arm to steady himself as he climbed. With the magic of the tower competing against the gravity below, it was more like crawling up an incline than climbing up a straight wall.

Finally, he dragged himself through window number one, tumbling onto the floor of his woodshop. He lay there, staring at the patterns in the ceiling while carvings looked down at him from every wall, no doubt judging him for supreme foolishness—nothing short of supreme foolishness would send a man leaping out a window year after year while knowing it would always end the same. But Dust could never squash the glimmer of hope, the slightest chance that his curse might possess a timeline Doll would never admit to, or have conditions that could shift without his knowledge. That chance was worth a try. So once a year, he ran with full strength, hurled himself into the air, and usually received broken bones for his efforts when the curse heaved him back to his cage.

A scratching sound came from the window. Dust tilted his head just in time to see Bumble clinging to the ledge, black claws digging to find purchase in stone as she heaved her chubby woodmunch body through the opening.

"Bumble, wait—!"

She plopped down on top of him, finding a soft landing on his stomach that left Dust gasping for air. Despite himself, he laughed—once he had enough breath to do so. He used his good hand to push her onto the floor, where she snuffled around before turning to face him.

Bumble had been hanging around Dust's tower since she was a cub; he'd never seen any sign of her parents. She was full-grown now, with shaggy black fur covering a rounded, squat body. Her wide, flat tail resembled that of a beaver, as did her protruding front teeth, though they were such bright orange they could be seen in the dark.

Dust sat up as the woodmunch gently nosed his limp arm, her watery black eyes filled with a condemning question. *What have you done now?*

"Just my annual holiday, friend. Don't worry about me. Hardly even feel it anymore." A lie—he'd already jostled his arm enough to leave him shaking. But he could mend it, at least. During each escape attempt, he carried with him an expensive healing sap, harvested from Doll's garden, sewn into his belt so it couldn't fall from a pocket.

With his left hand, Dust struggled to untie his fabric belt before working slowly at the stitched-in pocket. Bumble nosed his hand away and gnawed the cloth, leaving behind slobber-wet linen and an exposed glass vial. Dust pulled the cork with his teeth before smearing a thin coating of sap across his injured wrist, preserving as much as he could in the bottle.

The throbbing pain eased only a fraction. With reluctance, Dust continued adding layers of sap until the pain faded to a tingle. Just over half the bottle remained.

Bumble waddled off, distracted by the wood shavings beneath the workbench, her flat tail sweeping a wide, curving line through the sawdust on the floor. Dust's carpentry endeavors attracted many a woodmunch as they smelled the sawdust on the air, but they usually circled the bottom of the tower once, found no easy entrance, and left. Bumble had kept coming back as a cub, circling repeatedly with a sad, barking whine, until Dust had started tossing down wood scraps. It had apparently been motivation enough for her to learn to climb the tower, and he'd hardly been rid of her company since. He would never complain. She could eat as many wood chips as she liked, so long as she left the carvings alone. To that end, Dust kept one eye on the ravenous creature.

Turning his wrist carefully, Dust gave a satisfied nod that the break had healed. Doll's trees never disappointed, even if her prices did.

Outside, the spriggan chimes sounded.

Dust's head popped up along with Bumble's. The woodmunch gave a little snuffle in the air, her stubby, rounded ears perking as high as they'd go.

"Which direction is that?" Dust had already leapt to his feet, headed for window number two. "North? Northeast?"

Bumble swung her head a bit to the east, sniffing, then back. She thumped with her tail, sending up a thin cloud of sawdust. *North.*

"Thanks, friend. Don't eat that salamander while I'm on the roof."

Leaping out of window number two wasn't dangerous at all, thanks to the small balcony affixed to the tower wall outside it. Dust thumped across the balcony, following the wall until he reached the low railing. He stepped onto it, then planted his next step on the tower wall itself, heaving himself up so that he moved away from the balcony and into open air. The balcony counted as part of the tower, so if he fell while above it, the curse would let him have a hard landing. But if he climbed above nothing except the ground, the curse would stick him to the wall, as it had done before.

With strange pulls from ground below and tower beside, he scrambled up the gray stone, hunching forward to counteract the pull from below. He must have looked like a drunken squirrel, scampering up a tower-tree until he caught the edge of his upper balcony and swung himself onto it. Then it was a small jump from the railing to grab the beam he'd affixed just beneath the roof's extended lip. He heaved himself onto the roof.

The valley spread below him, green grass waving in the slight breeze, singing its gentle song just at the upper edge of his hearing. To the south were the knee-highs—a forest of dark green with bursts of purple leaves and blossoms—and beyond that, the Trader Swamp.

Dust hiked up to the roof's peak, toes curling around the slanted tiles. They felt warm beneath his feet. Everything in the fairy realm was warm; if not for the reminders in his morningdew mirror, he might have forgotten the existence of such things as winter snows and chilling rains. The highest point of the tower housed a sturdy pole, once used to display a banner. Dust had long since pulled down the banner and stitched it into a collection of other fabric scraps to make his bed covering. He held to the pole, swinging around to face north, squinting into the slight haze of the distant green air.

He'd scaled the tower quickly, so the chimes still rang. Alone, any one of them might have been melodious, but together, they produced a jangle to set his teeth on edge. That was the intention. It was a warning.

It meant: *Human in the realm.*

Carefully, Dust picked the sounds apart. The low, gong-type chords were earth chimes. The mid-range trill was fire.

His eyes swept the northern landscape, landing on a barren smudge of gray and black. *Ashpoint*. The most dangerous region in which a human could land.

The last time a human had landed in Ashpoint, Dust had been too late.

He set his jaw and dropped, sliding down the roof at an angle that landed him on the upper balcony with a heavy *thump*. In almost the same movement, he caught his tethered eel vine and slid down to the lower balcony, ducking back into the woodshop.

Bumble looked up guiltily, the tail and one leg of a carved salamander poking out from behind her bright orange teeth. Dust shot her a quick glare.

The chimes ended. Having guarded the realm's borders and sounded the necessary warning, the sky-dwelling spriggans returned to their hibernation until the next intrusion.

Earth had been the loudest chime, and though it might have been a trick of hope, Dust thought there had been a faint twinkle of wind scales in with the rest. Perhaps the human was right on the border between Ashpoint and Feather Fields. He could hope, but he couldn't count on hope to save lives.

He swept aside a row of carvings on a shelf, sending them clattering to the floor. He had just enough presence of mind to say, "Don't eat those, Bumble!" while he grabbed a fat wooden hedgehog and carefully pried apart the hidden seams, separating the dome of quills from the underbody to reveal a memmus bulb hidden inside. Dust tapped the round bulb three times with his knuckle, and it glowed faintly pink in response.

Then came the worst part.

Waiting.

Dust replaced the hedgehog. He returned the fallen carvings to their shelf. He caught Bumble's tail just in time to pull the woodmunch away from an unsuspecting Singer fairy that otherwise would have joined the ill-fated yellow salamander.

"Come on, Renny," he murmured. His nerves felt like a block of wood under carving, shaved thinner with every passing moment of delay.

Smicker arrived first—the Trader had heard the chimes and was always prompt. Dust could have drawn out the bartering process to get a better deal on his trade, but there was the carving-down of his nerves to consider—*Ashpoint*—and there was also the fact that Bumble hid under his workbench, quivering, the entire time Smicker sat outside the tower.

So Dust traded quickly, and in the end, Smicker flew away, leaving behind a rusted brooch bearing a portal enchantment. A one-way passage to the human realm. Whenever the chimes sounded, Dust made a trade to barter passage to the human realm, passage he could never use for himself.

Dust stared down at the brooch resting against his palm.

Where the metal must have once held pearls, it carried only empty sockets, crusted and brown. One end had bent upwards. Sad excuse for adornment though it might be, it felt weightier in Dust's hand than any monarch's crown.

Because if Dust weren't cursed, touching it would have transported him back to Everspring. Home.

Don't think on it, he ordered himself.

Useless. Without meaning to, he'd already closed his eyes, and his imagination flared with color. He saw Mother's garden, saw *her*. She stood from her favorite bench, arms stretched wide to receive him, voice breaking with tears as she said—

The sharp hum of wings broke his reverie, and Dust's eyes snapped open just as Renny swooped through window number two, coming to land on a painted white swan. The Planter's wings twitched. He darted glances at the window.

"Thanks for coming, friend." Dust smiled.

Renny's skin was such a deep cherry-brown that his faint swirls of wood-grain pattern were hardly visible. His wings took on the job of contrast all by themselves, a dark, unapologetic pink. If Doll was a yellow sunflower, Renny was a pink coneflower, though Dust had learned not to make the comparison out loud. No Planter liked being compared to something not in their garden, and Renny did not like being compared to Doll.

"Where?" Renny said, still looking at the window more than at Dust.

Dust took it as a blessing that he could decipher the chimes in a way few others could. Any fairy creature could hear the general direction, and some could pinpoint it more directly, like Bumble, but few could separate the individual chimes in the cacophony. For most, it was enough to stay away from *that direction*, but there were some creatures who carried ill will toward humans, and he was grateful for anything that slowed them down.

"Ashpoint, near Feather Field."

"They're melted," Renny said in his deadpan way. "Save your resources for the next one."

Ashpoint looked harmless, or so Dust had been told. With the open land and clear air, the thick coating of ash across the ground didn't seem threatening on its own, not like the immediately alarming nature of the Fanged Hills or Trader Swamp. But that ash hid a hundred different crevasses leading to an underground river of lava.

If Dust were to count his blessings, highest on the list would be how his tower had landed in a relatively safe region of the fairy realm rather than dropping straight into a chasm of lava.

"Take this." He extended the battered brooch.

Renny heaved a sigh. He liked to be clear how terribly their deal inconvenienced him. Dust was just glad he'd agreed to it at all. No other Planter would let Dust claim harvests—specifically, no other Planter would defy Doll. Renny did it secretly, but he did it.

"How about a rebel hyacinth?" Renny asked. "Gone in one use, no aches for a week."

He refused to do any *favors* or *errands*. Instead, ferrying an item from Dust to the lost human was simply part of a harvest agreement. It just had to be a harvest Doll wouldn't notice.

As soon as Dust nodded, Renny waved a hand. The movement produced his Planter basket from air, hovering before him. It looked to be woven from stalks of grass, though the stalks acted more like living tentacles. At Renny's command, the weave separated, opening a hole in the basket and twining green arms around the brooch. In just a few moments, the basket had widened enough to suck in the brooch, and then it vanished.

Renny stood, balancing on his bare toes, stretching his wings out wide until the pink feathers brushed the figurines to either side of his swan perch. It was a striking pose, good for a carving. Dust took note.

Before departing, Renny paused.

"With all your failed escapes," the Planter said, "you should resent these Everspring outcasts who return so easily through your efforts."

Dust had considered that before. But he said, "One of us ought to."

A quick movement caught his attention. He stuck his foot out just in time to block Bumble as she inched wide-open jaws toward an innocent mongoose. She pawed at his foot in a dissatisfied way, then returned to snuffling around the workbench legs, searching for overlooked wood shavings, though she'd picked the floor clean, even licking the grooves free of sawdust. Any moment now, she'd start gnawing on the floorboards themselves or take a leg off Dust's stool, as she'd done before.

When Dust looked back, Renny was already gone. All that remained of the swan he'd stood on was a blackened bit of sawdust on the shelf. Payment. He wouldn't keep anything made of wood from another Planter's garden, but without payment, there could be no harvest.

Dust swept the ash onto the floor, and Bumble licked up even that. She sneezed, then looked at him with accusatory black eyes. Dust chuckled.

"Thought you'd appreciate a new flavor," he said. "Roasted wood."

But he felt bad enough that he fed her a small bit of uncarved pygmy, peeling the bark first. Then he reluctantly shooed her out of the tower.

Once alone, he pulled his mother's letters from storage, scanning words he'd memorized. The chimes always made him nostalgic, and combined with a failed half-moon escape, the pain twisted his heart more fiercely than usual. He read his mother's words and saw her in his mind, tracing the shape of her in ink on the page. It was foolish. Like leaping out a window knowing there was only agony to come. But since he would not surrender to fate, he had to endure.

After a few hours, he worked up the courage to pry apart the hedgehog. The bulb inside glowed a soft, comforting blue; Renny had found the human. Dust breathed a sigh of relief.

One of us ought to escape.

He would not wish his own fate on anyone, and even as he helped other Everspring outcasts, he held to the faint hope that someday, help might come for him, too.

CHAPTER 6

ASTRA

Every portrait lining the hallway seemed to look down on me in judgment. The carpet dragged at my shoes, and the gray stone walls seemed to be the walls of a dungeon. The castle which had been so inviting from the moment of arrival now seemed an unsteady thing, waiting to collapse and strike me down as Lord Casserly had done to his rival. Would my blood be just as red across the gray castle stones or would I not even bleed?

After all, bleeding was not beautiful.

I followed the guards in a haze until they deposited me in a small room. While I'd expected a dungeon cell, the room was more akin to a study, with a wooden desk marked by inkwells and leatherbound journals. A single window permitted entrance to the sun's dimming evening rays.

With nothing else to do, I seated myself at the desk and waited.

The king hadn't called for my head or even a punishment, though I would surely be barred from court after causing such a spectacle. Thrown from Everspring only hours after arriving.

This was not what I'd wished for.

"I've been tricked," I whispered.

Despite Callista's warnings of fairies, despite the rumors I'd heard whispered by ladies at tea of this curse or that one, despite my own witness of Beauty's man-turned-beast, I'd fallen prey.

The pearl had looked so enticing that I'd taken hold of a boulder and sank myself in the ocean with eagerness.

Slanted light reflected off a hand mirror atop the desk, dancing across the wall, laughing at me. I lifted the object—squinting as it momentarily blinded me—then angled it away from the window.

The mirror spoke its message clearer than a barrel of water ever could: Truly, I was stunning. Perfection incarnate.

My wish could not be a curse. I would not accept it.

"Fairy," I said with determination.

A little *pop* sounded to my right, and she appeared, floating serenely as if suspended in water. Blue glitter trailed her every movement.

"Something is amiss with my wish."

The blue fairy tilted her head, surveying me. "Many wealthy men proposed, just as you desired. Are you not pleased?"

She had the audacity to grin.

"I was nearly torn apart in the throne room," I hissed, glancing at the door in case the guards heard me and re-entered. "Even *married* men vied for my hand. It was madness!"

The fairy pushed her bottom lip into a pout. Apparently she responded only to wishes. So be it.

"I wish for only wealthy men my *age* to propose," I said, "and they must be unmarried and handsome. As well as suitable husband material—no abusers, drunkards, or other unsavory types."

The fairy shook her head, sprinkling blue dust into the air. "Astra has been granted a wish."

"I demand another!" I tried to level a glare at the creature beside me, though it felt more like a sweetly concerned frown. "In the stories, there are always extra wishes."

The fairy's eyes were a cold, empty blue. "Am I a story?"

The world felt as cold as her gaze.

"This is not a new wish," I tried. "This is merely the amendment to the current one. A clarification for it. You must clarify it."

She ignored my pleas. "A wish has been made, and it may be undone only by completion. If you seek completion, you must be drawn to that which is ugly. You must see and treasure the wealth in it."

With that, she disappeared, leaving me with her useless riddle. I groaned, but when I attempted to slump in my chair, my spine deemed the action unbeautiful and held me with rigid poise. At the very least, I should be allowed to slouch when there was no audience to witness the slip in beauty! But the magic remained firm, my own body defeating my inner struggle.

Just to have some form of control, I stood, and at that moment, the door opened to admit the king himself.

"Your Majesty." At least enchantment covered my nerves. My curtsy came smoothly, even with muscles tensed.

Kenric's smile was subdued, though still present, as he regarded me with his own stiff posture, hands clasped behind his back. I braced myself for punishment.

"Interesting specimen," he murmured at last.

Specimen! Was I a crab at market, particularly long of claw?

"Beg your pardon?" I managed.

At his gesture, I stepped forward, and he circled me like a tailor taking measurements, hemming and hawing in the same way, as if noting regrettably narrow shoulders and bony ankles in need of covering.

"It's a bit much," he said, "but I cannot deny the effect. The shining hair is so . . . bold. We may try covering it. A queen's beauty reflects the good taste of her husband, but it should not overshadow the true monarch."

For the first time since coming to Everspring, I was the one staring.

"You will marry me," declared the king.

"I will not," I declared right back, shocking both of us.

I was a fool. One thing to dislike being evaluated like the day's latest catch, but he was a *king*.

Just as I began a correction, the king spoke first—

"Marry me. That is an order."

An order.

My jaw clamped tight while I wrestled with simultaneous urges to storm at having been ordered about and rejoice at having been chosen by the wealthiest man in the kingdom. Meanwhile, King Kenric frowned, absently rubbing his short beard.

He was handsome. He was certainly near my age. Most importantly, *he was a king*.

"How do you resist?" he asked.

Yet he also said things like that—as if *he* were the one with such striking beauty that I should be falling over myself to accept. I lifted my chin.

"You have not given me proper respect in the offer," I said primly.

If the competition of men was all my wish had truly bestowed upon me, then I would at least use that competition to receive a proper proposal rather than a pompous order. I was the daughter of a merchant; bartering was a game I knew well.

Daughter of a merchant. Dare I ever be a queen?

The king looked down, and his shift in gaze drew mine. I gasped to see that the floor had begun to grow around my feet. The pale wood fractured, reaching up with splintered fingers to hook my shoes in place. It grew even as I watched, inching up my laces, curling around my ankles. No matter how I yanked, I could escape neither the floor's hold nor my own shoes. When I clawed at the wooden tendrils, they did not break.

"What's happening?" I cried.

Too late, I remembered the warning of dear Piers, concerned for a stranger: *You must not encounter the king.*

Kenric shook his head. "A pity. Now I'll have to retake the search for a bride all over again, and it's such a tedious affair."

I began to sink, as if the wood had turned to quicksand. The branches grew thicker, reached higher, sucked me down into the shifting, molten floor. I grabbed for the desk, but the magic's hold was stronger than mine, ripping me away, sinking me up to my knees, then my hips. Kenric turned away.

The floor glowed with a bright green light from deep below.

Then—with one last gasp from me—it swallowed me whole.

CHAPTER 7

ASTRA

THE HEAVY AIR SMELLED MOIST. My mouth tasted like bark and wet earth. I coughed once, then blinked hard and sat up with a groan.

Only to tremble at the sight above me.

A green sky. Like sunlit leaves—a green so fierce it seemed to glow with inner light, and that light from every direction. No distinct sun. No clouds.

I lay on a bed of soft moss that moved unnaturally as I did, rippling as if it were suspended across water. Something darted past my eye, and I gasped, ducking my head before realizing it was one of my curls. The ends of my hair drifted gently in the air, the same way the fairy's did as she floated. Somehow, I was in her world now. It was the only explanation.

Unsteady, I climbed to my feet, sending the moss rippling in waves. Clumps of vibrant grass and spongy bushes dotted the ground at random, and in some places, the moss jutted up like an inverted waterfall, long and thin until it grew bulbous at eye level. Little homes were nested inside each mossy sphere. In the nearest one, I could make out a structure of wooden branches, with leaf-thatching for a roof and spaces left gaping like windows.

As I watched, a creature zipped out of a window. It might have been a dragonfly—if dragonflies were ever a blinding shade of purple, possessed of four sets of wings, and in the habit of carrying tiny baskets. Or if dragonflies ever cackled and said, "HUMAN, TRADE!" in scratchy little voices.

I ought to have shrieked myself hoarse, but enchanted beauty held back my voice, maintaining composure. Instead, I gave a delicate cough, covering my mouth with one hand and using the other to shoo the fiendish dragonfly on its way. It gave a little "HMPH!" before darting back into its house.

Then I squeezed my eyes tightly closed and attempted to breathe. My floating hair tickled my cheek. I realized my mistake as the world around me came to life with unnatural sounds. Buzzing, humming, a far-off roar. Faint chimes above my head.

I looked up, but the quiet tinkle of chimes ended. Perhaps I'd imagined them to begin with.

Moving seemed preferable to staying among the unnatural dragonflies that now peered at me from the window of every home, yet when I moved, I staggered on the unsteady moss, each step taking me farther than anticipated with less effort, like I weighed no more than a feather. A regular step sent me bounding over an entire bush as if I had made a leap.

I pressed both hands to my heart—which seemed to be attempting a staggered escape of its own—and wished desperately to be home. Of course, making a wish was what had led me here in the first place.

All I wanted was an uneventful life, a secure marriage,

financial stability, with no surprises and no misfortune. Safe. Protected. I'd thought myself in turbulent waters after Mother's death and Father's bankruptcy; now I knew what sinking truly felt like.

My hands trembled. I had to move. If I stayed where I was, I would drown.

"Hello?" I called out, my voice hoarse even without shrieking. Who did I expect would answer me? Talking dragonflies?

Then I spotted a familiar collection of wooden boards, buckled and broken as if something had ruptured through them. My sigh of relief nearly sank me to my knees. I inched forward, careful of the uneven ground and strange weightlessness. What grand irony that I'd spent all my life avoiding sailing only to walk across magical ground that surely rocked worse than the deck of any ship. At last, I reached a board and pulled it back.

It was not a castle room I saw beyond. It was, instead, a bed of green moss hosting a wicked beast. The creature looked up at me with soulless black eyes and a wide tail that seemed to have been flattened by a carriage. Then, with a low, rumbling growl, the monster took an entire board between its fearsome orange teeth. A sharp *crack* split the air, splintering one end of the board violently upward.

My stomach heaved upward with it. I nearly fainted.

Without waiting for it to crunch my bones next, I bolted. At least, I attempted to. My own legs strained against me and limited my pace. Running, I realized, would set my face afluster and muss my hair and clothes—such would not be beautiful, and I was ever-beautiful now.

Wonderful! I would be the most beautiful corpse this fairy realm had ever seen.

Just as my heart nearly gave out to panic, I realized the strange weightlessness was working in my favor. Though my pace was only a brisk walk, each step carried me three times the normal distance, and in moments, I'd lost sight of the boards and their hungry predator. The ground rolled beneath me like ocean waves, never in the same place each time I came down, but my enchanted grace compensated for the movement, and though I staggered, I did not fall.

At least not until I came to the cliff.

The sheer edge appeared without warning, moss rolling over it like a waterfall. Near-floating as I was, the ground fell away while I was still in the air with no way to avoid the drop—and drop I did, as all my normal weight returned in a rush.

I crashed down through reaching plant limbs, feeling the sting of whipping branches like thorns. They at least slowed my fall, and I landed with a *whump* that stole my air. But I was alive.

After lying still for a moment, trying to catch my breath, I moaned, rolling onto my back. I'd fallen into a forest, one that seemed *almost* akin to ours back home, with the brown bark of trees and the non-rippling moss of a steady forest floor.

If only it weren't for the eyes.

They blinked at me from a few trees, and I could not tell if they belonged to camouflaged creatures or the trees themselves Something giggled. A stubby tree stretched thick roots out into the soil, its bark dotted with violet flowers. Two of the flowers twitched, revealing themselves to be ears. From between them, a set of black eyes opened, regarded me, and closed again with another giggle.

I tried to curl into a pitiful ball, but enchantment

restrained my spine, instead posing me like a pitiful maiden in a tapestry, laid out in some forest grave for bards to sing about in mournful tales by firelight. I did not want to be a mournful tale; I wanted simply to be a person. The tightness in my chest and the throb of a headache spoke to oncoming tears, but they did not fall, nor even sting my eyes.

All my life, I had cried easily. It was perhaps the thing for which Beauty teased me the most, since she herself was so resilient. I cried when someone told of accidentally crushing a butterfly or losing wares to an unforgiving ocean. Beauty took such stories in stride and called them all pieces of an adventure, the disappointments along with the triumphs.

Crying was not Beauty's way, and magic clearly knew it, because the ache built within me until I felt my bones would surely break, but outwardly, I was only composed.

I closed my tearless eyes and let out a pitiful dry sob.

And then something dropped on me from a tree.

It felt like a small bean sack, the kind children threw back and forth in the streets, but I *knew*. I could feel the legs. Every muscle in my body seized, and I flew to my feet, flinging my arm out in an attempt to dislodge the massive spider. I caught a glimpse of it as it sailed into the trees, orange body and flailing legs. I nearly lost my stomach.

It had bitten me. My wrist burned around two puncture wounds.

I was going to die here.

"No, no, no," I clenched my teeth, yanking my sleeve down to hide the wound from sight. "No, this is not my future. No."

Before any other creatures could leap at me, I shuffled away as quickly as my aching body would allow. My spine stiffened again in regal posture. At a glance, I would appear to be strolling beautifully through the woods, and the giggling creatures would not know how terribly they frightened me. Unless they could smell it. Unless they were encouraged by confident prey and were, at this moment, slowly surrounding me, preparing to pounce with jagged teeth and—

I drew in a deep breath, fisting my hands in my dress. Only then did I realize I'd torn it horribly in the fall. The short gash along the left shoulder seam could be easily repaired, but the same could not be said of the gaping, ragged hole in the outer skirt.

I would have thought an enchanted dress impervious to harm, or at least expected it to mend itself after injury, but whatever magic existed in this realm must have overcome whatever existed within my dress. The pattern of black diamonds reflected green angles from the sky, as if they'd taken ill.

With no other option, I resumed my march through the forest, praying to find a shelter of some kind. All I found was a wide river with velvet-soft moss along its banks, the water carrying too much purple in its blue hue.

A green centipede the length of my arm scuttled down the river with the current, its needle-thin legs dancing across the water's surface. This was far worse than any scuttling crab. I watched it from the corner of my eye in horror, hugging my arms tightly around my ribs, though the self-hug offered little comfort. My wrist throbbed, and my fingers felt swollen.

At last, the trees thinned, and I found a sharp path upward. Leaving the forest behind, I rose into something resembling a field. The green grass waved without wind, creating swirling patterns that almost seemed to sing, but when I gave a gasp, it was not for them.

It was for the tower.

In a world of sickeningly bright green, the tower was constructed of gray stone, and I had never been so comforted to see the drab color. Though it bore the strange addition of two jutting wooden balconies connected with a vine, it had the same clay tiles on its conical roof as Castle Everspring. Perhaps a giant really had stolen the castle's tower. Plucked it right off the side of the structure before planting it in a fairy's field. I was not about to complain.

I struggled through the tall, entangling grass, forcing my way to the tower door—

Only to realize such a thing did not exist. After circling the base twice, even pressing at the most suspicious seams in hopes of finding a hidden door, I was forced to concede defeat.

"Hello?" I called up to a distant window. "Is anyone there? Please."

Perhaps insanity was setting in, because I conjured a fanciful hope that a human family lived in a doorless tower in the middle of a fairy realm. A kindly mother would come to the window and call down, "Oh, hello, dear! Do come inside. We have no spiders here." They would have a batch of hot tea and a cozy bed, just waiting.

That, of course, did not happen. No one answered my call.

With a sigh, I seated myself at the base of the tower. I would have to content myself with the stone against my back, even if I still felt exposed. Even if I imagined the endless number of things which could be, at this moment, slithering through that tall grass, creeping ever closer, dripping purple saliva—

A length of rope dropped into the grass.

I scrambled away from both tower and rope. Then I craned my neck to look up at a window far above me, the only one without a balcony attached. The rope had originated there. It dangled in invitation.

"Who's there?" I demanded.

No answer.

It was a realm of magic. Perhaps the rope was enchanted and had thrown itself down to answer my need. Or perhaps there was a terrible monster living in the tower, luring in delicious girls with its deceptively human architecture and ropemaking abilities.

Although, as I studied closer, I realized my mistake. What I had assumed to be rope was, in fact, another vine. Not green like the one connecting the balconies, but the shade of flaxen hair. It had the look of a braid, too—densely woven at the center, flighty wisps all around. Touching it, it had the moist feeling of a plant, but with a slight tackiness like that of dried tar. I wiped my hand on my dress. Surely this was a trick of some kind.

Just as I debated turning away, a low growl came from something close. The nearby grass rustled.

I seized the vine and began climbing for dear life.

CHAPTER 8

DUST

DUST HEARD THE SPRIGGAN CHIMES, but they were all wrong.

By the time he reached his roof, they were already gone, and they'd been too faint to begin with. Almost an echo of real chimes. Had they been from the south? Water scales? The Trader Swamp lay to the south, with its unsteady gravity and ground. Everspring outcasts had landed there before.

He squinted into the distance, biting his tongue.

He'd once dreamed of the chimes and woken in a cold sweat. To this day, he didn't know if he'd imagined them or if they'd sounded in his sleep. Imagination was the more comforting answer. Should he send Renny just in case?

The chimes had *never* been that faint, and for them to mark an intrusion in the swamp, of all places, they ought to have been near deafening. The swamp was just on the other side of the knee-highs. If not for the trees, Dust would have been able to see right into it.

He looked at the empty space beside him. Alone, with no one to offer insight or opinion. With a sigh, he slid down the roof, dropping heavily to his upper balcony. Just to be certain, he waited there for Smicker, but the Trader did not come. That was answer enough.

So he entered through the window and took the long way down to his woodshop, following the winding staircase from his bedroom, through his storage room, and into his workspace at last.

He'd been using his morningdew mirror when he thought he'd heard chimes, but leaving the basin had broken the connection and wasted his feather. A pity. He'd been viewing a small town through the eyes of an barn owl in flight.

Without morningdew, he returned to regular chores: crafting dyes for paint, sharpening knives, mending the new hole in his trousers. On second thought, he didn't care to do the mending, so he stowed the thread in the storage room and sat down at the workbench to continue his latest carving. He'd barely scraped the first curl of wood free along the ship's prow when he heard the grass outside begin a high-pitched, troubled song, as if . . .

As if something were tromping through his meadow.

Dust perked up, dropping his tools. He stuck his head out window number one and saw nothing, so he crossed the room, ducking onto the lower balcony.

A human.

Even with the distance, there was no mistaking the tiny form in a dazzling dress making her way through the tangled grass. The grass bemoaned her disturbance with a sound like buzzing insect song in summer. Dust only stared.

It *had* been spriggan chimes. That was all he could think.

While he stood paralyzed, the curse began to pull, reaching out with invisible hands to draw him back toward the tower. It had been so long since he'd seen another human, he'd nearly forgotten their effect on his curse.

For a moment, he was a child again, clutching a windowsill as he desperately fought the magic pulling him back. Mother had sent a knight to rescue him, a knight with a red-and-gray crest. The rescue had failed.

Gritting his teeth, Dust dug in his heels, as if his recent dive out the window hadn't taught him anything at all. But no matter how he strained, the curse dragged him back, just the same as when he was a child. He could not out-force it. He would have to outthink it.

Relenting, he ducked through the window before he could be shoved through it. Then he darted up the stairs to his storage room, overturning buckets and dried herbs in his haste as he searched. Faintly, he heard what might have been a voice calling up to the tower.

There! He gave a little "ha!" of triumph as he snatched up a bundled lee vine. Lee and eel vines grew on the same tree in pairs—one slick, one tacky—and Doll had included the full pair when he'd paid for a harvest. Dust had attached the eel vine to his balconies and left the lee in storage, since he found climbing the tower wall easier than climbing a vine. A regular human would surely feel the opposite.

He rushed back down the stairs—nearly tripping at the bottom—and crouched below window number one. The knight had brought his own rope, complete with a grappling hook, but even though Dust hadn't gotten a real look at the woman below his tower, he felt certain that dazzling dresses did not come equipped with grappling hooks.

Fortunately, one of his many escape attempts had included securing an iron ring to the floor, which was still there. He knotted the vine around it, throwing his weight on to be sure it held, before tossing the bundled end out the window.

Then he held his breath, waiting.

For a moment, nothing happened. Dust edged back enough that he couldn't be seen from below, so that the curse wouldn't do anything drastic to keep him out of view. The silence strained his ears.

"Who's there?" the woman called.

Better to answer or stay silent? Dust found his voice frozen anyway.

The vine tightened.

She was climbing.

CHAPTER 9

ASTRA

HAULING MYSELF ARM-OVER-ARM up a vine was not as easy as I'd imagined. Bracing my feet against the tower wall seemed to help at first, but mostly it pushed me away and twisted me around. My long, flowing skirts did nothing to aid, either, but I at last found a rhythm in trapping the vine between my shoes, one on top of the other, and using that leverage to shimmy up. The vine's texture was a large help as it clung to my hands and shoes, refusing to let me slip.

My arms ached fiercely—injured hand in particular—but my face displayed no grimace, and my breathing did not labor. I was inwardly strained but outwardly composed. A mask of beauty.

By the time I reached the window, my arms felt like floppy vines themselves, especially after I made the mistake of glancing down at the sheer drop. Quickly, I grabbed the ledge and heaved myself into the tower room beyond, rolling gracefully to my feet rather than landing in a disheveled heap. At least enchantment saved my pride.

The room was empty. To my left, the stone wall curved

away, following the shape of the tower, but to my right, a strange, milky wall divided the space, stretching floor to ceiling. Through it, I could make out only vague shadows.

The tower was not as dim as I'd expected. Light from the window brightened the floor, and in addition to that, the shelves held what looked like golden apples, scattered at irregular intervals, emitting a pleasant yellow glow. I could make out the room's interior quite well.

It was a mess.

Shelves lined every inch of the curving wall, and each shelf overflowed with wooden figures. The shelf nearest to me held a family of three large foxes, painted with orange backs and black-tipped ears. Under their bellies and between their paws sat a crammed collection of miniature ducks, owls, deer, finches, and turtles. Tiny foxes lined the backs and tails of the big ones, balanced precariously.

The other shelves were all similarly packed with carvings. Some figures were easily recognizable as depictions from the real world, but others could belong only to the fairy realm. I shivered at a carving of a talking dragonfly, complete in every detail down to the basket dangling between its spindly legs. Despite my repulsion at the creature, I leaned closer to peer at those delicate legs, suspended between body and basket like the thinnest of wires. How did anyone carve so delicately? I feared if I touched it, it would break.

The far left of the room held a sturdy workbench, its surface half buried beneath a collection of carving tools and blocks of wood waiting to be shaped, the floor beneath it littered with curled wood shavings and a thick layer of sawdust. It was obvious how the owner of this tower spent their days engaged.

"I am Astra Acton," I declared, pretending confidence. "If

any fairies live here, I'll thank you to keep to yourself for a moment. I promise to be gone from your home and realm as soon as possible."

A disembodied chuckle answered me, low and eerie. It seemed to come from the other side of the milky wall. I had *much* preferred the silence, but I was too weary to flee again.

Flexing my right hand, I found the joints stiff and the skin hot to the touch. Thin orange lines crept beneath the skin, reaching from the puncture wounds upward beneath my sleeve. Surely that did not bode well, but with no access to a physician in this wretched, murderous realm, I could do nothing except push it from my mind.

With no chair available, I sat on the stool at the workbench, carefully lifting my skirts to keep them from trailing through the sawdust. Though I meant to consider my options, my attention was instead captured by the carving in progress on the table. It had begun life as a thick slab of wood, and it had been carved as if it were a painting rather than a statue, the artist carefully shaving away layers of wood in choice places to create an image with depth.

In the center of the carving, a galley ship sailed directly toward me, its prow reaching forward as if it were coming to life from within the wood. Waves beneath it rolled in elegant curls. With care, I reached out to touch them, tracing the delicate ridges and indents. Faint lines etched by a knife marked places yet to be carved, outlining the point of the mast and the curve of billowing clouds, low in the sky.

I had never imagined anything could make me miss the ocean.

"This is stunning," I whispered.

"Pleased to hear you think so," answered a male voice.

I leapt to my feet. The room remained still, golden apples glowing on undisturbed. My heart began to calm.

"Excuse me, Mr. Woodcarving Fairy," I said crossly. "I've had a trying day. If you're going to speak, please tell me the quickest way to exit your realm."

Silence. Outside the window, I heard the rustlings of a savage world.

"Same way you came, I imagine," said the wood fairy from behind the shadowy wall.

Unlike my blue fairy, this fairy's voice was clearly masculine, slightly deeper than my brother's but with the same upbeat energy. I'd not thought much about my fairy's accent, subtle as it was, but the wood fairy spoke with a distinctly melodic sound. His voice danced from one letter to the next, clipping some, extending others, like the way he stretched out his *I* to have a little upswing. His vowels carried the same unnatural brightness as a green sky.

"The way I came," I repeated flatly. "I came by way of floorboard, and the floorboards have been eaten."

The wood fairy laughed at my plight, that same subdued chuckle as before. "By magic is what I meant. Astra, was it? Can you really hear me, Astra?"

"Yes, you've not gone anywhere. Though you're welcome to, if all you intend to do is mock me."

Unhelpful creatures, the lot of them. However, an unseen fairy behind a strange wall remained slightly preferable to the ones lurking in trees and slithering across water. Especially since this one seemed to be much the same as the one that had granted my wish, at least as far as intelligent conversation and lack of floorboard-eating tendencies.

"I'm Dust," said the wood fairy. "Always wanted to

introduce myself. Could you say 'pleased to meet you'? Always wanted to hear that."

Narrowing my eyes, I said, "I know better than to be tricked into saying what a fairy wants."

Then my face grew hot, thinking of my wish. I studied a shelf of carvings.

"I'm not a fairy," he said. "I'm human."

"You're in this fairy realm."

"So are you."

Perhaps he was some kind of mind-reading illusion fairy. I'd wanted a human structure and found one. I'd hoped there were humans inside, then lo and behold.

"Dust isn't a name," I said. I'd always thought my sister carried the crown for most ridiculous name, but Dust was even worse than Beauty.

"I worked hard to choose it. Takes more'n that?"

"To make me believe you? Certainly."

"That stings." It sounded like he meant it; his voice had softened.

If he was some kind of creature luring me in, he surely could have eaten me by now. Maybe he was a good fairy who just wanted someone to admire his carpentry skills. Or maybe . . . he really was as he claimed.

I shifted uncomfortably. The air felt stuffy, and the room seemed to have grown hotter since I'd arrived. Touching my forehead, I found it dry of sweat, but perhaps that was simply because sweating was not beautiful. Though I told myself not to look at my wrist, my traitorous eyes darted to the angry red skin just the same.

Focus on your possible fairy problem first, I told myself.

After a moment, I tiptoed over to the milky wall and prodded it with the fingertips of my left hand. It rippled at my touch, like the green moss of my landing place, and though it felt like a rough-woven linen, it carried solidness beneath. Were the creature on the other side a fairy, I would have assumed he wished to remain unseen. If he was human, what was I to make of the barrier?

One of the shadows on the other side of the wall fractured, splitting into two murky forms. I held tensely still as the larger shadow approached, stopping in a mirror of my position. Even standing mere inches away, I could not make out any features, just a formless blur, taller than I, like the shadow of a reaching tree over a frozen pond.

Dust knocked gently on his side.

I leaned back, then reconsidered. Hesitantly, I pressed my palm to the wall. It felt solid as stone when I tried to press through, and it rippled in faint rings around my hand, like water disturbed by a stone.

Dust did it again, three slow knocks, tremoring my hand. Each knock cast deep ripples.

I knocked back just the same, three times.

"Thanks," he said softly, and his gratitude was even stranger than my desire to answer his knock.

"If you're human," I said, "how did you end up here?"

He sighed, dark outline shifting. "That's a long story, 'n one I've never said out loud. Don't get much chance for real conversation."

"Up here in this isolated tower? You don't say."

Dust repeated his low chuckle. It didn't sound eerie this time. It sounded human.

"Did the king send you here too?" I asked.

"Of a sort."

I thought I heard him sniff. Perhaps his nose was as bothered by the sawdust in the air as mine—each step I took stirred more, and my new beauty would not allow me a relieving sneeze, so I was forced to hold my nose and breathe shallowly through my mouth until the feeling passed.

"You disobeyed the king," Dust said after a moment.

I huffed. "I momentarily rejected his proposal. I intended to rectify the situation—how silly of me for not realizing I was dealing with a spoiled child who banishes others to terrifying realms without warning."

"The king's married," Dust said. "Rather aging by now, with grown children."

"The late king, you mean. He recently passed. Kenric is the newly crowned disaster—and though this is hardly relevant, he's the only heir." I frowned. "How long have you been here?"

"The days blur," Dust said softly. He cleared his throat. "Shame about the king."

The emotion in his voice seemed too heavy for a passing condolence. I leaned back, eyeing the wall once more. The dark blur on the other side wavered gently but gave nothing else away.

"How exactly did you come to be here?" I asked.

At the same moment, he asked a question of his own, our voices colliding: "Why'd you reject the new king's proposal?"

A good question. Rather than allowing myself to feel foolish for having lost the greatest opportunity of my life, I justified, as I often did. "I did not appreciate his attitude, and since my options are plentiful, all of them impressively wealthy, I expect the proper respect, even from a king."

Stars, I sounded like the most arrogant woman alive. But if it was a choice between embarrassment and arrogance, I would always don the latter.

"Are the streets of Everspring so rampant with men just waitin' to be husbands?"

I snorted, then composed myself. "In my few short hours there, I received dozens of proposals. Therefore, yes, I'd say Everspring made for fine hunting grounds indeed."

Just as the fairy had promised. My stomach tightened.

Dust gave a low whistle. "Never seen *that* in the human realm."

With shock, I recoiled from the curtain, pointing at the unseen creature beyond it. "*Human* realm. You *are* a fairy! I knew it!" Tricked *again*. All it had taken was one lonely, emotional voice, and I'd swallowed hook and line with eagerness.

"I'm not!" he protested. The shadow moved, and a heavy thump sounded just above my head, making me jump back another step. "My head's up here, aye? You'll never see a Planter this tall!"

"No, I won't," I snapped. "Because there's a wall in the way!"

Just in case he had any ideas about changing that, I decided to take my chances out in the grass. I spun toward the window but slipped on a loose carving tool.

My enchanted grace saved me from falling—it could not save the shelf of foxes my arm crashed into.

CHAPTER 10

DUST

A SERIES OF LOUD CLATTERS ECHOED on the other side of the woodshop. It was a familiar sound from the many times Dust had collided with one of his own shelves, but he still felt a rush of panic.

"You all right, Astra?"

Her name felt strange on his tongue. There was another *human* in his tower—though apparently she did not like attention drawn to that fact. He'd never before had to worry about not sounding like a fairy; when the knight had entered his tower, his child self hadn't managed any words past tears. He'd never even learned the man's name, because he'd not had the presence of mind to gather information, only to grieve the sudden wall that prevented his rescue.

At least the knight had left behind the letters from Mother.

"Astra!" She'd still not answered. Was she injured? He pressed both hands to the wall, though it was pointless. It held as firmly as any part of the curse.

"I'm here," she said at last, voice soft.

Dust breathed again.

"I broke one of your carvings. I'm sorry."

That prompted a wry smile. "Never mind the carving—if you haven't noticed, there's at least a shelf to spare."

"Not anymore." Her voice lightened a bit. "I'll admit this *is* an impressive collection, Dust."

The sound of his name nearly stopped his heart. No other human had ever said it. He turned away from the wall, silently cursing the barrier while blinking a sheen of moisture from his eyes. Then again, perhaps the magic boundary was a good thing, at least for his guest's sake—otherwise he might have swept up a complete stranger in a hug.

Be a normal human, he ordered himself, well aware of the irony. *At least stop thinking* human *so much.*

"I'm sorry I don't have a way to prove I'm not a fairy," he said. "I can only hope you'll believe me."

Astra didn't respond, but she also didn't leave. The only answer was a series of gentle clicks and rattles as she replaced whatever had been knocked from the shelf. Dust listened to the melody, wishing all the while that her shadow was more than a dim wraith. She might have been missing a limb for all he could see of her shape.

Still, wraith or no, she existed. *Here.* In his tower. He tried not to cling to all the hope that fact ignited, but he found himself as successful in the attempt as a falling man trying not to cling to a rope.

"My father stole from a Planter," he said, finally answering her repeated question. "But the debt came calling, 'n payment was his firstborn child. That's how I came to be here."

Perhaps he should have been happy to hear the man was

gone. But all he felt was cold. *The late king.* What a phrase, late indeed. Too late to mend anything. Too late to hear from his father's own mouth whether the man regretted what he'd done all those years ago.

Dust had to admit the answer was plain, evident in the walls of his cage, evident in his growth to adulthood without ever having seen his family. Still. Even if his father had not regretted his actions, Dust had hoped to look the man in the eyes just once.

"Your family must miss you terribly," Astra said.

She spoke with an attractive confidence, as if she possessed every answer to be had. Dust wished it could be true.

"Can't you escape?" she asked.

He wished it could be so simple.

"Can't leave the tower, I'm afraid. Not for lack of trying. Also, you see what happens if someone tries to come get me." He knocked on the wall once again, three gentle taps. He didn't know why he kept using the same signal he used with Renny. Maybe because it was a call to save.

Astra gasped. "*I* caused the curtain?"

Did she think he always lived with an impassable barrier in his woodshop? Dust smiled.

"Blocked me off from all my favorite carvings," he said. "To be honest, I don't mind; I'd rather have the company. You're the first human to make it up here who's actually had a conversation with me. My knees have been shakin' this whole time, but since you can't see it, let's pretend I didn't admit it."

"Your first *ever* conversation?"

He chuckled at her mixture of shock and horror.

"You've *never* had a—how long have you been here? What of your parents? They just *abandoned* you?"

Offended on his behalf. Unexpected warmth spread through his chest at that. "A moment ago, you thought me a fairy. Still, I'll accept a good opinion from a friend—that's my price. We're friends now. No turning back."

He braced one arm against the wall, watching her shadow waver. He should have been rushing to help her return to the human realm—it was his usual response for an Everspring outcast—but she wasn't lost in the wilds. His tower was safe. As safe as anything in the fairy realm could get, at least. If he asked, would she stay a while?

He opened his mouth to ask, then closed it.

In the end, he said, "My mother wrote letters, even sent a rescue attempt. She wanted me. At least until she had her next son." She'd spoken of his brother only briefly in her letters and only by that moniker: *your brother*. Dust finally had a name to fill the void. *Kenric*. King now. They'd never even met. "What of your family, Astra? Are you expectin' heroic rescue from the fairy realm?"

For a moment, only silence answered. He saw the shadow tremble.

"No," she said softly. "I'm quite on my own, I'm afraid."

His heart twisted for both their sakes.

As if sensing it, she added, "There's no point to pity. I left my family willingly."

Dust frowned. "Who would do that?"

"Beg *your* pardon, but you have not met my family. They can be quite intolerable, particularly my youngest sister."

"I'd give anything to see my family," Dust said. "Broken a few bones in trying."

"If they abandoned you, they deserve no such devotion."

Confidence in every answer, even when she was wrong. Dust shook his head.

After another moment, Astra said, "It has been a trying day, and I find myself exhausted. I would be most grateful for a place to rest tonight."

"Oh, well, fortunately there's a very comfortable workbench on that side of the wall." Dust chuckled, then sobered. "There's nothin' I can do for a walled-off guest, I'm afraid, but you *are* welcome to stay. In fact, I'd love the company as long as it can last. Don't know if I'll ever get more."

"You are disconcertingly honest, has anyone ever told you?"

Dust watched the shadow meander from one side of the room to the other, as if she searched for a comfortable place to rest.

"No," he said, smiling wryly. "Can't say anyone's ever called me honest."

"Well, *I* am telling you. It is tactful to remain poised within conversation, never admitting fears, reserving private weaknesses for private confidences, and even then, understating their severity. One might say, 'The company is welcome' rather than admitting a dire need for it. Admitting a need gives power to the other party."

Fairy games. Dust could play them well enough; he'd simply lost himself in the rush of meeting another human. Her reminder was a good one, however—to both humans and fairies alike, a person was only as valuable as their use. Doll extended her help because Dust was useful. If Dust wanted any chance of help from Astra, he would have to prove himself just as useful to her.

Before that, though, he allowed himself one moment of

true honesty. "Playin' a power balance makes for lonely interaction, I'd say."

"Never mind, wood fairy."

He heard the scrape of stool legs across floorboards, then a shuffle of fabric as she settled. Silence.

And in the silence, a sound from outside the tower.

"Oh no," Dust said quietly, wincing.

The scrabbling sound of claws on stone grew louder, and then Astra gave a little gasp—no doubt as Bumble heaved herself into view on the window ledge. A moment later, the *thump* announced her entrance.

With the quickness of a Planter, Astra's shadow left the floor, leaping higher. She'd either climbed on his stool or his workbench.

"Shoo!" she said fiercely. "Shoo, beast!"

"It's just Bumble." Dust gave a sheepish grin she couldn't see. "She's harmless. To you, at least. But she'll eat all my carvings if you let her, 'n she'll make herself sick. Oi! Bumble. Out of my workshop. Come back later."

He gave the wall a sharp smack to emphasize his words, but he heard the shuffling sounds of an undeterred woodmunch.

Astra's voice held a distinct note of panic when she spoke. "I saw one of these fiends snap a full board in half!"

"Aye, they'll do that. Bumble, I mean it. *Out*."

In answer, the woodmunch emitted a high-pitched whine, which gave Dust pause. He frowned, listening. After another shuffle, Bumble gave it again. Squinting, Dust thought he could make out the creature's shadow beside his workbench, beneath Astra. Instead of the crisp snap of sacrificed carvings, he heard another keening whine.

"Please don't eat me," Astra whimpered.

"Astra . . ." Dust felt a cold dread, and he had to swallow before continuing. "Did you get bitten by something in the forest?"

"Yes, I—how did you know?"

"Bumble can smell it."

Blaze spider. They carried a venom that poisoned trees as readily as creatures, a venom that could kill a woodmunch if they ate the infected wood.

"Don't panic," Dust said calmly, "but you're set to die in about eight seconds."

CHAPTER 11

ASTRA

"Don't panic?" I shrieked back. Though enchanted beauty dulled the shrillness of my voice, it did not dull the thundering of my heart. I stared down at a black-eyed creature that whined back at me, head tilted in apparent concern. Or perhaps it was simply waiting for my corpse to drop so it could claim its meal at last.

"Quick as you can," said Dust, "fetch my healing sap. Closest shelves to the workbench, middle shelf, glass vial."

I glanced at the indicated shelves. From my perch atop the stool, I could not reach them. Once more, I eyed the creature waiting on the floor at my feet, with its wicked black claws and protruding orange teeth. My injured hand trembled, suffering jolts of pain, and my breathing had grown labored.

"This isn't a trap, is it?" I demanded of the shadow beyond the wall. "You aren't luring me down to be eaten?"

"I'm not . . . what?"

If his confusion was not real, my terror was, so I dropped to the floor at last. The wood-eating fiend shuffled backwards away from me, and somehow that was more terrifying than the creature itself, because if whatever smell I carried could scare such a monster, it surely *was* deadly.

In my haste reaching for the vial, I knocked a few carvings to the floor, wincing at the impact. The vial fit in my palm and carried a viscous liquid tinted blue.

"Do I drink it?" I worked frantically at the cork with my good hand.

"No, don't do that." Dust's calm did nothing to inspire my own. "Just spread it on the wound. You'll need all that's left. Hopefully it's enough."

Hopefully.

"You are *not* reassuring, wood fairy!" I snapped.

The cork popped free at last, and with my pointer finger, I scooped a large glob of sap onto my wound. Almost instantly, the pain faded, the heat soothed by a cooling touch. The thick orange lines of venom remained. I continued scraping sap, digging every drop from the bottle, rubbing it fiercely into the broken skin.

Slowly, the poison retreated and the punctures closed, leaving behind smooth skin once more. Not even a scar to mark the injury.

I gripped the vial, tears threatening once more, still held back by magic.

When something bumped my leg, I flinched, dropping the vial. It clattered against the floor but did not break. The black-furred creature ignored it completely, instead nosing the carvings I'd knocked down. I thought there had been three, but now I saw only two.

She'll eat all my carvings if you let her, 'n she'll make herself sick.

Quickly, I snatched the remaining two. The creature looked up at me with betrayal in her black eyes, but she did not try to substitute my leg for a carving. Instead, she snuffled off, thumping her flat tail on the floor, licking sawdust up to reveal intricate scrollwork patterns across the floor.

"Astra?" Dust tapped lightly against the wall. "You all right?"

No, I wanted to say. Hadn't I been the one to lecture him about not revealing weakness? I had never found it difficult to feign confidence in the past. Yet this realm made everything inside me whimper.

I'd nearly died. I still might.

"Perfectly fine." I swallowed. "My negligence cost you another carving, I'm afraid."

The fox cub I'd broken sat as two small lumps in my pocket, one body, one tail.

Dust said, "There's only one on that shelf I can't lose. 'Bout a hand wide, blocky shape."

It would have been just my luck if that had been the one eaten by Bumble, but I held it cradled in my left hand. "I wasn't even certain this *was* a carving. It's not up to the craftsmanship standards of your others."

"It's the first I ever made."

That explained it. With a new reverence, I regarded the clumsy angles, the stubby tail and off-center head. Thinking of my own first attempts at embroidery, I smiled.

"A bird?" I guessed.

"Surprised you can tell."

"It's better than I could do." I hefted the carving in my palm, tilting it to regard the narrowed point at the front of the head. "It's even got a beak."

"If you could put that one far out of Bumble's reach, I'd appreciate it."

Out of reach, he said. Out of reach of a creature who'd scaled the side of an enormous tower without so much as a vine for assistance. Human he might have been, but he was clearly not the brightest.

I replaced the second carving on the shelf, but the blocky bird I held on to. Eying the voracious creature as it munched its way through piles of wood shavings, I backed up slowly to the stool and seated myself once more. With such a creature on the loose, any hope of sleep had fled.

After examining the bird once more, I pulled the broken fox cub from my pocket to compare. Even missing its tail, the cub had a cheeky smile and perfect little pointed ears. Its fur was not defined by thick, angular cuts, like those that had made the bird. Instead, it bore a multitude of tiny strokes, some needle-thin, some thread-thin, all of them curving this way or that to show the ripples of the fox cub's fur across muscles and paws. I brushed the pad of my thumb down its tiny sloping muzzle, feeling the miniscule grooves.

Artistry if I'd ever seen it. I could not bear the thought of the cub wasted as kindling or worse simply because of my carelessness. So I tucked it in my pocket.

It was a weakness of mine; I never parted with my embroidery work either. Everything from fully embroidered gowns to meaningless fabric scraps, I'd always tucked neatly into a trunk in my room. Everything beautiful, I kept.

Then, after all that, my trunks and their contents had been sold along with the rest of my belongings after Father's bankruptcy.

Everything beautiful, I lost.

In Dust's woodshop, his artistry stood on proud display. If it were ever tragically lost, it would at least be admired first, so I had to admit his approach seemed better than mine, no matter the clutter.

Though it apparently attracted . . . pests.

"What kind of fairy licks up sawdust?" I crinkled my nose, regarding the furry creature as it smacked its lips and glanced back at me with what could only be called a smug expression.

"Bumble?" I watched Dust's shadow shrink and dim, as if he'd moved away to take a seat of his own. "She's what's called a fairy creature, not a fairy. Besides that, fairy is a general term, you know, groupin' them all together. It's not technically inaccurate, but it's like seeing a tree next to a blade of grass 'n calling them both 'growing things.'"

I raised an eyebrow.

"So there's Planters," he went on, "'n there's Granters. Traders 'n Raiders. Singers 'n Stingers."

"Charming rhymes," I drawled. It sounded like the sort of thing Beauty would have invented to tease me.

"The pairs are easiest to remember. 'Sides, no one wants to talk about depthfiends. There's a limit to the number of tentacles allowed in even disconcertingly honest conversation."

Flipping my words to his own purposes. That was clever.

"Explain this to me." I angled to rest my elbow on his workbench, squinting at the milky wall and the streak of shadow behind it. "If you've been trapped here all your life, and I'm the first other human to engage you in conversation, how did you learn skill in it?"

"I'm skilled? Really?" A little clatter echoed on his side of the wall, as if he'd dropped a single carving. Perhaps one he'd been working on. "Well, I've practiced extensively. In my head. Also been known to converse with the occasional woodmunch. Though Bumble can't answer back, so I'm forced to fill in the gaps."

"Perhaps skilled was too hasty an evaluation." My lips twitched.

"Can't take it back!" His grin was practically audible. I'd thought at first that he had my brother's energy in voice, but Rob would have dulled next to Dust, who could only be described as *boisterous*. Normally I might not have enjoyed such a thing, but he made it charming, perhaps because his brightness distracted from the terrors lurking just outside his tower.

Dust went on to say, "It isn't as if I spend my days *completely* alone. I talk to Doll and Renny—some of the other Planters, on occasion, though not as much as when I was younger. 'N Smicker, of course."

"Of course," I said dryly. In any given sentence, at least half his words were pure nonsense. Still. When he'd told me about being taken for his father's theft, I'd pictured devilish fairies carrying away a helpless infant, yet Dust had a grasp of human things that could not be attributed to an isolated upbringing. My curiosity burned.

I examined the shelf of foxes once more. "Have you ever seen a fox?"

"Aye, in quick glimpses. Skittish things. Love the color."

His experience surpassed my own. I did not wander in woods, and my familiarity with the creatures came from depictions of fox hunts within tapestries and paintings, not from any firsthand witness.

"Were you full-grown when the fairies brought you here?" Perhaps my imagination of the horror had been skewed, and he'd only been trapped a year or so. I could not imagine surviving a year in such a miserable landscape, but it was certainly better than a lifetime.

When Dust spoke, the enthusiasm had drained from his voice. "Just a child, I'm afraid."

I frowned. "A child who'd seen a fox?"

"There's the confusion. No, indeed. Mother's garden didn't have any foxes, 'n I remember that garden most. Playin' in the fountain. Diggin' in the soil. She always let me put the new bulbs in. I remember her, too, mostly when I look in the mirror—we have the same chestnut hair."

In my mind, I tried to add reddish-brown hair to the shadowy smudge that marked him. With a gentle smile, I said, "I look like my mother too."

Then I realized—

Not anymore.

What would she have thought of the new Astra? I had always prided myself on being my mother's image, from the same auburn curls to the same petite nose and brown eyes. New-Astra did not look like my mother. She did not look like anyone. She was wholly unique, and at first, I had loved her for that.

Now I simply felt ill.

CHAPTER 12

DUST

ONCE BUMBLE FINALLY LEFT—WHICH Dust achieved by coaching Astra to toss a block of wood through the window as a lure—Astra restated her intention to rest. She seemed mostly unbothered by her earlier brush with death, although based on her words about tactful conversation, Dust felt convinced that was an act. She'd certainly been afraid of Bumble.

Could he use that to his advantage? Likely not. Bumble was a gentle thing, much more likely to eat Dust's workbench than to help him manipulate Astra into some kind of deal.

"At least the floor is clean now," he heard Astra mutter.

Dust smirked. He'd seated himself on the edge of the staircase, one foot on the floor and one propped on a step below him, supporting his elbow as he idly whittled. The narrow block of wood in his hands, only a few inches long, had taken on the vague shape of a woman standing tall, but she remained faceless.

Astra's shadow settled on the stool once more, which

seemed to be her preferred spot. Fabric rustled. Then rustled again. The shadow moved, and some of the light wavered. As Dust rubbed his thumb across his carving's edge, gauging where to start the next cut, he heard a frustrated grunt.

"Is it always so *bright* in this place?" Astra asked. "Don't fairies care about a proper nightfall?"

"No sun to rise and set," Dust said. "There *is* a moon, a shy one, 'n temperamental to boot. Can't really spot it except for full moons, but whenever it's out, the color of the sky changes hue. It's subtle. Easier to tell nighttime by the routines. Traders won't fly at night, 'n the grass doesn't sing."

"The grass doesn't sing," she drawled back. "I ought to have guessed."

"If you tap the illimus bulbs twice, they'll go out."

"These glowing yellow fruits?"

"They're most certainly *not* fruit. At the risk of limb, do not eat."

She gave a little huff. The light beyond the curtain dimmed by degrees until the shadows blurred together, and Dust could no longer distinguish her outline. He sat with a quiet restlessness building in his stomach, each swipe of his knife growing a bit more jagged.

When he could bear it no longer, he spoke. "Astra?"

"Yes?" said her weary voice.

Dust winced. "Thought you might have left."

"I'll inform you before I depart," she promised.

That eased something inside. "Goodnight, Astra. That's how it's said, right? Always wanted to say goodnight to someone."

When no answer came, he thought she must have drifted off. Then—

"Goodnight, Dust," she said quietly.

Rather than going upstairs to his own bed, Dust sat on the curving staircase, unwilling to leave the room. After he finished his carving, he still didn't move. Just stared down at a faceless woman.

Astra would not stay forever, and even if she did, it was not just human friends he longed for; it was to return home. He'd already lost the opportunity to reunite with his father. Would he never see his mother? The brother he'd never met?

He needed to escape, now more than ever.

Which meant convincing Astra to kill Everspring's Peace Tree.

With a sigh, Dust stood at last, setting both knife and carving aside on one of his many shelves. He climbed out window number two, his bare feet padding softly across the dark balcony wood. They sky above greeted him with a pale green light. Cloudless. Ever constant. He thought of his mother's letters, but if he read them now, something inside might break.

Meeting another human was a dream come true—quite literally something he'd dreamed of on many a night. So it felt strange to admit that the emotion gripping his chest was not an overwhelming joy but rather a sharp ache.

Because Dust wanted so much *more*.

The most obvious path was to simply ask Astra for help, but in Dust's experience, help never came for free. In theory, he could trade her return to Everspring for her assistance, but such a trade would operate on trust, and there was no guarantee she would uphold her side of the bargain once he'd given his. Humans were not bound to fulfil bargains the way most fairies were, and by watching through his morningdew mirror, Dust had learned that one of the principles of human bartering was to never pay a full sum in advance for a service not yet performed.

He rubbed his hands over his face, wishing he had someone to discuss out loud with, someone to help him sort his thoughts and create a real plan. Even Bumble would have been nice. If he bribed her with a particularly chewy branch, she would lay across his lap while he spoke, allowing him to scratch her ears. It didn't take much of that for his legs to go numb beneath her weight, but he still enjoyed it every time.

Alas. All he had was himself and a silent tower. Four floors, three windows, two balconies, and one Dust.

Killing the Peace Tree would be dangerous. Every creature, human or fairy, did not risk danger to themselves unless they either sought a reward worth the risk or they feared something more than the danger.

Dust did not want to make Astra fear him. The very thought sharpened the ache within his chest, leaving him scarcely able to breathe.

But he had no reward to offer.

Poor Astra. Of all the Everspring outcasts, she was the most unfortunate. All the others, Dust sent home without cost, without expectation. On her, he was about to hang his entire future. She would hate him by the end of it.

Dust nearly retreated at that realization, nearly threw away his schemes in favor of just begging for help.

But then he saw a speck of yellow zipping toward the tower, and he realized he'd already delayed too long.

Astra was about to meet Doll.

CHAPTER 13

ASTRA

I SUFFERED A RUDE AWAKENING as something buzzed past my ear like an angry wasp. Jolting upright, I turned to face the workbench just as a fairy landed on its corner. I had no idea how long I'd slept propped up on a stool, leaning against a wall, only that the sharp pain in my neck testified it had been a mistake to do so at all.

This newcomer was not at all like my blue fairy. First, she was double the height—two hands high rather than one—but half the padding, more stick than creature. Second, she had wings, shaped like a hummingbird's, with long, drooping feathers of yellow. They trembled while she stood, as if eager to take flight once more. Finally, instead of solid-colored eyes, her yellow irises possessed black pupils, thin as an angry cat's.

"Where is your Granter, human?" she hissed, leaning her head forward on her twig-thin neck.

"My—my who?" I stammered, still trying to take her in.

She might have come alive from one of Dust's shelves—her skin was the golden-brown of a stained pecan wood, with the same dark pattern of swirled wood grain. In the places she might have worn clothing, she was instead coated in thin leaves, the green faded nearly to brown as if touched by autumn, growing directly from her skin and pressed to her shape. Had she been carved and brought to life? Or was there a tree in this realm that grew fairies?

"I . . ." My voice failed me once more, and my cheeks heated at the embarrassment. If she'd not startled me awake, I would have been more composed. I narrowed my eyes to match hers.

Dust called out helpfully. "Doll, Astra. Astra, Doll."

"Doll, really?" I crinkled my nose. "Dreadful name."

I hadn't even realized fairies would have names; I'd certainly never asked the blue fairy for hers.

"Astra," said Doll. Her yellow wing feathers tremored. "Call your Granter."

"You made a wish?" asked Dust.

I ignored him, keeping my focus on the fairy before me. "I don't know what you mean, and I'm not inclined to follow orders from strangers."

Worse than that, there was something unnerving about the fairy before me, something in the air around her that pressed against my senses, made me want to retreat. As if she were a beehive, and although I could see no danger, I could hear the buzzing of the storm inside. Her wing feathers vibrated as she continued staring me down like something she longed to sting.

"Do you not command your Granter?" Doll demanded. "Have they already moved on to the next wisher?"

"Enough!" I lifted my chin. "I'd like a moment alone, if you both please."

To my shock, Doll gave it. She leapt backwards off the

workbench, zipping out of sight through the open window. Not a moment later, I heard hushed voices on Dust's side of the wall, no doubt discussing me. Closing my eyes, I worked to tune them out.

Dust may not have been a fairy, but he kept company with the worst of their creatures. Twice now, I'd been threatened in the tower—first by an orange-toothed beast and now by a yellow-winged wasp. Perhaps it was all a trap.

My stomach clenched. When I pushed myself to my feet, my knees wavered.

What was I hoping for, hiding away in a tower? Hiding accomplished nothing except a delay, and there was nothing worse than floating in a pool of frigid fear, waiting for the inevitable drowning. I was responsible for my own fate, and I had to *do* something to set it right.

In the previous day's madness, I'd forgotten about my own fairy. She was surely the Granter referenced by Doll. I did not know Doll's purpose in trying to find her, and I was not about to trust it, but if I left the tower, if I could find a secluded place, I could call my fairy and demand she take me to Everspring again, just as she'd done when I'd first made my wish.

As quietly as I could, I crept to the window ledge and grasped the woven vine still anchored there. Then Doll zipped into view again, landing on the ledge, startling my heart into a thunder.

"Prisoner's escaping, Dust," the fairy said flatly.

"I am not a prisoner here," I snapped. "I am free to leave."

"So much for informin' me before you depart," said Dust. His drooping voice carried the heart-twisting whine of an abandoned fox cub, and twist my heart it did. I hadn't meant to lie. I'd simply . . .

I sighed.

"I cannot remain in the fairy realm," I said with practiced calm, fisting my hands in my torn skirt to stop the shaking.

The yellow-winged fairy tilted her head. "Leaving's easy. For how long?"

"For*ever*." As if there were any other option!

"Much harder, then." Doll smirked in a way that teased unpleasant secrets. She leaned forward, crouched on the stone window ledge, wing feathers reaching toward the ground as if even they wished to escape her. "Fearful little dearie, it must hurt to be in a place of such power, hurt to see creatures who could snuff you in an instant. I could help. Send you home, certainly, but there's more. I could make sure you never feel little again."

It did not take a shrewd merchant to know this was not a fairy to whom I wanted to be in debt. My skin crawled to hear the difference in her conversation compared to Dust's. While his unguarded honesty made me uncomfortable, hearing the real wood fairy's veiled implications made me more so, because hers was the tone of all society.

It was the tone of Mrs. Heartshire as she told me, "What a shame you're still not married, my dear. It's lucky you have such a stalwart father, caring for three unmarried daughters all alone."

What Mrs. Heartshire meant was, *You're a burden, Astra.*

What Doll meant was, *You're useless, Astra.*

I clenched my jaw, willing my voice to conjure a suitable insult. But it only locked in my throat.

Dust spoke instead.

"Doll," he said sharply. It was the first time I'd heard his tone be anything other than friendly. "Astra's not planting for you. Don't offer again."

Doll's yellow eyes turned their piercing gaze from me to the unseen figure behind the wall. Her wings shivered, and I heard the beehive come to life in the silence. My stomach tensed. I waited for a strike.

But the fairy shrugged, as if dismissing the matter. "Stay all you like, then. There's plenty of uses for a human around here." She shook her wings. One yellow feather tumbled loose, drifting to the floor.

"Morningdew, Dust." She smirked. "Shame you can't reach it. Astra—"

I stiffened at my name.

"Let me know when you really want help." Her smirk widened. Then she dove out the window, disappearing into a green sky.

My tension finally eased, fingers uncurling from my dress. I'd rumpled the silk, another thing I would have expected enchantment to prevent. Uselessly, I rubbed at the wrinkles, scowling.

"It's certainly no shame to see *her* go," I said sourly.

"Don't mind her," Dust said. "Planters are all abrupt. Did she leave a . . ."

"Feather?" I eyed the thing in question. The yellow of it looked sickly in the pale green light, and I could not help thinking of poison. Though it rested innocently against the floorboards, looking like any ordinary bird's feather, it could not fool me; there were claws beneath that shell.

"You should use it. Might see a fox."

I frowned. "What do you mean 'use it'?"

"There's a basin by my workbench. Drop the feather in the water, 'n you'll see."

I shook my head before realizing he couldn't see it. "No, thank you."

"Please. I pay a hefty price for these, would hate to see one go to waste."

He bought fairy feathers? And implied they let him see foxes? Grimacing, I sized the feather up once more, nudging it gently with the toe of my shoe. It did not shed trails of magic the way the blue fairy did.

"Doll likes to be intimidating," Dust said, as if reading my concern. "The feather won't hurt you, I promise."

Curiosity won out at last, and even though I scowled, I snatched up the yellow feather. It was stiff, prickly along the edges, and when I looked closer, I saw what seemed to be tiny water droplets beading along the shaft.

Even with instructions, it took a minute to find the basin, lost as it was in the sea of carvings. I let the feather drift from my fingers to the water's surface. Though I expected it to float, it vanished. Just a flash of yellow rippling out across the water.

And then the water became a window to another world.

The green was not that of a fairy sky but of a grazing pasture beside a river. Shepherds sat along the water, conversing with one another while they held to sheep with one hand and shears with the other. I saw an unfamiliar arm before me as if I were looking down at my own, and as it wrangled a sheep, I felt a strange disorientation to see my own arm moving without my command.

I was seeing through another person's eyes.

"What is this?" I gasped, leaning closer. The bleating of sheep filled my ears, along with the gentle trickling of the river and a conversation about "wretched Martha," whatever she'd done.

Dust said, “My one escape. I’d show you how to navigate it, but I can’t—wall ’n all. Took me years to learn it right, anyway. Planters gather morningdew when they fly. Usually, they only sell to Traders, but Doll lets me have a harvest, since my hair’s useful to her garden.”

“This is worse than books,” I murmured. It was a foolish thing to say, but I was caught between one reality before my eyes and another beneath my feet, and how could I manage both?

Beauty read books to expand her world—she’d told me that once. She drank in every mention of foreign lands, where people ate insects or sang along to strange drums, places so far from my experience that they all seemed to be invented. I chose to accept them as invented, because it increased my security to *know* the borders of my world instead of wondering how large the planet truly was and how infinitesimal I was by comparison.

Now my world of experience had expanded to include talking dragonflies, solid ground that moved like waves, creatures that could snap a tree in half with a single bite, and a basin of water that lived someone else’s life at just the price of a feather—things more ridiculous than any story Beauty’s books ever told.

“Astra?” said Dust. I’d lapsed into silence.

I peeled my fingers away from the basin’s edge, stepped back, and the sheep-shearing faded.

“These seem rare.” My voice cracked. I cleared my throat. “I ought to have saved it for you. For when the wall comes down.”

“They can’t be saved longer than a few minutes,” he said. “It’s a blessing, actually. Forces me to experience what I can rather than hoardin’ it away.”

"Right," I said softly.

"Astra . . ." He hesitated, then said, "I can get you home."

The whole of his human experience came down to bartered glances through a window—and *me*.

If I'd been in his position, would I have let my only human connection go?

I swallowed. "What did you have in mind?"

"There's a Trader settled not far from here. Smicker, good fellow. He'll have what you need to leave the realm, 'n he loves my carvings. There's a badger he's been, well, badgering me for. He'll be thrilled I'm finally ready to trade."

"There's no need for that," I said quickly. "I can pay my own passage." Or if I couldn't, a wealthy husband could. Surely this Trader and I could reach an arrangement.

I'd been mulling over a plan for my future, and in that moment, I decided it. The instant I was back on familiar ground, I would accept the proposal of the first wealthy man I met. It did not matter who. Even the toothless ancient was a good option—I need only endure his company a year or two before inheriting all the stability he possessed. No matter what, I would be married, I would be secure. And once I'd accepted a proposal, my wish would be fulfilled, so the other men would not be driven into an angry mob fighting for my acceptance.

When my wish was fulfilled, would I no longer be beautiful?

My hair felt hot on my neck. I bundled it into a familiar knot only for it to slip free and tumble once more across my shoulders. The magic must have made it sleeker; I would need a ribbon or hairpins to secure it.

"Very well," Dust finally said. "I'll call the dragon."

My heart stopped.

CHAPTER 14

DUST

"TRADER" WAS THE FAIRY NAME—the proper name—but Dust knew *dragon*. It was dastardly of him to drop the human term as he did while knowing what effect it would have, but Doll's visit could not have come at a worse time, and if Astra called the Planter back to accept a deal, she would make a terrible mistake with a terrible price, just as Dust's father had.

Before Dust would let that happen, he would get Astra out of the fairy realm, which meant he had this one chance to make a deal of his own. If that meant threatening Astra with a dragon, so be it.

Underhanded? Certainly. Dust had been raised by fairies, after all.

"No need to fear," he assured Astra, watching her agitated shadow pace beyond the murky wall. "Smicker's not a fire breather. Those're the fellows you have to watch out for—conversation can get heated."

"You will not summon a dragon here!" Astra squeaked. "I need only a moment of privacy and then—"

"You'll call your Granter?" Dust waited, letting the silence confirm Doll's words from earlier. Astra had claimed a wish from a Granter. "I've never met one, but I'll tell you this for free: Planters 'n Granters are mortal enemies. You're in Planter territory. Your Granter can't do anything to help you here."

Not that they would anyway; Granters had greater magic than any other fairy type, which meant they also had the strictest rules. If Astra had already claimed her wish, she'd exhausted all the help she would ever receive from that fairy.

Astra's voice quivered. "Then I shall simply have to return to the wilds and find my way to an exit."

The worst plan Dust had ever heard.

"The wilds," he repeated flatly. "Where *all* the dragons live. Not to mention the blaze spiders and the inkers and the trolls and—"

"You have made your point, wood fairy."

Her shadow retreated to the far edge of the room opposite the window, and then it shrank, like she'd sat against the wall with knees tucked. Dust felt a flash of guilt. But Smicker truly was harmless, as long as she didn't try to cheat or insult him. This was simply a show. A manipulation tactic. Since she didn't know how Trader bargains worked, he could strike a deal with her that included destruction of the Peace Tree, then say Smicker would come after her if the bargain was not fulfilled. It was the only motivator he could think of that might work.

Dust tasted something sour in his mouth. Wood fairy, she called him, and aptly so. But getting home was worth any cost.

Wasn't it?

Slowly, Dust followed the line of the shadowy wall. He

crouched down, which ought to have put them eye-level. He wondered what color her eyes were. They couldn't be green like his own, since his had taken on that shade across years in the fairy realm. When he'd lived in Everspring, they'd been hazel.

Full grown with green eyes—when he saw his mother again, would she even recognize him?

"You're a bit skittish, Astra," he said gently.

As expected, she huffed. Her voice gave no hint of tremor, only confidence. She was very skilled at that mask she wore. "Correction, wood fairy. I have a healthy sense of self-preservation. One which does not include encounters with ferocious, clawed creatures!"

"Traders are the most honorable of fairies, 'n they never break their word. Smicker's your best way to get home. I've bartered with him a hundred times."

Which means I'm your best way to get home. Dust allowed the unspoken a few moments to sink in before adding, "I think we can help one another."

"What do you mean?" Her suspicion could not have been clearer. It was as if he could see the narrowed eyes in her shadow.

"You need someone to trade with a dragon. I need someone to break my curse." Dust took a shaky breath. "Existence is a chord, every life a note. That's a fairy saying, one embraced by all types. Means everyone has a use."

"A *use*," Astra repeated scornfully. "I see it now. You've been inviting fairy creatures to your tower all this time to frighten me into breaking your curse."

Dust's eyes widened at the spear through the heart, one he couldn't deny. Raised by fairies, perhaps, but he was clearly not as skilled in their games as they were. Like a human pretending to garden.

With an empty smile she couldn't see, he said, "Only invited Smicker."

"I need no help from you," Astra said. "I am the daughter of a merchant, and I know how to barter. Dragon or no, I will deal with this Trader myself."

With perfect timing, the ground rumbled outside. The tower trembled, floor vibrating, and Dust put a hand against the wall to steady himself before standing.

"What was that?" Astra squeaked out.

"That'll be your Trader," he said. "Brace yourself. He's a wee bit big."

Just as he said it, a massive purple eye reared outside window number two, filling the sky beyond the balcony, the thin black pupil shifting side to side until it found Dust. The eyelid flexed open wider and then narrowed, exposing a ridge of sharp black spines above it.

"DUST," rumbled the dragon. His voice alone shook the floor, stirring particles of sawdust.

In dragonfly form, all Traders were roughly the same size, about the length of Dust's hand, but they put on their best face to make trades, and that face was the one that inspired dragon legends. That face grew larger with every successful bargain made.

Smicker had been making successful bargains long enough, he dwarfed the tower.

"Aye, Smicker,"—Dust grinned—"good to see you. Part of you, anyway. How're the little ones?"

The Trader snorted, rocking the tower. Dust adjusted his stance.

"You sound frustrated. They still keepin' you up all hours,

friend? I'm sure they'll fly soon enough."

"SOON ENOUGH," the Trader agreed. Then, straight-to-business, as was his style: "TRADE BADGER?"

"Not today, I'm afraid. I'd like you to meet another friend, Astra, who's hoping to make her own trade for a way out of the fairy realm. She's just around at window number one. She's a skittish sort, so be gentle."

The massive eye disappeared. Dust could tell the moment Smicker peeked in the right window, because from the other side of the wall came a sharp *eep!*

Despite himself, he smiled.

"TRADE," rocked the tower. Then there was silence.

"Astra," Dust said after a moment. "You'll have to make an offer. He's a Trader; it's in the name. If you'd rather I do the bargaining, just say the word. All you have to do for me is kill a tree in Everspring."

Please, he urged silently.

Considering how much Bumble had frightened her, he expected the view of a dragon eye to crumple her at once, but as it turned out, he'd not given her spine enough credit. She spoke to the dragon rather than him, even restraining most of the tremor from her voice, which must have taken an enormous effort of willpower.

"I—I have no coin with me, dragon, but I shall soon marry a wealthy husband—"

"COIN?" Smicker gave another snort with twice the power. Dust caught a carved butterfly just as it tipped from the edge of a shelf. Something on the other side of the wall was not so lucky, and he heard the clatter.

"He won't take human wealth," Dust said absently, his mind busy churning over her words. Astra had spoken several times of proposals and husbands. The king's proposal. A wealthy husband.

Perhaps he *could* offer a reward that would motivate her enough to break his curse.

Then he grimaced. He was trying to gain his freedom, and tying himself into marriage with a stranger was the exact opposite.

Better to continue with the Smicker angle.

"How else am I to pay?" Astra cried. "Wealth is the only—"

"CREATION."

"Traders have different interests. Smicker likes artistry. Don't suppose you paint, do you?" Dust expected a quick no and the opening for his counteroffer.

Apparently, he needed to stop expecting things.

"I practice embroidery," Astra said. "My skill is unparalleled."

A high art indeed, and one without local competition. Dust frequently had to barter his wood art against Finifugal's from the other side of the knee-highs. For thread art, Smicker would trade Astra anything she wanted. Dust sighed. So much for his underhanded sneaking.

Then she said—

"But I will not sacrifice any of my creations to a wicked monster!"

Dust's heart dropped to his stomach.

"Uh-oh," he said quietly.

"WICKED!" Smicker roared, shaking the very green of the sky. "*MONSTER!*"

The tower rocked beneath a fierce earthquake. Dust snatched another carving out of the air but missed the next three, too busy grabbing the edge of the staircase to keep from knocking his head against it.

"Well, I lived a short life, 'n I accomplished none of my dreams." He gave a dry laugh. "That'll go nicely on a grave marking. I leave all my worldly possessions to Bumble, may she find them through the wreckage."

"WILL NOT TRADE!" raged the dragon. Then came a great tearing of soil and branch, no doubt as Smicker's enormous tail took out a swath of nearby trees. Next a *crunch*—delay—*crash!* from what Dust guessed was his upper balcony smashing to the ground. That was a real shame. It was the first extension he'd built on the tower, and given his inexperience at the time, it had taken an eternity. Smicker knew that; scorned Traders were fearfully vindictive.

"Is he going to eat us?!" Astra's voice now shook like the tower around them. Her shadow pressed against the wall.

"He's certainly going to eat *you*," Dust said. If he'd been a fairy, he would have said it with scorn, since she'd cost him so much already—an expensive healing sap and a priceless balcony, among other things—and her fate was the result of her own stubbornness.

But he was himself, so he was already planning how to save her, whether she made an agreement with him or not.

Maybe Renny was right. Maybe he ought to have been more resentful of the humans who could come and go, leaving him with the consequences of their passing. For a moment, he felt a blaze of heat inside, a wretched burn like the hottest of friendship peppers.

He'd helped so many people. Just once. Just *once* . . .

"You told me I had nothing to fear!"

"That was before you insulted a dragon ten times the size of my tower!" Dust snapped. "This blame is all yours, my friend. What were you thinking?"

"I wasn't thinking!"

Despite himself, he smiled wryly. Honesty at last. The resentment he'd managed to scrape together melted beneath it.

"Astra," he said, "unless you have a year's worth of embroidery to offer up, he really will eat you. Please work with me. We can help each other."

Amazingly, she *still* managed a hesitation. She drove a harder bargain than the dragon wrecking the landscape. Outside, another roar shook the world. Dust's ears rang with the echo.

Finally, Astra gasped out, "I'll do it. I'll break your curse. I'll kill the tree or whatever. Please, make him leave."

Dust sighed in relief.

"Trade accepted," he said.

Now to get the real Trader to follow suit.

The tower shook again, staggering Dust on his way to the window. He hopped onto his remaining balcony. The eel vine hung free, dangling from the edge, snapped when the higher balcony fell. He dragged himself onto the wall, the curse shifting the gravity of his world, and he scurried up the stone until he caught hold of the roof.

"I'll trade!" Dust shouted.

Up close, the Trader's rampage was even more terrifying, considering Dust was not even the height of one of Smicker's talons. With those talons, the violet dragon had torn deep furrows in the green grass, exposing navy blue soil beneath, and he continued to dig furiously. The disturbed grass emitted an unending wail, almost too high to hear. Dust winced; that song would attract an inker infestation. One problem at a time.

"*Trade!*" Dust shouted again, loud as he could.

"*WICKED!*" Smicker roared back, barely shooting Dust a

glance. His purple scales reflected green streaks beneath the sky, bunching and stretching across his muscles with each new clawing motion. At least he kept his swirl-patterned wings folded along the black spines of his back—had he extended those with malice, he might have toppled the tower.

"You're not wicked, friend, 'n you're not a monster! You're the best Trader I know." *The biggest as well, unfortunately.* "Astra is very sorry!"

The Trader threw back his head with a howl. "LIES!"

Yeah, all right, lies. "I'll give you the badger, Smicker!"

The Trader paused his rampage. Without all the tremors, the world still felt wobbly.

"MORE," the dragon said at last.

Dust clenched his teeth. Before Astra's trading attempt, the badger would have purchased a portal to the human realm and then some. Now it couldn't even buy forgiveness.

"That badger has fourteen shades of brown in the coat, each hair defined. It's my finest work. I'll be heartbroken to part with it."

The dragon's head pressed in close to the tower roof, leaving Dust staring into a violet eye his own height as he clutched the tower's flagpole to keep himself from getting blown off the roof by the hot breath from Smicker's flared nostrils.

"MORE!"

They haggled. In the end, Dust was forced to offer up his prized badger, a beautiful snowy owl which had taken weeks to get just the right shade of white, *and* an exquisitely detailed depthfiend, the first and only in his collection. Getting the curves perfect on those tentacles had nearly cost him a finger.

But at last, Smicker said, "TRADE ACCEPTED."

Dust stood with weary shoulders and three wounds in his heart. After all the carvings he'd made, it should have been easy to part with a handful, but Smicker accepted only the best. There had to be real pain in the price; that was how trading worked.

Dust climbed back down to his woodshop, imagining how to direct Astra to the two carvings on her side of the room—

Only to find the wall gone.

And the room empty.

"*Astra?*" he shouted, panic lurching his stomach. He would have seen her leave the tower. She couldn't have . . .

Then he noticed the stairs, sectioned off at the upper landing, as if someone had thrown a blanket across the opening, except he could see murky shadows through it. The divider must have vanished while he was on the roof, and she'd taken the opportunity to explore—or retreat. Retreat was more likely.

Dust gathered the required carvings and hefted them with unnecessary force off the balcony. Smicker swallowed each one, forked tongue giving a satisfied snap across his scaly lips. Without any pleasantries, the Trader shrank to his dragonfly form and buzzed away into the slowly repairing trees.

Which left Dust to negotiate with a much scarier Trader: the woman he'd entrusted with his freedom.

CHAPTER 15

ASTRA

When the milky wall vanished, leaving me in a room with two gaping window-views to the thrashing violet monster outside, I fled up the stairs on instinct alone.

The next floor up was windowless and cramped. My enchanted beauty would not let me cower properly, but I sat pressed against the wall until the dragon's rampage seemed, at last, to calm. Sometime in the chaos, I'd found myself a needle in the disheveled storage around me, and I turned it anxiously between the fingers of my left hand. The thread winder it had been tucked through was clenched in my right.

After waiting a few minutes longer to be sure things had settled, I finally had the presence of mind to return to the woodshop, only to find the passage had been blocked.

Which left me alone in Dust's storage room. I'd thought his woodshop cluttered, but at least it contained beautiful displays. This circular floor of the tower was simply a maze of wood piles, paintbrushes, fabrics, dried flowers and herbs, buckets of water with questionable things left to soak, and whatever else the scheming little wood fairy had squirreled away.

Someone knocked on the milky barrier from below, and Dust's voice echoed in the staircase. "This is less ideal than before."

Regrettably, I had to agree.

"Is the dragon gone?" My voice was now composed, and he could not hear the residual rattle of my knees.

"Aye, he's flown off. Gave me what you need to return to Everspring."

Aware of the trouble I'd caused, I waited for him to make a laundry list of demands in return for my freedom.

Instead, he said, "I didn't tell you the full story, about my father."

Though it seemed a strange time for corrections, anything was a welcome distraction from the memory of a fierce dragon eye, pressed to a window and glaring down at me. I sat on the lowest step I could, just above the barrier that divided us.

"Yes?" I prodded.

Through his words, he painted for me a picture of a loving family, with a pregnant wife and a fearful soon-to-be father.

"Every father fears their child's exposure to disease and other things," Dust said. "Mine had slightly . . . weightier concerns. There were rumors in the kingdom—rumors of revolt, overthrow. Dark tidings."

I frowned while he pressed on, telling me how his mother was bedridden, how her safety and that of the child was threatened. His father grew desperate.

"There was a magic relic passed down in Mother's family,

a bell that could open passage to the fairy realm. Every generation was sworn not to use it."

"Oh no," I said softly, sensing the direction. How foolish —of course I knew where the story was headed. The evidence was on the very stairs below me.

Dust's voice grew softer as well. "Father held out as long as he could, I imagine. Dark times drive fear. So into the realm he came, 'n he found a seed that, if planted, brought peace 'n protection. Took it back with him."

Stolen. My heart twisted as I remembered a night months earlier, when my own Father had emerged from the woods behind our shack, trembling and ashen-faced, a stolen rose clutched in his hand. He'd taken it from an enchanted garden, never considering the consequences. Beauty had paid its price.

Dust had paid a father's theft just the same, with a price infinitely steeper.

"Such a fate should not come to anyone," I said quietly. Then I frowned. "You said you remember planting bulbs in your mother's garden. The fairies waited so long to claim you?"

Dust said, "Some debts don't come due right away. But they always come due."

"Why tell me this now?"

"Well, you've agreed to heroically rescue me. Thought you ought to know who you're rescuing."

He said it with emphasis, as if he'd revealed a great secret, but I was in no mood for guessing games. "And who is that?"

"What, that bit about overthrow didn't give it away?"

For a moment, my mind was still occupied by the dragon.

At his prompting, I finally pieced together overthrow's connection to a throne.

My eyes widened.

"Are you *wealthy*?" I blurted.

A low whistle answered. "What was all that earlier about tact in conversation?" Before I could do more than blush, Dust went on, "'Crown prince' is the preferred title, far as I know, but I suppose 'wealthy' comes close enough."

All this time.

Royalty?

When I spoke, it was with exaggerated calm. "I do not believe you, wood fairy."

He laughed. "Believe or not, I suppose, but you're standing in the evidence. Years ago, my father, *the king*, planted a fairy seed. Grew small at first, but you give it a few years, then the slighted Planter comes calling for payment—all at once, there's a castle tower in the fairy realm, 'n there's a great big fairy tree in Everspring."

A prince. I felt foolish for not seeing it, especially with his grief at news of the late king. Then again, the castle had a hundred servants—just because he lived in a stolen tower of it did not mean it should have been obvious to me that . . .

There was no point to justification. I'd not reasoned out his identity because I'd put no thought into the matter at all, even after having seen the tower. While I'd pitied his circumstances, my focus had remained on my own misfortune. It was how I'd always been, and for the first time, I wondered what else I'd missed seeing beyond my blinders.

Meanwhile, he'd saved me from death twice. First from poison and then from a dragon angered by my impetuousness. He could have left me to my fate.

"You put me in a corner so I'd help," I accused. I tried to let that make me feel less guilty about a dragon rampage that had nearly been the end of both of us.

"You're sharp, anyone ever told you?"

Him too, mirroring my own phrasing at every turn.

"I'm more often told I'm sharp of tongue," I said coolly, "than sharp of mind. And you might speak for yourself because, I suppose, you've gained all you hoped. I'll kill the Peace Tree. What happens after?"

"I'll go home. To Everspring."

He would be the true heir, with a birthright that superseded Kenric's. *Crown prince*. To say nothing of parental affection, how had the king allowed his heir to remain trapped all these years?

The answer, of course, was easy: He'd sired another heir. As if Dust were replaceable.

The way my parents had replaced Isabella with Beauty.

I clutched the needle and thread I'd found as memories reared cold in my mind, reminding me of a lost sister.

When Mother had carried Callista, I'd been too young to grasp the concept of a coming baby. But with Isabella, I was five. I understood I was getting another sister—and I was quite determined the baby would be a sister, no matter Rob's whining about lack of brothers.

When Mother made a baby dress, I would not let her do it without me. It was the first time I held a needle. With careful stitches, we affixed a row of lace. I liked lace at the bottom of my dresses, so I wanted my new sister to have the same. I asked to listen to Mother's stomach; I thought maybe I would catch the baby snoring.

Mother offered me names to choose between. She leaned

toward Beauty, but I crinkled my nose whenever she suggested it.

"Beauty's not a name," I insisted. "It's just a word."

"Names *are* words," she said.

By the time Father returned from his voyages, we'd decided on Isabella, and his own suggestions could not sway us. *Isabella, Isabella.* I repeated the name to myself like a chant. I played with a doll, pretending I cradled my coming sister, and I urged her to come sooner.

When the time came at last, I wasn't allowed in the birthing room, so I waited with my nose pressed right to the door. Rob and Callista quickly lost interest, following our nursemaid away to play, but I remained, wondering why sisters took so long.

Then I felt the change in the very air. The unknown sadness rested heavily on my skin. I heard it in the sounds from Mother's room, the shift in her cries, the tone of Father's words I couldn't make out. The silence which swallowed it all.

It was my first experience with death, and when it burned inside, no one gave me platitudes to soothe it. No one told me it would fade with time. No one talked about better places. Perhaps they thought a child couldn't truly understand death, so it couldn't hurt me.

They were wrong.

I carried it still.

"Does Kenric know about you?" I asked.

"He wasn't even born when I was taken," Dust said.

Something burned hot in my stomach. I felt myself drawn to memory again, to a confused time two years after Isabella's death when Mother called us all together to see a baby sister.

With Mother's hair damp and her smile bright, she tilted the new baby in her arms, and she said, "Her name is Beauty."

One almost-Beauty became one true-Beauty, and the dresses that should have been Isabella's went to Beauty, and the crib that should have been Isabella's went to Beauty, and every hollow of Isabella was filled by Beauty until there were no hollows left—until Isabella was never even spoken about, as if she had never existed.

She'd been replaced by Beauty.

"Astra?" said Dust.

I was not fool enough to blame my sister for her own birth. But knowing the logic did not ease the ache, the confusion. It never had.

Isabella could not come home. Dust still could.

I opened my mouth to speak, then clamped it shut. I was in dangerous territory. The place of revealing vulnerability, the place where hearts bled. And I was not willing to bleed before a stranger.

Besides, there didn't need to be anything personal in this promise. I would rescue Dust because I'd agreed to, because I owed him for saving my life.

Then what?

Once he was free and could see me, he would be a wealthy man under effect from my wish. He would propose. Did I want that?

A question for another time. First there was the matter of leaving the fairy realm.

"I was mistaken earlier, Dust," I said. "I think we can help one another after all."

CHAPTER 16

DUST

Since Dust couldn't reach Astra himself, he left the Trader's portal item on his workbench.

"I'll head back to the roof," he said. "Once I'm out of the room, you can come back down."

Just before he disappeared out the window, Astra's voice stopped him.

"There's a needle and blue thread here. I wonder if you would mind terribly—"

"All yours." Dust smiled. She would certainly put it to better use than he did.

He climbed up to the roof and waited longer than strictly required, just to be sure. Once he'd climbed back down, the wall had reappeared to divide the workshop.

"I knew you were a fairy creature," Astra said, her shadow rummaging over his workbench. "Scaling the outside of a tower like some sticky insect."

Dust raised an eyebrow. "I don't stick to anything; it's the curse that sticks to me. Now, remember not to touch it until you're ready. Soon as you do, you'll vanish. And if you break your word, you'll end up back here."

It seemed a kinder lie than saying a dragon would hunt her down.

"Yes, I understand, pesky wood fairy." The rummaging sounds halted. "This is really my path to Everspring? A handkerchief? I thought you might have been joking, but there's nothing else here."

"Has to be something that originally belonged to the human realm. Most common items are those that get lost in rivers 'n lakes, since Snappers like mud."

"You said he was a Trader."

"Who d'you think trades with the Traders?"

"Everything you say is an absurdity."

"But never a dull word."

She gave a snort of laughter, quickly smothered. Reluctant to make promises, reluctant to laugh. Something about that echoed familiarity to Dust; he wondered what kind of isolation Astra suffered to remind him of himself.

"It's not bad to laugh, you know." His face heated as he spoke, but luckily, she couldn't see it. "Took me a few years to accept that, but there's plenty in the world that's still good, even with the . . . curses."

Her shadow moved slightly, maybe as she turned to look at the wall. He didn't know what kind of response to expect, and in the end, she didn't give one.

"Unless there's something else," Astra said, "I'll be going now."

Dust had already filled her in on his history, at least relating to the curse. It required him to be in physical contact with the tower at all times, and although he'd found clever bends to the rule, such as extending the tower through vines and balconies, he'd never managed to break it. Trying to scale something all the way to the ground was impossible. The curse stopped him dead in the air just inches above the grass. Portal magic could not transport him directly from the tower.

But the curse had begun with a tree, and if the tree could be killed, it would end.

"The tree, you remember," Dust said, "can't be ended by—"

"Poisoning the soil, yes, your mother tried. Or so she said in a letter. No simple vinegar solutions for me."

Dust's strongest hope was his mother's knight. Though his curse history was severely lacking in names—his own birth name, first and foremost—he at least knew the knight's coat of arms, a gray serpent on red.

To that end, he said, "And the knight's crest—"

"A serpent, yes. While I understand your anxiety regarding freedom, you needn't fear my memory for details. Ask my sisters what grudges I still carry from our nursery years."

Dust's lips twitched. "I can only hope the knight's still in employ at the castle."

"And that he is not wealthy," Astra muttered.

"What's that?"

"Nothing. Let's just say I shall do my best to end this tree while avoiding a mob of violent, wealthy men."

"Jilted men?" Dust clarified. "Your—what was it—*dozens* of proposals from the fine Everspring hunting grounds, including my own brother?"

She gave a huff.

He smirked. Though he'd dangled the bait of his own wealthy station, at least by birth, she'd not taken it. So much for having a backup plan. She was not an easy woman to read.

"Why do you seek a husband, Astra?"

"I seek no such thing," she said primly. Before he could contradict, she added, "What I seek is security."

Security. Dust's brow furrowed. "What's that mean? Someone to protect you?"

"I need no protection."

Of course not. She needed nothing.

"Now I see why you called me honest," he said. "It's just comparative."

"I told you conversation is about tact and concealment. Particularly with strangers."

"We're hardly strangers now. Survived a fearful dragon together and all." Dust stepped right up to the wall, prompting her to do the same, her shadow deepening. He lowered his voice. "Tell me one honest thing, Astra. About you."

It seemed pointless to even ask. He fully expected her to refuse or to bluster. Her shadow thinned, as if turning away, and then it widened again. It looked like she raised her hand to rest it against the wall, so he pressed his to the same darkened spot.

"Very well," she said. "One honesty. Which you will not repeat to anyone, are we clear?"

Dust's eyes widened, and he found his curiosity burning.

"About that foolishness with the dragon . . ." She sighed. "Here it is. For years, my embroidery was an escape over which I had complete control. I decided when, and what, to stitch. Every piece, I kept to myself. Opening art to an outside view invites criticism, and I have always been poor at receiving such a thing. So I did not invite it."

Despite himself, Dust's lips twitched. Hers was such a *strong* personality. Were all humans such, dimmed by viewing through a mirror, or was she special? Either way, he felt fortunate she'd stumbled into his tower, even if it had cost him a balcony and his three best carvings. What was a collection of wood compared to the changing of his life?

"Then my father went bankrupt," Astra continued. "Everything I possessed was sold, every creation I'd stitched exposed to . . . unfeeling eyes."

Dust had only to think of Smicker swallowing a carved badger, and he felt the echo of that.

"Suddenly, I was expected to employ my needlework to make a living. When I could not bear to, my family thought me a villain, so I conceded at last. But I knew what would happen if I embroidered for others, and it happened with exactness."

She told of a Mrs. Heartshire—more aptly Mrs. Heartless—who commissioned a dress for her daughter, then had that very daughter embroidering in plain view when Astra came to deliver it. The woman proceeded to measure Astra's work against her daughter's, highlighting every perceived flaw. *Astra, your hand has grown tense. Oh, it's not your fault, dear. I can only imagine the stress of poverty. But see how Lara draws with ease.*

She promised to hire Astra again in the future, since their family was in the most pitiable circumstances, and Mrs. Heartshire was such a charitable woman.

Bitterly, Astra said, "The chickens at our cottage do not take nearly as much pleasure in their pecking order as do the women of society. I tried to adopt my sister Callista's humility, for survival if nothing else, but I . . . am not Callista. In the end, I vowed to never suffer someone else to claim my embroidery again. Then came the dragon."

"I understand deeming the cost too high," Dust said, "but you called Smicker a wicked monster."

"Yes, well, here is your honesty: I do nothing by halves, rejections or otherwise."

Dust's lips twitched. "I believe that."

She could have lied. She could have said anything, or nothing at all. Instead, she'd given him honesty when he'd asked. Her bold personality increased his confidence that she meant the things she said, and he felt hope rising within, threatening to consume him.

This could truly be his escape. After all these years.

"Anyway," said Astra. "I meant to thank you. Twice now. For saving me from both dragon and spider. It's burden enough for me to suffer being unmarried and impoverished; I am grateful to avoid adding *deceased* to the list."

Dust smirked. He swallowed down the emotion threatening to choke him and matched her dry tone. "For what it's worth, I may have exaggerated you had *nothing* to fear. Traders are a sensitive lot. Coming in Smicker's size, that can be fearful indeed."

"You faced the beast readily enough."

"He really is a friend—'n once again, you can't see my shaking knees."

"It's a strange list of friends you have, Dust."

"You're on it now, too, you know."

Her shadow wavered. "So you say. *You* should know I . . . have never been anyone's first choice of friend."

"I find that hard to believe, what with your quick wit and the way you admire carvings so much. Now, if you've been spendin' your time around society chickens instead of imprisoned carpenters, then I can see where you went wrong."

Strange, that—he never got much chance to tease fairies. They didn't take kindly to it. Astra responded with feeling, but not with threat of magic. It made Dust feel he could say what he wanted to rather than what he *had* to.

"I'd like to see those society chickens face down a dragon," Astra said, her smile practically audible. She cleared her throat. "Now, if you'd like to not remain imprisoned forever, I'll need to be on my way. Is there anything else before I leave?"

"One thing." Dust curled his fingers in, pressing his fist to the wall and leaning in close. Though the words pained him, he said, "Don't come back, Astra. You were lucky in your first landing, but Everspring outcasts can be dropped anywhere in the realm. Might land in the Ocean of Agony. I'm sure the name clues you in to its level of hospitality."

People die was what he couldn't say. He'd failed at least three outcasts for sure, probably more, and each failure haunted his dreams.

With all her strong certainty, Astra said, "I shall never return to this realm, thank you very much. When I swiftly and efficiently break your curse, you can meet me in Everspring's upper market, where you can buy me a necklace at the silversmith's as a show of gratitude."

Dust chuckled, standing straight again. "You say everything with such confidence. I find myself wantin' it all to be true."

"As do I," Astra said softly. For a moment, he wasn't sure he'd heard right, especially since she cleared her throat, as if attempting to erase the words. Her shadow lightened as she turned away.

"Goodbye, Dust."

The suddenness of it tightened his heart and seized his

voice in his throat. He pressed both hands to the wall, all his force useless against the cursed barrier.

On the other side of it, the light brightened. Astra gave a gasp. It was over in an instant.

She disappeared, and the wall vanished with her, leaving Dust to stumble forward into an empty room.

Alone once again.

CHAPTER 17

ASTRA

I DID NOT APPRECIATE magic's abrupt methods. It dumped me as unceremoniously in Everspring's lake as it had dumped me in the fairy realm, with one distinction—I could not swim.

Water crashed in on me with force, stinging my eyes and attempting to collapse my lungs. Only shock kept me from breathing. My skirts dragged in the water, twisting around my legs, and when I turned my head, all I saw was water in every direction with nothing to orient me.

Dragons were no better than fairies. Safely transported back, indeed, only to die to that most human-realm of dangers—the one that had claimed so many of my father's friends through the years.

Drowning.

While I desperately hoped my enchanted dress or forced beauty would aid me, neither turned out to be the case. Flailing was not beautiful, so I did not flail, but beauty did not tell me which direction was up nor how to keep yards of wet silk from dragging me down.

My saving grace was a hand through the water, catching me quite firmly beneath the arm, hauling me to the surface. My head burst from the lake, and I gasped in air.

"You're safe now!" said an urgent voice. "You're . . . your h-hair."

My hair was dry. It fell in luxurious curls around my face, floating atop the water like a sailor lounging on the beach, caring only about relaxation as if there had never been an arduous voyage to bring it here. It was such a strange sight that it faded the water's weight on my chest.

With effort—and a few slips beneath the surface—the man who'd rescued me pulled me to a jutting wooden dock where other hands helped us both up to safety.

While I wanted to collapse, my spine kept me regal, even as I dripped from every appendage and my gown felt heavy as iron. Voices kept insisting I was safe, and I laughed—not to mock them, but from sheer relief, because above us I saw a familiar sky, faded blue in early evening, the low sun just beginning to streak orange and pink through the clouds. Not a speck of green to be seen. Though the lake shore was dotted with boulders, I did not fear anything that might be lurking beneath them. Frogs, crabs, and worms could not compare to even the smallest creature in the fairy realm.

"I appreciate the—"

That was all the gratitude I managed before a matronly woman took me by the shoulders and steered me toward a small house by the lake shore, making soothing *shh* sounds all the while, as if I were a frightened child. Perhaps I ought to have asserted myself, but I was still too overcome by the relief of not having drowned and the joy of that sunset-colored sky.

The entire group moved with us into the house. They

were a motley collection, young and old, men and women. I counted eight once I had the chance to actually get a look at them. The only way I could tell which of them had pulled me from the water was that the young man's clothes dripped as much as mine.

I tried to catch his attention, but that same woman herded me in front of a fireplace, throwing a warmed blanket around my shoulders to sop up extra liquid, muttering all the while that she would find me a dress and get mine hanging and *oh dear,* what a *trauma* I'd just been through . . .

As she muttered and fussed, her hands shook, and her eyes kept darting away from mine. The others in the group stared openly, some with jaws hanging. I lost sight of my rescuer among them, but I heard the echo of his shocked voice in my mind. *Your hair.*

My stomach clenched. Strange how I'd nearly forgotten all about my wish while in Dust's tower. He'd treated me no differently from any other person.

Because he'd not seen me.

With a decisive movement, I shed the blanket and folded it in my arms, pushing it into the older woman's hands.

"While I appreciate the rescue," I said, "I'd now like answers more than I'd like care."

I craned to study the faces only to find my rescuer was no longer in the room. By firelight, all I'd really seen of him was brown hair and a sturdy build. Others of the group shook themselves and peeled away just the same, leaving only three —the motherly woman, a bespectacled man who might have been her husband, and a child, hiding behind the man's legs.

"We must get you out of the city quickly," said the man, glancing at the window even though the shutters were closed.

I did not budge. "Answers."

The woman took a deep breath. "Come sit at the table. We can spare a few minutes."

The Survivor's Guild, they called themselves. All of them had been to the fairy realm.

"Well, most," the woman said, filling my teacup as we all sat around the table. She was at least a dozen years older than me, betrayed by the thin laugh lines on her cheeks and a figure that had clearly borne a few children. "They're all gone, though. Out of the city. Elis and I are the only ones who stay, and the rest helping us know a survivor, so they volunteer, though they haven't experienced it themselves."

"We watch for the ones returning," said the man, his voice a deep rumble, "and we get them out."

It was a smuggling operation—one that smuggled people.

"They always land in the lake." The woman shook her head, settling with her own cup. She tucked a strand of blonde hair behind her ear, and I envied the way most of it rested in a secure bundle at the nape of her neck. I resisted the urge to hold my own hair off my neck.

"Strange," the man agreed. "Always a different spot in the green realm, but the same spot in Everspring."

Their youngest daughter crawled beneath the table, giggling, until her mother urged her to play in another area.

I tapped one finger against my teacup, still absorbing. "So the king banished you too. What for?"

Surely he could not have proposed to *all* these people.

The woman shook her head, finishing a sip of tea. "We don't speak of it. This is the purpose of the guild. We find the ones returning, and we ferry them safely out of the city, without royal knowledge. Then the whole matter is put behind us. Causing trouble would disrespect the freedom we've been granted in returning."

I scoffed, though it was not the harsh sound I intended. "You do nothing to *end* it? One thing to rescue survivors—a valiant thing, don't mistake me—but you continue to allow a wretched king to punish innocents simply to avoid *causing trouble?*"

Of course, I'd never been one to go looking for trouble either. That was Beauty's specialty. Was I getting ahead of myself?

The man made another one of his glances toward the window, and he must have seen something I didn't, because he and his wife exchanged a knowing nod.

"The wagon is ready," she said, standing to clear the teapot and cups. "I have a dress for you that will not draw such attention. You can be in Larkspur by morning, and—"

I set my jaw, and I said, "I'm not leaving."

They both gaped. The fire crackled, hissing around a log.

"Didn't Dust save you as well? It's no gratitude to leave while he's still trapped."

"Who?" the husband managed, eyes still wide behind his spectacles.

I frowned. "Then how did you escape?"

After unnecessary hesitation, the woman finally said, "A fairy with pink, feathered wings . . . gave me an old nail . . . said it would take me back. Said it was *secret*. It's the same for all of us, dear. Now, really, we can't speak of it further. The wagon—"

"Dust commands that fairy," I said firmly. No doubt it was one of his many strange *friends*. "He saved all of us, and I won't abandon him to the terrors of such a place."

There was no need to get into the specifics of my bargain. So while they protested, I made my way to the door.

"You'll be on your own," the woman warned. "We can't be associated. It would endanger everyone in the guild."

"I walked away from my own home," I said. "It's no sacrifice walking away from yours."

The man caught the door with my hand still on the latch. "The king."

"I have faced down a dragon today. King Kenric of Everspring does not frighten me." It was, perhaps, overselling the encounter. But I burned with a righteous fury I could not fully explain.

These people had seen firsthand that loathsome realm. Survivor's Guild indeed—survive and nothing else. One thing to help the people returning, but they did nothing to stop others from sharing their fate. They'd done nothing to prevent the hours of terror I'd spent, fearing for my life, dreading I would never see the blue sky again.

Only one person had really saved me, pesky wood fairy though he might be.

I said only one more thing before leaving: "Now, if you'd please point me to the upper market, I have a dress to sell."

CHAPTER 18

ASTRA

Before I could think about destroying curse-binding trees, I had to tend to my own immediate needs first, and what I most needed—as my stomach loudly reminded me—was a hot meal. I could only guess I'd been a full day without one while in the fairy realm. Unfortunately, meals did not come free. Therefore, my first task was obtaining money.

I possessed only one item to sell.

Following the guild matron's directions, I hurried up the hill to the upper market and ducked into the first dress shop just as it was about to close its doors for the night.

Then I froze, feeling the past rise behind me like a shadowed monster, grasping my ankles to hold me in place. Once before, I'd suffered the loss of everything I owned, sold along with the rest of my family's possessions to cover the debt of Father's lost textiles. I'd kept only one thing—the emerald necklace Mother had given me just before her death, the only thing I had remaining of her.

And when winter had come, and my family was starving, I'd sold even that.

"Welcome!" The owner of the shop glided over to me like the most elegant of swans, bedecked in silk and lace but with a few pins stuck through her collar to interrupt the perfection. When she got a good look at my face, she gasped. "Milady, you are truly a vision! How—how might my humble shop serve you?"

Once more, hunger would drive me to part with the only thing of value I possessed. Once more, I would be left with nothing. At that thought, I almost turned and fled.

But I had nowhere to go.

Finding my voice, I declared my intention to sell the silver dress I wore. The woman regarded the white embroidery with reverence, brushed her fingers lightly beside a line of black diamonds without touching them. The silk was still damp.

"It's very fine indeed," the dressmaker said after a moment. "It's a shame about the damage. This shoulder is easy enough, but I'll have to remake the outer skirt entirely, and that's no easy alteration."

"It's enchanted," I said.

"A family heirloom, is it? One of those relics of dwindling magic."

"There is nothing dwindling, I assure you. The enchantment is fresh and strong as any."

"Milady, enchanted fabrics shed dirt and water. Not to mention . . ." With a kind smile but clearly disappointed eyes, the woman plucked at the torn skirt. I could not explain that the damage had been done by even *more* enchantment within a fairy realm, so I restrained a sigh and asked her price.

Then I tried to keep my eyes from bulging at the insult.

"This dress is worth a hundred times that, if not more!" I protested.

"I'm the dressmaker here," the woman said sweetly. "It's my business to know the worth of any garment, and I've told you yours."

Her gentle smile and swanlike demeanor masked a *demon!*

I stood straighter. "Well, my father is the foremost silk merchant in the kingdom, and I know *my* business. Enchantment aside, you are not even paying me for the silk."

"This ruined silk, you mean?" She indicated the gash once more.

"Ruined nothing—there are yards of usable fabric left in this skirt, with the bodice and underskirt besides! And you show me a finer weave or color among any of your stock, I *dare* you."

No matter how I haggled, she refused to budge. In the end, time was against me.

"I'm closing shop for the night," she said, "and the offer will not last to dawn. Do we have a deal or don't we?"

Daughter of a merchant indeed. By wearing the very dress I intended to sell, I'd made it plain I had nothing else, and my claim at enchantment could do little to balance that when there were such obvious defects in the garment. The woman had no fear of competition, since I'd arrived at evening with no time for consulting a rival.

In short, I'd shown my desperation as clearly as the tear in my gown, leaving me powerless in bartering. To add insult to injury, my stomach growled loudly at that very moment.

The woman began counting coin, as if the matter was settled.

I lifted my chin.

"We do not," I said firmly.

Leaving her slack-jawed and gawking, I exited the shop into the night. I kept my head high through the entire market street, but by the time I reached the city square, I sat on the raised edge of a fountain with shoulders drooping—as much as elegance would allow me to droop. The pale gray of evening was nearing full dark. I had no food. No place to stay.

"I wish I were still in the tower," I murmured, the most foolish thought I'd ever had.

From behind me, a voice said, "Aye, it's warmer here, I grant, but the woodshop floor is just as hard."

Whirling, I stood. The fountain trickled gently from its single spout, the bronze statue above it remaining motionless. There was no one else in the square, though I could hear the distant evening sounds of the city as families bid goodnight to neighbors and occasional laughter echoed in the streets. Candlelight flickered in windows, casting long shadows.

"Dust?" I frowned as I said it, though I could not have mistaken his voice.

Then I looked down and saw a wooden fox cub beside where I'd been sitting. I reached into my pocket; my fingers found only a tiny tail. The carving on the fountain's edge wiggled tailless hindquarters and looked up at me with a smug fox smile, moving with a fluidity that belied its wooden substance.

I pointed its own tail at it. "Scheming wood fairy!"

"Told you there's a lot can be done with a morningdew mirror, though I'll admit this one surprised even me. Apparently, when I told you to use my mirror, it sort of . . . broke it. In the best way. Never knew that would happen, as I've never had the chance to let anyone else use it before."

If only I could say watching a carved fox open its mouth to speak was the strangest thing I'd ever seen. It was no longer even in top contention. As Dust spoke through the tiny fox's mouth, the orange fur of its face rippled, its black nose twitching. Its ears flicked back against its head, then forward again. The carving had been lifelike before; now I could hardly make the distinction at all.

Slowly, I lowered myself to sit beside him, still studying the marvel. "Is this how you pass your days in captivity—bringing to life human objects in order to spook innocents?"

"That *would* be entertaining!" His open-mouthed grin perfectly suited the fox. "'Fraid not, though. It's only because I created this little fellow that I get to control it. I think. Normally I'm a silent witness to happenings. Seems I should've been sendin' carvings to the human realm years ago." Clearly enjoying himself, Dust stamped his tiny black paws and turned a tight circle, chasing a tail he did not possess.

"I ought to have told you I took the broken carving." I felt a touch of guilt, since I'd asked for the thread but not the fox. "I couldn't bear the thought of seeing it thrown out just for being damaged. How did you know?"

"Reorganized my shelf, found one missing. It was either you or Bumble."

Straight-faced, I said, "I blame Bumble."

"Bumble would've eaten the evidence. That was your mistake—you should've swallowed the fox. Then I could've seen what a stomach looks like."

I laughed, halting myself just before I could snort. But the reality of my situation sobered me once more. Sleeping without shelter was something I'd not done even in the height of my family's poverty, and even if Everspring boasted a mild winter that lessened my danger of freezing, I *was* in for an unparalleled night of discomfort.

At least I would be under the stars.

"See that?" I pointed up. "A proper night sky."

The little fox tilted his nose up, then shook it. "Speak for yourself. I love a never-changing shamrock sky."

"*Really?*"

"Aye, it's blinding, 'n it leaves behind spots when you blink. Plus I can never be sure my paint colors aren't green-tinted. What's not to love?"

One thing I could not deny about Dust was that his companionship was enjoyable, whether with a wall between us or with him puppeteering a small carving. Besides his clever conversation, whenever we spoke, it felt as if I held every ounce of his attention while the rest of the world fell away. I'd never experienced that before.

"I'm named after the goddess of triumph." I smiled. "My mother used to tell me stories about the goddess Astra every night before bed. My favorite was when she made the stars themselves bow."

"Could see that happening," Dust said. "You certainly bowed the dressmaker."

"Yes, but stars can't bow."

"Never met a star, so who am I to put a limit on what they can and can't do?"

Lifting an eyebrow, I looked down at him. "And just how long have you been spying from my pocket?"

"Partway into your dress barterin', I believe, which was so fierce as to make Traders envious."

Thankfully, the warmth in my cheeks would not show in the growing dark. "All for nothing. Her offer could hardly be called that, but it would have paid for dinner and a night at an inn. I have been accused of being too prideful for my own good, and I believe, tonight, I proved it."

"The curse of pride can make a fool of anyone," Dust said. When I glared at him, he tilted his head, fox ears twitching. "But even a curse has its upsides. In the future, I believe that dressmaker will think twice before swindling anyone else."

"In the meantime, I sleep on the ground."

"Aye, well, even with upsides, a curse is still a curse."

I snorted, shaking my head.

"Goodbye, Astra," he said. "Didn't get a chance to say it earlier, when—"

He cut off abruptly, and when I looked down, the little fox sat motionless, trapped in its original position, smiling up at me with wooden features. I was alone once more, his voice echoing in my head. The way he pronounced my name had surprising allure—his accent added an H. *Ash-tra.* A touch of softness to a sound ordinarily so harsh.

And his visit had reinvigorated my purpose. Why spend a night miserable on the ground when darkness was the perfect time for criminal acts?

Such as burning a piece of royal property.

For being a capital city, Everspring was too lax in its precautions. I'd noticed it when first arriving—the way the city guards wore leather armor rather than plate, the way a strange woman could be escorted without question directly to the throne room. The king clearly depended too much on his banishing power to resolve threats.

The only entrance to the castle *seemed* to be crossing the bridge, which was guarded. Before my time in the fairy realm, I never would have considered the obvious alternative —the canal. The river passed beneath the castle wall.

With only the light of the stars to aid me, I crept down the canal's edge and eased myself into the water, finding it unexpectedly warm. I'd been too much in shock to pay attention to the lake's temperature, but I would have expected any body of water in winter to be frigid.

Warm or not, water had not increased its appeal. I held tightly to the canal's stone edge and followed the water upstream until I came to the castle wall and the iron grate which allowed the river's passage through it. Carefully, I edged myself away from the canal wall, wading with my chin just above the surface, my toes curling to find purchase through waterlogged shoes.

As I'd hoped, the bars were wide enough for me to slip through sideways.

Then I dragged myself from the canal and into the lower courtyard, which was mostly composed of animal pens and grass for grazing—part of the castle's food supply. I lay on the grass until I recovered my breath. In a soaked dress, I was forced to admit the night's temperature was *much* more comfortable than I'd anticipated. It did not feel like a mild winter so much as a full summer evening. Even wet, I did not shiver, and my breath did not cloud the air.

In fact, it felt reminiscent of the warmth of the fairy realm, and for a moment, I struggled once more to breathe. I looked up at the canopy of stars, drawing solace from a dark night sky.

And for the first time, I realized—

Dust had *seen* me.

I jolted upright, heart pounding, remembering my experience with his morningdew mirror. How clearly I'd seen the sheep, the shearers. Dust had looked directly at me through a fox's eyes.

He'd not said a word about my appearance. He'd not proposed.

What was I to make of that?

As my heart continued to pound, I realized criminal escapades provided neither the time nor the place for deep pondering, so I forced my questions down and focused myself on the task at hand. There would be time to think once I'd left the castle grounds.

I put effort to wringing excess water from my gown, then stood. At least silk dried quickly.

Following the incline up, I passed a sheep pen. A few of the animals greeted me with low, friendly sounds. I silently thanked them for not having orange teeth or snapping the boards of their pen in half. A discarded sack caught my attention by its deep shadow on the ground, and I found it to contain a stale chunk of bread, lost by a careless shepherd boy.

It was not a proud dinner, but I'd spent my pride in the dress shop.

I continued to the upper courtyard, which contained the king's stables and repair shops. Everything I needed for my crime was in the blacksmith's forge. I took iron and flint, then piled my free arm with kindling and a pitch-soaked rag. My shoes squished with every step as I made my way with great care to the Peace Tree.

With firsthand experience of the fairy realm, the tree's home became obvious. It even had the same kind of wet, prickly smell I'd noticed in the forest near Dust's tower. At least it did not peer at me with a set of eyes.

Crouching beside one of its hunched roots, I got to work, arranging kindling and covering it with the pitch-soaked rag. When ready, I took a quick breath and struck my flint.

Orange flames blazed to life.

With a smirk, I hurried away. By the time I reached the river, the guards still had not shouted, giving the fire plenty of time to find purchase. I felt a momentary flicker of worry, since my intention was not to burn down the entire castle. But the guards could not be *that* negligent. An alarm would sound soon enough.

I slipped once more into the water and made my careful way downriver, looking for shelter.

CHAPTER 19

DUST

"I DIDN'T LIE TO ASTRA," said Dust.

He stood at the broken edge of what had once been his upper balcony, waiting for his building sap to harden on the new boards and trying not to think about all the things affecting his fate in Everspring. At least fixing a balcony was within his control.

Doll darted in the air from board to board, criticizing his work and, occasionally, his life choices.

"You're a liar, Dust." She smirked up at him, sunflower wings a blur behind her. "You lie most about that. Sap is weak here; the board will break free."

Dust found himself scowling. "I was raised by fairies. If I happened on any schemin' tendencies, they're yours to begin with."

She cackled at that. "Raised by Granters, were you? Granters scheme."

"They'd say the same of Planters, no doubt."

Fairy pairs claimed to be mortal enemies with their

opposite, but except in extreme cases, "mortal enemy" only meant a slew of petty insults and complete avoidance of each other. Except Traders and Raiders. They killed one another on sight.

Dust tested the board she'd indicated, and under his weight, it did snap free of the one beside it. He grabbed for the plank but missed, and it tumbled to the grass far below. He sighed.

"Don't suppose you'd grab that?"

"For the right price," said Doll.

"For the sake of our friendship?" he countered.

"I can't grow friendship."

Planters. They cared about nothing beyond their own garden, and heaven help the man who trespassed on it. Or the son of that man.

With a *clunk,* Dust dropped his bucket of sap onto the half-finished balcony. He sat, dangling his legs over the edge. As long as he wasn't actually falling, gravity remained in its regular state, and he felt the pull of the ground below as a pull on his very heart, sinking it in his chest.

"I didn't lie to Astra," he said again.

Of course he'd lied to Astra. But the true lie was crafted for Doll, the careful one that played to the Planter's expectations.

Sending Astra home after Doll had seen her carried enormous risk. It could expose Dust's deal with Renny, could prevent him from helping future Everspring outcasts. But that was the trick—Doll didn't know Astra had gone *home*.

"Still can't believe she stormed off," Dust said dejectedly. "She'd rather be eaten than . . . well, she'd rather be eaten."

Doll knew he wanted to escape, knew he tried, so that

became an expectation to his advantage. He told her he'd asked for Astra's help to escape, promising her the wealth of a king as reward, but Astra had thought it a fairy trick and left the tower, wandering into the wilds.

Shaking her head, Doll said, "Shouldn't have claimed to be king. You don't want to be king."

That much was true. Living as a king in a castle was just imprisonment of a fancier nature. When he finally earned his freedom, Dust had no intention of trading one tower for another. He intended to travel, to witness with his true eyes things he'd only seen through mirrors. Things he'd only dreamed of.

"I'm a prince, aren't I?" he said. "Even without claiming the throne, I'm sure there's money in that. I'd have given her whatever she wanted. I just want my freedom."

Doll turned a spin in the air. "There's no need to justify to me. If anything, you didn't lie enough. Should've promised her a life of ease within a Trader's mouth."

For a moment, Dust worried *Trader* was an intentional barb, exposing his lie. But his face remained composed. This was their dance, always. Doll testing what he would reveal, him doing the same in return.

"Morningdew," Doll said, as if there had never been any other topic.

Rather than dropping a feather, she hovered. It could mean only one thing.

"You've run out."

Dust reached up to run his fingers through his hair, testing the length. Recently, he'd managed to avoid purchases beyond morningdew, but this was the one he could never do without. Especially now, since it gave him a window to Astra.

Besides that, he needed more healing sap, for the next half-moon.

He climbed to his feet. "I'll get the shears."

Dust hated the feeling of a haircut. He'd had enough practice not to leave himself raggedy or uneven, and he sold his hair so frequently, he was never losing more than an inch at a time. Doll was very particular about the cut—as she was about everything relating to her garden—so he could never trim too close to his scalp, else the hair would be unusable. All things considered, a cut changed very little about his appearance.

But there was something about trading away parts of himself that left his stomach queasy. Perhaps because he'd already lost his home, family, and freedom, yet still required more sacrifice to survive.

A little longer, he told himself.

Doll was right about the lies. He told them to himself most of all.

After checking himself in the silver mirror once more and running his fingers through the back of his hair to be sure he'd not missed any sections, Dust carefully swept the shorn hair into a bottle and capped it.

Stepping onto his under-construction balcony, he handed the bottle off to Doll, and her basket appeared to swallow it.

"Morningdew starts tomorrow," Doll said.

"Should have plenty now," Dust said tightly.

"Tomorrow."

She zipped off before he could offer further protest. For a moment, Dust clenched his fists, then forced himself to release them and breathe.

At least he'd been able to see Astra once since leaving—with an emphasis on *see*. Dust hadn't put much thought into his expectations for her appearance, but when he did finally get the chance to see her, he couldn't help the disappointment. She was lovely. Strikingly so. But it was clearly the doing of magic, and he'd had enough magic to last a lifetime. All he'd wanted was a connection with a regular human. He'd thought she might at least have a scar; he carried a permanent nick by his left eyebrow from a carving accident that had nearly cost him an eye, not to mention the multitude of small marks and gouges marring his hands after a lifetime of knife handling. Humans were like that—rough around the edges.

Astra was perfect. At least in appearance. It made him worry he'd trusted his fate to the wrong person, not that the options were plentiful.

There was also his morningdew mirror to consider.

By letting someone other than himself operate his mirror, Dust had apparently broken it—or, more accurately, locked it. Instead of randomly sending him into the eyes of any creature in the world, it now sent him to Astra. On the one hand, it was terribly convenient. On the other, only terrible. If his deal with her went poorly, the wide world had been closed to him, and he would be left with nothing but a view of her.

Enough brooding. Dust shook his head. He grabbed his bucket once more and returned to fixing his balcony.

In truth, he'd viewed enough of the world through a

mirror. This attachment to Astra gave him a chance, however small, to affect his fate in Everspring.

That was worth any risk.

CHAPTER 20

ASTRA

WHAT REMAINED OF THE NIGHT, I spent in a goddess garden. It was the kind of place where my mother would have worshipped, full of cobbled walkways and stone statues, interwoven with greenery. There was always one stone enclosure, marked by the goddess Bordia, patron of weary travelers, and I found a woolen blanket inside, courtesy of someone devout.

As soon as the sun peeked through the enclosure's window slits, I dragged myself out into a grassy area and fell asleep in earnest. It was a great irony that I'd camped beside a statue of the goddess Astra herself. Perhaps not irony—perhaps destiny. The irony was that I'd struggled to sleep all night with no success, only to manage it under the light of the morning sun.

As a result, it was mid-afternoon before I made my way to the market. I found it abuzz with gossip.

Did you hear? Someone tried to burn the Peace Tree.

Not as satisfying as I'd expected—no one said *burned down* the Peace Tree, but instead *tried to burn*.

Trumpets sounded in the distance, and a general stir of panic spread through the crowd. All at once, shopkeepers drove citizens from their shops with the urgency of shepherds driving off a wolf. People rushed through the street. Doors slammed. Even the stares directed at my beauty were fleeting because the ones giving them were more interested in *fleeing*.

"What is going on?" I asked one woman.

She ignored me, hurrying on. Through one shop window, I watched a man stuffing wares into a barrel, then forcing the barrel into a closet.

Possessed, every one of them.

I ducked out of the main street, into an alley. A wooden ladder stood propped against a shop wall, which creaked as I climbed. Once I was atop the flat roof, I had a better vantage from which to see what all the commotion was about.

A royal procession. The trumpets heralded the king.

Rather than walking or riding a horse, King Kenric was carried in a palanquin, flanked by mounted knights as the trumpeters played in the street ahead of the entourage. Even for a king, the display seemed a bit ridiculous outside of a festival, but perhaps that was my naïvety speaking. Our lord baron had always ridden a stallion when he went out. Perhaps the king preferred leisure.

The procession entered the market and came to a halt.

With my attention back on the market, I expected to find it empty, but to my surprise, a crowd of people milled, just as before. They did not seem to be *actually* shopping, only making a great show of it—bending over fruit stands, peering exaggeratedly in shop windows, commenting loudly on the fine offerings—all while darting glances at the king. The shops had reopened their doors, and I heard the voices of several merchants calling out hearty greetings, welcoming His Royal Majesty to their humble shops.

The footmen lowered the palanquin, and King Kenric descended into the market with his uncanny smile, graciously greeting his nearest subjects, waving at others. Irritation simmered within me at seeing him, but unless everyone in Everspring had taken a roundtrip to the fairy realm, I understood neither the earlier frantic reaction nor the forced calm now.

At least—

Not until Kenric began shopping.

Shopping was hardly the term for it; more colloquially, it would have been called *stealing*. He plucked fruit from stands as he walked by, dropping each into a basket carried by a waiting servant. He admired shop wares through windows and then ordered the corresponding merchant to fetch this jeweled brooch or that feathered cap. To a one, they obeyed without protest or even an attempt to ask for payment. Kenric certainly did not offer.

I watched with slack jaw. Had anyone asked me to describe the scene, I would have lacked words.

Because he was king, did he think himself entitled to anything he pleased?

Because he was king, did he think himself above law?

And no one protested! I'd refused to bargain with the dressmaker when her offer was too low, but she'd at least offered payment. If no one else was going to speak about the king's wrongdoing, I certainly would. I could not abide such an appalling scene with silence.

Then I thought of the fairy realm, and I hesitated. My stomach rolled as if caught in unsteady gravity. My skin crawled with the thought of creeping violet creatures.

Was I a coward?

The way I avoided the ocean, avoided vulnerability with my family, avoided so many things—I'd always called it sensible. And yet . . .

I forced away the uncomfortable thoughts as I caught sight of the knights. One young man on a speckled horse wore a red tunic with the crest of a gray serpent.

Dust had not mentioned the age of the knight his mother had sent as courier, but surely the man on the market street could not be older than my sister Callista. If he was the queen's courier, he would have been venturing to find a boy in the fairy realm while still a boy himself.

Yet he wore the right crest. He also attended the king.

I debated a moment more before deciding. Then I slipped across the roof to the ladder and tried to make my way back to the ground with as few creaks as possible. The king's entourage remained at the other end of the market street, and Kenric himself had stepped into a winery, so I ducked onto a side street and skirted the market, trying to keep my gaze down and the effect of my passage minimal. Luckily, everyone seemed to keep their focus on the king.

After circling around to the knight's position, I elbowed my way past a few women, ignoring their grunts of protest. The knight's horse stamped as I drew near, and he leaned down to calm the beast.

"Sir knight." I tried to keep my voice low but still audible. "I've been sent by Dust."

When the young man looked at me, he stared with the same senseless awe, which was growing tiresome. Likely he'd not even heard my words past the loudness of my face.

"In the *fairy realm.*" I tried to inject those words with all the emphasis I could muster.

Under the bright sunlight, the knight's hair was a rich hickory brown that seemed vaguely familiar. His brown eyes contained the same richness in a swirl of shades, darker rings fading inward to light, and they watched me with awe turning to something like panic.

"You!" My own eyes widened. "You pulled me from the lake yesterday!"

Quickly, he dismounted, handing his reins off to one of the king's footmen. Since we were beginning to draw attention, he motioned away, both of us ducking into the next street. At least Everspring's mazelike construction made concealment easy, and once we stood in the shadow of a building, I did not see any nearby peeping eyes.

"A lake? That's—I've never—don't know what you mean," the knight stammered. "Perhaps you've confused me with, uh . . ."

Enchanted beauty ruined my flat stare. "There's no confusion, sir. You're part of the Survivor's Guild."

He shifted, glancing at the street. "My lady, please keep your voice—"

"*How?*" I jabbed a finger toward him. "How does the king not notice that one of his personal *knights* has returned from the fairy realm?"

"Oh, I've—I've never been to the realm. My lady, might we discuss this in private?" He blushed suddenly. "Not in *private*, just, er, not here."

I eyed him from head to toe, lingering on his crest.

"Your name, sir?"

"Bastien Wolf, my lady. Although I'm more often called Fitzweller."

Fitzweller was a common nickname for the son of a fisherman, and a fisherman-knight was strange enough, yet he was also member of a secretive guild and the dowager queen's private messenger boy. Sir Bastien was more of a maze than Everspring's streets.

"The goddess garden, east of here," I said. "Are you familiar?" After his nod, I told him to meet me there. "The sooner the better."

Bastien gave a deep bow, turning to leave.

"Wait." I bit my lip. "The Peace Tree still stands?"

The knight frowned. "The—oh, the fire. Yes, it stands. Unharmed, apart from a few streaks of soot. But the king was . . . displeased."

I scoffed. "By what indication? Is His Majesty's smile a quarter-inch less wide?"

"No, it's more that he set his own fire in the dining hall."

While I stared, some noise from the market alerted Bastien, and with another quick bow, he hurried away. After gathering my senses, I reached in my pocket for the little fox but found it still wooden and immobile. I tucked it away once more and returned to the goddess garden.

Bastien arrived an hour before sunset.

On my way out of the market, I'd found a discarded ribbon, and with my hair hanging constantly on my neck and blowing into my face, I'd grown desperate enough not to care that the yellow ribbon carried streaks of dried mud or that it did not match my gown.

But my hair refused taming.

No matter how finely I divided the strands or how tightly

I wove them, every braid unraveled. No matter how securely I tied the ribbon, it fell to the grass. Though my outward composure remained demure, inside was a growing frustration until I nearly yanked a section out by the roots—not that it would have allowed me to do so.

Bastien arrived just in time to watch me ball up the ribbon and toss it into the statue Astra's face so my namesake could share in my frustration.

"Need help, my lady?" Bastien asked with chivalrous concern.

"It's no matter!" I huffed, then cleared my throat. "Thank you for coming, Sir Bastien."

What care did a wealthy woman have for untamable hair? It only bothered me now as I was trying to accomplish things while homeless and exposed to the elements. I would hardly notice it while relaxing in a vast manor house surrounded by luxuries.

I seated myself on the grass, arranging my skirts, and gestured for the knight to join me. He'd changed from his red tunic into a plain shirt and vest, perhaps to avoid the attention given a knight, though he still carried a sword in addition to a leather satchel. He lifted both out of the way as he seated himself with legs crossed.

"How many times have you ventured into the fairy realm?" I asked, seeing no need for preamble and hoping his vast experience would be more helpful than mine in knowing how to kill an unburnable tree.

Bastien sucked his lips in, then separated them with a small *pop*. "Never, my lady."

"Very funny, Fitzweller. Not only are you in the Survivor's Guild, but I have it on good authority that you've delivered letters from the dowager queen to her firstborn son."

"To whose . . . what?" His wide-eyed blink was so clueless, I found it hard to doubt the act.

"Please," I said, a word I did not employ often. "I know the guild has its *beliefs* about discussing the realm, but I am trying to save someone, and I need . . . help."

Dust had been the first to make me admit such a thing. Now he was forcing me to admit it again. Pesky wood fairy.

Bastien looked guilty. It did not bode well. His arms tightened around his satchel, and he scooted a bit closer on the grass, pitching his voice more quietly.

"I'm not actually a . . . survivor." Bastien winced as he said it. "And what's worse is I don't even *know* any, not like everyone else. I sort of . . . lied? To get in the guild."

Unbelievable. I was reminded that a nearby ribbon would be very handy for strangling.

"Sir Bastien," I said sternly. "Explain."

As it turned out, Bastien had nothing to do with queens or fairies. My instincts about his age had been correct, and at twenty-three, he was too young to have helped child-Dust, not to mention he had only recently been knighted.

"I'm just the son of a fisherman," he said, fiddling with the strap of his bag, "looking for my brother. My only lead is . . . well, fairies. So I, er, infiltrated the guild."

When I ordered him to explain his crest, he said it was a family coat of arms, but not his own family. It belonged to the household of the lord who had taken him in as ward.

Dropping my head into my hands, I groaned. My hair fell forward, ever a nuisance.

"I do wear it rightfully," Bastien said, his voice hesitant as if unsure he should be speaking. Surely nothing he said could make the situation worse. I'd been robbed of my one imagined ally, and my first attempt to kill the tree had quite literally gone up in flames. He went on. "I didn't . . . *take it from a corpse* or . . . or anything."

I lifted my head slightly, breathing against my fingers before I laced them beneath my chin. "Sir, that emphasis makes it sound as if you very much did remove it from a corpse."

"Yes, I realized after I said it. Anyway, I have heard of knights going into the fairy realm. At least one. Sir Reynolds? That doesn't sound right. Sir Ar . . . nold. Maybe. Lord de Berranger tells a few stories about him, says he spent enough time in the realm, his eyes turned green."

"Fascinating," I said flatly. Then, in a moment of panic, "My eyes aren't green, are they?"

Bastien leaned in with furrowed-brow focus. "I'm not sure they're any color so much as just . . . sparkle? It's rather uncanny."

"Well, I thank you for your honesty. Unfortunately, this has been a waste of time, and I am fearfully low on it already."

My stomach cramped with hunger, the previous night's scavenged meal long gone. I could scarcely think. No matter how low the offer, I would have to sell my dress, find a meal, and proceed from there.

Listening to my stomach's growl, Bastien's look turned sympathetic. He pulled an apple from his satchel.

Even my pride was starving. Rather than declining the offer, I said, "Thank you, sir."

As I crunched down on the sweet fruit, I could hardly keep the saliva in my mouth. Turning slightly away, I concealed my mouth with my free hand, though Bastien was picking at grass rather than watching me eat.

"I still hate being forced to serve the king," Bastien said, almost as if speaking to himself, "but the food is the finest I've known. When I was a boy, my father would bring—"

"Hold on." I struggled to swallow a lump of apple. "What do you mean *forced*?"

"Maybe I should start from the beginning."

Since he'd been kind enough to give me food without drawing attention to my poverty, I waved for him to continue.

"At sixteen, I left home in pursuit of . . . fortune." He rubbed the back of his neck. "Foolish fortunes. My mother and I used to fight about money, my future, my brother . . . everything, really. I thought I knew more than I did. After running off, I wandered and starved before—miraculously—Lord de Berranger found me. In his words, dying is a waste of young men, so he took me in as ward. I tended horses on his estate before he sponsored me first as his squire and, finally, as a knight. It's more than I can repay, and more than I ever deserved."

Despite myself, his clear humility made me smile. Wildly unhelpful though he might be, he was the most knightly of the knights I'd known. Growing up, I'd seen only the knights employed by our local baron, and they could hardly be called such. Men who lazed about with swords, waving them vaguely to keep the peace whenever a drunkard fell asleep at the docks, all while drinking into a stupor themselves.

"It's *his* crest," said Bastien, drawing a faint curve in the air with his finger, "the serpent. It's the de Berranger crest. Even though I'm only a ward, he insists I wear the family colors."

"Is Lord de Berranger here?" I asked.

"In Everspring? No. He never comes unless forced. It's

that way for half the court. The other half never leaves, whether by their choice or the king's."

He also hurriedly informed me it couldn't be Lord de Berranger I was looking for, since the man had lost a leg early in his knighthood, a notable feature Dust would have remembered. Only one of the lord's sons had been knighted, and only weeks before Bastien.

I took my next bite of apple with so much force, I nearly took my finger with it. Once I'd composed myself, I said, "You still haven't answered this business about being forced."

"Oh, right. Shortly after we were knighted, I came with Emory to present at court. The king liked my showing in the melee, so he told me to stay as part of his personal guard."

Blinking, I said, "That's it? Why not turn him down?"

Bastien smiled. Then he said, "Oh, you mean it! My lady, no one can disobey the king."

"Surely he wouldn't banish you for refusing an appointment to court."

"Well . . . he might not want to, I suppose. But the Peace Tree just . . . does it. While I was with the guild, I heard Elis say the king's a slave to the tree's magic as much as anyone —though that didn't seem to be a popular opinion."

The Peace Tree just does it. I nearly dropped my apple as the pieces came together in my mind.

CHAPTER 21

ASTRA

I'D THOUGHT IT STRANGE the king could send me to the fairy realm without a word, but it was not him at all. It was the same curse affecting Dust, a tree with roots spread in two realms, one set working to keep the true prince captive, the other banishing any human who defied its usurping master.

Kenric could walk down a market street, claiming any goods he liked without pay; he could command a knight to serve him, with no regard to the knight's desires; he could order me to marry him—all because the Peace Tree served the king. Fairy magic was the monarch's burly enforcer, casting out opposition with ruthless efficiency.

And because it was not the king himself, there was no riot in the street, no one calling for Kenric's head. It was simply *the way of things*. I'd seen it at home with my own father; when his textile ships were taken by hurricane, every sailor drowned, the widows did not come breaking down our door, condemning him for the foolishness of the voyage. They cried silently. Because although my father had ordered the voyage, he did not command the seas.

In Everspring, the Peace Tree was their force of nature, their ocean storms. They tiptoed to avoid it and resigned themselves to the times when it struck.

But just as my father had, at times, ordered a foolish voyage, out of season and against the advice of his captains, Kenric gave orders knowing the high risk of storms to come. When he could have paid for every purchase, offered his knights their positions, *asked* for my hand, he instead gave commands. He trusted fear to create obedience, and he embraced the tree as his tyrannical enforcer.

This was his own father's doing. What justification had the late king had? Fearing revolt, fearing his child's safety—that was Dust's claim, though I was not sure I believed such a thing. A king commanded armies. Perhaps the only reason revolt had been threatened to begin with was the king's selfishness. Only a tyrant would seek magic that could ensure continued tyranny.

The Peace Tree did not bring peace. It brought silence.

And if the rest were not condemnation enough, only a tyrant would choose such a tree over his own son.

Bastien must have seen something in my lapse of speech that worried him. He rummaged through his satchel until he produced a small bag of figs, handing them to me as he'd done with the apple. I realized my hands were trembling. Strange that I could not slouch, but I could tremble. Was a weakness ever considered beautiful?

"I will see that tree ripped from the soil," I said. I watched Bastien, daring him to argue.

"Why?" he asked simply.

My jaw clenched tight, refusing the answer. It was because I felt the shame of the old king's actions reflected on me. Just as my father gave reckless commands, he'd also stolen enchantment—the rose he'd taken from the beast's garden.

And yet . . .

My father was irritating, but he was not a tyrant. The moment he'd realized Beauty had taken his place in the beast's castle, he'd nearly lost his life trying to rescue her, only stopped by combination of an enchanted forest and the pleas of his remaining children. I remembered his nights sitting before the fire, beard damp with regret, praying to his God for Beauty's safety, even as he feared the worst.

I'd compared fathers as if they were ships made by the same craftsman, but Dust's father did not deserve to sail in the same ocean as mine.

However, *I* was not in a blameless sea. While I condemned Kenric for his dominating commands, I was guilty of a wish which made my own. The proof was in a mob of wealthy men, in Lord Merteberge's blood across the stones, all because I'd wanted to be *fawned* over. Because everyone's eyes had always been on my sister, I'd wanted them to be on me for once, with no thought to the cost.

Stars above. I was no better than Kenric.

The fig had turned to glue in my mouth. I found I could not swallow, could hardly breathe.

"People have tried," Bastien said. It took me a moment to realize he spoke of the tree. He lifted his shoulders. "It comes in waves. Someone tries to cut it down, but it can't be cut. There's a time of resignation before someone tries to burn it. But it can't be burned. Rope and mule can't pull it down. It's gotten too large to try that again anyway."

I swallowed at last, looking down at my lap.

"Poison," I said softly. "The dowager queen tried poison."

"That's one I hadn't heard. Her Majesty seems—I mean, I would think the tree suited her . . . purposes."

"I'm sure she benefits. But in a moment of weakness, she must have remembered her son. Her *good* son, I mean. Not the spoiled brat on the throne."

"Kenric is . . . spoiled," Bastien said, as if musing. He picked at the grass again. "But he's not overly terrible, I think. He has a temper, but it's half the temper of the late king. It was always strange to me that Osric wanted me in his court when I seemed to displease him at every turn. Except in tournaments, I guess—though the other court knights hate to be shown up by a Fitzweller."

I was only half listening while I ate.

Until he said—

"At the very least, it might be too early to judge Kenric. Six months is not long to be king."

Giving a slight cough, I swallowed. "Kenric was just coronated. I was under the impression the festivities were still underway."

"Oh, it . . ." Bastien's face reddened, and he could not seem to meet my eyes. "That's right, you were at the second ball. I was too. You made quite a . . . quite an impression. Anyway, it's—my lady, it's been six months since then."

I looked down at the figs as if I might find them spoiled.

"The ball was two days ago," I managed.

He shook his head.

I thought of the weather, much too warm for even the mildest winter. I thought of my trip through the canal at night, without my breath even clouding the air. Six months would have carried me from the frozen new year to the heated summer solstice.

I thought of Kenric's ease in the market, of the way

everyone had seemed to anticipate his patterns. Like they were . . . established.

"No," I whispered.

"The guild says it matters greatly where you land in the fairy realm," Bastien rushed to say, as if it might be comforting. "Most only lose a few hours before rescue, but there *are* some who . . . Well, Elis lost two weeks. He said one man lost a year."

"Hush," I said as everything inside bubbled strangely, threatening some kind of revolt.

"Silence, right. Yes, I'll . . . silence."

I turned my full attention to savoring figs, focusing greatly on the rich fragrance, the sweet juice, even the crunch of the seeds.

Six months.

I thought of my family.

At the height of summer, they would have already planted. There would be crops in bloom. Did Rob continue his apprenticeship? Was Callista married already? I'd never congratulated her on her engagement, only made snide remarks of jealousy.

And what of Beauty?

Had my youngest sister been in Everspring with me, she surely would have told two stories of killing magic trees and still had one left to explain the philosophy of why such a thing either made someone human or explained the universe or . . . No, it wouldn't be an explanation; it would be a question. Stars, I hated her questions. Ever since Father had first made the mistake of affording her philosophy lessons, she'd dogged my heels relentlessly with *questions*:

"Astra, is morality inherent in life?"

"Astra, is it sickness that gives meaning to health?"

"Astra, do memories exist if forgotten?"

To answer each question, I'd said things like, "Beauty, is there nothing but clouds in your mind?" Her philosophies had never made sense to me, and I had mocked her to avoid admitting so, because it stung to look at a sister years younger than me while realizing she'd left me behind long ago.

I cleared my throat, realizing I'd run out of figs and somewhere along the way ceased savoring them.

"It doesn't matter," I said, handing the empty bag carefully back to Bastien. "Time makes no difference in my purpose here, and the world is more pleasant in summer anyway."

Of course, killing the Peace Tree was not the purpose for which I'd first come to Everspring. I'd yet to turn my wish to my advantage.

In that moment, I realized—it was not wood I needed to kill, but rather magic.

And no one knew more of magic than a fairy.

Leaving Bastien where he was, I retreated out of sight to another part of the goddess garden. Once certain I was alone, I called for the fairy.

With a flash of blue, she appeared. Frowning.

"You stink of Planter," she said abruptly. "Shoo. I have lost my interest in you."

"Are you a Granter?" Dust was right; the pairs helped.

My fairy's eyebrows shot up over her solid blue eyes.

"Oh-ho, Planters have told you of Granters, have they? Spread all their nasty little lies? While Granters fulfil a noble purpose, Planters wander about in wide gardens, whispering to trees until wooden themselves."

"*Yes.*" I kept my expression serious, giving a deep nod. "Terrible, all of them. Ugly and feathered."

The fairy grinned, showing her tiny fangs. "Ugly and feathered. I like this. Planters do not float but rather *fly*."

"What would serve them right would be killing one of those trees you mentioned. How exactly does one kill a Planter tree?"

Admittedly, I had always lacked the patience to be sneaky.

The fairy narrowed her eyes. "Astra has been granted a wish."

"I'm not wishing for anything! It's called a conversation."

"A wish to know is a wish indeed."

I huffed. "Very well. If you'd like to speak of my wish, we can discuss once more how you mishandled it. My wish was to be beautiful, but I did not wish to look so *different*. You have removed in me everything that looked like my mother, to say nothing of the concerns we did not resolve involving married men and such."

The fairy mirrored my huff. "Your wish has been granted. Now I seek a new wisher. Though the boy is, so far, as stubborn as Beauty. I shall have to use lures."

"My sister has nothing to do with this," I said. "She never made a wish."

Which perhaps made her wiser than me, just as she had always been. I ground my teeth.

"No, this is the point exactly. Stubborn. Beauty knew the weight in a word. Her wish would have been most delightful to grant, but the delightful ones do not wish." The fairy shook her head, sunlight catching on the faint glitter shed from her hair with the motion.

Just watching her hair made mine itch. I bundled it in my hand against my skull, but even my hand could not hold it, and it slipped free to bounce across my shoulders once more.

"Don't compare me to my sister," I said heatedly. "Everyone compares me to my sister."

"Because Beauty is delightful, and Astra is ordinary."

Her words spread the heat. I jabbed a finger at the hovering blue nuisance.

"You are a wretched Granter—the worst, I imagine, to exist. I'd suggest taking up gardening with the Planters, but I doubt you could even grow a tree."

She froze in place, her glitter ceasing to fall.

See how you like it, I thought.

"You have ruined my wish," I said, "and I demand a correction. You insist it has been granted, but you didn't grant it *properly*. Have you any idea what I've endured in the last few days? Or months, as I've just learned. Wealthy men proposed, yes, I understand, but my wish was not to cause a riot of every man at court! And married men—*married* men—what good do their proposals do me? It's only an embarrassment to me and to all their wives."

Advancing on her a step while she was still unmoving, I pressed on. "I was banished to the fairy realm for *your* mistake! I spent a day in the most wretched place imaginable, where every creature was just salivating to swallow me. I nearly *died*. And where were you? The only kindness and help I've received since wishing has not come from my *Granter*, but from a man in more awful circumstances than my own, though I can hardly believe such a thing is possible!"

As I lost my breath to ranting, the fairy watched me with

soulless blue eyes, arms folded. When finally I paused, she gave a little scoff, revealing her pointed canines.

"You did not wish to avoid hardship," she said slowly. "You did not wish to never cause a riot or feel embarrassment. You did not wish for immunity to castle eviction."

I clenched my jaw. "You know very well—"

She only raised her voice. "Nor did you wish for the ability to blend in with salivating creatures or to possess an army of attendants falling over themselves to offer kindness and help. What you wished for was beauty to make wealthy men propose. *That*, I have *granted*. You are beautiful, and wealthy men propose at the sight of you."

I bit my tongue. Finally, I said, "It isn't the right sort of beauty. Do you know what's beautiful? Coiffed hair is beautiful. Gathered in delicate knots and ringlets, never hanging carelessly on a woman's neck." I twisted my hair to demonstrate, tucking it just as I'd done so many times in my life, but it unfastened itself, dropping every lock back down to cover my shoulders. "No woman wears her hair down and undecorated like this. It isn't fashionable."

The fairy heaved a great sigh, as I'd done to Beauty so many times over her philosophy questions.

"You did not wish to be *fashionable*," she said. "You wished to be beautiful."

"Beautiful *is* fashionable! That's the whole definition."

"Astra does not know the weight in a word." She came suddenly close to my face, nearly sending me cross-eyed. Despite myself, I leaned back. She said, "You wished for beauty to attract the wealthy. Have you no understanding of what is beautiful to a wealthy man?"

"A fashionable woman," I insisted.

"If so, it is because her fashion is made of expensive silks and lace, because she adorns herself with gold and jewels. What is beautiful to the wealthy is wealth—that which acquires it, that which demonstrates it."

Though I opened my mouth to refute her, my jaw hung wordlessly.

I was no better than a ball gown. Something to be worn in public, something to turn the eyes of all others. Every woman wore her hair fastened, so mine, therefore, escaped its fastenings—because I was not meant to blend. I was meant to draw attention. My every feature reeked of magic, and of all the wealth in the world, magic was the rarest and most valuable.

So I was uncanny.

I was uncomfortable.

Because that was beautiful.

If the world *did* bend to such a thing, would the cost be worth it?

"You'll do nothing for me," I said hollowly. It was not a question; I already knew the answer.

The fairy did not so much as furrow her brow in sympathy. She said, "Magic is not without purpose. I have granted your wish. If you regret, seek completion of it."

She disappeared, leaving me alone with my beauty.

CHAPTER 22

ASTRA

When I finally returned to Bastien, I found him dozing, propped up on one fist. He reminded me so much of my brother in the moment that I felt the urge to push him over in the grass as I would have done to Rob. I'd left my family behind with eagerness; how could remembering them cause such an ache?

It was because I still smarted from my conversation with the fairy, that was all.

"Wake up, Fitzweller," I said sharply.

Bastien started, hand dropping to his sword, as if pulling it while seated in the grass would do any good. He could triumphantly best a grasshopper.

"Go home," I said. "I have no need of you."

He blinked slowly, as if still waking. "You . . . told me to stay."

"Now I am telling you to go. It should hold at least as much weight as the first command."

"My lady, we'll figure something out. Perhaps the tree—"

"Have you gone deaf?" I snapped. "You have no obligation to help me, and I wish to be rid of you!"

I wish echoed in my ears with all the unpleasantness of a lingering smell behind a butcher's shop, a smell which said *something died here*.

I'd given no thought to my wish. I saw now the hundred opportunities I'd lost and the trap I'd set for myself. I'd wanted to change my future, and I had. Changed it forever. All because I'd charged recklessly headfirst into jealousy of my sister. Why had I not wished for wealth to secure a future? Why had I not wished for happiness?

Why had I not wished to see my mother again?

"I'm sorry," I whispered, closing my eyes, pressing one hand to my forehead, if only to keep my ridiculous hair back. My chest ached with the pressure of tears that enchantment would not let fall. "I made a mistake. Just . . . go. Please."

When at last I composed myself, I found Bastien standing before me, fiddling with the strap of his bag. He jumped when my eyes met his.

"I can't," he said.

"Can't what?"

"Can't let you be rid of me."

I resisted the urge to sigh.

"You are a . . . bold person," he said.

In response, I gave him as much of a flat stare as my face would allow. "That was not your first adjective of choice, sir. The unspoken one no doubt would have been more apt."

Rather than correcting his insult, he said, "What I mean is . . . you are so direct, it makes me feel as though I might—perhaps I could do the same. Be direct."

"A tip to assist would be finishing the sentences you begin."

"Right. Yes. I've said some careless things in life, you see, so I'm trying to be more . . . deliberate. Less careless." He drew in a deep breath and held himself a little straighter. "My lady, I joined the guild because I thought I might find clues to my brother's whereabouts, but I'm now convinced that such clues may actually lie in helping you."

"Bastien, if I knew your brother, I would have told you."

"Yes, I realize. It's—see, when other options failed me, I sought the aid of a soothsayer, and he directed me—"

"A *soothsayer*?" I could not restrain the scorn in my voice, and only after speaking did I realize the irony. How much stranger was help from a soothsayer than from a dragon?

"Lady Astra, please." Bastien actually laced his fingers to plead as if we were children and I had the final slice of pie. "It's been eight years since I've seen Andre. After my knighthood, I finally made it back home to see my mother, but Andre wasn't there because he had gone searching for me. *Yes,* I have grown desperate enough to rely on soothsayers, desperate enough to chase a riddle about fairies and beasts. Because I . . . because I have nothing else."

My heart chilled at the words.

"Beasts?" I repeated.

His brown eyes caught the spark of hope. "Does that mean something to you?"

Andre Wolf. The enchanted beast at the castle . . . had Beauty mentioned his name was Andre? I'd never had much ear for my sister's words, particularly concerning what I deemed fanciful things.

"Possibly," I said with hesitation.

Bastien dropped to one knee as if I'd felled him with his own sword. He pressed his right fist to his chest in a salute. "I will take any possibility, my lady. I beg you. Please allow me to assist you on your quest while I pray it brings the answers to mine."

"Yes, fine, very well. Get up." My face heated at his earnestness and my own uncertainty. One matter at a time. "My only quest at the moment is to sell this awful dress. It reminds me of fairies."

I would buy a hot meal and a night at an inn, and come morning, I would find a way to see the king—because while the Granter had been unhelpful on purpose, she'd nevertheless reminded me of something.

Completion, she wanted me to seek, which she'd earlier explained as being drawn to ugliness. The opposite of my wish. If Dust's curse used fairy rules, then whatever magic the Peace Tree had bestowed on Kenric, I had to enact the opposite of it.

If the king's *wish* was to be obeyed, then I had to convince him the people's disobedience was better.

It was only a small matter of turning a tyrant into a supporter of free will.

The next morning, I examined my new dress. Since the room I'd rented was more closet than bedchamber, there was hardly room to stand between the bed and the wall, and I had to turn back and forth to properly see hemlines and laces.

A second attempt to sell the silver gown—to a different dressmaker—had still resulted in a low offer, and being drained of patience as I was, I had solved the matter quite efficiently by saying, "I am watched over by a fairy, and unless you pay me double, I shall curse your shop to never sell another dress."

After taking another look at my enchanted face, the dressmaker apparently decided not to take chances. I'd received my double payment—still ridiculously low for an enchanted silk gown—and immediately purchased one of the dressmaker's stock dresses to wear out of the shop.

The new garment was actually two: a gray linen chemise with a green woolen overdress. The overdress was split along each side with a lacing of leather cords for adjustment, so it needed no tailoring to fit a specific form. It was a practical garment, meant for daily work and wear, not for elegant social functions. The chemise was a loose, boxy style that received its shaping from the overdress.

There was no elegant swishing when I walked, but neither was there any danger of tripping, not when the dress did not even brush the floor, instead falling an unflattering inch short of my ankles. There were no gems, embroidery stitches, or other embellishments. This dress would not draw attention as the other had; although I would certainly manage that on my own.

In short, I hated it. Much as I hated everything about my current impossible situation. How did one convert a tyrant?

The inn offered a breakfast of pottage and bread, simple but filling. Unfortunately, I had no strike of inspiration as I ate, so by the time Bastien arrived, I was no closer to a solution than I'd been the night before.

But I had to try.

"I fear this won't work," Bastien said nervously as we approached the castle bridge. He was dressed as a knight once more, bearing his coat of arms, though he escorted me on foot.

"The king trusts his enchantment too fully," I said, glancing up at the gray turrets, ominous against a cloudy sky. "His security is lax, as is his general sense of danger. We'll have no trouble reaching him."

"No, I meant the . . . part that comes after."

With false confidence, I said, "It's a simple matter. I'll make the king see the logic of how his selfish actions damage his kingdom. No sound mind can resist logic."

Liar, said my own sound mind, which resisted it even now.

"So you'll . . . talk."

"Yes, Bastien, I'll *talk.*"

"And if he orders you to stop talking?"

I lifted my chin. This was my alternate plan, and in all honesty, I hoped it might sort the curse all on its own. "Then I'll disobey."

Bastien stiffened beside me, his eyes wide and panicked. "You'll be sent back to—"

"I'll break the curse," I said firmly. "Last time, I was not aware of the Peace Tree's magic, so I did not defy Kenric with purpose. That's the difference."

Magic is not without purpose, the fairy had said. In all Callista's stories about fairies, she'd always said details and intent mattered to magic. I ought to have heeded her warnings sooner, but I could at least employ them now.

Bastien fell silent as we marched past the guards. They did not halt a king's knight, although they certainly gawked at me.

I'd warned Bastien ahead of time—and he'd witnessed the ball himself—so we made our path through servant corridors and back passages. Twice, he motioned for me to wait while he scouted the next hallway to be sure it was free of wealthy lords. At one point, we waited in an alcove while a pair of lords took a generous amount of time chatting jovially outside private quarters.

"Have you any friends within the castle who might aid us?" I asked, pitching my voice low.

Bastien lifted one shoulder, his brown eyes keeping a sharp lookout. For all his awkward conversation, he'd shown no lack of skills elsewhere. He said, "Lord de Berranger's family members are my only true connections. Most people take offense to my station. My advancement, I mean. Lords and ladies think I'm, uh . . . beneath them. Because of the fish. Servants think I'm . . . well . . ."

"They're jealous," I supplied.

He nodded tightly. "The other knights tolerate me well enough, but we're not . . . friends."

"Fools, the lot of them. That advancement is the most impressive I've ever heard; it can only mean you're a most impressive person."

He flashed me a smile, showing slightly crooked teeth. "All it took was some starvation and near-death."

"Quite simple. It's a wonder the son of fishermen everywhere don't flock to follow suit." After a brief return smile, I sighed. "It's a shame you aren't the lord's son. You deserve a better regard."

"Lord de Berranger has sons aplenty," Bastien said. "The real shame is that my father only had two, and his eldest is a fool."

Though I could sympathize with sibling problems, I frowned. "Why search desperately for your brother if you think him a fool?"

"Oh, me. I—I'm the eldest."

I raised an eyebrow, and he rubbed the back of his neck.

"Andre's always been responsible," he said. "A little too responsible. He had to make up for me. And I search desperately because I . . . want to tell him that. I want to say I'm sorry. For all of it."

His eyes darkened with a clear sorrow, and I shifted uncomfortably.

If I saw Beauty tomorrow, what would I say?

"They're moving," said Bastien.

The voices in the hallway faded at last, accompanied by the click of a door. Bastien stepped out first to be sure, then gestured for me to follow, and we continued making our silent passage through corridors until, at last, we neared the king's study.

Bastien had timed our arrival to be just after the king met with his prime ministers and advisors. After the upper court adjourned, Kenric took an hour to rest in his study.

Just around the corner from our destination, Bastien caught my arm.

"My lady, are you certain? I would hate for you to—to put you in danger, I mean."

I smirked. "The only thing I'm not certain about is your ability to distract the guard. It's not too late for me to set a fire."

Once again, his expression grew pained at the idea of a fire within the castle.

"Bastien, if you stutter, he will not believe you." I tried to say it gently, though I had never been skilled at tact.

The knight did not seem to take offense. "He'll believe me. Here's the key."

He drew his sword, and I saw immediately that he was right—an unsheathed weapon spoke a hundred words.

"Don't impale anyone," I said. "Least of all yourself."

That he seemed to take offense to, with the same pained expression as before. I shrugged. After a fisted salute, he stepped with haste into the hall, and while I dared not peer around the corner, I listened intently. Bastien's footsteps thudded dully against the long rug, and then a click of heels snapped the guard to attention.

"Intruder in the castle," Bastien barked. "Did he pass this way?"

"No, Sir Bastien. I've seen no one."

"Then help me look."

I spotted the flaw in Bastien's plan at the same moment the guard brought it to light.

"If there's any danger of violence, I cannot leave the king. We must summon the rest of the guard."

Wincing, I pressed my fist against my forehead. There would be no way to reach the king if his entire guard surrounded him while on alert.

"What are you—danger?" Bastien scoffed, stumbling over his words. "There's no danger to His Majesty!"

My wince only grew deeper on the clumsy knight's behalf.

Until he said—

"The intruder is a snake."

Certainly, the guard blinked with the same confusion as I did.

"A snake?" the man repeated dully.

If Bastien stumbled, he at least did so with confidence. "Yes, that's . . . you heard me. You're worried about *assassination*—what's in danger of being assassinated is the king's favorite carrier pigeon! He won't be pleased. Let's not have another fire. Now, come on. If we move quickly, I'm sure we can catch it just around the corner."

After only a moment, the guard grumbled his agreement,

still taking a moment to complain that Bastien had not been clear from the start. But when they moved off, they did so with urgent footsteps.

I waited a moment before I slipped inside the king's study, latching the door behind me.

The king sat at his writing desk, staring at me, quill dripping a slow, extended dollop of ink onto the parchment below. His dark eyes held a shine of wonder.

"All right, Kenric," I said curtly. "Let's talk."

CHAPTER 23

DUST

It seemed to take an eternity for Dust to get his next morningdew feather. Once he had it, he almost overturned the basin in his haste to get the mirror working.

He saw first through Astra—the world moved in a disorienting blur as she opened a door and ducked into a room—before Dust circled his finger through the water, turning the viewpoint dark, since the fox carving had only the interior of Astra's dress pocket to look at.

Anything with eyes, that was the requirement for the mirror. He smiled, amused at how he'd never considered the painted eyes on a carving. Morningdew was remarkable indeed.

At least one upside of his curse was his frequent enjoyment of magic. Perhaps he would miss that in the human realm. Perhaps he would carry a tiny spark of magic with him. Or perhaps there would be enough ordinary wonder that it would never matter, one way or the other.

Just as he was about to direct the carved fox to wiggle free, he heard Astra speak.

"All right, Kenric, let's talk."

On second thought.

Dust returned to Astra's view.

"Extraordinary," the king murmured. A smile overtook his features. "You escaped the fairy realm."

Thanks to his crown, Kenric was instantly recognizable. Unfortunately, Dust had hoped he might recognize something else—an echo of himself in face shape or feature. But where Dust had his mother's chestnut hair, Kenric's was solid black. Where Dust's face was narrow, Kenric's was broad. And where Dust's eyes carried the eerie green of a fairy sky, Kenric's held the rich depth of brown earth.

Takes after Father, then. Dust remembered his father as a commanding figure with an air of authority, suited to the crown he wore. Like the man Astra now faced.

Although Dust's father had certainly never smiled like Kenric.

Astra folded her arms, and from the shift at the edge of the mirror's view, she'd no doubt tilted her head.

"I'd hoped you might be ignorant of your own actions," she said to Kenric, "but since you are aware of the realm and what your own decisions cost other people, I feel no regret saying what someone ought to have told you long ago—you are a horrible tyrant. Your brother suffers in that very realm, for *what*? Magic that allows you a free hat whenever you please?"

Goosebumps rose on Dust's arms. Using morningdew had never before felt like *spying*, not when he was in the view of animals or among strangers. Now he was in the middle of a conversation discussing himself.

And he held his breath for what his brother might say.

"Brother? You've lost me there." Kenric tidied his desk, setting quill, parchment, and inkpot aside before standing. He cut a regal figure, broad-shouldered and sturdy. "You must tell me, are there dragons in the realm? I've always wondered if there are dragons."

"As a matter of fact," Astra said heatedly, "I encountered one larger than this castle. I'd be delighted to introduce you to the back of its teeth."

The corner of Dust's lips twitched, but mostly he was caught in the echo of Kenric's words. *Brother? You've lost me.* Was he putting on a show for Astra's sake?

Or had their parents never mentioned Dust at all?

"Oh-ho!" Kenric chuckled, wagging his finger. "Lady Astra learned no deference in the fairy realm, I see. Surprised I remembered your name? I tried quite earnestly to put you from my mind after our last encounter, and yet, I found myself unable. All other candidates pale next to a specimen such as yourself."

"Specimen?" Astra spat, echoing Dust's thoughts.

"Your return is fortuitous for us both. Let us resume where we left off. Lady Astra, I *respectfully*—there, see, I am not so inflexible—I *respectfully* order you to—"

The room's second door opened to interrupt, admitting a well-dressed man who might have been one of the king's advisors.

Dust realized his stomach had gone tight, and he'd curled his fingers too-tightly at the basin's edge.

"Oh, what *is* it, Conrad?" Kenric turned, his genial smile melting to an expression of annoyance. "I'm in the middle of something."

Before Dust could rethink it, he swirled the mirror once

more. A flick of his finger directed the little fox carving to paw at Astra's pocket until she reached in and extracted him.

She lifted him on one palm, and though her eyebrows drew down, the expression did not look disagreeable. Up close, her face was simply dazzling, hard to look at, even. Dust nearly glanced away.

But her voice was a welcome one: "Wood fairy, your timing leaves something to be desired."

From somewhere outside his view, Dust heard the advisor offer apologies and say the matter was urgent, something about a venomous snake in the castle.

"If you want, I'll leave," Dust said, which was the most foolish thing to say. He didn't want to leave.

Astra gave a dainty scoff. "He's *your* brother."

She set the fox on her shoulder, giving Dust a view of the room once more, and that was that. He smiled, the tension in his shoulders easing.

"A *snake*?" Kenric's face had reddened. "You call this matter urgent? Is it the responsibility of a *king* to enforce snake removal within his own castle?"

Conrad's eyes had drifted to Astra. Though he still spoke to the king, he seemed to do so in a daze. "No, Your Majesty. I only worried . . ." He stepped forward, right past Kenric, reaching for Astra. "Forgive me, my lady, but your beauty. It is breathtaking!"

Astra did not seem to take it as a compliment. She took it with a heavy sigh.

Then the advisor dropped to one knee. "Please, my lady, marry me! I feel I must have you or die!"

For the second time, Dust nearly overturned his basin on accident. The edge of his hand dunked into the water, knocking the fox from Astra's shoulder, but she caught it and pushed the carving gently back into place with one hand while she tugged her other hand from the advisor's grip.

"Yes, I'm sure you feel that way," she said, as if it were no shocking matter. "However, I must decline. Kenric, I am hoping there's a shred of reason within your selfishness, enough to consider—"

But Kenric wasn't looking at her. He was looking at Conrad.

"Get up," he said with a voice like ice.

The advisor leapt to his feet immediately, though he still made an attempt to reach for Astra's hand. "Please reconsider! My lady, I—"

"Stop this at once!" ordered Kenric. "She's to be my wife. The arrangement is made. You will not pursue her again."

"There's been no arrangement made at all!" Astra protested. "And I'd sooner marry whatever snake is loose in the castle, thank you very much!"

Dust had once viewed a *valanga* through his mirror. It was the only word he had for the event, because it was the only word he'd heard spoken when it happened. One moment, he'd been looking through the eyes of a man at a snowy mountain. A single rumbling sound shook the mountain, like thunder. Then the face of the snowy cap cracked. At first, the rush of snow looked harmless—puffy and languid, like clouds billowing gently across the ground. But it grew.

And then it wasn't harmless at all.

Conrad dripped with the sweat of exertion, and his eyes were those of cornered prey. He did not look like a man in love so much as a man under death sentence. Clearly, he struggled against magic; Dust recognized the signs he felt in himself whenever he fought his own curse.

He felt like he was back in that moment on the mountain,

watching a rush of snow growing to consume the poor human right before him, painfully out of reach.

"You *must* marry me!" the advisor burst out.

And like a summoned executioner, the floor opened to swallow him whole.

CHAPTER 24

ASTRA

THE FOX FELL from my shoulder a second time, and this time, my grab for it came too late. It clattered on the floor, a motionless carving. My stomach twisted in knots. Carefully, I gathered it and tucked it once more into my pocket. Perhaps Dust's morningdew had simply run out.

More likely, he now saw me as my family did—as the villain. Perhaps that was my true identity after all. Conrad's final shout still hung in the air before me. If not for the magic of my wish, he would have obeyed the king's directive. He would have been safe. But my wish had forced his obedience as surely as the Peace Tree.

I *was* no better than Kenric.

"Now." Kenric smiled, content as if he'd opened the shutters to a beautiful morning. "We may discuss the rest of our arrangement without interruption."

"He was your friend," I spat. Any beautiful expression my face would bestow was too good for him, so I turned away.

"Friend? A king does not have friends. He was a good advisor, which is a pity, although I'm still baffled he qualified news of a snake as urgent. To the matter at hand. Lady Astra, after due consideration, I respectfully order you to marry me."

I glanced back only to find him looking pleased as a peacock.

When I gloated over my siblings, did I wear the same expression? Perhaps I *should* marry him. We could make each other miserable and at least spare our respective families.

"I feel faint," I whispered. It was not wholly accurate to describe the churning storm inside, but I worried that without a chair, my knees would buckle.

I need not have worried—enchanted beauty did not buckle.

Kenric clapped his hands in clear delight, his grin spreading to the same obnoxious width it had sported at the ball. "Yes, you are most overcome, I'm sure! Excellent. To details. A wedding in front of the Peace Tree, I think, during the summer festival. Mother will be pleased, and she can at last quit harping on this marriage-and-heir business."

"She values family?" I raised an eyebrow. "Yet she's abandoned her firstborn son in favor of you, a spoiled centipede."

Kenric was busy adjusting his crown. He waved his free hand. "You've said this nonsense twice now. I am an only child. The most delightful boy ever born, in my mother's exact words. Also." He lowered both hands, fixing me with an icy stare that belied his flippant nature. "You'll not insult me again."

I'll insult you as often as I please.

Except I could not speak the words.

With that too-wide smile, Kenric stepped closer. "That's settled. Now, tell me more about this dragon, my lady."

As I struggled to find words against him, something came to life in my stomach, a terrible pull, as if I held tightly to a pole and someone had hitched a rope around my middle to wrench me away.

Kenric snapped his fingers in the direction of my face. I looked up with irritation.

"Answer me," he said. "More about the dragon."

I tried inviting him to stab a quill through his own hand. What I said was, "His name was Smicker."

"Dragons have names? How extraordinary! Do they think themselves people?" He laughed uproariously at his own humor.

The pull had come and gone again, before and after my answer. It was not illness. It was magic. I'd never considered that my first denial of the king may have been a fluke, that perhaps in my newness to Everspring or my own bearing of fairy magic, the Peace Tree had not yet taken hold to make me subservient.

It seemed my unknown luck had now run out.

Why did I continuously charge forward without thinking? Magic was the most volatile power known to man, and in all my years of trying, I had not even managed to harness the normal ones—anger, desire, jealousy. Now I danced with fairies and kept thinking I could direct the music.

I will not marry you, I ordered myself to say.

"I will not ma . . ." I swallowed, feeling as if the action upended every organ inside me. I grabbed the edge of Kenric's desk as if to steady myself, though I needn't have bothered. My elegant posture paid no attention to the swirling tempest inside.

Kenric had returned to wedding planning. He spoke of

wildly elaborate decorations and his own lack of perfect attire.

"I'll need to go shopping," he said, eyes glittering at the prospect.

That was enough. It was true that I'd never learned to harness my anger, so I let it break free, hoping it might drag me to a resolution.

"Did your father never tell you the origin of the Peace Tree?" I demanded.

"Only as every bedtime story." Kenric rolled his eyes. He deepened his voice. "Once upon a time, son, the grandest king in the world secured the grandest blessing in the realm and built the grandest city in the kingdom." Another dismissive wave as his voice returned to normal. "He told me all about trading with fairies. Do you know what he didn't tell me? Dragons in the fairy realm. *He* told me dragons were a myth. Hah!"

I narrowed my eyes on him. "Trading—is that what he called it? Did he think the loss of his firstborn a fair price for the power to indulge his own crass selfishness?"

Kenric's smile dimmed. "Tread carefully, Lady Astra. I loved my father."

The bridle inside struggled to contain me. I gripped the desk with white knuckles. With all the spitfire spirit that was in me, I willed myself to break Kenric's command not to insult him, willed myself, by the same stroke, to break the curse. Then I said, "He was clearly an egotistic fool, and he raised you to be the same."

This time, the victory smile was mine.

Kenric stared. "Impossible. How do you manage to resist? And *why*? I've been told the fairy realm is an awful place, that it's—"

I jabbed a finger at him. "What's awful is this kingdom under your rule. You treat the people around you like yesterday's wardrobe, casting them off without a second thought. You should consider how they will cast off such a king if only given the chance. And you should know I represent that chance."

The floor rose up beneath me as I spoke, grasping at me with wooden tendrils, sinking me into a glowing green light. I held to the desk as long as I could, and my eyes never left Kenric's, rewarded by the growing fear reflected in his. Robbed of his smile, his jaw hung slack with terror.

"Mark me, Kenric." I gave my most dazzling smile. "I am Astra, the goddess of triumph, and my triumph will see your Peace Tree pulled down."

I did not hear his response before the fairy realm dragged me in and sealed the exit.

It was not the swamp I'd landed in this time. Instead, I found myself lying along the very edge of a mountain cliff, one foot dangling over the precipice. The air felt hot and dry in my throat. The green sky leered down at me. Very slowly, I scooted away from the cliff's edge, my rough dress scraping against the dusty stone.

A gray lizard scurried beneath my arm, scraping my wrist with its scales. It had eight webbed feet. Hopefully it did not possess the same venom as blaze spiders. After a moment of holding my breath, I noticed no change in my arm, and the scrape had left only thin white lines without blood.

"Welcome back," I murmured to myself. All the bravado I'd displayed with Kenric vanished in an instant, sliding off the edge of the mountain while I could focus only on inching my way back to solid ground.

Once I could finally stand, my legs wobbled. I picked my way over discarded castle floorboards and then onto a gravel-strewn path, hugging the mountain to avoid any sheer drops. At least my green peasant dress was more suited to travel than my silver gown had been; it did not drag on the ground. Yet there seemed to be little point to travel when every direction was the same craggy stretch of gray rocks beneath a sickly green sky.

"Nit!" something barked at me. I jumped.

What looked to be a little bald man scurried out from beneath a low outcropping. His arms dangled to his knees, every joint knobby and pronounced. His nose looked like a bulbous mushroom on his face, and his skin carried the same color, tone, and texture as the rocks.

"Nit!" he shouted, waving at me with a rock in each hand. "Nit, nit!"

I didn't bother with negotiations, just held up my hands and hurried on until he seemed satisfied, retreating back into his outcropping.

I'd chosen *this* over marrying a king? Kenric had been right to question my sanity.

Bastien would hear about my fate. Would he blame himself? I ought to have told him my suspicion about his brother, even if it turned out to be incorrect. He'd been so desperate for any lead. As usual, I'd been selfish.

A dry wind blew hot against the barren landscape. One would think lack of a distinct sun would make the fairy realm more tolerable, but the opposite proved true, since the light and heat seemed to beam down from every corner of the sky at once, without even clouds to filter it. I sighed, seating myself on a boulder free of lizards and Nit-monsters. With both hands, I combed my hair out of my face and held it trapped against my scalp, fingers interlaced. It did very little to cool me, and sweating, it seemed, was not beautiful.

I'd managed to disobey the king with purpose, yet I'd still been sucked into the fairy realm. Without seeing, I knew—the tree still reigned. I'd changed nothing. Even if I made it back, there seemed to be no path forward. Kenric would not change his ways. I'd seen the truth of our similarity, and when had I ever bent my pride to reason?

With a groan, I released my hair. For a moment, I had the impulse to call for the blue fairy, but I resisted, not even sure why. Pride, most likely. With me, it was always pride.

Or perhaps I was tired of demanding solutions from others. When we'd fallen into poverty, I'd expected Father to set things right. The rest of my family had distributed burdens, done what they could to help, but I had not. I'd waited. I'd sulked. In my search for a husband, I'd whispered with Callista at balls and waited for men to approach *me*. I'd blamed Beauty for stealing Stephan, but I'd made no attempt to engage him first. If I had, perhaps he would have considered me, perhaps not, but I could have been proud of the effort. Instead, I resented lost opportunities—and my own sister.

"This is a dreadful landscape for self-reflection," I griped to the rock beneath me, half-expecting it to come alive as some hideous troll. Thankfully, it did not.

I pulled the fox from my pocket, cradled in my palm. Though missing its tail, it still held a playful pose, front paws extended, haunches up. The orange of its fur could not have been more perfect—dusty yet vibrant, something belonging to a creature both wild and playful. Knowing myself, there was no surprise in how deeply I admired the artistry.

There was, however, surprise in how deeply I ached to meet the artist.

Dust was a fool to trust me. My own life was a shambles, as I was coming to realize, and he would be better off enlisting the help of the little Nit creature brandishing rocks. I carried the very same failings as Kenric, the same pride, the same selfishness. I even wielded a magic which enforced my will upon others.

Was it too late for me?

I stood, slipping the fox once more into my pocket beside the thread winder and needle. To my right was the mountain face, to my left, the sharp drop-off at the path's edge. In the distance, I could see a green valley, with purple trees and a spiral-shaped lake. It would take days of hiking to reach it.

The path's edge loomed in my vision, reminding me of pearl divers and a hundred feet of sinking. The mountain seemed to press in from above. I was not Astra, the goddess of triumph; I was only Astra, the dry-mouthed girl stranded without water in a fairy desert.

I nearly curled up on the ground right then, dissolving into a puddle of self-pity, but I thought of a lost prince in a tower. He didn't have anyone else. Just me.

Stars, he had the worst luck in existence.

With a huff, I squared my shoulders, lifted my chin, and began marching down a mountain.

CHAPTER 25

DUST

DUST BROKE FROM THE MIRROR EARLY. It was the first time he'd ever had warning of a human in the realm faster than the spriggan chimes could give it, so he signaled Renny first, then scouted from his roof to find Conrad's location. Water chimes to the west. That would be Spiral Lake.

And at the back of his mind, his thoughts lingered on Astra, circling ideas like *Granter, wealthy husband, enchanted beauty.* Though he tried not to draw conclusions, they practically drew themselves. They were not pleasant.

He'd tempted her with the knowledge that he was a prince, not realizing he was walking himself into the grasping tentacles of a depthfiend. Based on what he'd seen in the castle, the instant there was no wall or morningdew barrier between them, he would lose all his senses, begging for marriage. She intended to free him from one curse only to enslave him with another, and he'd encouraged it.

Making assumptions, he warned himself. Yet he could not stop.

He was naïve—that was the problem. No matter how

much interaction he had with fairy creatures or how much he looked through a sad little mirror, it was no substitute for existing in the human world. He saw humans trick each other more often than fairies, and he'd assumed having that knowledge gave him the advantage in laying his own trap. He thought he'd been the one manipulating Astra, steering her to help him.

Instead, she'd been enchanting him with her confidence, with her stories of embroidering for Mrs. Heartshire that made him feel like they shared something in common, like she knew how it felt to be left without options and taken advantage of. She'd made him feel like he could be himself. Like he could tease. Like he could even . . . love. Maybe.

Naïve, indeed. He was a fool. Doll would have said so.

Smicker arrived, shaking the tower, and Dust climbed onto his balcony to trade.

"How're the little ones?" Dust asked without any heart to the question.

"SPEEDY," grumbled Smicker. He lifted one taloned foreleg and made some vague grabbing gesture. "OVER HERE, OVER THERE."

"Hard to keep ahold of, are they?"

"IMPOSSIBLE."

Before Dust could think better of it, he asked, "Smicker, do you love your mate?"

The violet dragon puffed up, scaly plates rippling across his chest. The black ridges above his eyes stood at proud attention. In a more booming voice than before, he said, "BEST TRADE."

Of course. Trader mating wasn't exactly romantic. They bartered for each other just as they did for anything else. If the trade-off to Dust's freedom was marriage to Astra, would it really be so terrible?

But if he didn't choose it himself, it was no freedom at all.

"TRADE SINGER?"

Dust dragged himself back to the present, haggling through a few carving options. He made the trade for Conrad's return, and just as they finalized the agreement, he heard the faintest tinkle of chimes in the air.

His heart took up an unsteady rhythm.

"Did you hear that?" he asked, pointing up. A slight breeze ruffled his hair, confusing the sound of chimes in the whisper of leaves from the knee-highs and the whine of his meadow grass, still injured from Smicker's rampage.

Smicker lifted his head into the sky, then snorted and shook it, clearly dismissive.

The spriggan chimes had acted strangely upon Astra's first arrival in the realm. This was even worse—not only could he not make out the individual chimes, but he could not even guess what direction they'd come from. It might have just as easily been a moment of Dust's ears ringing without any chimes at all.

But if it wasn't . . .

Naïve.

Foolish.

"One more trade," he said to Smicker.

CHAPTER 26

ASTRA

I HEARD THE BLESSED SOUND of trickling water before I saw it. The smallest stream in existence dribbled down a tumbled collection of rocks on the mountain side, and I had to balance precariously just to reach far enough to gather a thin pond of it in my hand. But as I brought it toward my lips, a deadpan voice spoke from behind me.

"I wouldn't drink that."

Startled, I slipped, but elegance converted the movement into a smooth dip-and-turn rather than a set of skinned knees. The water splashed to darken the stone path, leaving my hand slick. I shook off the remaining drops and then wiped my palm on my green skirt.

A Planter hovered at eye level. He was darker than Doll, with stunning pink wings that blurred as he hovered. Knowing just who'd sent the fairy, I smiled.

"I'm grateful for your timing. What's wrong with the water?"

"Slow-acting acid," the Planter said. "It would melt your insides over the course of a year. You're Astra?"

"Even the water in this realm . . ." I shook my head, but even after a narrow miss with death, I could not bring myself to complain too much. Such circumstances were becoming commonplace for me. "You're the Planter all the survivors see. Dust's friend."

"I suppose he would use that phrasing." As a green basket appeared in the air before him, woven tightly closed, he gestured at himself. "Renny. That's me. Horseshoe and bag, that's you."

The basket expanded and pulled apart as he spoke, extending thin green tendrils wrapped around a small linen bag and a rusted horseshoe. I hesitated.

"I'd hoped to see Dust." Or as close as we could come, anyway.

Still hovering, Renny raised an eyebrow. "Why?"

"Well, because I—" A light blush heated my face. "What business is it of yours to know my motivations, Renny?"

"It's dangerous for Dust," he said.

My turn to raise my eyebrows. Renny was not like Doll, nor even like my fairy. He did not carry himself with the same pretention.

"Dangerous?" I repeated. "I'm not any danger to him."

"Doll is."

At that answer, quiet dread sprouted like vines in my heart, squeezing tight. The more I learned, the more tangled Dust's curse became.

Nodding to myself, I said, "She's the one his father stole from."

"The one he harvested with," he corrected me.

"What's the difference?"

"A harvest is a harvest."

Riddles. Perhaps he was similar to other fairies after all. I nearly reached for the items, then paused once more.

"Can you tell me how to break Dust's curse?" It was certainly worth asking.

For a moment, Renny sagged in the air. Perhaps it wearied him to remain hovering in one place, or perhaps he was tired of keeping the basket out, since he made an impatient gesture toward it. When I remained unmoving, he turned his palms up in something like frustration.

"I am only a Planter," he said. "This magic is beyond us. Doll's garden flourishes; she grows in the human world. She does things Planters cannot, and her secrets keep themselves. She grows more dangerous, makes threats. The others fall in line. What am I to do?"

He made the same gesture again, and for the first time in my life, my heart softened for a fairy.

"Thank you for helping me," I said.

"I help Dust," he corrected. "Because what's done isn't right. But your gratitude may do him good, since I believe he had to barter for your location as well as your safety."

I didn't know what to make of that. In the end, I said, "I'm glad he isn't alone."

The pink Planter certainly enjoyed correcting people, because he said, "He is alone."

"You fairies are all baffling to me." I huffed. "It's a wonder Dust hasn't gone mad."

To my surprise, Renny grinned. It was a fleeting expression, gone as quickly as his wings beat.

"He is mad," he said.

"Now you're just contradicting me for the sake of it. Here's something I don't understand—if Granters grant wishes, and Traders trade with people, it seems like fairies have a purpose to interact. But Planters just hole up in gardens, growing things?"

"We grow," he said, "and we harvest."

"Yes, but interaction with others—"

"Our gardens grow, and human plants have morning dew. Humans harvest, and we have morningdew."

"Thank you, Renny, that's just as helpful as I'd hoped." I rolled my eyes. Then I bit my lip. "You're certain I can't see Dust?"

Renny shook his head. Then he gestured toward the basket. "The horseshoe returns you to Everspring. It is the ongoing harvest agreement Dust and I hold, to return every human outcast to Everspring. The bag is new. A gift, he said, for Astra."

I took the bag but didn't open it. Several small lumps rested inside. I could not imagine what he might have sent me, and I found my heart pounding at the mystery. No matter what, it could not be a bad sign that he'd sent me something he didn't send anyone else, could it? Even after seeing the magic of my wish with his own eyes, he was still choosing to rescue me rather than leaving me to my own foolish choices.

"Everyone the Peace Tree banishes," I repeated, "Dust sends back?"

Renny nodded.

I remembered the guild woman's story, of a fairy and a secret. It wasn't only my rescue Dust had coordinated; it was everyone's. The entire Survivor's Guild. He was responsible for it all.

Scheming wood fairy, acting as a guardian angel for people who didn't even know he existed. Dust had no reason for loyalty to Everspring, yet without ever touching a crown, he did more to help its people than its coronated kings. The kings banished. The lost prince saved.

I gripped the bag.

"I have to set this right," I said.

Though Renny couldn't have known what I meant, he nodded again. Bracing myself for a sudden drop in a lake, I held my breath and grabbed the horseshoe.

My second attempt at swimming proved better than my first, though it didn't hurt to have guild hands helping me onto the dock once more.

"Oh, it's you," said the guild woman, her face pale in the dreary morning light.

"Oh, it's me." I flicked a water droplet onto her nose and smirked. "You can set your mind at ease—I didn't breathe a word of your guild to the king. I won't be the undoing of all Dust's sacrifice."

She clearly thought me unhinged, though that may have been more a result of my second trip to the fairy realm than my words themselves.

The woman and her husband were the only members on the dock this time, though a second woman waited near the house, clearly serving as a lookout. They ushered me into the house as though bringing in a plague carrier, and I would have declined, except for one thing.

"You need to know who's behind your guild," I said, "and also, you need to send for Bastien."

I didn't bother with all the details of Dust's situation,

since it wasn't my story to tell, only that there was a lost prince, sacrificed for the Peace Tree, watching over his kingdom all the while. Bastien arrived just as I was finishing, and he rushed toward the table, stumbling over apologies until I stopped him.

"How long?" I asked.

He blinked. "How long for—how long you've been gone, you mean? Just since yesterday."

The woman had said Conrad was returned as well, already hustled out of the city. Six months had been an irregularity, then, just as Bastien had guessed. I breathed a sigh of relief, pushing back from the table.

"I know you have rules," I said to the husband and wife. "Silence. Obedience. I know you have reasons, too. But if you *are* grateful to be survivors of the fairy realm, at least consider the man still left behind."

After sweeping an elegant curtsy, I took my leave.

It turned out Bastien was even less impressed with my new plan than he'd been with the old one.

We strode up the hill together, pointed toward the castle. On every street, people stopped to stare and whisper. More than a few pointed at me blatantly. I found myself wishing for a hooded cloak or perhaps a face veil. No doubt my magic would have shed both and left me revealed no matter what I tried, so I focused on Bastien at my side and ignored the rest.

"Marry the king?" Bastien demanded, looking ill. "How

exactly—I mean, unless you just *want* to, I suppose. Do you want to?"

I tried to wrinkle my nose, but my face barely twitched. "Not particularly. At best, Kenric's an odious barnacle, at worst, a raging tyrant."

"Then . . . why?"

At the point of the hill, the castle's banners flapped in a summer breeze, warm and encouraging, not the stifling heat of the realm's mountainous desert. The white hawk above every turret seemed to be soaring in earnest. Free.

For so many years, I'd looked after Beauty, chaperoning her when Father and Rob were at sea, when Mother was busy, when Callista was too young or too permissive to keep our wild sister in check. I'd begrudged the responsibility, begrudged every day that robbed me of opportunities to pursue my own wants and interests.

I'd finally pursued my own wants, and where had it led me? For all the times I'd accused Beauty of recklessness, it turned out I was no better. We were Acton sisters, both of us.

I set my jaw. "Because for the first time, what I *want* is to help someone else."

Besides, odious barnacle or not, Kenric was certainly wealthy. I would have a secure life, wanting for nothing. I could hardly even call my plan a sacrifice. It was the obvious option, for both myself and Dust.

The confusion remained clear in Bastien's expression, but he fell into true form as a knight and asked how he could assist. I smiled.

"Widow's Point," I said. "That's where I'm from. It's a port city on the western coast. If I'm not wrong, you might find your brother there."

Bastien halted in the street. I was forced to stop and look

back, where he stood with stunned brown eyes, as if he hardly dared hope.

I shifted uncomfortably. "It's only a slim chance, Fitzweller. Don't hang all your hopes. But there was some business with fairies a while back, and there was an enchanted beast who became a man—the point is, you can search out Beauty Acton and ask her all about it. She'll gladly regale you with every detail."

"Acton is your name," he said slowly, the unspoken question clear.

My face heated. "Yes, I suspect my sister may have fallen for your brother. As I said, feel free to ask her. Now, if you'll excuse me."

I turned forward once more, hands pressed to my cheeks, hoping my cool fingers could dispel a blush. After only a few moments, Bastien hurried to catch up, and his only response to my frown was a sad shrug.

"I'm grateful," he said. "Truly, beyond . . . beyond what I can express. But the king's knights are forbidden to leave the city. I'll send a messenger to Widow's Point, and in the meantime, I'll escort you to the king. It's the least I can do."

He was trapped too. Imprisonment was the Peace Tree's bountiful fruit, it seemed. No wonder the survivors fled the city as quickly as possible. That wagon ride out seemed more tempting than ever—and I had been offered it once more by the guild.

But I pointed my eyes toward castle and king.

CHAPTER 27

DUST

DOLL WAS LINGERING in the tower more than usual. As if she suspected something.

"It wouldn't hurt you to help out a bit," Dust called up.

The Planter sat on a tile of his roof, her thin legs dangling over the upper balcony as he worked, yellow wings splayed behind her. She ate quite casually from a handful of lekon seeds.

"Or at least share the seeds," Dust grumbled, scooting on his knees to attach the next board.

Renny's signal had confirmed Astra's safe return. Dust still couldn't reason out why the chimes hadn't heralded her correctly. His only guess was that the Granter magic affecting her appearance also confused the chimes, though it shouldn't have made her any less human.

"What d'you know of Granter magic?" he asked, since Doll didn't seem inclined to converse on her own.

The Planter stiffened, pausing with a seed in hand. Still in the shell, it filled her whole palm. "Why ask?"

"Thought I might make a wish to leave the tower."

Doll cackled. She squeezed the seed until it popped open with a tiny cracking sound. Then she flicked the shell at Dust. When it bounced off his cheek and stuck in his newly spread sap, he glared up at her, and she returned a grin.

"Granters live one hundred years," she said. "Only the first two years within the realm, the rest among humans. Slaves to humans, the lot of them. You'll never catch one here, not unless they follow their wisher."

"How come they can do magic in the human realm when other fairies can't?" Dust carefully used his paddle to lift the lekon shell out, then pressed the next board into place. The balcony was nearing completion.

"Other Planters would say it's because Granters are lesser. Are they right or are they jealous?" Doll crunched her seed, shrugging.

"What do you say?"

"I say your board's weak. It'll fall."

Dust sighed. "Whose fault is that, I wonder?" But he pried the board free, reapplied the sap, and pressed it without delay this time.

"Shame about Astra," said Doll. "She could have lured in her Granter for you, if you hadn't scared her off."

The back of Dust's neck tingled, as if he could feel her piercing stare. He kept his eyes on his work, and his voice was cool as he answered, "Or for you."

"Planting for me's a better fate than death."

"Depends on the plant." Dust looked up, smiling. "Depends on the death."

Doll sniffed. She crunched the next seed. "Cheeky human."

"If I am, where'd I learn it from, aye?"

With satisfaction, Dust held the final board in place for a

moment, then stood. He'd need to add a railing still, but the balcony floor was finished. It wasn't anything grand to look at; even with enchanted materials, he could only build so far outward without supports. But it was enough. Four floors, three windows, two balconies.

"Morningdew."

Doll zipped away so quickly, the feather she left spinning drifted off the balcony completely. By throwing himself forward, Dust managed to catch it, held to the wood more by the curse than by his own effort.

Did she suspect his deception, or was she only irritated at having lost what Astra might have given her?

Feather in hand, Dust made his way to the mirror, but he stood without dropping it on the water. He listened for the sound of returning wings. He'd never before hated having two open windows in his woodshop.

In a moment of decision, he tucked the feather into the laces at the front of his shirt, and he lifted the basin of water from its stand. Careful steps took him up one curve of stairs, until he sat in a shrouded nook of his storage room, where he set the basin down. Only then did he activate his morningdew.

The little fox wiggled out of Astra's pocket and thumped to the floor.

"Here I thought you'd forgotten me," drawled a feminine voice.

Dust craned the view to look up, realizing he'd dropped all the way from a chair to the floor. Astra sat in a wicker seat beside a fireplace, her fingers busy with a needle and thread along the hem of her gown. She quickly tied off the thread and stowed the needle.

Turning a slow circle, Dust surveyed the lavish room. He

recognized the gray-stone interior of a castle. As himself, he reached out to his morningdew mirror and traced the knuckle of his middle finger across the water. In response, the fox carving trotted across the floorboards and leapt onto a dark oak chest, scrabbling for purchase along the edge before managing to fully climb up. From there, he got onto a window ledge, which opened a view to the courtyard below.

At the far right of the visible space, he could see a ring of broken, weathered stones that had once marked the foundation of a tower. Tree roots had overtaken most of the space, with the branches reaching into the sky and curling into the castle stone.

"Is this the first time you've seen the Peace Tree?" Astra asked.

She'd come up behind him. He tilted his head back to see her chin, then returned his gaze to the tree.

"I managed to see through the eyes of a stable boy once. Tree was much smaller then, quarter of the size, at most. No fruit." Dust rubbed the knuckle he'd dipped in the mirror and found all his fingers had gone cold. "It looks awful."

"Hideous," Astra agreed. "I doubt it's ever seen pruning shears. If there were any justice in the world, it would have died from neglect, and it would have served the old king right."

Planter gardens did not abide by human rules of watering and fertilizing and trimming. They thrived or died by magic. The Peace Tree was overgrown, sagging under its own weight, every branch laden with fruit. It was thriving.

The curse was thriving.

Dust turned the fox and hopped to the floor where he could no longer see the tree. "Taken up residence in Castle Everspring, have you?"

"Temporarily." Astra shifted to kneel gracefully beside him, spreading her green skirt across her legs. "I find it offers the best arrangement for curse breaking."

Hunched over the basin as he was, Dust's neck ached, and he found himself without patience to decide her motives. He had a better method than conjecture, anyway.

"Renny gave you the bag?" It was hardly a question.

"Yes, and what exactly is the purpose in a handful of discolored strawberries?" As she spoke, she pulled the small bag from her pocket, loosing the drawstring. "I worry about this one in particular. It seems to have blackened with frostbite."

Dust refused to allow her charming banter to soften him. He opened his own matching bag.

"Friendship peppers," he said. "It's a Planter game. Thought we might play a round."

Astra raised one sleek eyebrow, and he could not read whatever emotion rested in her dazzling eyes. Perhaps it would not have been so difficult if not for all the layers of magic; it was as if there was still a wall between them.

"No one ever invites me to games, wood fairy. I've a poor temper upon losing."

"Then I'll brace for poor temper. Start the game by eating the pink one."

If she picked up on his frosty tone, she didn't comment. She also didn't protest the game further, only lifting the pink pepper by its stem and popping it off daintily with her teeth.

"Awfully sweet for a pepper," she commented.

Dust didn't bother telling her the spice was on its way. He felt a bit foolish, simmering in his bitterness, but he also felt something deeper, a burn in his gut that had nothing to do with the pepper he'd just eaten. It had to do with the memory of Conrad and a swallowing rush of snow and Dust's inescapable naivety.

"Game's on," he said. "From here, we take turns askin' each other questions. Any question you like. After each answer, we eat a pepper in order of color, all the way up to purple. I trust you can follow your rainbow."

Astra poked a finger in her bag, eyeing the contents. "That makes six questions, but there's—"

"Black to finish," Dust said. "If you make it that far."

She plucked the red pepper from the others, twirling it between her fingers by the stem. "Ask your question, wood fairy."

"You have a Granter. What did you wish for?"

Her serene expression gave nothing away, and her voice held the usual assurance as she said, "I wished to be beautiful."

But when she bit into the red pepper, she doubled forward, pounding her chest as if she meant to cough, though she made no sound. Her face took on a delicate blush.

"These are death on a stem!" she finally choked out. One dainty cough escaped, more hiccup than anything.

"Means you didn't tell the truth," Dust said grimly. "You skewed it or concealed a part. Only full honesty'll save you from friendship peppers. Care to have another go, to ease the heat?"

"Friendship indeed!" She seemed embarrassed, ducking her head. "I wished to be so beautiful that wealthy men would propose at the sight of me."

There it was. Her ongoing enchantment against others, the explanation for her appearance, painted with magic.

Dust's stomach twisted itself in a knot.

"Your question," he forced out.

After a moment of composing herself, Astra turned back. She met his gaze with a clear determination, and even across the distance of magic and mirror, Dust shivered.

"Now I see how the game is to be played." She smiled. "Tell me your biggest regret, Dust."

This game, perhaps. There was a reason he never committed to real questions with Doll, but he was in it now, with no intention of retreat. Dust rolled his own red pepper between his fingers.

Trusting you. That wasn't it, not really.

"First time a human landed in Ashpoint," he said. "I was still learning the regions, 'n I was slow on the chimes. I'd only just made the deal with Renny. All that to say someone died when I could've saved them."

The pepper gave a crisp *snap* between his teeth, and the burst of juice across his tongue was nearly citrus, lacking any heat.

"After savin' me," he said, "did you think I'd be forced to marry you?"

"This is a jolly game," Astra muttered. She straightened, holding an orange pepper. "Yes, when I agreed to save you, I was very aware the effect my wish would have on a wealthy prince, once we met face to face."

Even knowing it, Dust's stomach tightened. "That's all you wanted, then? That's all you cared about?"

"I'm afraid you must save your questions for the next pepper. It's my turn," she said primly. When she bit, she gave no evidence of pain. She seemed to chew an extended time before settling on a question. "What makes for a good carving knife?"

Frowning, Dust said, "Short blade. Keeps its edge."

"How do I even know you're eating peppers, little fox?"

"I suppose you'll have to trust me. Must be difficult for you, bein' that you're so untrustworthy yourself." Dust bit his pepper too hard, barely tasting it. Then he said, "What's your worst quality?"

"My unrelenting arrogance, I imagine. My desire to be seen at any cost. Perhaps my exhaustive list of fears, from the ocean tide to a mountain nit-monster." Astra hesitated with the yellow pepper held just before her parted lips. She looked away. "My worst quality is that I'd rather inflict pain on others than experience it myself."

She ate in silence before asking, "What's your best quality?"

Dust gave a quiet snort. "Carving. It's my only real skill."

But as he ate his next pepper, it raked his mouth like knives, and he coughed.

With a lilt of song, Astra said, "Somebody is lying." She smiled. "Far more impressive than any carving is the way you relentlessly help others while gaining nothing in return. You're a hero, Dust. The very best I could imagine."

His face burned, residual from the pepper. He rubbed the back of his neck.

"A time you've been dishonest," he managed.

"After Father's bankruptcy, our family had to sell all we possessed. Father risked debtor's prison if we could not pay the full sum. All the same, during the auction of our belongings, I kept back my most expensive necklace." She plucked a green pepper from the bag. "'Why,' you ask?"

Dust's lips twitched. "I've been told it's one question per pepper."

Ignoring him, she said, "Because it was my mother's final gift to me before she died, and I thought Father deserved prison after his negligence. Was I sentimental, or was I spiteful? I cannot separate the two. All I know for certain is that winter came, and I sold the final remnant of my mother. Spite and sentiment both have their limits, it seems."

The empty pepper stem waved between her fingers like a flag.

"If you could travel anywhere," she asked, "where would you go?"

"The ocean," Dust said. "Why did you leave your family?"

"Because I have been wildly jealous of my sister all my life."

If the incomplete answer hadn't given her away, the frantic fanning of her hands after eating the blue pepper did. Amazingly, her eyes did not water, and her face held only that light blush. Dust knew better than anyone the ways magic could limit a person.

Do you regret your wish? he wanted to ask. But he had only two questions left, and he found himself reluctant to ask anything at all. There was more discomfort in this game with Astra than he'd ever felt before, and yet, in a strange contradiction, he wished to extend it a hundred peppers, to live in this place of honesty forever with her.

"How do you know when you can trust someone?" Astra asked quietly.

Dust's heart thumped strangely in his chest. He realized he'd forgotten about the fox entirely, not moving it since the game began. Astra hadn't moved either. It almost felt like she was in the tower beside him, or he was in the castle with her —or they were together in some unknown place, holding a moment in time.

"Wouldn't know. I've never trusted anyone, not really." Dust swallowed. He trusted Renny, didn't he? Or was part of him always waiting for Doll's power to make Renny bow just like all the other Planters?

The pepper's mild flavor gave the answer.

"I hope you might trust me," said Astra.

The words stole Dust's breath.

She shook her head, smiling faintly. "It would be foolish of you, all things considered. Because I did know what my wish would do. Because a large part of me hoped to marry a crown prince and didn't think much about the person behind the title. But to answer your other question—no, that isn't all I cared about. That isn't why I'm here now. So it would be foolish of you to trust me, and I will no doubt disappoint you, as I've disappointed my family, but all the same . . . I hope you might."

"I might." Dust struggled to keep his voice unaffected. "Have you ever been in love?"

Silence answered him first. He wished his heart would pick a rhythm and stick with it.

"I've never considered love," Astra said at last. "Had I written my life's plan, love would have been pushed to the back, perhaps overlooked entirely. Marriage? Certainly. Because beautiful girls ought to grow up to marry handsome men, and since childhood, I've put all my care into being a beautiful girl, into some imagined life in which I knew all the rules and everything fit together as it should and I had nothing to fear. But love is a fearful thing."

Dust felt the echo of that sentiment in the trembling of his fingers.

"Lately, though . . ." Astra seemed to catch his eyes through the mirror. "I'm considering all sorts of new things."

On impulse, Dust reached for her hand.

His fingers hit water, rippling the illusion, reminding him

of the stone prison enclosing him on all sides. Slowly, he curled his fingers to his palm, and a drop of cold water slid down his wrist.

"Was there anything you didn't tell me about your curse?" Astra asked.

Dust had no chance to answer. The last of the morningdew magic faded, leaving him staring into a basin of ordinary water, trying to hold a moment that escaped his grasp.

CHAPTER 28

ASTRA

THE FOX FELL ABRUPTLY STILL, just as before, and I could not tell if Dust had been pulled away by magic or if I'd scared him with my question. I looked down at the single black pepper remaining in my bag, then tucked the bag away, along with the fox.

Not a minute later, a knock came at my door. After brushing my skirts off, since they'd gathered dust from the floor, I crossed the room. The king himself stood in the hallway—though I supposed I should get used to calling him my fiancé.

"As agreed." His dark brown eyes sparkled above a wide smile. "Shopping."

When I'd walked directly into the throne room after a second trip to the fairy realm, Kenric had made no jibe about "specimens." He'd only paled.

"Your Majesty, I will marry you," I announced before he had a chance to issue orders, "but I have conditions."

Since the wealthy men in attendance were already beginning to salivate, my first of three conditions came quickly: *You must order the men of your kingdom not to look at me.*

That one ached, particularly as it took effect and Bastien's brown eyes turned away. But my granted wish had been for wealthy men to propose at the sight of me. No sight, no proposal. The same shield that protected Dust.

My second condition: *You will not place any order on me.*

Though Kenric had gladly accepted the first, he turned his nose up at the second. "Who is king here? I'll give any command I see fit to any person in my kingdom."

"I thought to make peace," I said, fluttering my eyelashes. "Is that not the clarion call of our beloved tree? But if you insist on war, I'll visit the realm a third time, and I'll return riding a dragon. Never fear—he can tell you all about himself before dinner."

Kenric stood from his throne, fuming. His mouth worked soundlessly, then closed.

"Conditions of my own!" he cried at last. "You will neither insult nor threaten me, or the whole wedding is off!"

"I'll consider it of my own free will," I said, "but you'll not forbid me."

Then my third condition.

You must pay a fair price for everything you buy.

It was a dangerous line I walked. With Kenric's temper, a sudden push could override the whole agreement, and despite my blustering, it had been nearly impossible for me to refuse him the second time; I knew I could not hope to manage it a third.

But just as he had his tree, I had my wish. Even now, I saw the desire in his eyes, the pull that drew him to propose as any other wealthy man.

I could not demand he break from his tree all at once, but I could begin with a single matter of selfishness. A difficult sacrifice, but not impossible. If my wish could win this small victory over the tree, I would continue to tug, little by little, and in the end, I would pull the royal family's curse out root by root.

In the end, Kenric agreed. And for the first time in my life, I felt the power to accomplish something with true meaning.

Kenric frowned. "All that time to settle into your room and get ready, yet you wear the same peasant dress?"

While I could have pointed out it was the only thing I owned, I said, "I favor this dress."

"Well, you'll need better for the wedding, that's certain."

He tried to order a palanquin for us both, but I insisted on walking. Kenric grumbled about my stubbornness, and I chided him for not spending enough time among his subjects.

"Do you even speak to them at all?"

He seemed amazed at the question. "What could they possibly say?"

Clearly, ours would be a very harmonious marriage, if I could only resist strangling him for the rest of my life.

Though Kenric finally agreed to walk, he would not

compromise on his trumpets, so the market heard us coming long before we arrived, and the announcement was repeated enough times to grow wearisome. The marketgoers did not bother pretending to shop; they gawked openly. No doubt word had spread of our very unusual engagement.

Kenric took to the shops with enthusiasm, his usual servant scurrying along behind to gather everything that caught his fancy.

With only one difference—

"What is a fair price for this?" Kenric demanded after choosing each item.

I smiled. This was a victory. It was a difference. Glancing over my shoulder, I saw the top branches of the Peace Tree just above the wall of the castle, and I thought they looked shriveled in the light.

But there was something shriveled inside me as well. My fingertips brushed the fox carving in my pocket, and although it was smooth wood, I felt the prick of splinters.

Have you ever been in love?

I'd not mentioned the engagement to Dust. He'd been rightly horrified at seeing my effect on men; no doubt he would hate me for using his brother. But for Dust to have any hope of freedom, Kenric needed to change, and I could see no other way to accomplish it.

My sister was right to think me a villain.

"You've not bought anything," Kenric said, startling me. He'd filled a basket already, and the servant hurried to bring a new one.

"I have need of nothing," I said stiffly.

"You have *desperate* need of a new dress. And jewelry. And perfume. You smell like a dragon."

I narrowed my eyes on him, but Kenric pushed me

forward with a servant of my own, informing me that my appearance reflected on him now.

"Something refined but not too opulent," he called out. "The queen should not outshine the king, after all."

Through glass windowpanes, I saw the wares of a silk merchant and a silversmith. A large carpenter's shop displayed furniture, carved in intricate detail—though not as detailed as anything in Dust's workshop, including the workbench itself. One of the stands held a collection of fruit that sweetly scented the air. At each shop, I garnered the stares of women and the averted eyes of men, and I could practically hear the whispers traded from ear to ear, whispers saying, *That's her!*

I was a known entity now. The future queen. Though I should have felt triumph at that, I felt a strange discomfort cramping my stomach, like I'd overindulged at dinner.

In a perfumery, I sampled oils of myrrh and clove, rich scents that lingered even after I'd stoppered the bottles. The shopkeeper tried to tempt me with flower perfumes, but I'd never understood the appeal. My mother had loved rose scents, reflecting her name, and Callista favored anything relating to lilies, but I preferred woody scents and something that spoke to the solidity of the earth.

"This is my finest offering." The shopkeeper proudly displayed a perfume bottle that seemed to be empty, rushing to assure me that it was *enchanted*. The final drop of perfume would never run out. It was not only a worthy scent, but a charm of good luck, one befitting a queen.

I gathered the single drop of perfumed oil on my finger and spread it at the base of my neck. Sandalwood. For a moment, I breathed in a tower with carvings on every shelf and the thick grit of sawdust in the air.

When I looked down at the bottle, the drop had not replenished.

"It appears someone has deceived you." I handed the empty bottle back to a stunned shopkeeper. "Some things are not meant to continue."

Face aflame, he rushed to hide the ordinary bottle and offered me other perfumes of a sandalwood scent. I declined.

"My lady, is nothing to your liking?" The poor shopkeeper was sweating; I'd been about to exit without buying.

I had the king's wealth at my disposal. There was no concern of the sellers not being paid for their wares. And a future queen should certainly look—and smell—the part.

This is what you always dreamed, I thought. More than I'd dared to dream, in fact. I'd once set my sights on the heir to a mere barony. Now I was marrying into the greatest title and wealth in the kingdom.

I lifted my chin, and I shopped in earnest. By the time I left the market, I'd purchased a dozen necklaces, a collection of brooches and earrings, a ruby ring, and six bottles of spiced perfume. Beyond that, I had a wardrobe of silk dresses on the way, a collection of the softest fur wraps, and a shawl for each day of the week. Kenric stood beside me proudly, as if my use of his wealth made me more valuable.

Once I was resettled in my guest quarters, I admired each purchase, trying each necklace, bundling my hair in my hand and pretending it could be fastened to better display my earrings.

This was my life now. My husband's wealth would buy me any adornment I desired. I could have anything in the entire kingdom.

Yet it felt like nothing at all.

CHAPTER 29

ASTRA

THE NEXT DAY, the dowager queen summoned me to tea.

As I approached the appointed music room, plucked harp strings came ringing gently on the air, reminding me of the mysterious chimes in the fairy realm before I recognized the tune.

Why do you march
Silly soldier girl?
The war's not yours
The war's not yours.

The song had been one of my mother's favorites, but the lyrics spoke to me ominously. All the same, I marched into the room.

Large windows let in the afternoon sunlight, which fell across a few narrow reclining couches. The ladies in attendance were not seated on couches but rather around a tea table, slowly turning their attention to me in the doorway. The servant at the harp cast me a wide-eyed glance but was skilled enough that her fingers did not convey her surprise, instead continuing the melody uninterrupted. As I'd once been in my silver gown, I was dazzling to match my enchantment, dressed in a blue silk gown with teardrop sleeves, wrists and neck draped in sapphire jewelry.

The queen was not difficult to spot; she wore a crown, after all. The lady to her right had the look of a vulture considering prey, due mostly to the way she bobbed her head at the end of an extraordinarily long neck. To the queen's left, the elderly woman had nodded off over her saucer, and beside her, in the final occupied seat, it may as well have been Mrs. Heartshire. She wore the same expression of overt sweetness masking something ugly beneath.

The queen lowered her teacup, smiling in an echo of her son's favorite expression. "My son's newly acquired fiancée! My dear, you're a few minutes late. I hope you don't mind that we started without you."

Though she could not have been many years beyond my father's age, her hair had turned completely white, and she wore it pinned beneath her crown.

Of course, all the ladies had their hair pinned. Except me.

My neck itched beneath my curls.

"Forgive me, Majesty," I said. "I was not aware of my tardiness."

They'd arranged it that way, of course. A basic rite of passage for any social circle—the newcomer put in her place.

I took the last available seat. The queen herself poured a cup for me, and though I'd charged in with fierceness, I found my edges withering. I'd sat at many tables like this before, and though the company was dressed with twice the finery, it felt familiar all the same. A circle of faces scrutinizing me for flaws.

With as much enchanted grace as I could muster, I lifted my cup and took a sip.

The tea was awful. Bitter and over-steeped. I nearly laughed. After facing a dragon, why should I fear a queen?

"Your Majesty," I said with a smile. "I have been so curious to meet you after hearing your son talk of his fond memories."

"Oh, Kenric does go on." The queen swatted vaguely across the table at me, sharing a look with the would-be Heartshire while the vulture bobbed and the other woman snored. "Though I was not aware you had spent much time together. That spectacle at the coronation ball certainly can't count, nor yesterday's spectacle in the throne room. My, I can't help noticing you do cause a scene wherever you go."

"No, I meant your firstborn," I said smoothly. "He spoke of the letters you wrote to him—not addressed by name, of course. With him gone so many years, perhaps you forgot it. The letters were addressed only to 'my darling son.'"

In the silence, I forced myself to take another long sip, as if unaffected. At least magic covered the disgust.

But when I peeked at the faces around me, my triumph faded.

I'd expected the queen to pale with shock, perhaps even show the guilt on her face. Instead, the women all stared at me with vaguely confused expressions. Even the vulture had ceased bobbing and instead cocked her head.

The harp played on, plucking out the notes of my awkwardness.

"Kenric's elder brother," I said. "Your firstborn son."

After sharing another glance across the table, the queen's expression turned pitying. "My dear, are you quite well? It sounds as if someone has deceived you. If I'd given birth to two sons, I assure you, I would be *quite* aware."

She and her friends shared a tittering laugh.

My stomach tightened. Had Dust lied to me all along?

Just as quickly, I dismissed the thought. His tower had come from the castle—that much was plain to see—and the fairy tree in its place served the king. There could be no mistake.

I set my teacup down with force as I stood. "While you were expecting your first son, the late king entered the fairy realm and stole an enchanted seed. The king got his Peace Tree, but the price was your firstborn, taken as a child in the very tower removed from this castle."

Her pitying smile was not even slightly disturbed. "Oh, my dear, that's not at all how the story goes. Someone *has* been deceiving you."

Heartshire said, "The king of Everspring *traded* the castle's tower for the Peace Tree. Everyone knows that."

The vulture bobbed. "It has blessed our kingdom ever since. Two hundred peaceful years."

I'd just opened my mouth for a heated retort when I stopped cold.

"Years?" I repeated. I could not seem to manage the first part.

The dowager queen said, "In fact, this very summer marks two centuries since the tree's planting and the renaming of our city into Everspring. Just next week, we'll hold the grandest festival the kingdom has ever seen. I've been planning it ever since I became queen. You ought to know this, dear—Kenric has ordered your wedding be part of my festival."

Slowly, I sank back into my seat. Even with the cushion

for support, I felt part of me was still sinking, right down through the floor.

My first visit to the fairy realm had cost me six months. When the second did not follow the pattern, I'd brushed off the discrepancy without additional thought. Yet Dust had grown to adulthood there. *Years* of possibly warped time. I'd never considered . . .

Clearly, *he'd* never considered. He was fighting to return to his family, to see the people he thought were his mother and brother. But his family had been gone a hundred years or more.

He was alone.

My heart twisted, pinching around the empty space that held my mother's absence. At least I'd spent twenty-one years in her company, knowing her opinion of me even when it was frustration. *Astra, you speak opinion without honey.* How many times had she said that to me? Fewer times than she'd said, *My little goddess, you'll make the stars bow.*

Dust would never hear his mother's praise or censure—or anything else.

She'd not even left him with his name.

The pressure of tears built in my chest, tightened my throat, and strained my breathing, but my eyes remained clear. Enchantment concealed the emotion. That was the fairy way, wasn't it? A callous outward display. In all of Dust's years without his family, I doubted anyone had cried for him. I doubted anyone had held him.

I was glad he could not see me, because he would have thought I cared as little as the fairies he called friends.

In truth, I'd never cared more about anything than I did about him in that moment.

"Do you have any records from two hundred years ago?" I

asked hoarsely. "Any . . . books, perhaps, that detail what happened?"

I could not believe I was hearing a request for *books* come from my own mouth. Beauty would have been thrilled.

The queen smiled broadly. "Well, I don't carry them around with me, now do I?" Like birds along a fence, she and her friends shared their titters once more before she went on. "If you're curious, my dear, you'll have to check the royal archives. That's rather the point of them. But be warned, anything you do find will be dreadfully boring. Better to let the bards tell it at the festival."

Without care for how it reflected on me, I rose from my chair, curtsied, and left without response.

Bastien had told me I could find him in the knight's courtyard if needed. He was sparring when I arrived, and both men quickly looked away. The other knight hardly had a chance to introduce himself before Bastien and I were already on our way out. I told him I urgently needed the royal archives.

"Right this way," he said without hesitation, taking the lead. Since he could not look at me, he walked a few steps ahead, eyes forward.

"You're the most valiant knight of this kingdom, Bastien. I hope you won't ever let the judgment of others deter you." I was still emotional, it seemed, leaking out sentiment I normally would have reserved.

Bastien's ears pinked, and he gave a slight, happy laugh. "What do you hope to find in the archives?"

"The history of the Peace Tree." I left it at that.

The archives were kept in a tower. Following the symmetry of Everspring's castle, it stood exactly opposite the empty space where Dust's tower belonged. Bastien introduced me to Lord Iveral, the white-haired keeper of the royal archives, who watched the ceiling rather than me.

"My lord, if you would be so kind," I said, "we need documents regarding the founding of Everspring or the planting of the Peace Tree."

He moved off at my request, steps firm and swift despite his cane. Bastien and I followed him into the archive room. Shelves of parchment greeted us, stacked in sheaves and gathered in leather bindings. A few shelves held fully bound, illustrated manuscripts, but much of the crowded room had an air of disorder. Tiny dust particles littered the air, glowing faintly in the light from the room's two windows.

Pausing, I stared at the nearest window, thinking of the parallel to another room, crowded not with forgotten parchment but with sawdust and carvings.

Would I hurt Dust more by digging for the truth?

In my pocket, I felt the hard lump of a small, uneaten pepper. One that burned dishonesty.

I set my jaw.

Lord Iveral led us to a set of shelves recently cleaned and neatly organized, then bowed and left us alone to peruse. Some of the parchment had been lovingly folded and unfolded so many times, the creases had worn ragged to the point of disintegrating. No doubt this topic was revisited more than any other in Everspring's history.

The details of its founding.

CHAPTER 30

ASTRA

I'D NEVER BEFORE READ with dedication. King Firmin—Dust's true father—had left behind more paper trail than any person had a right to. The personal missives were the most worn and faded, making it difficult to glean anything from their contents. The king's journals were more promising, though there were five thick leatherbound volumes, as if the old king had enjoyed writing nearly as much as my sister enjoyed reading.

"Take this one," I said, handing a volume to Bastien. "Skim for any mentions of the tree or the fairy realm."

"I'll tr—I'll do my best," he said, with all the confidence he usually offered conversation.

Two oak tables stood arranged to catch the best light from the room's windows. I took my journal to one while Bastien occupied the other. After I grew accustomed to King Firmin's slanted penmanship and archaic capitalization, the journal became easier to parse at a glance, and I soon finished flipping pages, having found nothing of use. A single page of the journal could have sufficed to tell the entire story of it: *I am the grandest king of all the kings. I am incredible. There has been no king like me.*

The king himself was, of course, more flowery in his presentation of such a message. It should not have surprised me; if he ever would have humbled himself, he would have saved his son.

As I exchanged the journal for another, I saw Bastien, hunched over his table, only a few pages into his volume, brow furrowed and lips moving as he murmured soundless things to himself. I raised an eyebrow.

"Can you not read, Sir Bastien?"

He jumped. Then he rubbed the back of his neck, his eyes on a bookshelf rather than on me.

"There's no shame in it," I said.

"I can read," he said. "Just . . . not well. It was the weakest area of my training as a knight."

"Then you've lost nothing. Here, study this instead. I doubt Dust will have any presence in it, but it's worth a look." I carried to his table an illustrated manuscript which detailed the royal lineage. It landed with a *thump*.

Bastien smiled in the other direction as I made the swap of study materials. "My lady, you're a more considerate person than I first thought."

My heart panged. "Am I?"

No doubt my family would not have shared the sentiment.

He blanched. "Not that I—that sounded like an insult! I didn't intend it to be. I only meant—"

I snorted. "You're incapable of a proper insult, Fitzweller. Study the lineage."

Returning to my table, I placed his volume next to the

one I'd chosen earlier. By the time I'd perused both, my eyes began to ache. Perhaps this was a pointless endeavor.

But I selected one more, and I found, at last, a mention of the tree.

"Bastien!" I said, waving him over, though he couldn't see.

Just as quickly as my excitement had grown, it faded. King Firmin's journal held nothing but a spread of lies.

We have made Grand Advancement for Our Kingdom, it read. *By sacrifice of a Tower of Our Beloved castle, given in Goodwill and Harvest to fae folk of the Realm, We have been Bestowed, in turn, with a Tree. This Tree shall be for the Great Peace of Our Kingdom, springing forth Evermore, and henceforth, this Name of Everspring shall mark the Remembrance.*

How ironic that Everspring had nothing to do with the fair weather of the city, only with an eternal spring of the founding king's greed.

"I was a fool to think he'd record the true history, even privately." I closed the journal's pages with force, my fingernails pressing into the leather cover. What would I tell Dust?

"My lady, look here." Bastien stepped into place beside me, his head turned away awkwardly as he spread his book across the table. It occupied nearly double the space of one of the journals, with wider and taller pages. One page held cramped text, detailing the history of royal families. On the opposite page, illustrations stood out in bold color, crests and coats of arms, with extravagant calligraphy marking each.

"Did you find Dust?" I hardly dared hope.

"I found your knight."

He pointed to a familiar crest, the gray serpent on red. It

branched and split across the page, joined by others, but Bastien held his finger on the largest, the origin, marked by the name *Sir Reynard Baillairgé*.

"The de Berranger name came later," he said. "But over here, it says the queen bestowed the crest."

He pointed to the beginning of the page of text. Sir Reynard had been a cousin to Her Majesty Queen Emmeline, wife of King Firmin, and for Reynard's notable services on her behalf, she'd bestowed him a new coat of arms—the serpent—along with an impressive landholding. The book did not say what those services had been.

I pursed my lips in thought.

"We've gone about this wrong," I said. "We need the *queen's* journal."

Dust's mother had cared, if only for a time, and if anyone had recorded the correct history, it would be her. But though we sifted every document of founding, we discovered nothing belonging to the queen.

"Then it's on another shelf," I said, "separated from the rest. It must be here. Keep looking."

Bastien had his eyes on the window. I'd not noticed the light beginning to dim.

"Lady Astra . . ." he said hesitantly. "No doubt the king will expect you at the evening meal. Making him wait would not be . . . fires could be set, I mean."

For a moment, I watched the slanted light across the floor. Then I clenched my jaw.

"I'm not leaving without that journal," I said.

We resumed the search. At one point, I heard distant shouts within the castle. Bastien touched the hilt of his sword, shifting nervously.

"You should leave," I told him.

He said, "I'm unable to help my brother. But I can help here."

Not even a stutter. "You're a good man, Bastien Wolf. Now stop looking at the door and start searching that corner shelf."

I began checking a line of cabinets, one after another. Export recordings. Citizen counts. The most uninteresting documents of the kingdom. And then—

"Found it!" I declared.

It seemed every queen of the last two centuries had been relegated to the same forgotten cabinet, all their relics crammed together in one stockpile. Foregoing care, I began pulling at journals and letters, dropping them at my feet, sifting for anything marked by the name Emmeline.

"I'll buy you time," said Bastien. I barely heard him. From beyond the tower door came the shout of guards and the rush of booted footsteps.

My darling son—

I glimpsed the words, then swore as I realized I'd tossed the letter before fully processing. I dropped to my knees, digging through discarded parchment.

From the hallway, I heard Bastien's voice. "Everything's under control, Captain. There's no need for such a show of force."

A muffled voice answered him. I caught Kenric's name and something like *The Enchanted Woman*. Charming moniker.

Finding the right letter, I shoved it back into the thin journal I'd pulled it from, winding a leather cord to secure it. The whole bundle went down the front of my gown. Then I grabbed another parchment at random just as guards filled the room.

The captain of the guard—if the collection of knots on the

man's uniform shoulders were any indication—stood before me, flanked by six of his tunic-men. Though they tried to look stern, the effect was somewhat lost as they had to find bookshelves or room corners *near* me to look at rather than staring directly.

"Forgive me, Captain. I didn't mean to cause trouble, only to investigate my future husband's lineage. I'm about to become queen, you know. Can you blame a woman for being eager?"

The captain's eyes darted to the mess of parchment on the floor behind me. Suspicion clearly struggled to overcome my enchanted charm.

In the end, he said, "Records are forbidden to leave the archive."

I extended my lip in a little pout, then realized there was no point to the act when he couldn't see it. I bent to release the parchment in my hand, pressing my other hand to my stomach as I did so, discretely holding the most important record in place.

Then I strode out of the tower with poise. The guards hurried to fall in line, pretending they'd led me all along. Bastien ought to have taken the opportunity to disappear, but he fell into step beside the captain.

"An insult!" Kenric raged. "Do I marry a woman with no sense of propriety? With no respect for my position—my very *crown?*"

It took all my self-restraint not to roll my eyes. "Your Majesty, I lost track of time, nothing more."

We stood in the castle's private dining room—private being a relative term, since the table could still seat twelve people without brushing elbows, and there were at least as many servants and guards attending. From the open kitchen door, I could smell roast pheasant and spices. My stomach rumbled. But the king was more interested in booming out his grievances than sitting down to a meal.

"It is certainly more!" he roared. With all the temper of a spoiled child, he took his goblet from the table and hurled it into the fireplace. It might have made an impressive burst of flame if not for the fact that wine had not yet been served. Kenric seemed to realize that, his face flushing with even darker color.

"I promise a strict punctuality in the future," I said, "if you promise to spare innocent goblets. Now, may we proceed to dinner?"

Kenric's eyes caught the firelight. Rather than reflecting from without, they seemed to be raging within.

"You will not take dinner with me this evening or any other." He pointed at me with menace. "In fact, you will not leave your room until I allow it."

Dread took hold of my heart and squeezed, but with a fire to match his, I snapped, "And *you* will not issue orders to *me*. Such was our agreement."

I realized my own mistake too late. I was accustomed to dealing with the tempers of siblings or peers, and my own was more often on display than theirs. There was not a peacemaking bone in my body.

What had made me think I, of all people, could reform a tyrant?

"I am the king of Everspring." Kenric straightened, the rubies of his crown flashing in the light. "And Mother was right; I should never have bent to your threats. You will marry me because I command it. You will obey me, just as any citizen in this kingdom. And you will not so much as *speak* to me unless I allow it."

I willed myself to speak, but the pull inside reared greater.

Bastien stepped forward and attempted to speak on my behalf, but Kenric silenced him at once. At least it was no more severe than that. The king's anger was focused solely on me.

Once again, I'd been a fool.

When Kenric ordered the guards to escort me to my room, I had no choice but to follow.

The king made his orders explicit. The guards at my door—four of the castle's burliest offerings—would not allow me to leave under any circumstances until Kenric himself came to get me. I'd hoped he would offer me at least one opportunity to renegotiate things before our marriage ceremony, but he showed no inclination for such a thing. Meals were brought to me, and the servants ignored any request I made. I was kept alive. Nothing more.

I was a prisoner. Just like someone else I knew.

Though I placed the little fox carving on my window ledge and watched it closely, after four days, it still remained motionless.

Bastien spoke to the guards; I heard his muffled voice through the door. They would not even permit him a conversation with me. Still, it was noble of him to try when it easily could have led to a punishment.

Everything at the will of the king.

I returned to wearing the peasant dress, refusing the wardrobe purchased by Kenric, and I embroidered the hem of my overdress with Dust's blue thread. The faded blue was not a good match for the forest green, clashing in a way that made it seem as if the thread melted into the wool's stronger shade. I did not care. I wanted only to keep my hands busy. Sometimes I turned the needle between my fingers even without making a stitch, because although it was a silly thing, a needle in my hand was the only comfort I knew.

Five days. The fox did not move. Two days remained before the wedding. I knotted my thread and pulled the needle smoothly with my left hand.

At home, I'd learned not to embroider while in direct view of others, else I'd be ridiculed for my oddity—it was said to be bad luck to favor the left hand, a sign that a woman would be a crone of a wife who burdened her husband and produced ill-featured children or worse. The specifics of the curse varied depending on the person delivering them, but all the superstitious parties agreed it was certainly a fool who favored the left. My mother had tried for years to convince me to hold utensils and needles with my right hand, and I made some concession for utensils, but my right hand could never satisfy me with precision in stitches. So I let my left hand accomplish them in private.

Perhaps that was the answer to everything—the wrong turn I'd taken and the source of the path that had led my life astray. It was simply the bad luck of a left hand. How wonderful that I was not at fault for my own poor choices.

I smirked, glancing at the fox, who surely would have had some clever response to that. It did not move. So I kept sewing.

My family became obnoxiously constant within my thoughts. One of the first sewing tasks my mother had given me was mending a hole in my brother's shirt, and after the patch fell off, Rob never let me forget it. Even now, when I received the highest praise on my needlework, Rob had to remind everyone of a time when "Astra couldn't even patch a shirt." Surely I did not miss that. I simply missed the sound of a familiar voice.

Each time I bent over my embroidery, my hair fell into my face, and I had to spare a hand to push it back. Though my frustration mounted, I did not allow it to pass through my needle.

Beauty's remembered voice mocked me more than Rob's. I could practically see her, sitting across from Stephan at our family's dinner table, the night she'd brought him over for dinner. I remembered her laughing as she said, "I'll speak slowly next time, Astra. I forget you can't follow a topic without a needle to guide it."

I'd never invented a sufficient comeback for that, not even now, revisiting the memory.

The worst part of everything was that even as I conjured all the reasons I should hate my family, I just kept thinking of the queen's journal hidden beneath my pillow, with a letter that had never been sent.

I'd asked the servants for letter-writing materials and been denied. What if Callista's final memory of me was my cruel mockery of her engagement? What if my argument with

Father was the last time we ever spoke? What if, for the rest of my life, I was nothing more than a glittering ballgown on display in Everspring, the most beautiful woman in the kingdom, unable to utter a word of unhappiness?

Why had I already wasted so many of my life's words on unhappiness?

I finished a row of pleated stitches, knotting my thread to match my knotted thoughts.

Though I'd avoided it for six days, I retrieved Queen Emmeline's journal. When I untwisted the leather tie, the letter fell into my lap, and my eyes caught sight of things like *express my heart* and *your brother* before I forced them to respect privacy. I tucked the letter against the back cover before turning the pages of the journal.

Unlike the letter, the journal was addressed to no one. It was simply the echoing voice of a woman long gone, a fragment of her life left behind. Most of it was useless. Entries about gardening. About her second son.

I watch Crispin with pride. He is a thoughtful boy, and he will make a great king.

Did she tell herself such things as consolation?

The bigger the flower, the more he loved it. He helped me plant iris bulbs.

I paused, remembering something Dust had said about planting bulbs in his mother's garden. Tucking my feet beneath me, I leaned forward on the quilt, the journal splayed as I flipped pages, my hair curtaining around my face.

He. The mentions appeared everywhere. Never a name to explain the pronoun, never the story of his birth or even a brief account of the Peace Tree—King Firmin had said more on the matter than Queen Emmeline had. But Dust littered her journal, all the way to the final entry.

My mind is weak. I entrusted Crispin to keep the irises. I love the irises desperately, but I cannot remember why.

When I removed my hand, the journal's back cover drifted slowly closed. My chest ached.

In the morning, I would wed King Kenric, and of all the multitude of problems surrounding that, the one my mind repeatedly came back to was the fact that I waited desperately to hear from a lost prince.

But after six days, the fox still did not move.

CHAPTER 31

DUST

PART OF DUST'S AGREEMENT with Renny was to limit their contact; he only signaled the Planter if there was an Everspring outcast to be saved. It was safer that way, since Doll had ordered the other Planters to stop allowing Dust harvests.

But after Dust's pepper-conversation with Astra, he needed advice from a friend, and Renny was arguably the only real one at his disposal. So he signaled the Planter. Three taps on his memmus bulb. He waited.

The call went unanswered.

Dust sent the signal again, then began to worry he'd done something to offend his only ally. If so, it was the worst possible timing. Unfortunately, there was nothing he could do except wait.

He started on the railing for the upper balcony, carving the posts first, a methodical, repetitious work that dulled his anxiety. Wood curls gathered beneath his bench, growing higher with each finished post, like a gathered sandpile on a beach, waiting for the tide that was Bumble to wash it away.

After a full day, Renny did not appear, and Dust signaled again.

He began attaching posts to the balcony, but after adding only two, he found himself resenting the structure entirely. An extra ten feet of space to walk was no freedom, and it was only in lying to himself that he found the illusion of it.

Dust fumbled the third post, and it rolled free of the edge. He watched it sail down to be enveloped in the waiting grass.

Following Smicker's rampage, the grass now held an inker infestation, just as Dust had predicted, and the dark, locust-like insects swarmed at the post's disturbance, turning the grass around them a sickly yellow as they squirted out poison. Normally, Dust would have dealt with them immediately, but he'd been preoccupied with Astra. Why should he care about an infestation? Why did he bother tending to grass he couldn't even touch? He wasn't a Planter. The inkers couldn't hop higher than a foot or two and certainly could not climb a tower, so let them kill the grass if they pleased. Dust was tired of staring at so much green anyway.

Astra's final question had been about his curse. Perhaps she'd found something in the castle that contradicted his sweet story about a man protecting his wife and unborn child, a story which made the fairy out to be the sole villain, stealing an innocent, while Dust's father was only a victim of terrible, unforeseen consequences.

The story was, of course, a lie. Beyond carving, it seemed to be Dust's only skill.

Though hazy, Dust remembered the truth. His father's worry had been real; there *had* been rumor of uprising in the kingdom, but the king worried only for the safety of his crown. Dust remembered bitter arguments that left his mother crying while his father stormed out.

“Garden, Mother,” Dust had urged her, his childlike equivalent of *Don’t cry.*

They knelt in the soil together, planting bulbs and admiring butterflies, until she smiled again.

Dust remembered the day his father had smiled. The king had found something magical, something that would end the worries, that would “make the people listen.” He wanted to plant it, but he wouldn’t let anyone help, even though Mother was the only one who ever planted things.

“Watch,” he ordered Dust. He told his son just where to stand, at the window of a castle tower. Alone.

Then Dust remembered the earthquake, the awful wrenching. Darkness.

And afterward, a sky of green.

In a world where he controlled nothing else, Dust controlled his words. He constructed his own life’s narrative. He called enemies friends. He pretended four floors and three windows could be remade into a pleasant world if he only constructed it right. Empty words. Lies.

“I’m terrified,” he whispered. That was the truth.

Humming sounded from beneath his balcony, and a Planter burst into view. “Don’t be scared! You’ll build it right. You’re so good at building things.”

Dust leapt to his feet. It wasn’t Renny; it was Welly. She perched on the second of his two attached posts, her gray-speckled wings reminiscent of a snowy owl. She was the palest of the Planters, with skin barely a shade darker than birch.

“Hoped you were Renny,” he said with a sigh, though he should not have admitted it.

In her usual chipper way, Welly waved a hand. "That's what I came for! Doll told me to tell you: Renny met winter!"

The words came as a blow to Dust's stomach, only increased by her bright tone. He staggered back, steadying himself with one hand against the tower.

Fairies felt eternal. But nothing was eternal.

Dust swallowed. When he managed words, his voice cracked. "How long ago?"

"A few days? I didn't count."

"How did Doll know?" Though Dust tried, he couldn't silence the voice inside that whispered something insidious, that remembered Doll's growing complaints about her rival. Renny had been the only Planter to resist Doll's instructions, to question her authority. Dust's knuckles whitened against the tower stone.

Welly's expression faltered for just a moment, like a withering illimus bulb. Then it returned to brightness. "There was a little tiff over his garden. See, I thought *I* would get it—next garden to the right and all, that's tradition—but Doll reminded me that *she* should have it."

Dust closed his eyes, breathing shallowly.

Renny. Gone, just like that.

"I'd so hoped to have it," Welly continued. "Renny's garden grew such beautiful illimus bulbs, and I could never grow those in mine no matter how I gathered the moonlight."

The last time they'd seen each other had barely even been a conversation. All of Dust's focus had been on Astra.

Welly blathered on as Dust sank. "I would have torn out the clary onions, of course. They stink! And the rebel hyacinths, too. But those illimus bulbs are so glowy and fun!

What does Doll need bulbs for, anyway? She grows trees, mostly."

"Renny *died,*" Dust snapped, "'n all you can say is that within the hour, you'd've torn out everything he worked his whole life to grow? How is that—how—" He opened his eyes. The view had grown blurry. "How do you *justify* yourselves?"

Holding fairies to human standards. He really ought to have learned better by now.

The white-winged Planter cocked her head and blinked. "Justify what?"

"Get out of my tower."

"Cranky!" she said. "Hope you feel better soon!"

Without another word, she flitted away, over a field of slowly suffocating grass. She never looked down.

There was no ritual for a Planter funeral; for them, it was enough to fade back into the soil. Fallen leaves had no funeral, so neither did Planters. Dust, however, was human, and he may not have mourned leaves, but he mourned friends. He did the only thing he could.

He carved.

With careful strokes of a knife, he whittled a memory—Renny standing on bare toes, face upturned, stretching his pink wings out wide. Dust could not bring himself to paint it, or even to keep it in his tower.

He called for Smicker.

Perhaps it was an insult, trading away his only memorial.

Dust chose to believe Renny would have approved, named as he was after perennials. Perennials did not fade in death. They renewed.

"I need someone to smuggle items to lost humans in the realm," Dust told Smicker. "Has to be either Planter or Trader, willing to work with me."

"HIGH DEMAND." Smicker shook his head, but his violet eyes glittered, and his voice carried a note of hesitant whimper. He'd already seen the carving, seen all the broken heart and unshed blood Dust had cut into every angle. He wanted the trade.

In the end, the waver of his bobbing head made it clear he could not resist. Dust hoped Smicker might volunteer himself to help, but that was putting too much stock in their friendship.

"WILL SEARCH," the dragon promised.

Before he could leave, Dust asked him about linking spells. The Trader grew restless, clawing briefly at the ground, sending inkers hopping in every direction.

"HIGH DEMAND," he repeated at last.

"Can I trade for both?"

"TOO HIGH."

"Maybe I won't trade, then."

A high-pitched whine echoed from the violet dragon's throat. His head drooped on his neck, but he did not change his evaluation at the threat. The carving of Renny was the best piece Dust had ever made, by Trader standards. Every aching beat of his heart carried an echo through the shaped wood in his hand. But every payment had its limit, and Dust had to choose his priorities.

"Forget the linking spell, then. Find me a smuggler."

Shortly after Smicker left, Doll finally arrived. She'd not

made an appearance since Welly's visit, no doubt rearranging her new garden extension to remove any trace of Renny.

"Thought I might starve before you showed up," Dust said. He sat on his bed, mending his shirt, attempting to hold the needle the way he'd briefly seen Astra do it. She'd moved so quickly, so confidently, yet with such finesse.

Dust pricked his finger. He grimaced, shaking his hand. Perhaps one day, she could give him a better demonstration.

After swooping once around the room, Doll settled on the rounded knob of his bedpost, her favorite perch. Her ruffled feathers conveyed her high spirits.

"So dramatic, you humans. Couldn't have run out more'n a day ago."

Her basket appeared, dumping a bundle of fruits and vegetables across his patchwork blanket, along with a bag of grain. Dust raised his mending to avoid having it overrun.

"Enjoying your new garden?" he asked, focusing on his stitches. The thread creaked beneath his forceful tug.

"Eh," she said. "It's nothing groundbreaking, but then, Renny never was."

Dust stiffened. He looked up.

"Did you kill him?" It was foolish to ask, but something ran cold inside, slowing his logic. He gripped the needle, the point facing the Planter on his bedpost.

Doll scoffed. "Planters can't kill, you know that. We're not lesser forms like Traders and Raiders."

It didn't mean she couldn't make clever arrangements. She'd arranged her way out of other rules in the past. But even if the very worst he suspected was true, what would Dust do about it?

Everyone avoided upsetting Doll. Even Dust. Everyone except Renny.

Now Renny was gone.

"Gifts!" Doll clapped her hands. "From my new garden."

Her basket dumped another assortment of plants onto the bed. Dust recognized white clary onions.

"Haven't grown enough for a cut," he said warily, running his fingertips through his hair.

"*Gifts*, I said." Doll beamed, waving a dramatic arm.

Planters didn't give gifts. It was always a harvest.

Obviously sensing his reservations, Doll heaved a sigh. "You're not terrible for a human, you know. Sometimes I appreciate the variety."

Not a compliment by any stretch, but Dust found himself wondering if he'd misread Doll's antagonism toward Renny. She had a strange relationship with all the other Planters, and none of them had met winter in his lifetime. Sometimes death just happened.

How do you know when you can trust someone? Astra's voice whispered in his mind.

Since Dust didn't know what to do, he said, "Thanks, friend. Clary onions'll make good dye. Always tricky to get a strong white."

Clearly the response pleased Doll. She perked up and chattered for a few minutes about her new garden, making space for trees, finding uses for what was there. At least she didn't seem intent on ripping everything out like Welly.

When she finally left, a yellow feather remained behind.

Dust stared at it. Dewdrops glistened along the shaft.

Maybe he wouldn't be so unhappy in his tower if he didn't keep looking at an outside world, if he didn't keep longing for things he couldn't have. Maybe he should accept the boundaries of his world rather than constantly fighting to expand and redefine.

And the worst thought, the very worst *maybe* of all—

Maybe his efforts to leave had gotten Renny killed.

The feather trembled. One of the droplets disappeared, vanishing into a pinprick of mist.

Dust surged to his feet, pulling on his shirt, scattering vegetables in every direction. He grabbed the feather and rushed it down the stairs to where his mirror was still tucked away in the storage room, and he wasn't sure whether to be proud of his bravery or ashamed of his cowardice. All he knew was the truth.

He wanted to hear Astra's voice.

CHAPTER 32

DUST

"YOU'RE LATE," she said.

Dust's heart twinged at that—good or bad, he couldn't tell. Everything around Astra was a tangle. He maneuvered the fox to the edge of the windowsill and leapt for the bed where she sat. He would have fallen a bit short, but Astra caught him.

"There's been some . . . things here." The rest of any explanation stuck in his throat.

"Here too," she said.

He couldn't tell what explanation might have gone unsaid on her side.

She lowered her hand to the quilt, and he hopped down. Then her fingers gently followed a line of thread leading from her dress to a fallen needle. With some awe, Dust tilted his fox head and followed the view from the bottom hem of her green overdress to where she'd nearly reached her hip.

A pattern of creeping blue flowers filled the space. With just a single thread color, she'd managed to create a scene so vivid that Dust felt he was gazing at real flowers, pressed by magic into the fabric itself. Stitch variation alone created the illusion of depth and shadow, separating petals from flower centers and flowers from vines, buds, and leaves, all of them twisting along their path in mesmerizing swirls.

"This is stunning," he breathed.

The corner of her lips tilted in a smirk. "Pleased to hear you think so."

He'd echoed her first words to him without meaning to. Heat touched his ears. "This can't be what you felt lookin' at my carvings. I've never made one half so skilled."

"No, I imagine you never have. Every carving I saw in your woodshop was full-skill and then some." She turned the edge of her dress to reveal the underside of the embroidery, as clean as the front, and she wove her thread until it disappeared, then pulled the needle free.

Hearing her confidence made breathing easy again. Had a Granter been present, Dust would have made a wish without a second thought, a wish to walk right through the mirror to be with her.

"Forget me not."

He blinked. "What?"

Astra gestured at her embroidery. "Mother called them mouse ears, but I always preferred the name forget-me-not."

He gave a breathy, distracted laugh. "Right. The flower."

"You're less boisterous than usual." She raised an eyebrow. "What's happened?"

He faced a choice of how to use his words.

"Bad batch of clary onions," he said at last. "Worried they might be poisoned."

"Well"—Astra scoffed—"at the risk of limb, do not eat."

Dust didn't know how he managed to laugh while his chest ached so deeply.

Normally, when he viewed things through the morningdew mirror, he was able to lose himself entirely in the viewpoint, and especially while controlling the fox, there had been times he'd truly felt as if he'd left his tower behind, if just for a moment.

But he felt it beneath him now more solidly than ever, the chain holding him in place.

Astra's eyes drifted to the window. Pink light tinted the glass, either sunset or dawn. The fingers of her left hand rotated the needle absently, as if she'd forgotten she held it.

"Kenric hasn't forbidden me from stabbing him in the eye with a needle," she said. Not forgotten, then. "Optimistically, it would not count as defying him."

"What's this, now?"

"The king has ordered me to marry him today."

She said it so calmly, Dust almost didn't catch the meaning. Then, as if on cue, a trumpet sounded, and Astra jumped, dropping her needle once more. This time, a faint clang marked the moment it hit the floor. She did not bend to retrieve it.

"I think that's my wedding call," she said, eyes wide.

Dust's heart stopped.

He scrambled to get the fox back to the window. In the courtyard before the Peace Tree, a canopy had been raised. Minstrels waited with instruments at the ready. Servants bustled around the corner and out of sight. The entire courtyard had been strung with ribbons, banners, and jeweled decorations, glittering in the pink light of dawn.

"You were so calm!" he accused, looking over the fox's shoulder at Astra. "How could *this* be what's happened?"

"It's a façade," she shot back. "It's always a façade, and I told you—you're late!"

Dust used the fox to pry at the window, but tiny carved paws accomplished nothing. No doubt Astra had already tested it in the night. She wasn't a fool. He whirled to face her, heart pounding. He'd been so thrilled to discover his new control through morningdew, but in a moment that mattered, he could control nothing at all.

"Please don't marry my brother," Dust said. What a time for honesty.

Astra looked pale, perhaps a touch ill. Amazingly, she managed to wear the illness with beauty, like a woman fainting in a strategically arranged pose.

"Kenric isn't your brother," she said. "Your brother's name was Crispin."

Voices echoed in the hallway just outside her door.

Dust blinked. "What?"

"There's something I meant to—well, you didn't visit, and then I didn't know how to say it, and I was a bit preoccupied this morning with *this morning*, plus you were already upset—stars, I sound like Bastien!"

She stood with abruptness, facing the door just as it opened.

"Astra—"

Dust caught a glimpse of the guards, and beyond them, a king with black hair and gold crown. Then the mirror rippled, erasing the image. By delaying earlier, he'd shortened his morningdew.

And he'd abandoned Astra.

CHAPTER 33

ASTRA

As Kenric entered the room, I glanced at the wooden fox on the window ledge. Before I could retrieve it, Kenric smiled and said, “Lovely day for a wedding. Perfect weather. Come along now.”

The pull of the magic strained against me, the same strain I felt while trying to run or do other un-beautiful things. Between the king’s commands and the foolishness of my own wish, I was no better than that wooden fox: just stiff limbs and a painted smile.

As we exited the room, I cast another glance back at it. No matter how I tried to dig in my heels, I walked forward, leaving it behind.

The castle had come alive with the movement of servants. Woven strings of flowers decorated the halls, hanging from the rafters along with silken banners, all in white and yellow for the king’s crest. Kenric himself wore a yellow robe lined in white ermine fur, and his usual ruby circlet had been traded for a much grander piece of gold and diamond.

Shockingly, he did not protest my wedding attire—the plain peasant dress.

Even one of the female attendants commented on it, questioning "the future queen's choice of presentation."

"She favors that dress," Kenric said. "And half the kingdom cannot look at her anyway."

The message was clear: Nothing I did mattered. Only he mattered.

Beneath the loose dress, I'd secured the queen's thin journal to my stomach with a wrapped scarf. It was not the most flattering alteration to my figure, but with my face and hair on display, I doubted anyone would notice the padding at my stomach, and I could not leave it in my room to be discovered.

As we entered the courtyard, servants released a flock of trained doves, which circled the Peace Tree and brought cheers from the gathered citizens. Kenric basked in the attention, grinning widely and waving at his subjects. I saw the dowager queen standing among other courtiers, all of them dressed in bright robes and hats, sparkling with jewels. Trumpets played once more, announcing the king's arrival. The crowd's roar was near deafening.

Perhaps I should embrace it. My own attire notwithstanding, this was the finest celebration I'd ever seen, and it was a marriage to a king. He may have been the most selfish centipede alive, prone to fits of temper, but he did not seem to be overtly corrupt. If anything, he was merely foolish, caring more about enjoyment and vanity than about topics of true weight.

I glanced at Kenric, his arm linked through mine while he winked at some courtier. He had no care for me, but at least he was honest in that. Since he had not yet given me permission to speak, I was now convinced that he never intended to—a mute wife made a better ornament. Having told him dragons existed would be my biggest contribution to our marriage.

Please don't marry my brother. I winced, Dust's words still echoing in my mind.

The moment the fox had twitched, my heart had surged to see him; it still pounded at the memory. Somehow, the conversation had passed in moments, gone before I'd said anything of purpose at all, and now I carried his mother's final letter while he still didn't know it existed.

I could not abandon him.

But I'd stepped into this cage myself, and I had no option of escape.

Performers charmed the crowd, dancing with ribbons behind a man with a booming voice as he told the story of Everspring's founding. Noble King Firmin and his wise fairy trade, obtaining for the kingdom an everlasting peace.

That is not the story. They all cheered a lie. Children giggled and danced circles around their parents, hands aloft, pretending to hold ribbons of their own.

Kenric smiled as if he were arrogant King Firmin himself.

At the front of the crowd, Bastien stood with the other knights and a line of guards, ready to hold back anyone grown too eager or intoxicated. I knew if I called for him, he would come running, but what would that accomplish? At best, an easy restraint. At worst, an execution. I could summon my Granter, but she would offer even less aid. At best, she would smile wider than Kenric, pleased to see my wish fulfilled by the wealthiest proposal.

Once more, the trumpets. Then the king led me down a carpet of yellow and white rose petals toward the Peace Tree while minstrels played at one end of the courtyard, their violins raising a chorus in the air.

Without meaning to, I stared at a young violinist, remembering Beauty practicing in our manor's music room. No matter how her tutor reminded her of strict posture, she could not resist swaying as she drew the bow. In recent years, our only friendly interactions had been when we made music together, me at the harpsichord and her playing violin. When we spoke, we inevitably traded barbs, but with music shared between us, we smiled. Sometimes Callista joined to sing, completing the sisterly trio, and all our differences—age or otherwise—harmonized into a moment of unity.

My throat burned, but the tears would not come. Foolishly sentimental, that's what I was.

"Place your hands upon the sacred tree," said the priest. Rather than any familiar religious symbol, his vestment bore the symbol of a tree with branches spread wide. Apparently Everspring *worshipped* the tree, as if it was not their gruesome jailer.

Kenric stepped over an arched root and pressed his hand to the ridged bark.

I remained in place, willing my body to grow roots of its own.

"Hand on the tree, my bride." Kenric smiled as he gave the command. Vanity aside, there was a definite streak of malice within him, an enjoyment at ordering people while knowing they could not resist. Could a man born into two centuries of tyrannical tradition even *conceive* that what he did was unjust? That his authority ought not have been absolute law?

Be sewn to the ground, I commanded my feet.

The king won out. I stepped forward and lifted my hand.

Though there were no visible insects on the tree's bark, I felt my skin crawl just the same. This close to the tree, it smelled wretchedly moist, like the greenery of the fairy realm, and even in early morning, the summer air grew uncomfortably hot.

The priest drew his palms together at his chest and spoke with a sickening reverence. "This tree of peace marks the hope of every union! We must all remember . . ."

He went on, but I was thinking of my family again, thinking of the day we'd moved to a run-down shack at the edge of an enchanted forest. Beauty had stood with axe in hand, ready to venture into a forest no one else dared enter, ready to prove she was braver than the rest of us, and I'd said, *Let her go. Beauty accomplishes things. Perhaps she'll clear the whole forest.*

In return, she'd smiled with eyes hard as flint. *Perhaps you'll water the whole land with your tears.*

Now I could not cry at all, and I would have given anything to see Beauty with her axe. I knew just the tree to which she could apply it. My memory taunted me so vividly, it was almost as if I could hear my sister's voice now.

"Astra!"

That *was* her voice.

Heart in my throat, I turned to face the crowd. Bastien looked up as well. His eyes went right past her, but I saw.

I saw my sister.

Why should I be surprised to see Beauty in Everspring? She was ever unpredictable and—by the goals of ten years previous—still missing two adventures. Disrupting a king's wedding would surely fit her criteria.

"Astra!" Beauty shouted again, forcing her way through the crowd. She wore an undecorated linen dress, as she had since Father's bankruptcy, which was not the fashion crime it ought to have been because she would be vibrant in a potato sack. She'd bound her brown hair in a loose twist, and at a glance, she seemed taller than I remembered.

The guards stopped her, and she shouted fiercely, "Let me through! That's my sister!"

"Do not move," Kenric ordered me, his smile dimming.

I'd not intended to. Perhaps I ought to have been happy. Perhaps I should have seen Beauty's devotion as the forgiveness of things that had gone before. But all I felt was a shriveling inside. Despite all my thoughts and wishes, I could not face her.

Bastien made his own way forward with urgency, and though Kenric relaxed, clearly expecting his knight to dismiss the interruption, I realized what truly moved Bastien.

I'd been so focused on Beauty, I'd missed the man next to her. Her beast-turned-human, overly tall, wore a subdued expression. But now that I saw him next to Bastien, I realized they shared the same hickory hair and sloped jaw.

Andre. I thought it at the same moment Bastien choked it out. In an instant, the brave knight was overtaken with the expression of a lost child. Andre was moving, too, seizing his older-but-shorter brother in a strangling embrace. Bastien wept.

Over the shoulders of guards, Beauty watched me without words. I'd never known my sister to be without words. Did she hope for an embrace just the same?

I shrank closer to the tree.

"Enough of this," said Kenric, smile absent now. He raised his voice. "Fitzweller, back in line. You two, whoever you are, remove yourselves from my sight."

Clearly thinking the matter sorted, his smile returned.

Bastien stepped away from his brother, anguish apparent on his face. He returned to position. Andre said something too quiet to hear, and Bastien shook his head as he responded. He jerked his chin toward the city wall, and after a moment's hesitation, Andre took a step into the crowd, reaching for Beauty's hand.

The moment before it happened, I saw my sister's expression, her set jaw, her defiant eyes.

"Beauty, don't!" I said sharply.

Either she did not hear me or did not care. The latter—it was always the latter.

With a quick, darting movement, Beauty dove beneath the outstretched arm of the closest guard and rushed toward me, her steps scattering yellow and white petals. She caught my free hand in hers, and my fingers trembled at her touch.

Kenric's eyes widened. "Is this orchestrated rebellion?" He watched me, as if expecting my own defiance at any moment.

I could not take a single step.

"Your Majesty," said Beauty, clear and unbending. "I was invited by a knight of your guard, and I will not leave without speaking to my sister. I've not seen her in months; surely you can spare a moment."

Seeing Beauty's actions, I knew—the secret to the Peace Tree's hold on a person was time in Everspring. My exemption had never come from my wish; I had only been buying time while new to the city. My time had run out.

And I knew what was coming for my sister.

"Listen to him," I ordered Beauty, trying to summon a harshness in my expression that would not come.

"Have you been here all this time? Astra, you didn't even *write!*"

In desperation, I shouted, "I don't want to see you! Get away from me!"

Beauty reared back, releasing my hand. But she did not step away.

And it was too late.

I watched the ground swallow my sister just as I'd once watched her fall from atop a boulder. My sister was there and gone. Her scream was there and gone. Under my right hand, the Peace Tree stood firm throughout it all, as continuous as an ocean tide, the spring of everlasting peace for one man and no one else.

My fingers clawed into the ridged bark. Though my enchanted eyes could not convey the seething inside, I turned my gaze on that tree, and I felt it tremble beneath my palm.

Andre's agonized voice shouted Beauty's name. I could only hope Bastien's brother was not as reckless as my sister, that he could be convinced to retreat, even if Bastien had to drag him into it.

"Honored guests!" said Kenric. "It was only a momentary draft to dampen the warmth of this grand event. We shall continue on at once!"

Bark pressed sharply into my uncalloused fingers, shooting a tingle deep into my bones, as deep as the magic's pull. We dared one another, the curse and I, to see whose stubbornness was stronger, both of us unparalleled in our reigns. For the sake of pride, I would sleep homeless and hungry. For the sake of a sister I sometimes hated—

I would die.

"No, Kenric," I said. "We shall not." My voice wavered as I dragged in unsteady breaths, my very organs pulling to separate from my body. I took one dragging step forward, hand still on the tree.

The wood of the Peace Tree groaned as if bent beneath a hurricane's gale. Its branches shivered, casting off purple fruit like lumpy hail. One landed at my feet. As Kenric looked up, one struck him in the eye. Watching him double over felt an awful lot like seeing the stars bow.

It all proved too much for the king, and he fled, calling for his knights.

Roots broke from the soil around me, tangling my legs. I kept my own fingers tangled in the tree until it asserted its victory at last and dragged me into a whirlpool of wet earth.

CHAPTER 34

ASTRA

My eyes opened to a green sky.

For several minutes, I lay, unable to move, with a weakness so deep, it felt like I'd slid several years closer to the grave. Groaning, I finally clambered to my feet, surveying what fresh torture the fairy realm had concocted for me. I saw neither swamp nor mountain, only an endless stretch of gray ash and open sky. The ash clung to my woolen dress no matter how I shook the material. The palm of my hand stung, reddened and puffy where it had touched the Peace Tree's bark, like a collection of bee stings.

"Beauty!" I called out. Turning, I did not see her.

My sister was lost in the fairy realm.

I remembered Dust's warning about the Ocean of Agony, about being dropped anywhere in the realm. Beauty had been standing right next to me. Now she might be on the other side of the world.

And where was I?

Green smudges marked the horizon in two directions, while there was only gray giving way to rocky black in the other two. The faint chimes that usually greeted me were conspicuously absent, and I did not trust any change to be a good thing in the fairy realm.

Ashpoint. During our pepper battle, Dust had said something about that. Someone had died there. My weary knees wavered.

But I could not remain paralyzed forever, and if Dust was busy saving Beauty—which I could only hope he was—then the best assistance would be for me to roll up my sleeves and save myself for once. I'd just taken on the Peace Tree; certainly I could take on a few other magical dangers.

"Trade!" I called out, the only thing I could think of. I cupped my hands, trying to amplify a voice that would only let me shout at a beautiful volume, never reaching a screech. "*I wish to trade!*"

After repeating the call in all directions, I waited.

And to my shock—

A purple dragonfly came flitting over the ash, carrying its dainty little basket.

"*You're* a Trader?" I managed.

With a happy buzz, the dragonfly zipped forward and tumbled in the air, growing larger and larger before landing at my feet as a true dragon—a lumpy, stubby-winged thing barely the size of a cat.

Why had my first Trader experience been with a *mountain?*

"TRADE," the lumpy cat-dragon squeaked.

At least Smicker had been majestic. This little thing had bulgy eyes with pupils that did not align; one almost managed to track me while the other wandered off to follow ash flurries. But I could not afford to be choosy.

"I need three things. First, a—"

"TOO HIGH."

"Beg your pardon?"

"TOO HIGH. ONE THING."

"You've not even heard the requests."

"TOO HIGH!"

With great patience, I restrained my sigh. It only made sense that lopsided cat-dragons could not manage the trades of grand, majestic mountains.

"Fine," I said through gritted teeth. "One thing. I must be transported to Dust's tower within this realm. He lives in a meadow of waving grass, surrounded by trees, near a swamp. I'll find my way forward from there."

Scratching its floppy ear with dull talons, as if in thought, the dragon panted and huffed before finally squeaking, "TOO HIGH!"

"Pray, tell—is there anything you *can* do?"

It perked up. "TELL LOCATION."

Knowing Dust's location would do me no good if I could not reach it, and knowing my sister's location would not help me assist either of us. This was the whole problem with books—knowledge was practically useless on its own. It served only to taunt with what could not be reached.

I rubbed my forehead. "That does me no . . ." A pause. Then, "Very well. If you can manage nothing else, you must inform Dust of *my* location."

Renny had said Dust traded for my location, and the first time I'd arrived, I'd startled him in his tower. If it took a sacrifice of resources for him to find someone, I prayed this might help, in whatever small way.

"GOOD TRADE," squeaked the dragon.

Finally. "For payment, I have only one creation, though it will require—"

The dragon reared back with a squawk, overturning on its

lumpy tail and sending up a puff of ash. After wiggling in ash for a moment, it waddled around to face me once more, leaving streaks behind with its movements.

"FINGER. TRADE FINGER."

I blinked. "You can't be serious."

"NOSE?"

"I'm not feeding you any of my body parts, thank you very much, and if you continue in this pattern, I may crush one of yours."

"KISS."

The very word caused my stomach a flip, the kind experienced while smelling a bloated fish carcass washed up on the beach.

"KISS," it repeated. "TRADE KISS."

While I deliberated an unthinkable option, the cat-dragon wandered, weaving in a drunken line. Then it pounced, diving unexpectedly a few feet away.

The ground gave way beneath it.

I could do nothing but stare while it vanished in a cloud of ash. So much for—

The buzzing of wings brought a dragonfly into view, and then the lumpy monstrosity was at my feet once more, looking up at me as if nothing had happened. Edging sideways a bit, I peered down a chasm at a now-revealed river of lava, bubbling far below in a hot, hissing orange. Slowly, ash melded to cover the opening once more, leaving no trace of the danger beneath.

I squinted at the lumpy Trader.

"That was very shrewd," I said. "Showing me how I might fall to my death."

It admitted nothing. Its purple scales could hardly be called that, more the texture of craggy skin, with green edges like mold. Its fleshy wings made a sticky sound when flexing. One eye still wandered.

I needed the trade. Beyond that, in the back of my mind, I remembered the blue Granter telling me that to complete my wish, I must seek that which was ugly. If I could break my wish, then Dust would not be forced to propose once he was finally free. We could have honest conversations. We could see each other truly, and perhaps even . . .

With a huff, I said, "Fine. You tell Dust my location, and I will deliver to you, in return, one kiss. Given by me while you do not so much as *twitch*, understand?"

"TRADE ACCEPTED."

The dragon straightened as much as any lumpy creature could, stretching its neck upward. I crouched and delivered a swift kiss to its forehead, quickly scrubbing my lips afterward, lest I'd transferred some kind of disease to myself.

While the dragon bounded in happy circles, I touched my hair, but it was still unnaturally smooth, my skin flawless.

I'd changed nothing at all.

Except the dragon, apparently—as I watched, it grew several inches taller, and a row of tiny black lumps popped into existence down the center of its back.

"GOOD TRADE," it chirped. Then it stopped to claw briefly at its forehead where I'd kissed it. "HOT. HOT."

"Our agreement," I reminded it.

In a moment, a purple dragonfly buzzed off to find Dust.

CHAPTER 35

DUST

WHEN DUST HEARD THE CHIMES, his heart fell; he'd not yet finalized the trade with Smicker, and there was no one to fill Renny's place.

At least the Trader arrived promptly.

"Smicker, it has to be you," said Dust. "I've got no one else."

The dragon whined and hunkered down on all fours, burying his snout in the trees, his tail wrapping forward to drape across his eyes. "LITTLE ONES," he protested. "TIRED."

"If I weren't desperate, I wouldn't ask. Please, friend."

Would Welly be willing to help? She'd not even stopped Doll from claiming Renny's garden; she would never defy the stronger Planter. Vine was lazy, and Gard hated the very idea of Doll's "pet human" to begin with.

"TRADE ACCEPTED."

Dust started. Even after pleading, he'd not expected Smicker to actually agree.

"Why?" The question escaped without permission, and

Dust found himself tense, as if he'd stepped into a dark room, feeling blindly for a trap.

After clawing at the ground a bit, Smicker snorted and tilted away.

Without looking at Dust, he said, "FRIEND."

Despite the urgency of the matter at hand, Dust broke into a grin. He had to force a deep breath before he could speak properly.

"Chimes came from the Fanged Hills. Let's hurry."

Once trades had been made and Smicker was on his way to find the lost Everspring outcast, Dust thought he might have a moment to relax, but his mind could only think of Astra's wedding to Kenric. He sat down to sharpen his whittling tools, then thought better of doing it with a distracted mind.

"ASTRA!"

Dust whirled. One thing to be preoccupied with longing thoughts, another to manifest voices entirely.

With a deep buzz, like that of a fat bumblebee, an unfamiliar Trader entered through window number one before tumbling across the floor as a dumpy little dragon, landing in a pile of wood shavings. It snorted, sending up a cloud of sawdust.

"ASTRA," it squeaked.

"Did she trade with you?" Dust could not help the grin that spread across his face. If she was in the fairy realm again, she'd defied the king, and beyond that, she had such a grasp of things, she was now summoning Traders on her own. He felt a swell of bittersweet pride.

Until the Trader said—

"ASTRA, ASHPOINT."

Ashpoint. That single word rattled Dust's very bones.

There'd been no chimes at all. How long had she been stranded?

"TRADE?" the underdeveloped dragon said hopefully.

Dust crouched to look it in the eye, shaking his head. "Doubt you'd like me as a barterer, friend. I always seem to need high trades." Like the one he would need to save Astra.

With clear disappointment drooping its wings, the young Trader zipped away.

Dust remained crouched, his mind churning desperately, his heart pounding. Smicker was occupied, with no way to send a message or call him back, and he had a human of his own to rescue. *Ashpoint.* Sweat broke out across Dust's palms. He remembered the last outcast, remembered his failure.

No matter the cost, he could not bear to fail Astra.

So even while knowing it was the most foolish thing he'd ever done—

Dust signaled for Doll.

CHAPTER 36

ASTRA

It was not until I was alone—unable to move for fear of dropping to my death down an unseen chasm—that everything began to sink in. I sat heavily, sending up a puff of ash, uncaring that it dirtied my dress.

My mind conjured for me horrors untold—moving trees and monstrous ogres and tentacled depthfiends, all clamoring to prey on my sister. Even the innocuous things could not be trusted, the fairies that looked like flowers or trailed glitter like rainbows. They could ruin a life.

"Granter," I called softly.

She appeared in a tiny shower of sparks, as blue in the fairy realm as she had been in my own, unaffected by the surroundings—except to wrinkle her nose as she looked around.

"This is Planter territory," she complained.

"I regret it," I whispered. Everything inside twisted at the truth. "I regret my wish. Undo it. Please."

The fairy said, "A wish may be undone only by completion."

"I don't understand what that means!" I raked my fingers through my hair, holding it clenched at the back of my head. "The Peace Tree forces all to obey the king, so I thought completion would be a defiance of him, but I've defied three times now, *with purpose,* and changed nothing. You spoke of pursuing ugliness, but I kissed the ugliest creature imaginable yet still—"

"You defied the wisher king?" Her empty eyes caught a spark of something. Curiosity, perhaps.

"I thought you would know."

"I said I have lost my interest in you."

As much glare as my face could muster, I gave her. Her response was an unapologetic shrug.

"You could not defy the wisher king," she said. "Planter magic would not allow it. Planter magic grows deep roots."

I snorted. "It's no unique thing. So many people are sent to the fairy realm for it that they've formed their own guild."

Blue shimmers twinkled around her face as she shook her head. "Before the roots grow, you could defy. While they are young, perhaps defiance with great effort. But after they sink deep, there is no defiance. There is only growth of magic."

I frowned. "How long to 'sink deep'?"

"Three days of wisher time? No more."

I'd certainly spent longer than that in Everspring, awaiting my wedding. Slowly, I released my grip on my hair, fingers tingling.

"I was fighting for my sister." It was the only explanation I could think of. "So I was stronger than the curse."

The fairy snickered. After looking me over head to toe, she said, "Astra is not stronger than magic."

I huffed. "Astra is bigger than you."

To prove that point, I reached out and poked her in the

chest. It was a light thing, but she doubled over as if I'd punched her. Then she hissed, "*Hot!*"

I thought of the cat-dragon. "What did you say?"

The Granter looked up at me with wide, solid eyes. Murmuring inaudibly to herself, she walked closer on the air, making me lean back as she observed me once more from head to toe, apparently seeing something different. She reached out to jab my shoulder, and her poke did not have nearly the same effect mine had. I did not feel it through my dress. But she shook her hand fiercely, as if she'd touched a fireplace coal.

"There's something wrong with me," I said, swallowing. I'd suspected it for a while. "When I touched the dragon, when I touched the Peace Tree . . . I did something."

More than that, I'd *felt* something. A kind of tingle inside, the kind that came from leaning on one hand for too long and then moving the fingers.

"Something is amiss in your wish," the Granter admitted.

"I knew it! Stars, didn't I *tell* you that first day in the castle?" I shook my head, a breathy laugh escaping. "Whatever it is, just set it right so I can end this wish."

"A Granter cannot alter a wish."

It was a struggle not to swat her right out of the air. "You just admitted you made a mistake!"

"The mistake is not mine. I granted your wish. But your wish is dangerous because of the weight in a word—Astra wished, not to be 'beautiful *enough*,' but to be '*so* beautiful.' Enough is a limit, but so is never-ending."

I'd accused Dust of speaking madness, but he did not compare to true fairies. For two hundred years, this had been his life? Surrounded by confusion, forced to learn the rules of a nonsensical realm from the most unhelpful creatures imaginable.

For another moment, I stared at the fairy. Then I said, "Why do you grant wishes?"

She did not protest my change in topic. She only hovered in silence, blue sparks trailing from her bare feet like falling stars, fading before they touched the ground.

"I see wishers in need," she said at last, "and I wish to help."

"Help?" My scoff was only a pretty smile around an airy laugh. I scraped my hand across the ground, sending a puff of gray ash billowing toward her. "What help is this?"

She flapped her hand to dispel the ash before her face, displaying the scowl I could not. "How am I to know if a wish will make you happy? I cannot create your happiness. Only you can. If you wished for the wrong thing, it was not my words or will but your own. Why did you not wish for that which would make you happy?"

"I thought it would!" My chest ached, and my cheeks strained beneath a magic that would not allow them expression. I'd turned the attention of entire crowds with my beauty. I'd spent the wealth of a king. I'd stood on the cusp of queenhood. Never in my life would I have imagined such a circumstance could *be* unhappy.

But I was miserable. And in truth, that had started long before my wish.

There were plenty of years I'd been happy with my family, but they were not recent. After Mother's death, I had grown bitter, even more so when the rest of my family had seemed readily able to move on while I'd stood rooted in place. I'd given them the honesty of my feelings, but I'd given it as a weapon—*I am miserable,* not to seek comfort but only to say, *You should be too.*

They'd managed to thrive in our terrible circumstances when I could not, and that had left me with the sourest of all feelings.

Jealousy.

That was the heart of all of it. My jealousy. It was the turn I'd taken, veering off the well-worn path and over a cliff. It roared like an insulted dragon, tearing ruts in my happiness, uprooting any lasting trees I might have planted. Over the years, I had let it swallow me, and then I'd pretended I did not live in its stomach. Pretended the walls around me were of a different material, placed there through no fault of my own. Pretended my every misery was someone else's doing.

But it had always been my own.

I took a shaking breath, setting my fingers in ash. The horizon of green seemed so far away as to be unreachable.

"I don't know what would make me happy," I said. "I don't even know where to begin."

It was more a matter of *stopping,* but just as I'd cowered helplessly before a true dragon, I did not know the right words to stop the rampage of the beast inside me. I'd looked Beauty right in the eye, and I'd turned away. I could not face her.

I could not even face myself.

The fairy sniffed. "Perhaps the starting point should have been considered before wishing."

"Wretched fairy, you enjoy taunting!" I choked on a sob that could not be voiced. "That's the true reason you grant wishes—and the reason you won't undo them! You claim to have rules and restraints when all you have is an unfeeling heart. When my sister found you in the forest, you cleared our land of brush so it could be tilled. There was no wish made for that. You would use magic to clear a meaningless spot of dirt but not to help me!"

After a moment, the fairy sank in the air, drifting down to land at my feet like an upright doll. She was the right size—a toy that every human longed to carry around. Even telling stories of the dangers in wishes, we could not deny our own greed. I'd not been able to.

The fairy said, "To every wish is given magic. A Granter may also wish, but only to grant wishes."

"*Riddles,*" I hissed.

"I desired your sister to wish. Therefore, I could clear the land because Beauty had to *see*. Beauty imagines magic in every corner, so true magic had to be seen. Wolf needed no evidence. Astra needed no evidence. An available Granter was evidence enough."

I drew a long breath through my nostrils, exhaling it in a sigh.

"To solve the riddle," I said, "what you mean is that you can't do magic unless it's either fulfilling a wish or persuading a person to wish."

"Magic is not without purpose. To the Granter who forgets, they are forgotten. To the Granter who refuses, they are refused." She tilted her head, hair drifting softly. "I knew one who refused a wish, and I saw when magic refused him."

Perhaps my heart ought to have panged in sympathy, but I shook my head. "Rules, I understand, but it's no excuse. You could still be helpful beyond magic, but you speak in riddles, and then you mock misunderstanding."

Her lip pushed forward in a pout. I did not offer apology; I was thinking of Dust. While I'd grown to adulthood surrounded by a family who loved me, even if they said it through things like, *Astra, beware the path that leads to pearls,* he'd been surrounded by *this*.

"Astra draws in beauty," the Granter said.

I frowned down at her.

"It is the danger in your wish. You wished for beauty to attract the wealthy, but not beautiful *enough*. Not a limit. Rather, *so beautiful*. There is no end. When Astra contacts beauty, she draws it in. She increases, growing *so beautiful*."

The blue fairy was clearly trying to help, and it was more effort than she'd given thus far, but my brow remained knitted in confusion. "I don't understand."

She stamped one foot, sparking like a tiny flash of lightning. "*So beautiful!* This is the weight! A mending gown is beautiful. An endless perfume is beautiful. A cultivated tree. I see these drawn in. I feel the heat."

Stepping forward, she pressed her hand to my ankle, then drew it swiftly away.

With effort, I forced back my frustration. I tried to sort her words. *Mending gown*—my silver gown, the one that had torn in the fairy realm. I'd expected it to mend itself, yet it hadn't. *Perfume*. I remembered the scent of sandalwood, a bottle that ought to have maintained an eternal drop but didn't. The Peace Tree.

"Oh," I said softly.

In her grin, the Granter showed tiny fangs.

I'd worn an enchanted gown that lost its enchantment, handled a perfume that did the same. Before defying the king during our wedding ceremony, I'd held my hand to the Peace Tree.

"*Oh*." I gave a small gasp.

Of all the wealth in the world, magic was the rarest and most valuable. My beauty was in magic.

And I drew in beauty.

"I do wish to help," said the fairy, almost petulantly.

In return, I said something that seemed a grand irony. "Thank you, Granter."

Pushing off from her toes, she lifted into the air, hovering before me. "No wisher has complained so much. Wolf did not speak enough words to fill a cup." Then the corner of her lips twitched. "No wisher has called me Granter."

"Do you have a name?"

"The Malcontent."

That seemed wildly appropriate.

Before I could respond, she spoke again. "Astra still does not know the weight in a word. What is beautiful to the wealthy?"

"Magic," I said.

She stuck her hands on her hips.

"Wealth," I said.

"Then what is ugliness to Astra?" she asked. "What is the wealth in it?"

"Riddles. Just tell me."

"Some riddles cannot be told. If you seek completion, you must be drawn to that which is ugly. You must see and treasure the wealth in it."

She vanished, leaving a trail of blue in the air like the spray of an ocean wave.

CHAPTER 37

DUST

"YOU NEVER SIGNAL." Doll's first words. She stood on a corner of his workbench, smirking as she always did when knowing she held something Dust needed.

He held a knife and block of wood, but it was for show more than anything. Perhaps for comfort. He was just scraping away layers without an end in mind. Inside, his stomach churned, and he kept his eyes on his carving as he spoke.

"Funny thing," he said, attempting to keep his voice empty of feeling. "Just a bit ago, a new Trader tumbled in here, brought a message from Astra."

"The Granter girl?" Doll's breezy tone could not mask the spark in her yellow eyes.

"Regrets leaving. Thought you might give her a way back."

"I could be persuaded. Where?"

"Stumbled her way into Ashpoint, it seems."

"Dangerous place, that." Slowly, Doll tilted her head. "There's something you could do for me. A little thing."

A little thing. That was always how she phrased it, though her prices came in blood steeper than any Trader. *A little thing*. The payment she was about to demand was not little at all; it was his very soul.

But Dust had known. When he'd signaled for her, he'd known the price she would demand.

"Name it, then," he said.

"Stop trying to escape."

There it was, plainly stated—the contract for his soul, simply awaiting signature. Doll had teased such a thing twice before, in times when they'd each tiptoed around things they wanted, and both times, he'd found a way out of the corner.

But this time, he had no other option, and he would not risk Astra's life.

Dust sank his carving knife deeply into the block, feeling the resistance of the wood pushing back against him. With a twist of his wrist, he cracked the block wide open, splintering its side, leaving it gaping. Like a ribcage cracked to expose a heart.

"It's settled, then." He met Doll's gaze. "Bring her here, 'n do it fast."

"Of course." Hovering above the workbench, smile brighter than the yellow blur of her wings, Doll said, "Just one quick stop first. She should see my garden."

Then she was gone.

CHAPTER 38

ASTRA

TRAVELING WITHIN THE FAIRY REALM was not like traveling to it. There was no violent whirlpool to suck me down. Instead, the world around me simply melted, like rainfall off tree leaves, blurring colors and dragging everything down until I blinked to find myself in new scenery.

"All right," I said, dropping the sprig of lavender Doll had given me. "Lovely garden. I've seen it now."

When the yellow Planter had appeared over the ash field, she'd smiled to tell me of her agreement with Dust. Supposedly, he wanted me to see her garden. I very much doubted that.

The garden we'd entered had no walking path, only the peek of navy-blue soil between plants. Those plants came in all varieties—wide, flat-petaled flowers next to puffy turquoise bushes. Trees were the most numerous, bordering the immediate plant rows in what seemed to be an entire forest. Most of the trees had a familiar look—green tops and flowering trunks—but some were a vibrant orange with needles like pine. I even saw a line of narrow trees with pink bark.

"You've seen nothing." Doll laughed, the same tittering sound shared between the dowager queen and her tea friends. "This is barely a corner of what I cultivate. Impressive, aye?"

Flattery might make her more pliable, if my lessons in society were anything to go by. I could play the part, heap upon her praise and flattery like the perfect little sycophant, hoping to charm her into liking me, to avoid the danger she posed. I could correct the mistake I'd made with Kenric, soothing rather than antagonizing.

Flatly, I said, "I'm sure another Planter has a more impressive offering. Renny, perhaps."

And I thoroughly enjoyed the way her smile turned to an irritated squint.

"I'm the most powerful Planter in the realm," she said.

"How lovely for you. If you're so powerful, I'm sure it's no bother to get me to Dust's tower."

"How lovely for *you*," she parroted, watching me through thin pupils. "In a rush to reunite with your true love."

A sudden breeze through the garden brought the heavy scent of flowers in bloom, and I wondered if she'd done it on purpose. Heat blossomed in my cheeks. "He's not—"

"Human obsessions, they are. Truth. Love. It's a shame there's not much power in them."

Plainly, I heard the unspoken: *I can give you power.*

"Whatever you're offering," I said, "I'm not interested."

She purred, "You haven't even heard the offer."

Zipping away, she rustled turquoise bushes in her flight. Flowers burst to life along each disturbed branch, tiny blossoms the same yellow as Doll's wings. A quiet melody hummed to life in the air before fading. I felt a deep sense of calm wash in like the foamy tide.

Every part of the fairy realm was like a sleeping monster, except Doll's garden. Here, there was a sense of magic the way magic ought to be. Enchanting. Beautiful.

Doll turned, hovering in the air, gesturing me forward.

With a smile, I followed.

Flowers reached up to brush my fingers as I passed, their petals soft as silk. Little drooping blossoms rang with the sound of crystal bells. Leaf and stalk alike parted to avoid my footfalls, then sewed themselves together again after I passed. Trees lifted their branches to avoid catching my hair. The entire garden was alive and welcoming.

"Fearful little dearie." Doll smiled. She hovered before a greenhouse that had not been visible before. "My offer is to plant for me."

The small, ornate greenhouse—barely taller than I was and only my arm-span wide—looked as if it belonged in a castle yard. Carved marble pillars framed the structure, with gold-latticed glass filling walls and ceiling between. Viny flowers of muted red grew across the ceiling, creeping slowly even as I watched, filtering the green light to become soft yellow.

I stepped close to the glass, peering in. A single wooden planting box marked the center of the greenhouse, positioned to catch the warm yellow light. At first, I thought it was empty. Then I saw—two petite seedlings had burst the soil, barely the size of my fingertip, like tiny hands reaching for the sun.

Doll sat on the curved glass roof, legs dangling beside my head. She leaned down and spoke tenderly, as if we shared a secret.

"If you plant for me," she said, "I will give you a seedling, never before dreamed of. The entire world will proclaim your beauty. Astra the Alluring. Astra the *Goddess*. Your family would not dare look down on Astra the Goddess."

As she spoke, I felt a swell of emotion, a swell of *rightness*. My mother had given me a name with meaning; I *deserved* to embody that.

But something was missing—like I was sewing without a thimble.

Leaning closer to the glass, I squinted at the seedlings. The soil around the little green sprouts was not the same deep blue color as the rest of the garden. It was, instead, reddish-brown, swirled in a familiar hazy texture.

Hair. Clumped and discarded, the way mine littered the floor after Mother trimmed it.

"Dust's hair," I whispered. He'd mentioned it only briefly, but the thought had sat uncomfortably with me even then, the idea of the fairies taking from him a part of himself after everything else.

The inner calm shattered, like ocean wave meeting rocky shore.

"*You*," I hissed, rounding on Doll.

She leapt to her feet, wings twitching.

"This is what you did to King Firmin! Lured him in with calming spells and false promises, made him believe he should be the greatest king in the world, no matter the cost!"

Doll heaved a sigh. "This was so much easier with a Granter. Humans can't resist the sparkle."

"You orchestrated the Peace Tree!"

"As if it's such a terrible thing!" Doll spread her hands, leaning down toward me, balanced on the edge of the greenhouse. "Always, Granters and Planters at odds, despising one another, spitting insults, but *I* had the vision to see past it! I worked *with* a Granter to make seeds, and *such seeds*. Seeds of magic that grow in the human world, if planted by a human hand. Seeds of magic that grant a wish lasting beyond a single human, lasting generations!"

She flew straight up and swept an arm in a full circle, gesturing at the land surrounding us. "Just *look,* human! Look at the reach of my garden. A single tree has given me *this,* more power than any Planter in the realm."

The boiling inside me did not lend itself to words, but rather to action, so I stepped across her carefully cultivated plants until I reached one of those stark orange trees. Though it tried to dodge me, I grabbed hold of the closest branch, ignoring the sharp prick of the needles against my hand.

Under my touch, the tree began to wilt, losing its vibrancy. Branches drooped. Bright orange needles faded to the color of molding pumpkins, then plummeted to the ground below.

"Stop that!" Doll shrieked, diving toward me.

I stuck out my other hand, blocking her, and as her shoulder collided with my pointer finger, she gave a hiss of pain, drawing back.

She was so proud of her beautiful garden. How fortunate that everything beautiful, I kept. Now more than ever.

"Don't speak to me," I said, "of joyful collaborations and magical breakthroughs. What you've done is despicable. You tricked Dust's father, and Dust, you've . . . you've . . ."

I released the tree, but it did not regain its color.

"You've made him suffer," I whispered. "Two hundred years, you've made him suffer."

Doll said, "I tend a garden. Not human emotion."

Nodding, I bent to search the ground, my fingernails catching soil, my gray chemise staining deep blue at the hem.

"What are you doing?" Doll asked, since I'd clearly not given an expected reaction.

"Finding a rock," I said calmly.

I straightened, and with all the power I possessed, I lobbed the palm-sized rock in my hand toward the greenhouse. The shattering of glass echoed against the trees. Red petals rained through a hole in the roof.

With purpose, I strode toward the greenhouse.

"*No!*" Doll squealed, blocking my path, though she drew back when I moved to touch her.

Sharply, I said, "I tend to human emotion, not gardens. And if you want anything in *this* garden to remain standing, you will tell me how to kill the Peace Tree."

She trembled, bobbing in the air.

"It's one tree or your entire garden, Planter. Tell me now!"

When she still hesitated, I crouched once more, sinking my fingers into a turquoise bush. Its humming melody wilted into the screech of an untuned violin. Leaves dropped from every branch. "Greenhouse seedlings next, Doll!"

"The king must make reparation!" Doll cried. "To kill the Peace Tree, reparation must be made for its benefits."

Pulling my hand back, I stood. My fingers prickled with pain. "I could kill the tree, just like I'm doing now."

Doll narrowed seething yellow eyes. "You would wither first. Two hundred human years, it's grown roots, the strongest Planter tree in existence. You have no roots, and a human can only withstand so much magic."

Considering my experience at the wedding, I'd feared it might be something like that. Especially since the stinging pain in my hand still had not faded.

"Why Dust's hair?" I asked.

"Because they must be stabilized while I wait for true planting."

"No, I meant . . . did you start using him because he was conveniently here, or did you arrange him to be *payment* so you could use him?"

Her silence told me enough, even before she said, "He's Firmin's blood. A linking spell requires something to be the link."

"Come closer," I said, smiling a dare.

Wisely, she darted away.

If I stayed any longer in this garden, I *would* wither it all, and there was no telling what that would do to me. If I was going to destroy myself battling plants, there was an overgrown tree which took priority.

I had only two things to do first.

"Send me to Dust's tower," I said, leaving no room for argument in my tone.

Doll seemed as glad to remove me from her garden as I was to leave it.

CHAPTER 39

DUST

DUST HAD NEVER BEEN SO RELIEVED to have a sudden milky wall nearly take his head off. He picked himself carefully off the floor, watching shadows on the other side of his woodshop.

"Astra?" he called out, heart in his throat.

"Always this workbench," she said. "I know the tower has other floors, and I wouldn't mind seeing beyond the storage."

Dust laughed. He stepped up to the wall and leaned his forehead against it, breathing in the moment. Finally, he asked, "You all right? Heard you might've visited a garden. Could be spiders."

"Just one angry yellow wasp."

His stomach pulled back against his spine, but he kept his voice light. "Sting you, did she?"

"She tried. I put a hole in her nest."

His eyebrows shot up at that. "You might need to explain beyond the metaphor for that one."

"First, I have to ask." Astra's shadow drew close to the wall, mirroring him. Despite not being able to see her, Dust's breath caught. "My sister," she said. "She was sent to the realm before me, and—"

"Safe." Dust smiled gently. "Didn't meet her, of course, but I made arrangements with Smicker. It's why I couldn't send him after you. Hope you can forgive me."

"Thank you," Astra whispered, the slightest wobble in her voice.

"For you," he said, "anything in the world."

The proof was in his promise to Doll.

Dust hesitated, then reached up to knock gently three times. Astra gave no hesitation of her own in knocking back.

"Are you married, Astra?" Despite his best efforts, his voice cracked.

She snorted. "Despite my best efforts, I have been unmarried twenty-five years. It does not happen easily, and both of my younger sisters, I believe, have beaten me to it. Though I can hardly complain anymore since I left my would-be husband at the tree."

"I'd very much like to hear that story."

Surprisingly, he was met with silence. Then he heard the soft crinkle of parchment.

"There's something else we should discuss," she said. "Something I learned at the castle."

"The name Crispin, is it?" Though she herself had been his foremost worry, he'd not forgotten what she'd said through the mirror. He pressed one hand to the wall, fingers tense.

"I found . . . records," she said at last. "Your mother's journal. Her final letter, I think. Her name was Emmeline. Your father's name was Firmin. I told you about your brother Crispin, and no matter how I searched, I could find no record of your name. Perhaps the records were destroyed to preserve a false history, or perhaps they've just been lost."

After another pause, she finished: "Record-keeping across two centuries is not easy."

Dust said nothing. He did not move.

"It's on your workbench," Astra said. "I'll wait in the storage room."

He carved.

The letter sat at the top corner of Dust's workbench, folded but never sealed, the top third dipping gently in every light breeze from the windows. He'd pulled it from his mother's journal but then been unable to read it. It haunted the corner of his eye while Dust focused on the small chisel in his hand, tapping it into the wood, cutting a hollow with careful precision because what was removed could not be replaced.

Astra was waiting on him. Occasionally, he heard the muffled sound of her footsteps above his head.

He set down his chisel. Then he picked it up again.

Two hundred years.

He tossed the chisel away from his workbench. It clanged across the floor, leaving a trail in the sawdust. With decisiveness, or perhaps desperation, he unfolded the letter at last. It showed the weathering of age and abuse—crumpled corners, a tear at one edge, faded ink.

My darling son,

This final letter is too often begun and never finished. The words to express my heart do not seem to exist. If they ever did, they have left my mind. It fails me more often with each passing day. Today, I looked for your father, though it is four years since his passing.

Had I told you? I am sorry. He was not a kind man.

Your brother rules well. He cares for the irises. Were he not forbidden, I think he would ask about you, the way he did as a child. He has his own son now. I forget the boy's age.

Do you have children? Are you well?

Perhaps you are gone already, and I am a selfish mother for hoping my Cypress will greet me when I pass. I am told not to use names in a letter which might be intercepted by fairies. Was my son not already intercepted by fairies? At death's door, as I am, superstition seems foolish to me now.

Cypress, my love,

The letter ended abruptly, without signature or even a conclusion to her final sentence. Perhaps she'd tucked it in the journal to finish later. Later obviously never came. Dust read the message six times. Then he flipped through the journal, lingering on pages, his fingers trembling. In the end, he set both letter and journal on his workbench.

He retrieved his chisel, turning it in his hand the way he turned his mother's words in his mind. Two hundred years. His mother, brother, father, all dead. Two hundred years.

Two hundred years.

Dust placed his chisel carefully, beveled edge vertical to the wood. With precise, steady mallet strikes, he drove the chisel into the center of the galley ship he'd been carving, *tap* by steady *tap*, until it reached the handle and could go no further, fully embedded in the heart of his work. Perhaps he'd driven it all the way into his workbench beneath.

Then he left it behind.

He climbed out window number two. The curse took hold as strongly as ever on his climbing—tethering him to solidity when what he wanted was to fall—until he reached the tower roof, and the world shifted.

He did not sit for long, only long enough to call out for Astra to return to the woodshop.

He could not stomach the view of a green sky.

Again, Dust carved. His single answer to everything. He sat on the staircase, a four-inch block of wood in one hand and his oldest knife in the other—the knife he'd received as his very first harvest from Doll. It felt too small for his hands. After two hundred years, it only made sense he'd outgrown some things.

"I'll trade Smicker for your way out," he said, "but it'll

have to wait a few hours. Traders won't fly at night, you remember."

"It's night?" Astra said with some wonder.

He smiled.

She'd said she couldn't find his birth name, which meant she hadn't read the letter. She'd carried it all the way into another realm for him, protected it from Ashpoint and Doll both, and she'd never read it. He almost thanked her for that, but it would have meant talking about the letter, so he said nothing.

Cypress. His mother had named him after a tree. No wonder she'd never used the name.

Astra's shadow wandered aimlessly in the room. She'd stopped twice by his workbench, then moved on.

"We found the knight as well," she said. "Record of his lineage, anyway. Sir Reynard. He was your mother's cousin."

Dust snorted. *Reynard,* like the fox. Through a mirror, he played fox in the human world, after one had failed to rescue him from the fairy realm. Life really was laughing at him.

"It would help to talk," Astra said.

Tilting the block in his hand, Dust blew a woodchip off his thumb. It added to the carpeting across his floor.

"Nothing's changed," he said.

"There's a cruelly impaled carving on your workbench that says otherwise. I quite liked that ship."

"I'm sure I'll make another one." What else was there to do in an empty millennium? He was already two hundred years old. Might as well go the next eight hundred to see if he collapsed the tower under the weight of carvings.

Astra's shadow did another circuit of the room. She always came back to the fox shelf.

She said, "We just have to make Kenric want to set things

right. If we could somehow organize a full-scale rebellion, a revolt in the city—"

"I don't want that." Dust pressed his knife deeply into the block's side, severing the grain. A second, angled cut removed the entire triangular chunk with a *snap*.

"Well, why not?" Astra demanded. Her shadow had grown easier to read; she had her hands on her hips.

"Because Everspring's still my home, so I don't want violence in the streets. Because it's hard enough returnin' one human at a time, so I can't risk a whole parade out there in the fairy wilds. Because it wouldn't break the curse, 'n because I don't want to break it, besides. I could go on."

"What do you mean you don't want to break it?"

"I'm sure you heard me clear enough."

"What do you *mean,* Dust?"

By accident, he made a cut against the grain; it split. Dust took a moment of disappointment, then flicked away the chip and resigned himself to carving a woodmunch with one stunted leg.

"I mean leave it here, Astra. My family's gone, so there's no point to going back. Besides that, my payment gives the whole kingdom peace. It's a fair trade. It's worked for two hundred years."

"No, it hasn't! People dread seeing their king in the streets. They fall over themselves to keep him happy, to pretend whatever they have to pretend in order to minimize the damage of his displeasure."

Dust made his refining cuts with hardly a thought, guided by instinct. "Sounds like any monarch to me. But what an ordinary monarch *can't* do is keep a hostile foreign ambassador in the city a few days, then order him, *You will not attack this kingdom,* 'n have things settled just like that. Every curse has its upsides. The upside here is two centuries without war."

He took a deep breath, glancing up at his circular walls and the shelves that lined them. Three windows, four floors. "Truthfully, this isn't a curse at all. Just a circumstance. People live in difficult circumstances all the time. If I were any kind of crown prince, I'd have realized years ago that if one life in a tower can buy a thousand years of peace for a kingdom, it's not just an easy trade—it's a duty. A privilege, even."

For a moment, the only sound was the scraping of his blade as he worked.

"*Privilege?*" Astra scoffed. "The privilege would be a kingdom that gets to know you. Everspring has no idea what it lost."

His heart twisted, and he nearly cut his thumb. But he shook it off and kept carving.

Astra was not finished. "It's lucky for you I have a great deal of practice hearing absurd philosophies, thanks to my sister. Peace for two centuries, perhaps, but the kings of those centuries have been drunk on their own greatness, on a lie King Firmin established as truth. He preached it so much, they started a *religion*. How long before someone whispers in a king's ear that he ought to share Everspring's greatness with the world? How long until the king conceives the idea himself? Maybe Kenric is satisfied to waste his power collecting baubles and scaring off the occasional foreign dignitary, but will his son be? This kingdom *will* go to war because, as I understand it, war is the way of the world. If we don't repel it, we'll begin it. It's a matter of time, Dust.

"So the question becomes: When your home does go to war, do you want it to go with an unchallengeable tyrant at its head, one who sacrifices his own people without a second thought, or do you want a king who's had to struggle and compromise, who suffers consequences for his actions—a *real* king?"

"All right," Dust said softly, his hands slowing, "I understand."

"I could go on," she said.

He gave a dry laugh. "*I understand.*"

Her shadow stepped directly up to the wall. After a moment's hesitation, Dust set his carving aside, then went to stand before her, watching the dark outline and imagining he could meet her eyes.

"It is a curse," she said, so full of that Astra-certainty. "Breaking it matters. *You* matter. I don't care what king or fairy says this is a fair trade; it isn't. Because you're a person, not a coin, not a creation. People were never meant to be traded. Not for any price."

Dust pressed his hand to the wall. He lifted his fingers slightly and curled them, but before he could knock, Astra did it first. Three slow times. He savored each vibration against his skin.

Then she kept her hand in place, a shadow through a murky wall. He covered it with his, pretending he could feel the warmth, the touch. As his eyes stung, he slid them closed and let his forehead rest against the wood.

"I just wanted to go home," he whispered.

"I know," she whispered back.

Perhaps they stood for another hundred years. Astra never dropped her hand, never so much as rustled her skirt while shifting positions. Dust refused to pull away long after his back had taken up an ache. Just as he pretended he could feel her warmth, he pretended the moment could last an eternity.

But eventually, he had to move, and then it was only a matter of direction.

So he decided to move forward.

Dust cleared his throat, blinking hard. His voice still carried a touch of hoarseness. "A hard woman to argue with, you are. Has anyone told you?"

Astra shifted at last, her shadow thinning as she lowered her hand.

"My siblings," she said. "Daily."

"What's your family like?"

"Infuriating." She sighed. "And better than I."

"Can't imagine that."

She mistook his meaning. "The infuriation is my failing, not theirs. I'm afraid I am full of such failings."

"I'm no perfect prince myself." Dust winced as he said it. "In fact, I . . . owe you apology for several lies."

To his surprise, she gave a breathy laugh. "If you're referring to the story about your own family, you owe me nothing. I had my suspicions from the start; desperation makes for a transparent bargainer. And I understand the reasons."

"Lied about a few other things . . ." He swallowed. "I tried to manipulate you, 'n I've never wanted to be king."

"If I could make a confession of my own, wood fairy, we are both guilty of the first, and concerning the second, I'm not sure royalty is all it's proclaimed to be. I did have the chance to become queen just this morning and made a rather dramatic exit."

Before Dust's smile could get away from him, he said,

"Cypress. That's my birth name. You're welcome to read the letter; there's a reason I left it on that side of the room."

"Cypress." She paused. "Do you like it?"

"About as much as I enjoy a shamrock sky."

She laughed in earnest. There was so much character in her laugh—a little snort and very little restraint.

"It's a fine enough name, I suppose," Dust admitted. "It just doesn't feel like mine. I fear I'll remain Dust forever."

Because an entire lifetime could not be forgotten so easily, and though he ached for what might have been, it was not the path his life had taken. If he was being honest with himself, perhaps he'd forgotten his name on purpose all those years ago; perhaps he'd known, even then, that Cypress was gone. Turned to Dust.

Astra said, "Keep it, then. It's no stranger than my sister's name. And besides, I've grown accustomed to Dust."

Hearing her say as much shot a thrill up his spine. The ache of everything lost sat heavily on his bones, but even so, he began to feel there was something to say for what he'd gained.

CHAPTER 40

ASTRA

We spent the night in conversation until Dust said something about morning, and I realized I had to get things moving, else I'd stay in comfortable conversation forever. I asked him to call for Smicker but said I'd handle the trade.

"I have a plan," I said. "For the Peace Tree."

Given, it wasn't a very *good* plan, so I didn't outline the details. There was not much elegance in saying, *I'm going to grab hold of a tree and desperately hope it dies before I do.*

Instead, I said, "It's certain to work."

During our conversation, Dust had stretched out along the bottom of the wall, and his shadow looked more relaxed than mine, due to the fact that even in reclining, I had to be beautiful. Once I'd found a squat turtle carving to prop my head, that helped, though a wooden pillow certainly left an ache.

What made the position worth it was my view of the ceiling. In my first visit, I'd not noticed how the tower itself had been carved, every inch. Spirals and birds decorated the ceiling, circling in dizzying patterns. Although mostly hidden by sawdust, the floor carried swooping patterns of its own, and I enjoyed tracing the grooves with my fingertips.

"While I love your confidence," Dust said, "I don't love the idea of having you leave."

A little shiver climbed my back at how easily he said the word *love*. I adjusted my head on the turtle, resisting a smile.

"You'd rather I moved in here, then? You'd never have your workbench back."

"Built that one. I can build another."

He drummed his fingers on the wall, as he'd done a few times through the night. I let the back of my hand rest against the wood, feeling the vibration and watching his movement send out ripples.

"It's a full tower, you know," Dust added. "Three windows, four floors. Whenever you need a change of scenery, I'd be more'n happy to hop on the roof."

I nodded. "By all definitions, it *is* living in a castle, which was always a childhood dream. And I've no doubt whatever I might need in life, you have tucked away in some corner of that storage room."

"Plus you'd teach me to sew. I'd teach you to carve."

"Oh, I would, would I?" I raised an eyebrow, smile growing.

"I'm in desperate need. If you could see the holes in this shirt."

He chuckled to himself, and a sudden pinch caught my heart. I turned toward the wall.

"All this time as a prisoner," I said softly, "and you manage to laugh. Even after the news last night. How?"

That low chuckle was now my favorite sound, one that tickled my spine and made me ponder ways I might draw it out more often.

"Suppose it would make more sense to be miserable," he said. "As a boy, I cried plenty. Then I realized misery's no way to really live. So I learned to make do."

"You make it sound as if it's a choice. As if it's *easy*."

"I don't know about easy, Astra, but I do think there's choice in it. I've had to direct my own life at every turn; there's no one else to do it. Maybe misery's the safety of people with family."

Or maybe misery was the wedge that drove families apart. After Father's bankruptcy, my siblings and I had all been miserable at first, but then Beauty found her castle, Rob found his apprenticeship, and Callista found her fiancé. While my family had adjusted to life's hurricanes, I alone had kept drowning, and I'd thought it made them uncompassionate people, the way they'd left me behind. Maybe they'd waited for me as long as they could.

One of the last times we'd seen each other, Beauty had asked me if I was happy. I'd told her no one in my circumstances could be. It felt shameful now, to think any of *my* circumstances—with home and family and love—were worse than the ones belonging to the man on the other side of the wall.

Did the world truly bend to beauty, or did it simply bend to those who dusted themselves off after disaster and resumed walking? Perhaps that was a type of beauty I'd never considered.

"I don't care what you look like."

I'd said it too abruptly; it sounded unfeeling. I winced. "What I mean is I've always cared what men—what *people* look like. What *I* look like, even. Cared far too much. So I'm only saying . . . I like you as you are, Dust. Without caring what you look like."

Had I been lacking enchantment, my face would have stained like a tomato. I covered it with both hands, tilting away from the wall even though I couldn't be seen.

Dust chuckled. I'd always hated feeling laughed at, but he didn't make it sound mocking. It sounded more like I made him happy. How that could be true was unimaginable.

Then he said, "I like you too, Astra."

His heavy tone seemed to carry twice the words actually said, and in that moment, everything inside me buckled under a sudden pang of longing. I wanted him to *see* me. The real me. Without enchantments.

But I did not know how to find my way back to that girl; I knew only how I might save a lost prince in a tower. And he'd waited long enough.

"I think it's time we call for Smicker," I said.

The massive eye filling the window was worse than I remembered, and Smicker clearly remembered me as well.

"WICKED." He snorted, quaking the tower. "MONSTER."

"I'm deeply sorry for my insult," I said. Only after Dust gave his support to the sentiment did the dragon's purple eye squint in what seemed to be consideration.

Per my request, Dust had allowed me to be the one to trade. Hopefully we would not regret that.

"I have a creation." With trembling hands, I showed Smicker the blue embroidery along one edge of my overdress. I'd had to clean it of ash and sawdust before he arrived, and despite my best efforts, a few pesky splinters still clung in places.

Even so, the dragon's pupil dilated at once, widening from a slit to a wide oval, and I did not have to be overly familiar with the creatures to know he was a Trader at market who'd just found a priceless ware. It brought my confidence surging back.

"TRADE!"

I bit my lip and tilted my head toward the wall, nearly bragging to Dust that a *dragon* liked my embroidery. If only petty Mrs. Heartshire could witness—though she'd likely die of a heart attack at Smicker's mere appearance.

You have only one chance, I reminded myself. Since it would not do to reveal my own excitement, I reserved both my smile and my bragging.

"It comes at a high price," I said.

Smicker withdrew at that, his eye narrowing as it edged away from the window. A ridge of black spikes lined his brow, each one capable of impaling me like a knife. But I did not intend to insult him again, only to drive a hard bargain, so I held my ground against the Trader. And I began my pitch.

"This is the most important piece of embroidery I've ever sewn. It was made in a time of desperation, stitched with thoughts of my mother and all my longing to hear the advice she can no longer tell me. It was stitched with regret, because I seem to have ruined my own life at every opportunity, but also with relentless hope and a stubbornness to continue forward, because I am nothing if not stubborn. It is the capturing of imagined beauty, and it is the capturing of silent rebellion, sewn in a single color because I did not have multiple, because the waves of life had driven me under, and I'd lost all I had."

My breath caught, and I had to swallow before adding, "Sewn in a single color because this thread was the kindness given me by the best man I've ever known, given without hesitation or second thought, just as he gives every sacrifice. Smicker, I daresay, this embroidery is no longer thread at all. It is every moment that led me to lifting my needle and every event which came as a result. The converging of the path. A tapestry woven with the essence of an entire life. It is the symbol of all I've done and become. The perfect representation of *Astra*."

The Trader's eye pressed tightly to the window once more, practically bulging. With every word, I found myself drawn in just the same, more attached to my own stitches, clutching my dress with white-knuckled fingers. After vowing to never again part with my work, I was about to sacrifice the most important composition I'd ever made.

And ironically, that was not at all what I'd thought of it at first. Between the clashing colors and my own distracted mind as I'd waited to wed a king, I'd thought it my *worst* embroidery for a time. Now I knew.

There was power in what I'd done. It would tear my heart to release it.

But what it would purchase was worth any sacrifice.

Lifting my chin, I said with finality, "Trader, I am not offering you mere embroidery. I offer you a *creation*."

The dragon whined, a high-pitched sound too pitiful for a full-grown mountain. I had him. When I told Smicker I wanted two things in trade, he urged me at once to speak.

"First, a return to Everspring."

"AGREEABLE," rumbled the Trader.

"Second, a standing trade agreement for Dust. Whatever he next needs, you provide. No questions asked, no further bartering."

Behind the wall, a shadow moved, as if startled. "What?" said Dust.

"TRADE ACCEPTED."

Abruptly, the eye vanished from the window, followed by a streak of purple that might have been a wing. When I peeked out, I saw the dragon waiting patiently, sitting on a bed of yellowed grass and hopping black locusts, seemingly unbothered by the tiny insects. From his posture, it seemed I would have to be the first one to deliver on our trade.

Though I'd not seen it in our first encounter, there was certainly a majesty to the violet dragon, with his armored underbelly flexing as he breathed, his posture as rigid as magic kept mine. Perhaps someday I would embroider the swirled pattern of his wings.

For the moment, I took a knife from Dust's workbench, and I carefully cut away the long, wide strip of dress I'd embroidered. I held it gently, brushing my thumb across twisting stems and raised forget-me-nots.

Then I took it to the window.

The dragon perked up, lifting slightly on his hind legs. With no other option, I dropped the embroidery, sending it fluttering through the air, and in one swift movement, Smicker's monstrous jaws opened and snapped shut again, swallowing the fabric. It was a miracle he didn't take a large chunk of the tower along with it.

My jaw dropped in shock. "He ate it!"

From behind the wall, Dust laughed.

"TRADE COMPLETE," thundered Smicker, rising to all four feet, tail whipping into the misty green air.

He vanished, leaving a large purple blot in my vision when I blinked. A tiny violet dragonfly buzzed up to the window, a woven basket dangling between its spindly legs. While I was still trying to catch my bearings, the basket opened, dropping a pottery fragment on the window ledge. Then the dragonfly zipped away.

I'd not realized how much I was shaking until that moment. Feeling behind me as I went, I backed myself into safety on the stool.

"That trade," said Dust after a moment, "put to shame every trade in realm history."

Though I rolled my eyes, I also felt a flush of warmth. "You exaggerate."

"I'm not all-knowing, I suppose, but it put to shame any of my trades, that's certain. From now on, I'll have you as my royal negotiator, thanks."

I shook my head, glancing at the pottery fragment on the window ledge as it innocuously waited to whisk me back to the human realm. A small, selfish part of me hoped it might tumble off and disappear.

"Why trade for me?" Dust asked. His voice was suddenly guarded, as if I'd offended him, or was about to. Perhaps he was waiting to hear what I expected in return.

I meant to say things about Doll and her garden, about how I feared for his safety. What I found myself saying was, "You've always had to do it yourself, and you've helped so many people. If I could ever help you, in even the smallest way, I think it would be the best thing I've done in my life."

My cheeks burned again. I stood abruptly.

Then, realizing this might be my final opportunity to take it in, I cast my eyes around the woodshop, appreciating the creatures of two realms sharing one home, the creations of an incredible man who found joy in the dimmest circumstances. Though every piece was remarkable, I had to admit my partiality to his foxes. Something about the squinty eyes and mischievous smile. I felt I didn't need to see Dust to know him; I'd seen his foxes.

"Can I have a new fox cub?" My voice cracked. I cleared my throat. "I was quite fond of the one I lost."

"You can have any carving you like," said Dust.

Just as I tucked one into my pocket, he spoke again.

"Thank you." He'd come right up to the wall. I thought I could make out the curve of his arm as he perhaps leaned on it. "For all of it, Astra. All of it."

More than anything, I wanted to tear down that wall.

And I would.

"For you," I said, "anything in the world."

As much as it hurt to leave him, I turned away, and I grasped the pottery fragment.

Dumped in the lake again. I surfaced, treading water gracefully now, my unaffected hair floating all around me. The sky was black above and the water black below, but a light on the dock gave me my bearings.

With difficulty, I dragged myself to the woman holding the candle, and she did not seem surprised so much as wearied.

"It's you."

"It's me." I laughed as she helped me out. Then I wrung my dress in the places I could and swiped water from my face. "I don't suppose you've seen my sister? We look nothing alike, but she may have mentioned Astra."

As it turned out, Beauty had also refused a smuggling out of the city. She and Andre had instead taken up residence at a local inn, courtesy of Bastien.

"That boy asks after you daily," the woman said.

No surprise from the considerate knight. "What's your name, madam? I'm embarrassed to say in all our meetings, I've yet to ask it."

Hanna Everly, she told me. I thanked her for helping the Everspring outcasts because I thought if Dust were present, he would have offered such gratitude. And they were truly diligent to keep watch even through the night.

"How long since my failed wedding?" I asked.

"Four days. The festival still runs under the matron queen's command, but no one's seen the king since the . . . er, ceremony."

I couldn't help a smirk at that. Whether he was cowering beneath a bed or setting fires in the dining hall, I did not care.

Reparation, Doll had told me. Surely Kenric possessed the means to pay back all his frivolous shopping, but he'd inherited the crown he wore, and I felt a dread certainty that it came with a weighty debt piled across two centuries.

Before ending the Peace Tree, and in case my attempt ended poorly, I'd resolved to do two things. The first had been accomplished in telling Dust the truth of his family. The second was to apologize to my own family. Yet even knowing where Beauty was at this very moment, I felt myself rooted in place.

If I could not even repay the debts of two decades of

selfishness, how could anyone repay the debts of ten times that?

So my foolish plan was truly the only hope.

"Have you a place to spend what's left of the night, milady?" Mrs. Everly asked, gesturing with her flickering candle toward her own home.

I smiled at the offer. "Just Astra, please. If there's a meal included as well, I can promise the best sewing hand in the kingdom applied to your mending."

It was not the shrewdest trade I'd made that day, but it felt fair nonetheless.

CHAPTER 41

ASTRA

IRONICALLY, BEAUTY AND ANDRE had taken lodgings at the same inn I'd previously used. Mrs. Everly had given clear directions, and I found the building with ease, though it was not as easy to enter. I found myself pacing in a circle which took me onto a neighboring street, then back to the inn, then away again.

This was ridiculous. If I did not have the spine to enter, better to make for the Peace Tree and be done with it. The longer I lingered in the city, drawing stares and whispers, the sooner Kenric would hear of my return.

Just as I made such a determination, I caught sight of Bastien, hurrying down the street. I did not follow fast enough, and he ducked into the inn before I could reach him.

Rather than continue my pacing, I lurked at the building's side window.

Andre and Beauty met the knight in the inn's main room, all of them within clear view of my hiding place. The brothers embraced, and Bastien laughed about something. He mussed Andre's hair, the action requiring him to reach up, since his little brother was nearly a head taller than he was. While Beauty spoke, Andre stood taller still, at least until she gave him a little jab in the side to deflate.

I had been caught in a spider's web, unable to enter, unable to leave. I only watched.

After a few minutes of friendly conversation, the three of them took seats at a table, Beauty and Andre together on one side while Bastien sat across. The table's surface already held scattered sheets of parchment, which Beauty made half an effort to gather with one hand while her other reached for a quill. Andre slid the inkwell closer. Then Beauty set her quill to writing while the brothers spoke.

I turned away from the window only to find a woman staring at me from the mouth of the alley I occupied. Having been discovered, she quickly scurried off.

Within my pocket, something pawed at my hip.

I freed the fox and set him gently on the window ledge, raising an eyebrow rather than showing the smile I might have. Dust had no such emotional restraint, openly grinning at me, tail swishing behind him. It *was* better for a fox to have a tail.

"You have morningdew," I said. My stomach tightened, and questions about Doll pressed on my throat. Who was I to give Dust advice regarding the fairy who held him captive? I understood only the barest threads of the situation.

He pressed his paws to the window, squinting in. "Is that Bastien, there? You're not with him?"

The morningdew was surely a tense topic; Dust never ignored me. And I of all people understood how complicated a relationship could be.

"That's my sister," I said, nodding to Beauty.

As Beauty spoke, she gestured with the quill in her

hand, flinging tiny droplets of ink across the rest of her writing. Her eyes were up, no doubt imagining something no one else could see, translating it in her grand, sweeping gestures. Sitting beside her, Andre listened with a faint, crooked smile, until he finally caught her hand and kissed it.

My ache grew sharper.

"We never finished our game." I pulled a single black pepper from my pocket, turning it slowly between pointer finger and thumb. "If I understand the rules, these must be the two most difficult questions to answer honestly."

The fox carving watched me, silent.

Perhaps I overstepped. Perhaps both of us were better off not confronting certain things.

Then Dust said, "Why can't you face your sister, Astra?"

I took a deep breath.

"Before I left home," I said quietly, "Father reprimanded me. Beauty had the attention of a man I desired, and my jealousy drove ill-considered actions. Father tried to turn me from my path. He claimed I did not know the entire story."

There was no honey to soften this truth, no fairy magic that could twist my insides worse than the guilt of it.

"He claimed Stephan forced my sister. But I knew Father's information would have come from Beauty, so I dismissed it."

Beauty told stories. She made every moment a drama. If she did not want to marry Stephan, it would not be a matter of simple choice or preference. She would make it an imposing reason, make it unfathomable to disagree with her.

"I knew it had to be a lie," I said. "My sister lies."

Everyone lies. Dust and I had done it to each other. Manipulation and veiled intentions and half-truths—these were the tools of society, the interactions we all employed to protect ourselves.

The itch beneath my skin increased. My hair irritated my neck. Still clutching the pepper, I used my other fingers to twist my hair, feeling the pressure of roots pulling scalp, the intertwined attempting to separate.

How often had I lied to myself? Pretending I was justified in all matters while closing my eyes to the evidences around me. I treated concerns as sand on a beach, with a clear line of distinction between truth and error that was as easy to see as the line of tide-soaked sand meeting dry. But these issues were more like the tangled knots of embroidery, all one color, all one image, separated only by a shape that had to be seen and felt.

As children, Callista and I had often imagined ourselves at a court tournament, choosing knights to be our champions. We'd borrowed Mother's handkerchiefs from her wardrobe, stood upon chairs, and tossed them as *tokens of favor* to the gallant knights waiting below.

Then we'd grown. Callista had decided she had no love for tournaments, and I'd declared real social events more exciting than invented contests. By the time Beauty had aged enough to join our games, we had left them behind, and I remembered seeing her once, standing on a chair with one of Mother's handkerchiefs, blowing a kiss to an imagined knight below. All alone.

My sister grew in our shadows, and she found ways to entertain herself. She found stories.

I remembered Beauty waving an imaginary sword beneath our apple tree. I remembered her battle cry—*Taste the wrath of Ruiner!*—followed by her exaggerated death rattle, since she played the part of both hero and dragon. When Mother forced me to instruct Beauty in needlework, my sister turned the needles into tiny swords and tried to stage a battle, only giggling at my irritation.

Beauty cared for swords and heroic quests. She wanted battles and glory and every whimsical nonsense. They made her happy. Just because I thought it childish, just because my happiness was found in other places, what right did I have to dismiss my sister?

Everyone lied. But everyone told the truth as well. We were, all of us, a tangle of deception and honesty, simply trying to understand and be understood.

Suppose Father finds a white-sand shore. I remembered the Beauty of ten years ago, standing atop a boulder on the beach, stretching her fingers toward the horizon. *Suppose the fountain of youth truly exists, and it's guarded by a dragon, and every story is real. Can you imagine?*

Can you imagine, Astra?

"Dust," I whispered, my heart breaking. "I fear this story was real."

We stood in silence while I struggled against tears I could not express. In the end, I ate the black fairy pepper, and it burst in sweet juice across my tongue, the confirmation of all my fears.

"It's your question," Dust said quietly.

I rubbed my eyes, though they remained dry. "I don't want to hurt you."

"What hurts," he said, "is the truth existing. Not the admitting of it. At least not to you."

Nodding, I folded my arms, still watching my sister and her companions through the shaded inn window. It took me a minute to speak.

"Do you know why Doll uses your hair?"

The fox sat still as a carving. I worried he was gone, but if so, it would be his right.

"I know," he said at last, pointed ears twitching. "I know just about all of it. Planters 'n their gardens—she can't help but brag." After a pause, he said, "Whenever I make her unhappy, tower life gets . . . difficult."

It was a useless gesture, but I scooped him off the window ledge and held him to my heart. The fox curled in my hand, looking up at me with painted eyes that seemed to betray real pain.

"A coward 'n a liar," he said. "That's me."

"No," I said sternly. "You've been surviving, and you made do with what you had. I just hope . . ."

What promises dared I make? Every time I'd gone against the tree so far, I'd failed.

But even so.

"I hope you know you have better now. At the very least, when you call someone 'friend,' they should be worth it."

"You are, that's certain." The fox's mouth curled up in a smile, eyes squinting. "From one friend to another, your sister's right there, 'n she may be a wee bit scarier than Smicker, but I have faith in my royal negotiator."

I raised an eyebrow at him, and he flicked his tail, then settled.

"Might be selfishness speaking," he said, "but my

brother's gone. Don't let her go. I know reparation's pain, just like truth, but it's better than the alternative."

My heart began to pound at his word choice, at the idea it sparked in my mind.

A little stunned, I asked, "What did you say? Reparation?"

"I mean if you did wrong, you can make it right. It's not—"

"Reparation," I repeated breathlessly. Leaning in, I peered through the window, something taking root inside.

If I drew in magic, perhaps I could also draw in a curse. If that curse could be passed by inheritance from one king to another, perhaps it could be *stolen* by me. And if I could make my own reparation while holding it, perhaps I could end things once and for all.

"Dust, I—!"

I looked down, but the fox had gone still. Fearing for us both, I cradled it in my hands one moment longer, then slipped it into my pocket.

And before I could run from the fear, I charged into the inn.

CHAPTER 42

DUST

DUST'S MIRROR RIPPLED, the colors fading. Always too soon.

Astra's appearance had changed—the near-glow of her skin increased, the shimmer of her hair a little brighter beneath the sun. Subtle changes, like the hue of the fairy realm's sky shifting from day to night. Perhaps someone else would not have noticed, but he noticed. And he feared.

She said she had a plan for the Peace Tree. After he'd told her to leave the curse be, she fought against it more strongly than ever.

Meanwhile, he'd promised Doll not to try to escape. When the Planter had come by to bring morningdew, her sour expression a clear sign that she simmered about something, Dust had done what he'd always done—he'd soothed her. He'd put on a smile and made small talk. All out of fear that he might lose his only connection to the human world.

Coward, he thought.

No, said Astra's voice, echoing in his head.

He sighed, running one hand through his hair. Then he stood.

Just as he entered his woodshop, a familiar scratching came at the window, and Bumble heaved her thick body over the stone ledge, tumbling into the tower. She snuffled against the floor, then looked up at him with a satisfied gleam in her black eyes.

"Aye, Bumble"—he smiled—"there's enough for a snack."

Herding a woodmunch gave him opportunity to think, and by the time Bumble had licked the last bit of sawdust from between the floorboards, Dust had made the most frightening decision of his life.

"Here." He crouched beside the woodmunch and offered her the ruined ship carving, having already removed the chisel. While she splintered the waves and gnawed on the galley, he stroked her head. Her dark fur was soft, if a little grubby, but he'd be a hypocrite to cringe at dust.

"You've always been a good friend, Bumble," he murmured. "Some others . . ."

The woodmunch bobbed her head, as if in support. Dust smiled.

After Bumble finished snacking and began her slow climb back down the tower, Dust signaled Smicker. He waited for the Trader on his upper balcony, tossing down three dried toothwort leaves from Renny's garden, watching them flutter and spin in the air. Thanks to Doll's gift, he had a bottle on hand, and even the smallest amount of toothwort leaf would poison the inkers ingesting it. Their cannibalistic nature would take care of the rest. His infestation should be clear by the next quarter-moon. Toothwort would poison the grass, too, but crettle grass was sturdy, and without the inkers, it would grow back.

He held a leaf between finger and thumb, studying the dried veins and cracked edges, the spiny points that separated toothwort from its non-poisonous cousins. The irony was not lost on him—Doll's gift was poison.

He flicked the leaf. It tumbled to the grass below.

Dust missed the arrival of the little dragonfly, but there was no mistaking the moment of transformation. Smicker settled onto his hindquarters, violet tail wrapping around the base of the tower. He flexed the spines of his back and brought his head in close enough that Dust could have leapt the distance from the balcony to the dragon's snout—if he weren't tethered by a curse.

"SO SOON?" Smicker asked, as if he knew exactly the direction of Dust's mind.

Dust shrugged. "A lady made a bargain on my behalf. I'd hate to waste it."

While Doll's gift was poison, Astra's might save him. If he let it. If he trusted.

"Had a recent conversation about linking spells," Dust said. "Thought we might revisit that."

It was a high demand, and Dust could not have paid it on his own, not with all his recent trades. Rebuilding creation stock was tricky business, since he could never tell until a carving was finished how much of his heart would be in it. Perhaps he would have been waiting years to make something Smicker found worth the price.

The Trader turned his head to examine Dust up close from the other eye, exhaling a wave of hot air beneath the balcony as he passed.

"HIGH TRADE," he said, possibly with a meaning beyond actual trade price.

Dust nodded.

"CERTAIN?"

"Not fully," he admitted. He gave a shaky smile. "It'll change everything, Smicker. Everything. But I think I've cowered long enough."

The dragon snorted, the edges of his violet lips curling to reveal jagged white teeth. "GOOD. TRADE ACCEPTED."

When the dragonfly buzzed away, Dust held a small corked vial, the inner side of the glass reflecting a pink sheen, like the light of a human dawn.

Even having taken the first steps, Dust hesitated on the path. He might never see Astra again, might never see anything beyond four floors, three windows, two balconies. But his conversation with Astra lingered in his mind, a conversation about tyranny. No matter the benefits, no matter the dangers, it was not right.

You matter, Astra's voice whispered in his mind. *Because you're a person, not a coin, not a creation.*

At last, he curled his hand around the vial, and he went inside to summon Doll.

CHAPTER 43

ASTRA

As I ENTERED THE INN, Beauty saw me, gasping my name as she lurched from her chair, but Bastien was closer, and he caught me in a hug before he seemed to realize what he was doing.

"I was—we were worried," he said quickly, releasing me. He kept his gaze on the wall, and he moved his hands restlessly, as if he didn't know where to put them, before finally folding them across his chest.

Though he couldn't see it, I smirked. "At ease, Sir Bastien. I'm alive."

"We were making plans to break into the fairy realm. Sneak, I mean. If we could. Your sister has a theory about Sir Reynard's travels, but there wasn't much evidence to—"

"Bastien," said Andre quietly. He gave his older brother a look of significance before nodding toward Beauty.

"Right." Bastien pinked. "I should let you catch up." He took a step away, hesitated, then turned back. As he'd done once before, he went down on a knee, fist pressed to the center of his chest in salute, head bowed. "My lady, thank you for helping me find my brother."

As he stood, he grinned at Andre, and that smile lit the room. I couldn't help smiling in response, though it dimmed as I turned my attention to my sister.

Beauty had kept her eyes on me since I'd entered, uncertainty in her gaze.

"Can we go somewhere to talk?" I asked her. "It's important. It's a . . . quest."

My sister's eyes widened, and she glanced at Andre, perhaps waiting for him to pinch her awake. When he only gave a shallow nod, she gestured for me to lead the way, following me into the street.

Beauty maintained her silence all the way to the canal. When I climbed down the steep side and lowered myself into the water, she hung back.

"What you said of a quest—you're mocking me." She squinted. "Or you're a fairy disguised as my sister. The Astra I know would not even allow the tide to touch her shoes."

"The Beauty I know would not hesitate to chase that intrigue."

Without looking back, I pulled myself along the canal's edge, following it toward the castle wall and iron grate. I heard the little splash of water when Beauty decided to follow. Since we were not under cover of night, I glanced at the castle bridge downriver, but I could not see the guards, so I trusted they could not see us.

Beauty was shorter than me by several inches, so when I waded toward the grate with the water up against my tilted chin, I worried for her. But I'd forgotten that, unlike me, my sister had always been a confident swimmer, and before I reached the grate, Beauty touched it, righting herself in the river and smiling back at me with water streaming down her face and hair. She swiped it out of her eyes, then ducked through the iron bars.

"Infiltrating a castle," she said. "The evidence for 'fairy replacement' grows by the moment."

She reached the bank before I'd even passed through the bars. While she wrung out her dress and hair, I made my way carefully to shore, holding back an irrational tension. Then I worked at my own dress, my hair needing no attention, the wet fabric itchy against my skin. The more often I was drenched, the more I remembered my aversion to water existed for many a good reason.

We tiptoed through the lower courtyard. All it would take was one shepherd boy to sound the alarm, but the closest one dozed outside his sheep pen with a straw hat over his eyes, and we continued into the upper courtyard without challenge.

"Where are we going?" Beauty whispered, sidling up to me as we crept past the stable wall.

"*Shh,*" I hissed back, ducking as I thought a stable hand had begun to turn.

This was an impossible task. Even with the opportunity to practice my words in silence, I found they all deserted me. Getting to the tree could only delay us so long. Once there, I would have to speak.

To prove my point, we rounded the edge of the courtyard, and the Peace Tree loomed ahead.

With exaggerated care, I picked my way over roots until I reached the shadow of the far side, closest to the castle wall, nearly secluded.

"I can only guess we've arrived," Beauty said at last, keeping her voice low. She eyed the tree, no doubt remembering the last time we'd been here. "Astra, what's going on?"

I had to try. Feeling foolish, I touched the fingertips of my left hand to the tree's bark and drew in a deep breath before saying, "Beauty, I'd like to . . . repair things."

Beauty eyed me, then eyed the low-hanging branches, heavy with sour-smelling fruit.

Before I'd left home, she'd apologized to me for unkind things she'd done and said while we were growing up. I'd thought she was lying, trying to appear humble to show she was the better person. Everything done to gloat over me.

Rather than assuming the worst of her motives, I could have apologized in turn. Perhaps it would have been easier in that moment, before I added more time and distance and grievances. The deep roots of the Peace Tree seemed to be my own, binding me down to years of built-up resentment and misunderstanding.

"Repair what?" she finally prodded.

"Us." The word came from between my teeth. I felt foolish and exposed, hiding in the king's own courtyard, awaiting discovery at any moment, petting a tree. "I'm sorry. *There*—I'm sorry."

I looked up, but the overhead branches did not so much as tremble.

Beauty sighed. "Well, that's . . . I can't say why I expected any different."

I scowled. "What does that mean?"

"What do you think it means, Astra? It's been months, you never wrote, you yelled at me to leave, and now you made up some kind of quest, which is clearly just a game to you. A game to mock me, as usual. *I'm* trying to mend things —and also trying to remember why I wanted to, since the last time I saw you, you tried to ruin things for me and my husband."

My heart chilled. "You married Stephan?"

"No!" The disgust on her face could not have been clearer if she'd eaten raw eel. "I married *Andre*. The same day Callista married Thomas. You missed the wedding."

Still smarting from my clear oversight, I said, "Well, it's not as if I received an invitation."

I was horrifically bad at this. It was a good thing no one's life hung in the balance, like, say, a lost prince in the fairy realm.

My fingers tingled against the bark.

"Why do we do this, Astra?" Beauty's voice broke. "Why do we treat each other like enemies? I just wanted to see you again."

Even now, she was apologizing, admitting responsibility, and I was fixed in place, as stubborn and unmoving as an overgrown, rotting tree.

I strained, willing the roots to break.

"Because I can't tell you there's something wrong with me," I managed, "so instead, I tell you there's something wrong with you."

Deep inside, my stomach churned like it would empty itself. I felt a flush even though it wouldn't show on my face. My palms grew clammy.

What *was* wrong with me?

"I don't know how to apologize!" I sank my fingers more deeply into the bark, feeling the prick of it. "I don't know how to apologize, because I'm still upset. It's terrible of me. It's petty and selfish, but it's the truth of my feelings. How are you . . ." I shook my head, feeling the pressure of tears I couldn't shed. "How are you so much *better* than me?"

Beauty stood before me with a patient, earnest expression. For my sake, she'd defied a king, endured a fairy realm—though it did not escape my notice that spending time in the fairy realm and meeting a dragon had not entered her list of complaints against me. She'd probably thrived in that terrifying realm. Ever the adventurer.

"I'm not better, Astra." Beauty lifted one shoulder, half a shrug. "I'm just different. We've always been so different, you and I, with our rough edges always clashing. There was a time I *did* enjoy mocking you, when I let Stephan bring out the worst in me, and there have been plenty of times your sharp words have made me bleed. But you're my sister."

Despite our turbulent history, she loved me.

I felt the same, but I could not speak it. Everything within her reflected as beauty while the same things within me made me shrivel. I may have been outwardly beautiful, but inside, I was as twisted and overripe as the tree shivering beneath my hand.

In truth, I was *ugly*, and that thought made me look down, unable to meet my sister's gaze.

Ugly.

Astra still does not know the weight in a word.

My eyes widened.

At the same moment, a shout went up in the courtyard.

CHAPTER 44

DUST

DUST CALLING FOR DOLL a second time clearly put her on edge. When she arrived, her wing feathers twitched violently after landing. She crouched on the corner of his workbench, eyeing the posts spread across the floor and Dust kneeling beside them. He'd decided to finish his balcony.

She huffed. "If you don't mind, I'm in the process of repairing a greenhouse. I *just* gave you morningdew. What more could you need?"

As if he were a bothersome pet. As if he were unreasonable for needing anything at all.

Dust expected to feel angry, but instead, he felt a strange calm inside—like when he sat down to begin a new carving with no evidence it would turn out except a clear vision in his head and a sharp knife in his hand.

He used that knife for a precise cut by saying, "Doll, I won't be harvesting from your garden anymore."

Even her twitching wings fell still. She watched him with unreadable eyes. "Whatever the Granter girl told you is a lie."

Dust smiled, raising his eyebrows. "There's some irony."

He stacked two completed posts together, then moved for the next block of wood, but Doll zipped down to stand on it, halting him.

"I have morningdew." She stretched her wings, yellow feathers splayed wide. "This very wood"—she stamped a foot on the block—"comes from my garden. Everything in this room came from my garden."

"Purchased fairly," Dust said. "Shaped by me. You're trying to create a debt, but there isn't any. I owe you nothing."

Her eyes narrowed. "When you were new to the realm, who pointed you toward carving? Who kept you company? I did, Dust. I always have."

"Who brought me to the realm? Who took me from my family?" Dust felt the stir of anger he'd missed before. He took a deep breath.

Then he stood, towering over the Planter, forcing Doll to look up. "You've always given me what I purchased, aye. In your own way, I think you even *have* been here for me through the years, 'n I'm grateful for the good, but it can't erase the bad. You take more than you give, Doll. It's the worst of fairy ways."

"I've kept you alive!" She darted into the air, hanging at eye level for a moment before dropping onto his workbench once more.

"For your own purposes, Doll! I'm nothing but a pet sheep, chosen for my wool 'n sometimes pampered before shearing."

As he said the words, he felt the humiliation of them, the burning deep inside. He drew the linking spell from his pocket, displaying the pink-tinted vial. Before she'd arrived, he'd cut a lock of his hair and sprinkled it in. Followed by a poisonous toothwort leaf from Renny's garden.

All that remained was to break the vial and link them.

"Dust . . ." Doll's wood-grain pattern vanished for a moment as she blanched solid brown. Her yellow feathers trembled.

Despite everything, it made him hesitate. The most foolish part of his mind thought if she gave an apology now, if she meant it, then . . .

Then what? That most foolish part of his mind wanted to continue enduring pain for the meager benefits because an unknown future without them was like stepping into the wilds. There might be an Ashpoint just ahead, waiting to burn him alive.

Against better judgment, he found himself saying, "Just kill the two seedlings, Doll."

Even if she didn't remove the Peace Tree, there would never be another like it. Could he be satisfied with that? If he used the linking spell, the poison would spread to her entire garden, drawn through the soil. Was he honestly trying to protect—himself and others—or was he only lashing out in revenge?

Doll burst into the air again. "You've no understanding of what I've accomplished! You should be *honored* to be the smallest part of it!"

He smiled sadly, realizing he may not know the dangers ahead, but he knew the ones at hand. For so long, he'd painted them with a nicer face than they truly carried.

You've been surviving, Astra had said, *and you made do with what you had.*

Funny how a single sentence from her gave him permission to admit things he'd never dared. To strip away the lies he'd painted on and see the carving beneath, the sharp cuts that were still bleeding, that would keep bleeding unless he did something to stop it.

"The *smallest* part?" he repeated hollowly. "Doll, what you've accomplished can't exist without me. You're the one who made that link, 'n I'm tired of abiding it. Tired of bowing to a tyrant."

"You ruin my garden"—Doll's eyes threatened hidden lava—"and I'll ruin you. I'll see to it no one deals with Dust again. No harvest from Planters, no barter with Traders. How will you *live*, human?"

That most foolish part of him cracked under threat, screamed at him to stand down, to offer platitudes, to let everything pass like water around a boulder, interrupted for only a moment before returning to the regular current. Doll would let him. It was what she wanted, no deviation from the current course.

But what Dust wanted was a new life, and he could not become new without risk.

Though his insides quaked, and his knees along with them, he gripped the vial.

"I wish we could have been real friends, Doll. I always wanted to. But as you say—you can't grow friendship. As for me, I can't grow a garden. Guess you used the wrong hair."

He shook the vial twice, stirring the pink inside to a light mist.

"You think the Granter girl will save you," Doll snapped. "She won't. She cares only for her own vanity."

Astra's voice echoed in his memory. *I like you as you are, Dust. You matter.*

Dust smiled at the Planter. "Now who's lying?"

He shattered the vial against the floor. The glass vanished, leaving a swirl of pink mist that turned green as it absorbed the hair clipping and poison together. Like a great sigh, it gathered and then dissipated. Linking spells were precise, so Dust had no fear of being poisoned himself, but any of his hair that had been cut free—no matter where it existed in the realm—would carry toothwort to whatever it touched. It would poison Doll's soil and kill every plant. Some might regrow, like the perennials in Renny's garden, but anything delicate, like Doll's prized saplings, had no chance.

The yellow-winged Planter sank to the workbench, staring at the floor where the spell had vanished. Her wings trembled, dropping a few feathers as her shoulders shook with grief, and despite himself, Dust felt a clenching guilt. It was not simple to stop caring, even knowing he cared for a venomous creature.

"I'm sorry," he said, and he hated that he said it. What he'd done was for himself and for Renny. For Astra, too, because weakening Doll would weaken the Peace Tree. It was right to do.

But right was not easy.

Doll looked up with hateful yellow eyes. "From the start, I've known your true name. Every human who knew is dead. Now you'll never know."

Spitting venom. It should have made him hate her in return, but all he felt was an ache.

"Cypress never suited me anyway," he said.

She reared back. "You've always known! And you accuse me of deception!"

"Not always. It was brought to me recently, by someone who cares."

That was enough to ease the ache. Whether Astra succeeded or failed, she fought for him, and she'd already given him more than anyone else in his life. If there were unknown dangers ahead, the fear abated to know Astra stood with him.

Having played her last spiteful card, Doll zipped out the window, vanishing in a green sky. No doubt there was retribution coming, but Smicker had proven himself an ally, and Dust dared to hope that with help from those he trusted, he might stand through the approaching storm.

Leaving the workshop, he stepped onto his lower balcony.

Though nothing visible had changed about his tower, the air tasted just a bit like freedom.

CHAPTER 45

ASTRA

WITH ONLY MINUTES until the guards arrived, I tried frantically to solve a riddle, my hand growing hot, prickling against the bark of a tree, the moist air heavy in my throat.

What is ugliness to Astra? my Granter had asked. *What is the wealth in it?*

"Father told me an infuriating story before I left home," I said, speaking with the distracted ramble of insanity. "A pearl diver who brought on his own foolish death. But why is it foolish? Why is it judged from the outside as *greed* or *pride* just because someone has the comfort to not be sinking? I'm sure he wanted to provide for his family. I'm sure he was afraid. He feared his rival would put him out of business, so he felt he had to compete. Why is that a cautionary tale?" I gave a dry, humorless laugh. "Isn't it just a tragedy?"

Beauty frowned. "Astra, you're pale. And did you . . . did you put real thought into analyzing a *story*?"

The Peace Tree's bark stung my hand like the jab of so many steel needles, but I did not remove my palm. I clawed my fingers into the ridges, and I allowed the fight to motivate me. For so much of my life, I'd deflected and hid. No more.

When the fairy had told me to seek ugliness, I'd thought of ugly appearances; my own wish had made me outwardly beautiful, after all. But it had done so because I had never been able to manage the ugliness inside. I'd wished to cover it. A beautiful tapestry thrown over a broken mirror.

I closed my eyes, struggling to breathe. I thought once more of my jealousy, burning like acid inside me, eating away at all my best parts until it threatened to leave only the ugly.

What is ugliness to Astra?

"Astra?" Beauty stepped forward to grab me as I sagged. Her outline seemed blurred in my vision, like a mirage in summer heat. "Astra, what's happening? You're *glowing*."

She tried to guide me away from the tree, but I grabbed a branch, clinging. Heavy fruit dropped from the branch to the ground, rolling and catching on roots. The shouting of guards drew closer.

This riddle was beyond me because I thought of everything too literally. Lines of division in the sand. *Astra does not know the weight in a word.*

"Beauty, I need your philosophy," I managed, grabbing her hand with my free one as I met her eyes. "What is ugliness?"

Her own eyes widened, staring in horror at whatever she saw in mine.

Horror. Ugliness was feared, despised, rejected. While beautiful things beckoned, ugliness repulsed. What repulsed me? What did I fear?

Well, that was a poor question. Oceans, monsters, insects, the list went on, and I struggled to think beyond the heat carried in my blood. My hand felt as it once had under the venom of a blaze spider, and I ached to let go, to find remedy.

If I let go, there would never be a remedy.

Above us, the Peace Tree shook, raining fruit. Beauty raised her free arm to shield her head, still holding tight to me with the other. I heard the panicked shouting of guards, the creaking of bark.

The pain in my hand increased, needles sinking down to pierce bone, the burning so cruel that I whimpered, expecting to smell my own flesh cooking. But through it, I held to the tree with stubbornness.

Unyielding stubbornness, one of my failings. Selfishness, insecurity. But if those were ugliness to me, my wish would have ended long ago. They were a comfort. What I clung to.

To me, in my foolishness, they'd been beauty.

Consideration was the ugliness, the thing I fled. A pure joy for other people with no comparison to myself.

If you regret, the fairy had told me, *seek completion.*

I'd been seeking it all this time.

It had begun with caring for Dust, seeing his best features beyond handsome appearance or wealth, beyond any benefit to me. It had continued with my realization about Beauty.

But it would not be finished until I could release my jealousy, until I could say that *any* advancement of my sister was beautiful, no matter how it left me behind. If she married before me, if she possessed a better mind, if she was kinder—these were not crimes against me. They were simply Beauty.

"Astra!" Beauty shrieked, pressing in close. A branch above us snapped, crashing down with only the castle wall to prevent it from striking us.

I stumbled under a wave of lightheadedness. My blood

pulsed with fever. But my fingers clamped around the tree with a fervor that would not release, not until one of us ended.

"I'm sorry, Beauty." My voice seemed too quiet for the storm of whipping leaves around us. "I'm sorry for ever hating you. For imagining your worst instead of seeing your best. For speaking cruelly of you. For leaving. For all of it."

And most of all—

Beauty looked at me with frightened brown eyes. For a moment, she might have been eight, and I might have been fifteen, both of us frozen on a beach in a moment of slipping.

"I'm sorry," I said, "for Stephan, and for choosing to hurt you when I could have helped."

Something cracked like thunder. It might have been my spine. As my left arm went numb from fingertips to shoulder, I flinched beneath a spear of pain through my entire skeleton.

When I opened my eyes again, they met the cold blue of a Granter's.

"Here is completion," she said, sparkling in my blurred vision. "Never again may you benefit from a wish."

She flicked her hand, and I felt the relaxation in my skin, the return to myself. Beside me, the Peace Tree had fallen still, sheared straight down the middle of its trunk as if struck by a bolt of lightning. The courtyard echoed with dazed voices from guards tangled in fallen branches, slipping on discarded fruit as they tried to stand.

The Granter tilted her head, a faint smile lifting one corner of her lips. "Astra has learned the weight in a word."

Astra had learned a lot more than that. My left arm was still numb, and my ears rang with more than the voices around me, but I blinked my vision clear. With my right hand, I touched my hair, feeling ragged texture rather than silkiness. The true evidence of change came in the form of tears dripping freely from my eyes.

"What was that?" Beauty whispered breathlessly.

I threw my arms around my sister, nearly toppling us both, and I sobbed in unabashed ugliness.

Around us, the Peace Tree withered and shrank. When I finally managed to see it through my tears, it was little more than a sprout in the ground before even that vanished, leaving barren earth marked by fallen leaves, like remnant tears of healing.

The guards may have arrested us if not for the lingering Granter. Thanks to her appearance, a crowd gathered, spreading the rumor from person to person—King Kenric must have angered the fairies, and in response, they'd taken back the Peace Tree.

Amidst the commotion, Beauty and I slipped beneath attention and made our way out of the courtyard through the mob of curious citizens pouring in to see the fairy for themselves. One unlucky soul would no doubt seize the opportunity for an ill-conceived wish. I wished them the wisdom I'd never possessed.

Halfway across the bridge, I began stumbling, and Beauty practically had to drag me to the end before we met Andre and Bastien on their way with the rest of the crowd. Bastien caught me as I collapsed, and I had only a moment of irritation realizing I'd not properly met my brother-in-law before Andre's face slid out of focus.

In one brief glimpse, beyond the castle wall, I saw a tower where a tree had once stood.

"Wait . . ." I rasped, reaching for it.

But the world was still sliding, and it dropped into darkness.

CHAPTER 46

DUST

AT FIRST, DUST THOUGHT the tremor was Smicker's arrival. He set aside a balcony post, already wondering if Smicker could barter with another Planter for morningdew or if there was perhaps a better solution to let him interact with the human realm.

Then the tremors doubled, bringing Dust back to his knees. Even the sturdiest carvings tumbled from their shelves. He threw one arm over his head just in time to avoid being knocked unconscious by a falling life-size owl, and he hissed at what would surely be a nasty bruise down his forearm.

The light of the sky extinguished, plunging him into darkness save for the glowing illimus bulbs, rolling across the floor.

At last, he remembered another earthquake, another darkness, and his heart leapt into his throat, strangling him with hope.

The quaking finally ended, though Dust's bones quivered still. The light returned, warm and yellow, streaming through windows one and two from a blue, blue sky.

Better than even the blue sky was the door. There was a *door* in his woodshop, sitting at the halfway point between windows, as quietly innocent as if it had always existed. After all the effort and the years imagining, it felt too simple a thing. Dust stared.

Then he scrambled to his feet, and he threw the door open.

Outside it, the castle was in chaos.

He couldn't stop grinning. Guards demanded his identity; the court was in uproar; the king himself came to see the newly returned tower, all while Dust grinned. A few times, he wiped tears from his eyes.

"King Firmin's son?" demanded the royal archivist. "Im—Impossible! Crispin of Montmor, His Royal Majesty, has been dead over a century!"

Dust showed the man a few of his mother's letters, and the archivist confirmed it to be Queen Emmeline's hand. As a result, half the castle was overturned in search of a history that didn't exist. King Firmin had left no record of his first son.

"An imposter!" cried some.

"But the tower!" argued others. "Returned as the tree was taken! And his eyes—the most startling green ever seen. Truly, he's lived in the realm."

Dust had not expected his first experience back in the human realm to be a trial over his very existence. He stood in the throne room among a court in session, growing weary listening to arguments, until he dared to say, "Does it really matter who I am?"

That set them all off again.

"Perhaps while the court discusses," said a new voice, "His Majesty might see to our guest's needs—shoes at least, I mean. Sorry, Dust."

The last thing he'd expected to hear was his name. Dust grinned at the approaching knight, dressed in a red tunic with a serpent crest.

"Bastien Wolf?" he said. "Heard stories of you, sir."

The knight gave a salute, then leaned in to speak with a low voice. "Astra thought you might need support. Not that she doesn't think you're capable, but she worries—not too much, I mean, just a normal amount of caring. She certainly hasn't told me otherwise."

Dust glanced at the door, as if he might see her striding in at that very moment. "Where is she?"

Bastien's expression faltered. "She's . . . well, see . . ."

Kenric stood from his throne and gave commands. Immediately, Dust found himself being firmly escorted by a handful of servants to a dressing room. The only reason he didn't dart away was that Bastien came along with him.

"Is she all right?" Dust demanded, refusing to enter the room until he had an answer.

"Yes," Bastien said. "She's sleeping. It's . . . the tree really took a toll on her. But yes, she's all right. She's with her sister."

At that, Dust finally smiled. Confident Astra. She'd faced her fears. Though he wanted to rush to her side, she deserved a moment with her sister—and he was convinced the court would break into civil war if he snuck away.

He endured a bath and a proper set of clothing, finding the shoes nothing short of a torture. With a grimace, he told himself to adjust. Every upside had its curses.

Then a cry set the castle in upheaval once more: Records had been found.

Though King Firmin had left nothing behind, the same could not be said for King Crispin. Before his death, Crispin had formed a guild—the Survivor's Guild—and left a record of their founding. A woman called Mrs. Everly brought it forward, trembling all the while. She'd never read it; the guild leaders of the past several decades had all been illiterate, but they'd protected the original record.

When Dust finally had a chance to see the journal himself, he thought his brother's handwriting looked very much like Mother's.

Crispin wrote of a lost brother and of his own father's command never to speak of it, a command enforced by the Peace Tree. He also wrote of his determination to voyage into the fairy realm.

Mother's relic allows five journeys, he wrote. *One by Father, two by Reynard. Two chances remain for me.*

For years, he planned and prepared; then, in his early twenties, he entered the fairy realm. Unable to find the tower, he exhausted his supplies and was forced to return.

A failed attempt, just as Sir Reynard's first. I will not fail again.

Dust had to admire his brother's determination. Unfortunately, that second journey landed him in the Ocean of Agony. Sir Reynard had been lucky beyond measure to have one landing at Spiral Lake and the other in the knee-highs, both only mildly dangerous regions. Dust pitied his younger brother, trapped in depthfiend territory, where the sea churned beneath an ever-present storm and the islands sank at a human touch. To make matters worse, Crispin lost his relic to the ocean.

I knew it would be my death, he wrote.

But even before reading it, Dust had an idea how the story ended. He remembered his first successful rescue of an Everspring outcast—working with Renny to save a human from the Ocean of Agony. He'd had no idea who it was he'd saved.

Crispin gave him credit. *Though it was a fairy bringing me the means of passage, he said he did so as part of an agreement, and certainly no fairy in that place had a care for me. It could only be my brother.*

Without a way to return to the realm, Crispin did what he could; all his life, he struggled to give no commands that could not be obeyed, and when he mistakenly sentenced an innocent to the fairy realm only to find the woman safely returned, he formed the Survivor's Guild.

Though we cannot speak, he wrote, *silence shows our gratitude to Cypress.*

It was not perfect, but Dust could not fault his brother's efforts. In fact, he cherished them. And the record of Everspring's second-greatest king could not be disputed. Dust was finally recognized as the missing crown prince of two centuries past—Cypress, son of Firmin.

He still hated the name.

CHAPTER 47

ASTRA

I WOKE FIRST TO THE smell of fresh bread. The pleasant aroma was not quite enough to distract from the ache in every muscle, and I groaned as I shifted in bed.

"The heroine awakes." Beauty smiled, seated in a chair at my bedside with a loaf of bread in one hand and a small jar in the other. "It's only a proper quest if you faint from wounds at the end of it and then awaken to hear news of your success."

She *would* turn my hard-won triumph into nothing more than a story.

"Breakfast smells good," I rasped, throat dry. But I could not find the energy to even reach for it. My arms seemed dead at my sides.

Beauty said, "This is *my* breakfast. You'll have to get your own."

At my sour expression, she laughed. Then she tore off a piece of bread for me, spreading it with what turned out to be mashed figs in honey.

"It's a local specialty," she said. "Only a few short days, and I've fallen in love."

I still could not lift my arms. Her brow creased in concern at my struggle. Finally, I realized it was not both arms—only my left.

Beauty reached out to take my left hand, turning it in hers. I could not feel her touch, and my eyes widened to see a webbing of scars across my palm that reached all the way to my fingertips, pulling the skin, leaving my fingers curled as claws. I could not flex them when I tried.

"That's your sewing hand," Beauty said softly.

My eyes burned, but I breathed deeply and held the emotion back. There would be time enough for all concerns—better to focus on the most pressing first.

"The tower?" I croaked.

I feared she would frown in confusion, but she only nodded. "It's all anyone can talk about. Tower returned, lost prince found, all of it."

With relief, I sank back into my pillow, though I'd hardly lifted to begin with. Every ache had grown sharper.

"You," she said, "have had *quite* the quest. Bastien told me some, but I would love to hear all of it . . . if you want to share."

"Fetch me a cup of water, and I'll talk."

In honesty, the last thing I wanted to do was talk. I wanted to break down the castle gate to see Dust. But the mere thought was exhausting.

Before Beauty could make it through the door, I called for her to wait.

"You heard me at the tree, right?" I swallowed.

Beauty smiled. "Yes, I heard. All of it."

"Good."

She left quietly, and I'd just drifted off when a knock at the door roused me again. Bastien entered, perching at the edge of Beauty's seat with clear worry. I managed a mild scowl for him, pleased that if I could no longer command my hand, at least I could command my face again.

"Lady Astra, you're—"

"Not a lady," I said. "Just Astra."

"Astra." He smiled briefly, then resumed the worried frown. "You're pale. How are you feeling?"

I could have mentioned my paralyzed arm, but I said, "Like I made the stars bow."

"I'm heading to the castle," he said. "There's quite the . . . uh, bedlam happening inside, from what I understand. But I wanted to be sure you were well first."

He plucked gently at my hand. I'd not realized I'd been struggling to move it again; I must have achieved something. Bastien turned my fingers in his, brushing his thumb across the scars.

"What happened?" he asked, brown eyes wide.

Rather than answer, I swallowed. "Sir Bastien, there's something I ought to have addressed sooner. I apologize if I've given any false encouragement to a . . . stronger relationship between us. While I am grateful—"

"What?" He blanched. "Oh, no! I—no, *I'm* sorry if I gave any—in Lord de Berranger's household, there's a young woman I—"

"Very well, don't find an early grave." I laughed, though it turned to a cough. "It seems we both have interest elsewhere."

His face had gone red, but he smiled along with me. "I'm grateful for you as well. Not just for the reunion with Andre.

I believe your efforts have made it possible for me to go home again."

"Half the effort was yours." And despite *my* best efforts, my eyes would not stay open. My chest felt heavy on my lungs, every bit of me sinking in bed, but I forced one final thought. "Hurry to the castle; there's a lost fox in need of a friend."

"He's your, uh, interest, isn't he? Dust." Bastien nodded knowingly. "I'll do my best."

That was the last I heard before weariness claimed me, mind and soul.

CHAPTER 48

DUST

THE APPEARANCE OF A should-have-been-king upset the entire government, and judging by the way court debated, Dust could have sworn they loved an upset. They debated an endless list of questions: Who did the kingdom belong to? If they supported King Kenric, would it anger the fairies clearly serving Prince Cypress? If they upheld the lost prince, would it divide the kingdom into civil war?

In the end, Dust found himself closed in a room with Kenric, as if court hoped the two royals might battle things out to the death, with Everspring awarded to the victor. Dust had no interest in fighting, nor even in arguing a case for himself as king. He had interest in just one thing, but Bastien told him Astra was still recovering. Though he'd nearly sought her out anyway, it was a selfish impulse.

She needed rest; he needed to settle his kingdom.

Kenric stood at the window, brow dotted with sweat as he watched units of royal guards struggling to contain a mob at the castle gates, the gathered people demanding to know what Kenric had done to upset the fairies and cause the Peace

Tree's removal. Ironic that the city did not seem to understand what a blessing the loss was—though there were plenty calling for the king to repay what he'd taken from them in stolen wares, unjust taxes, and so on.

Dust was busy enjoying finger pastries provided by the castle cook and testing the way his leather shoes sank into a bearskin rug.

"You've come to take my crown," Kenric said at last. "You sent the Enchanted Woman first, warning me with stories of a lost brother-in-arms, and when I paid no heed, you sent the fairy to reclaim the tree."

Dust saw the shadow of his father, searching for rebellion in the shadows.

"All I'm interested in," he said, "is living."

Kenric clearly did not believe him. He turned from the window with desperate eyes. "We can reach a compromise. If you're unhappy with the direction of the kingdom, I'll change its direction. I'm worthy of the tree—you'll see. When you're pleased, you'll return it."

With a pitying smile, Dust said, "Wrong priorities, friend. What you need isn't magic. It's good advisors 'n a dose of patience."

"An advisor, yes! Splendid idea! You shall be my advisor!"

"That's not what I—"

"With the Fairy Prince guiding, the people will see I still have favor. The tree's loss was not my fault."

Fairy Prince—it was the moniker for Dust adopted by most of the castle. If linking him to fairies motivated a positive change within the city, he could stomach such a thing. It was not wholly inaccurate, after all, though he did not command armies of fairies as they seemed to assume.

With deliberate steps, Dust crossed the room to stand

directly in front of Kenric, looking him in the eye. The king leaned back, clearly unnerved by the unnaturally bright green of Dust's irises. Everyone was.

"Kenric," he said softly, "why do you want to be king?"

"I was born to it," Kenric said. His gaze faltered as he seemed to realize Dust had been born to it too.

"Why do you *want* it, I asked."

"I . . . well, I . . ."

Dust let him flounder. The fact that he hadn't said *I deserve to be* or *I want the wealth* or something equally foolish boded well.

After another few moments of watching the king fall into internal crisis, Dust said, "I think you want to be a good king, despite everything. You've just never known what it means."

Kenric's gaze returned to the window, to the mob with angry fists raised high.

When he responded at last, the king's voice was stricken. "I cannot be king without the Peace Tree. No one will obey me. At least you . . . you have fairy magic. Perhaps you . . . should . . . wear the crown."

The words seemed to cause him physical pain, but he said them.

For the first time, Dust considered it seriously—taking his father's throne. He could help the people of Everspring, and perhaps there was something left of Cypress to be found in resuming the path his life had been meant to take.

But those people at the gates were not demanding answers of Cypress. They were demanding answers of Kenric. Disappointed and angry though they might be, they were turning to the king they knew, and a seizing of the crown would not serve Everspring.

What the kingdom needed was peace. Dust had been the payment of a false peace; now he could be the enactor of a true one, starting by making peace with Kenric.

"My time's past," said Dust with a smile. "You're king, Kenric. With some effort, we'll make a good one of you yet."

They sat down together, and they built a compromise. In addition to the position of advisor, the king gave Dust a court title, announcing it came with lordship over any section of the kingdom Dust desired, up to half the kingdom's entirety. Though it did not please everyone in court, just the fact that Kenric was acting decisively settled some of the unrest. After Dust coaxed him through a speech to the city's frightened citizens, it settled further—all of it helped along by Dust's public renunciation of his own claim to the throne.

After two days, Everspring was no longer on the verge of collapse, and Dust finally allowed himself an act of selfishness.

He left the castle to find Astra.

With Bastien as escort, Dust made it to a familiar inn. He no longer had the viewpoint of a small fox on the window ledge; now he viewed it with natural eyes. It was the most beautiful two-story, plain wooden building he'd ever seen.

Though it could not compare to the woman who stepped out its front doors to greet him.

"I'll give you a—some privacy, I mean," said Bastien.

Dust nearly clapped the knight on the shoulder but hesitated. All his life, he'd waited to embrace other humans, and now that he was finally surrounded by people, he found himself unable to touch a single one—as if convinced they were only an illusion, and the moment he reached out, the illusion would shatter. He'd be back in his tower, alone.

With a quick bow to Astra, Bastien ducked inside the inn.

She looked different. She looked *human,* no longer bleeding magic from every feature. Her auburn hair was braided and bound with a green ribbon two shades lighter than her dress. No longer flawless, her skin was nevertheless smooth and infinitely more charming for the occasional freckle. Under his scrutiny, her small nose scrunched up, and she squinted through brown eyes edged with green. Exposure to the realm had changed her just as it had changed him.

"The Fairy Prince finally comes to visit," she said, lips twitching in a half smirk. "I was just on my way to break down the castle gate."

Her left arm hung awkwardly at her side, and she tilted to conceal it behind her dress. She lifted her other hand to touch him.

Without meaning to, Dust took a step back.

Astra paused. "Dust?"

The sound of his name stole his breath.

She was the most beautiful woman in existence, and if he touched her only to realize the last few days had been an elaborate trap, a revenge from Doll or something else, he would never recover.

All the same, he took one step forward to reverse his retreat, then one more to close the gap. She watched him with a raised eyebrow but said nothing to chide his strangeness. Perhaps she understood the reasons behind it; it would not be the first time she'd understood things he couldn't say.

Gently, Dust reached for her concealed hand. She let him take it. He brushed his thumb across the knuckles, slowly enough to catch each peak and valley, turning at last to the webbing of scars where her skin appeared melted and deformed.

She did not disappear at his touch.

"Was this for me?" His voice cracked.

"Trees fight with unfair advantage, as it turns out," Astra said, lifting her right shoulder in a shrug. Her gaze lifted to his and held. "It's still worth the result."

All that confidence. Seeing the woman behind it, he loved it even more fiercely.

Catching her other hand, Dust trailed his fingers up the outside of her arm, first to her wrist, then her elbow. The nearness of her threw off every rhythm inside him, but he drew closer still. The green and brown of Astra's eyes swirled like a whirlpool, pulling him down into an unknown realm, and he welcomed the journey. He tilted his head, leaning forward to whisper, changing his mind at the last moment.

He brushed a kiss against her cheek that sent shivers down his own neck.

Then he did whisper. "I worried you wouldn't be real."

She'd closed her eyes, and she drew in an unsteady breath before whispering back. "Give me a moment—I'm not sure I am anymore."

Dust could not tell if his own breathing was unsteady or if it was only the thundering of his heart shaking his lungs. He pulled back just a bit, cupping her cheek. She pressed her right hand to his.

"Pleased to meet you," Astra said. "Something tells me you've always wanted to hear that."

Dust's smile bloomed. He kissed her in earnest, and she held him fiercely, her uninjured hand tangled in his short hair. He could have lost himself forever and still been found.

But there was a matter left to tend.

Reluctantly breaking the embrace, Dust pulled a bottle of healing sap from his pocket.

"Brought some fairy realm with me," he said. The way Bastien stammered around Astra's recovery had been clue enough that it might be needed.

"I should have known you'd have something squirrelled away." When she smiled, her jaw trembled, and when Dust reached for her crippled hand, she did not pull away. As he applied the sap, he thought of all his failed half-moon escapes, every disappointing moment that had led him here.

As Astra said, the scars were worth the result.

He used everything in the bottle, and then he watched her rotate her wrist and flex her hand. Slowly, the fingers drew in and out, though they retained a bit of claw shape. The sap had disappeared, taking with it most of the scarring, leaving only a thin web covering the center of her palm.

Dust's heart ached. "If I had more, it—"

"Hush, wood fairy." She looked up at him with tears shimmering in her eyes. "And thank you."

He tucked a loose strand of her hair back, resting his hand along the curve of her jaw. When he leaned forward, she beat him to it, capturing his lips.

For the first time in his life—

He felt like he was home.

EPILOGUE

ASTRA

FOOLISHLY, I'D THOUGHT ALL my difficulties behind me—until Andre and Beauty announced they were returning home. They did not have the funds to stay forever, and Beauty missed Father.

"At some point," Beauty said, "every adventure must make way for a new one to begin."

Bastien promised to visit when he could. Only I remained.

"Are you coming home?" Beauty asked.

Father deserved a reconciliation of his own, and I longed to speak to Callista. But my mind could not shake off the Dust of it all.

He was free now, and he'd renounced any claim to the throne. With dread, I waited for the moment he would set off to travel the world, as I knew he longed to, as he *deserved* to. It would be selfish to hold him back, and I'd promised to devote myself to consideration.

But the ever-present tingle in my left hand did not bother me nearly as much as the thought of losing him.

With Bastien's help, I located Dust in the castle. It was

only he and Kenric, bent over records in the royal archives, and when I entered, Kenric grew flustered, gripping a thick manuscript like he might use it to fend me off.

I lifted my chin. "I'm terribly sorry, Your Majesty, but the Fairy Prince has taken ill."

Dust smirked, bringing out the foxy mischief in his bright green eyes. "Have I, now?"

"Dreadfully ill. He shall need a fortnight's recovery at least. Fortunately, the cure may be found in only a short journey to the western coast."

"A fortnight—!" Kenric stopped his protest short, eyeing me.

"Think you can manage a few weeks?" Dust asked, gripping the king's shoulder.

For a moment, though they carried no physical resemblance, they looked almost like brothers. To my shock, Dust asked me to give him a moment to confer with the king. I paced outside until he came at last to tell me he'd meet me at Widow's Point.

"Few things to tie up here first, is all," he said.

Too late, I realized my mistake. I'd invited him to a port city. He would climb aboard a ship and disappear forever.

"Take your time," I managed.

Andre, Beauty, and I made our way home by hitching rides with merchant caravans. I found myself frequently cornered by my obnoxious younger sister, who sat beside me in wagons, forcing a needle into my deadened hand until I finally relented and tried a few stitches.

I knew immediately.

It was like seeing a childhood friend after they'd grown. Familiar enough to recognize, but changed in every way. I could grip only weakly, needing the tilt of my wrist to accomplish even that. Though I could hold the needle, there was no precision for stitches, no dexterity for the thimble.

"There's the answer," I said, voice trembling. I returned the fabric scrap to Beauty's hand and leaned away, watching the countryside pass as the wagon rolled.

I should have remembered my sister's tenacity.

Our journey took four days, with nights spent in towns along the road, and each day, Beauty brought the needle back.

"Woe is me," she bemoaned. "I find myself in the dire straits of being a young woman with *no* instruction in embroidery. If only there were a master seamstress to teach me."

At her goading, I tested my options, even holding the needle in my right hand, but nothing returned what I'd lost, and on our final night of travel, Beauty pushed too far, forcing a needle on me as we relaxed from the compounded aches of several days on the road.

"Enough!" I shouted, tossing the needle at the inn's fireplace. It made a soft *ping* against the floor; I could not even direct a needle through a gaping hole in the wall, much less the miniscule space between fabric threads.

Andre sat at the table with us, scribbling some new parchment. He and Beauty seemed to write love letters even though they kept a constant company.

"Can't you control your wife?" I snapped at my new brother-in-law.

Andre dipped his quill, carefully scraping the excess ink. Without looking at me, he said, "I'm only a cabin boy, trusting direction to my pirate queen."

They were certainly made for each other.

Beauty retrieved the needle and tried to hand it to me again. "My sister did not overcome so many fears," she said, "to surrender here."

"Enough," I said, softer now. "I'll relearn it, whatever that looks like now, but I won't relearn it in a single night."

She bit her lip. Then she sat beside me with a sigh.

"I'm sorry." Pink colored her cheeks. "I just know embroidery means everything to you."

She wasn't wrong, at least about the old Astra.

"Not *everything*." I gave a quiet huff. "I have room in my heart for plenty of things."

"Plenty of Dust, perhaps."

I took a swipe at her, but my hand was as inaccurate in sister-swiping as in needle-directing. Beauty settled beside me with a smug expression. For a moment, we had companionable silence.

But my mood deflated as I considered how easily my temper had flown loose. After everything we'd gone through together, I still shouted at my sister, even when she tried to help me.

Pretending I had one of Dust's fairy peppers, I said, "Beauty, I'm afraid to go home."

She reared back in protest. "Father misses you! Every time I see Callista, she asks—"

"I'm afraid," I said quietly, "I'll go right back to who I was."

A gentle warmth wafted from the fire. Autumn had crept in, with cold fingers in the evening, and I felt a strange mixture of goosebumps on my neck from a window's breeze and prickles across my legs from the fire's heat.

Andre gathered his parchment and stood, kissing his wife goodnight. For me, he gave his usual quiet nod, and then he padded up the inn staircase toward the guest rooms.

After a stretch of silence, Beauty said, "For decades, philosophers have debated how much change humans are capable of—if they leave a dark cave, will they learn to appreciate sunlight or go rushing back to shadows? Malthea said it best, I think. She's a female philosopher who wrote—"

"The world bends to beauty," I said.

My sister turned so quickly, she nearly slipped off the bench. "First you go on quests, and now you're a student of philosophy?"

I rolled my eyes. "You're the one who taught me. Ten years ago, the day you nearly died on the beach."

"I've never—you mean that time I slipped? I was not in danger of *dying*."

"Of course you wouldn't think so."

She shook her head. "Anyway, I meant to say, *Fate is helmed by purpose*. That's Malthea's most famous teaching. And since you already know what she said of beauty, you should also know she taught that nothing is so beautiful as a person who has embraced purpose despite hardship. Such a person can bend the world itself."

So I'd misread the text. I sighed at having carried a misunderstanding for so many years. Though I hoped to increase my humility, it was still new, and I said, "Perhaps her purpose should have been in expressing herself more simply so she could actually be understood."

"She's one of the most accessible philosophers. I read her writings as a child."

My glare did nothing to wilt my sister's smirk. She scooted closer to me on the bench and rested her head on my shoulder.

"If you return home to drift," Beauty said quietly, "then no doubt, you'll slip back into familiar habits. But if you return home with purpose, you helm your own fate. You don't have to be who you were, Astra. You'll be who you decide."

For a while, we sat without speaking, just listening to the fire's peaceful crackle.

Father welcomed us home with enthusiasm, sending immediately for Callista and Thomas, lingering when he held me.

"I'm sorry, Father," I whispered into his neck. "I went chasing pearls."

Rather than lecturing me for all the heartbreak, he only held me tighter.

Considering my father's forgiving nature, his hug was no surprise, but Rob's was. It may have been a disguised assassination attempt, since the force of my brother's embrace left me struggling to breathe.

"Glad you're home," he said, really seeming to mean it.

"I missed you," I said, and I meant that as well.

We settled around the cramped table, and though I still found the space constricting, there was at least a touch of coziness to it. Rob demanded stories of the fairy realm, though he preferred Beauty's description of Smicker over mine. Hers added the falsehood of fire-breathing and made the Trader double the size, as if he wasn't mountainous enough already.

Callista arrived at last, pale as a ghost—which she quickly informed us was not due to malaise but to a coming baby. Her tree of a husband loomed behind her, ready to fall on any perceived threat, bracing her up whenever needed. I hugged my sister, whispering a heartfelt congratulations in her ear. A touch of her color returned.

While I enjoyed the warm glow of family, the effect was dampened somewhat as I thought of one more person I would have added to the table.

Dust arrived three days later. He must have caused an absolute riot in the city, since he came by way of royal carriage and full escort.

"Courtesy of Kenric," he said, face reddening as he glanced back at the procession on the road. The whole lineup dwarfed our cottage and sent the chickens into a squawking flurry. At least there were no trumpets.

At a command from Dust, the entourage returned to the city to find an inn, leaving only one knight as guard. Bastien Wolf.

"I said I'd visit." The knight grinned.

Since Andre was at the shipyard working, Bastien

contented himself with Beauty's company. Meanwhile, I introduced Dust to my father.

"Father, this is the scheming wood fairy who saved me from spider poison, monstrous dragons, slow-acting acids, and rivers of lava, among other things." With a smile, I added, "Dust, this is Robert Acton, a better father than I deserve."

When Dust attempted a bow, he got pulled into a hug.

"Thank you, son," said Father. I did not think he used the term of address by accident.

For a moment, Dust held stiff. Then he seemed to collapse into the embrace.

It was certainly underhanded of me to hope that sharing my family might encourage him not to leave, but while I battled full selfishness, I could not resist a few underhanded tactics.

Two, to be exact.

For my second tactic, I took Dust to the beach.

Waves crashed and seagulls cried, the symphony I had grown up with and always avoided, suddenly beautiful as I saw the wonder it sparked in his eyes. He stared out at the rolling waves, his lips parted slightly in a dazed smile.

"It's so much bigger in real life," he whispered.

Taking advantage of his distraction, I dropped a handful of sand down the back of his collar, and then I ran. Dust chased me down the shoreline, me shrieking with laughter, before he caught hold, sweeping my legs up, his other arm secure across my back. His chest warmed me through his shirt, and I found no desire to escape, caught up as I was in the swirls of his bright green eyes.

I kissed him while he held me, and our hearts thundered along with the pounding waves.

Like children, we played in wet sand and foamy tide, digging out shells and walking barefoot in the shallows. As my dress grew soggy and sand clumped beneath my fingernails, I endured without complaint. I only prayed it could be enchantment enough to persuade him to stay.

Once we'd both grown exhausted, we sat together on dry sand. I snuggled against his chest, enjoying the blanket of his arms around me while he rested his chin on my shoulder, and for a while, we watched the ocean.

At length, he said, "Sunset's coming on. I'll have to leave soon."

Stiffening, I turned in his arms. "You only just arrived! Father's expecting you for dinner."

More tricks. My stomach twisted, and when he winced, I felt the guilt of it. Could I not just give him his freedom? Hadn't I learned the price of selfishness by now?

"Should've been clearer with my plans, sorry." He gave a sad smile. "If I could put it off a night, I would."

As if his entire life hadn't been on hold long enough already.

I willed myself to practice a calm control, but it was like straining against fairy magic, and without permission, a tear dripped down my cheek.

"Astra?" Dust's eyes widened.

Abruptly, I stood, turning away to swat at the watery betrayal.

"It's fine," I lied. "You'll want to hurry. My father's

captains were known to leave passengers behind rather than delay the ship."

Dust came up behind me, wrapping his arms gently around my waist, resting his chin on my shoulder once more. I breathed deeply his sawdust scent.

"Much as I'd love to go sailing," he said, "it's not my plan tonight. The baron's invited me for dinner at his manor. As a visiting lord, it would be a slight not to recognize the local one."

Confusion furrowed my brow. But in the end, I said, "You're not leaving?"

"Not with any permanence, anyway." Catching my elbows, he turned me to face him, looking down with a smile. "When you thought I was climbing aboard a ship tonight, what did you mean to say? The thing that made you cry."

I shook my head.

"Astra." His green eyes were an enchantment in themselves, a pull I could not resist. "Friendship-pepper honesty, if you please."

"Don't go," I whispered at last.

He gave a mysterious smile, and he kissed me in a way to steal my breath. If not for his arms to steady me, I would have lost track of the very direction of the ground. Resting his forehead against mine, he said, "I'm only seeing the baron because I thought someone ought to tell the poor fellow he's been replaced."

My dizziness hadn't quite faded, and my mind struggled to solve the riddle. "When you said you were a lord . . ."

"Kenric's offered me any landholding I please. First time here, but this seems a nice area. The ocean, at least—that's better than I ever imagined."

"You . . ." I shook my head. "Scheming wood fairy."

The evening sun cast a red-orange glow in the sky behind him, drawing the red from his brown hair. He kissed my forehead, and I slid my arms around his waist, resting my head against his shoulder while he held me.

"From what I hear, Baron Galliford deserves a dethroning." Dust tensed for a moment. "If it's overstepping, I—"

"Hush," I said.

The rumble of his low chuckle vibrated my ear.

"I know you wanted to travel . . ." I struggled with the words. "After all that time trapped, you deserve to—"

"Hush," he murmured gently.

I smiled into his shoulder.

We held each other until the last possible moment, and even then, I clung to his hand, walking back with him along the sandy path.

"I meant to buy you a carving knife," I admitted, "but I couldn't find one of satisfactory quality, so the ocean visit had to do."

"Here I thought I was the one smuggling gifts."

I blinked. Dust kept one hand tangled in mine, revealing that his other held a necklace, a strand of tiny, delicate beads, curled across his palm. Though mostly emerald green in color, under the fading sunlight, they shimmered with a rainbow hue.

"Mydar," he said. "Tree pearls. It's not exactly the silversmith's necklace I owe you for your swift 'n efficient breaking of my curse—"

I laughed, ears heating.

"—but I hope it'll do just the same."

He fastened the necklace and kissed my neck just above the clasp, raising goosebumps on my skin.

"Thank you," he whispered, breath tickling my ear. "For all of it."

Something inside me burned to be said. The admitting of it would change me; it would demand of me a higher standard, a dedication to the new person I'd become, with no excuse to retreat.

An ocean breeze danced around us, heavy with the scent of salt, teasing strands of my hair free before Dust tucked them once more behind my ear. My hair accepted taming now, the evidence I carried daily of a change I'd already made.

So rather than fearing the future, I took the helm, secure in my hands even if one of them struggled to grip.

I would be who I decided to be.

"I love you," I said.

ACKNOWLEDGMENTS

This book has had a bumpy road, and it would not have arrived at any kind of destination without the stalwart support of these people.

My beta readers: Brooke Adams, Brianne Bird, Rachel Bird, Megan Dunn, McKenna Gillette, Alyssa Green, Melissa Hokanson, Lindsy Isackson, Brady Lowham, Karen Lowham, Ashley Nicolaysen, Ashlie Olson, and Moriah Pond. Several of you suffered through drastically different versions of this book, and I'm grateful for your time, patience, and for your continued support of my work.

My critique group: Allison Mathews, Bri Stephens, and Katie Stone. Thank you not only for your detailed feedback but for your emotional support through this entire process. You guys rock.

A special thank you to Rebecca Gage for helping me workshop the beginning, and for offering that help on such a tight deadline. I cannot wait to meet you for *reals*. Many thanks to Emily Poole at Midnight Owl Editors for ensuring I didn't make a fool of myself in verb tenses. Thank you to Danyelle Ferguson for saving my life with her swift formatting and to Aamna Shahid for having the most incredible design team and making the impossible possible.

Finally, a most heartfelt thanks to Cindy Gunderson for answering my endless parade of questions with a fountain of patience. You really made me feel like I could accomplish this, and here we are. Also thanks to the Superstars Tribe at large, who came into my life at just the right time, who were all massively supportive when I felt overwhelmed.

I bet Smicker would love to trade with any one of you.

DISCUSSION QUESTIONS

1. This story was written as a gender-bent Rapunzel retelling. What aspects of the Rapunzel fairy tale do you see in Dust's life?
2. The fairy realm is full of a variety of strange creatures. Which was your favorite and why was it Bumble?
3. Dust struggled to find his own fairy name. What would yours be?
4. Why do you think Astra was afraid of so many things?
5. Dust says even curses have their upsides. We might call that finding silver linings. When did the characters make the most of a bad situation?
6. Before Astra left home, her father told her the story of the pearl diver. In what ways did she fall into the same trap as the unfortunate pearl diver? Do you think it was a cautionary tale or just a tragedy?

7. Do you think Dust's father was a villain or was he simply tricked by fairies?
8. Siblings play a big role in the story. What are the similarities and differences between Astra/Beauty, Bastien/Andre, and Dust/Crispin?

ABOUT THE AUTHOR

Elizabeth (Liz) Lowham dreams of a future house that is seventy-percent library with at least three lavish window seats. Her reality is five bookshelves and a rocking chair, which isn't so bad. She is the author of *Beauty Reborn*, which is the story of Astra's whimsical sister, as well as the upcoming YA fantasy novel *Casters & Crowns*, releasing Fall 2024. She lives with her husband and son in Loveland—the most appropriate place any romance fan could hope to live—and has a BA in English from BYUI.

Learn more at elizabethlowham.com